a field guide to
burying your
parents

a field guide to burying your parents

Liza Palmer

NEW YORK   BOSTON

5 Spot
Hachette Book Group
237 Park Avenue
New York, NY 10017

Visit our Web site at www.5-spot.com.

5 Spot is an imprint of Grand Central Publishing.
The 5 Spot name and logo are trademarks of Hachette Book Group, Inc.

Printed in the United States of America

First printing December 2009
10 9 8 7 6 5 4 3 2 1

Library of Congress Cataloging-in-Publication Data

Palmer, Liza.
  A field guide to burying your parents / Liza Palmer.
    p. cm.
  ISBN 978-0-446-69838-2
  1. Problem families—Fiction.   I. Title.
  PS3616.A343F54 2009
  813'.6—dc22
                                    2009003638

For Alex

acknowledgments

I am the proud owner of a very special dog with very special needs. Recently I realized that—not unlike how dog owners start physically resembling their dogs—I am very similar to Poet in many very special ways.

My epiphany came when I realized that it was the care and feeding I received as a child from a very special mother that made me the moderately functioning person I am today. Another set of parents and...well, I'd be out in the back biting some wooden fence in the rain. Looking back on my childhood, I think there should be a Nobel Prize for Parenting.

The people that follow are the village it took to turn me from the idiot who gleefully dwelled within its walls ignorant of the stories I had to tell.

Thank you to my family: Mom, Don, Alex, Joe, Bonnie and Zoë. Christmas mornings with cowboy breakfasts and television yule logs are memories I hold near and dear to my heart.

Thank you to Megan Crane, Jane Porter and Paz Stark: the three women who had the unfortunate task of reading the first drafts of this book. Your dear friendships are something I treasure—until you say my writing sucks, then...we'll just play it by ear.

Thank you to Kerri Wood-Einertson: my shiny penny of a friend—and to her family—Siena (the milk of human kindness) and Erik (thank you for the inside dish on corporate America).

Thank you to Christy Fletcher: for talking me off ledges and giving me a reason to buy little pink baby shoes. Thank you also to the amazing team at Fletcher and Company—a truly class act of an agency.

Thank you to Caryn Karmatz Rudy: the bestest editor a girl could have. I mean—I think she may have a bone to pick with a few of my English teachers growing up, but...I'm sure it was them and not, you know, my...uh...lack of educational... ahem...okay, I was a horrible student and now poor Caryn is paying the price. There. I said it.

Thank you to Araminta, Sara and Isobel: another dinner of unexplainable cocktails is definitely in order—followed, of course, by a trip to Wagamama.

Thank you to Marissa Devins and Howie Sanders at UTA for everything they've done...it's exhilarating just having agents in the same part of the country.

Thank you to James Newton Howard for writing "The Healing" off the *Lady in the Water* soundtrack—final tally, I listened to your song 460 times during the writing of this novel. Genius.

Thank you to Lyn Nierva at Auntie Momo Web Designs for an awesome website.

Thank you to Kim Resendiz and posse, Lynn and Rich Silton, Bill Gallagher, Juanita Espino, Judy Kelly, Henry Glowa, Norm Freed, Michelle Rowen, Levi Nuñez, Kristin Harmel, Carrie Cogbill, Larry, Ricca, Matthew and Adam Wolff, Peter Riherd, the Bad Girls' Bookclub, Marilyn Marino, Phoebe and Dave Einertson, Pauline Callahan, Nita Millstein at the Peach Café (more her Belgian waffles, but...), Susan and Tim and finally the staff at the Starbucks for putting up with me hour after hour after hour after hour after hour...

And my mom wants me to thank her dogs—Lulu, Leo and Roxy—because "when they read the book their feelings will be hurt if they're not mentioned."

"I'm fractured from the fall, and I want to go home."
—*Ryan Adams from* Two

Once upon a time we were a family.

chapter one

Aaaand to the left," Tim instructs, bending over his outstretched leg. His salt-and-pepper curls, now soaked from the torrent of rain, dribble down over his forehead. I pull my hood tightly around my head and can't help fearing I resemble a giant sperm. Just the professional message I want to send. I look at all the members of Tim's team following his every move. This Fun Run was optional—the brownie points, however, were too good an opportunity to pass up. Tim Barnes is a name partner at Marovish, Marino and Barnes and, in their eyes, not a man to disappoint. To me, he's the man I've been dating for several months and am confident have already disappointed on a far more personal level. Tim leads his entire group of sodden money managers down into the deep stretch.

Something about being ordered to bend left makes me want to bend to the right. I let out a sigh as I envision the chaos that could result from such a rebellion. Tim shoots me a look of deep concern. Apparently, I'm not taking this "stretching circle" as seriously as he'd hoped. It's a *5K*, honey, we're not carrying the Olympic torch. I press out a smile and lean *slightly* to the left. Tim softens, smiling to himself as we all are finally able to bend to the right.

With my head to my right knee, I feel the vibration of my BlackBerry in my pocket. I'm surprised the damn thing still works, considering how sopping wet my entire body is. I let it go to voice mail as our group is allowed to return to a standing position. We all start walking toward the now deflated red-green-and-white balloon arch that stretches languidly across Santa Monica's Ocean Avenue, marking the beginning of the star-crossed Fun Run.

"Are you one hundred percent, *Grace*?" Tim asks as we approach the starting line. Even after several months of dating, far beyond the time we could credibly keep the relationship a secret from our coworkers, his voice still drops when he says my name.

"I'm just not awake yet," I say, grabbing my ankle behind me and stretching one leg and then the other, like this will somehow show a higher level of commitment. My BlackBerry vibrates again. I let it go to voice mail, shaking it off...get your head in the game, Grace. The rain and the wind are now whipping sideways. No hood in the world can stop them from stinging every inch of my face. That and I feel suddenly compelled to run toward some giant ovum I know is waiting for me at the end of this race. Resigned, I pull the hood off and let the rain fall.

As the crowd settles in behind the melancholy, sagging balloon arch, I pull my BlackBerry out of my pocket, trying to shield it from the rain, and listen to the messages.

"Grace, it's Abigail. Dad's had a stroke. It's time to grow up and join the family again. I'm serious. Call me back."

No. This cannot be. My stomach drops. My legs feel numb, my fingers waggle around the keypad, fumbling with threes and ones, unable to stop atom bomb number two from playing.

"Grace—Abigail again. I *will* keep calling. And I won't stop like I did when Mom died. Like we *all* did before. Not going to happen. We need you. This family needs you. Call me back. Talk to you in another ten minutes wh—" I finally control my digits enough to successfully stop the message from continuing. This is *not* possible. I simply can't let it be.

I turn my face back to the group as the announcer cuts in, "Welcome to the Winter Fun Run!" Tim motions for me to fall in with the rest of the crowd. I oblige, but can't focus. The messages. I'm not surprised it's Abigail who's urgently summoning me now—about *Dad*, of all things. It's been—well, since Mom died, so, almost five years since I've spoken to her or either of my brothers. When I pictured reconnecting, it wasn't over a man who was no father to us when he was healthy and certainly doesn't deserve that distinction now.

The announcer continues, "Runners! Phase One! Phase One are the runners who will finish the 5K in eight minutes or less! Please approach the starting gate! Phase One! Runners who will finish in eight minutes or less!" I get as far away from Phase One as is humanly possible. Tim and two of his hangers-on leap forward.

"Is this your first?" asks an older woman holding an umbrella. Could her umbrella possibly be aerodynamic?

"Oh...yeah," I answer, hopping up and down trying to keep warm. Concentrate. All I can picture is Tim and his cadre of ass-kissers getting trampled by the legitimate Phase Oners when the starting gun sounds.

"Me and my husband are getting ready for the LA Marathon in March. He's running the half-marathon today, but I'm not there yet," she adds, motioning to the steadily approaching herd of runners who are waiting their turn. Wait...twenty-six miles?

"The LA *Marathon*?" I ask as the announcer tells Phase Two to approach the starting gate. Phase Two are the people who will be finishing the 5K in twelve minutes or less. I take yet another step back.

"I walked it. Took eight hours, but I finished," the woman exalts.

"That's awesome," I say, absently.

"The rain's nice," the woman adds. My normally straight blonde hair is hanging in spaghetti-like tendrils around my shoulders and I'm sure my face has the pallor of a long-term shut-in's. Is this woman retarded?

"Phase Three! Runners who will finish the 5K...well, runners who just plan on finishing! Phase Three!" I wave at the umbrella-ed marathon machine with a forced "Good luck!" and approach the starting gate shaking my frozen legs out one at a time. Get my head in the game. I can't...I still can't focus. The vibrating reminder on my BlackBerry indicating I have yet another message is driving me slowly insane. It hasn't even been ten minutes.

"On your mark! Get set! Go!!!!" My mind clears. My legs start moving. My breathing steadies.

The rain *is* nice.

Thirty-two minutes, twenty-seven seconds and six messages from Abigail later, the drenched volunteer cuts the time chip from my shoelaces. I find the group after being presented with my little medal and a complimentary bottle of water.

"I pulled a groin muscle," Tim announces to all who will listen. No medal. No complimentary water.

"You gave it your best," a particularly buxom money manager oozes.

"Thanks, Laura," Tim replies politely.

As I down my complimentary water, I can't help but marvel at the hardest-working sports bra in the Los Angeles area. That Fun Run couldn't have been easy on it. Laura takes this opportunity to shoot me a particularly pointed look. I wipe my mouth with my sleeve and sigh—taking Tim's hand in the process. He pulls me close. Laura crosses, or at least *attempts* to cross, her arms across her chest. As one of the lowly mathematicians at the firm, I'm technically not even supposed to be here. This Fun Run was for money managers, not for us quants who formulate the models and earnings reports for the money they manage. It's because of my relationship with Tim that I'm here. And everyone knows it. Laura looks away.

I've grown accustomed to Tim's iconic heartthrob status with the women at the firm. Our relationship seems to have zero impact on this phenomenon. Suits me fine. The few times I've sat among Tim's harem in the break room, I've been tempted to stick stale donuts in my ears just to make their cloying voices stop.

"You're going to have to share that medal," Tim jokes, as we walk to his car later.

"Absolutely," I answer, reaching up to his sopping wet face and smoothing a rogue salt-and-pepper curl down with the rest. He smiles and walks back to the trunk of his car. He pulls two large towels out, passes me one and folds into the driver's side. I take the towel and can't help pulling my BlackBerry out of my pocket. Six missed calls. All Abigail. Delete. Delete. Delete. Delete. Delete. Delete. I shove the phone back in my pocket and look up, letting the rain sting my face. I pull my hoodie tight, set the towel down on Tim's leather interior and climb into the passenger side. We follow the caravan of luxury sedans to the predetermined Noah's Bagels right next to the freeway on-ramp in nearby Westwood.

As we drive, Abigail's messages become this echoing symphony somewhere deep in my consciousness—like I'm standing on the street outside an opera house listening to the faint music. By the time we find a parking space, my brain has already processed and compartmentalized the information in an almost Chutes and Ladders type of way—sending her voice down, down, down—through a trapdoor and into the depths, out of reach. After five years of tamping, repressing and numbing, I have it down to an exact science. Not even Abigail can pry that trapdoor open. Not even Abigail can make me buy a ticket and hear that opera live.

Maybe this is an evolution. Maybe time does heal all wounds. Maybe now I can move on and somehow forget that I've lost my mom. It's been difficult, but I've managed to put it away for five years now, split in two like a magician's assistant without that whole other part of me: past, history, family.

Maybe I've come to terms with things? Or maybe I've finally snapped and completely shut down every emotional response I ever possessed? Whatever the truth is, Abigail's relentless calling means I'm about to find out.

chapter two

"Can I help you?" the man behind the counter says.

"I'll have a plain bagel with lox and cream cheese, please. And a large coffee," Tim says, handing the man a twenty-dollar bill.

The man turns to me. "Can I help you?"

"This is for both of us," Tim adds, motioning at the twenty-dollar bill.

"I'll have a blueberry bagel with just really light...like *super*-light cream cheese—" I say, making a bizarre sweeping hand motion. Apparently, this is now the international gesture for "schmear." "And a...what black teas do you h...okay, the Earl Grey."

My BlackBerry buzzes again.

"They're just going to keep calling," Tim points out. I didn't even know he noticed. Tim takes his change. I pull my Black-Berry out as the man behind the counter hands me a large cup and an Earl Grey tea bag.

"It might be important," Tim urges, squeezing my shoulder. The BlackBerry buzzes again. The man behind the counter points me in the direction of the hot water. In a haze, I check the caller ID. The phone buzzes again. I look back at Tim. He nods at it emphatically.

"You really should get that." Easy for you to say, I think. You're not the one about to vomit in public. The phone buzzes again. A chill runs up my spine as I check the caller ID. Abigail's sent in the Closer.

"Hello?"

"Grace." Huston. My big brother. Without Abigail in my life, I quickly realized I couldn't fold a bedsheet by myself or do much of anything practical. Fine, no one need see the pandemonium that lurks within my linen closet. But with no Huston, it was worse. Without Huston, I couldn't believe in heroes.

"I know, okay?" I sputter, finally stepping out of the line, clutching my large cup and eyeing that hot water like it was the North Star.

"You know about what?" Huston presses.

"I know about Dad. The stroke," I say as the activity of Noah's Bagels buzzes around me. Tim looks over. A look of genuine concern sweeps across his face.

"Abigail says you won't take her calls," Huston accuses.

Huston's voice cuts through a chink in my armor. I can feel the tip of the sword sinking in deeper and deeper. Noah's Bagels melts away. It seems like only twenty minutes ago, not twenty years, it was just the four of us sitting around a game of Sorry!, absorbed in what we were certain were the important issues of the day. Abigail's voice cuts through the din.

"Grace isn't going to do her own laundry! She'll just wear my stuff! And then I won't be able to wear it anymore because she stains everything!" Abigail yells at Huston.

Mom is at the flower shop. She's their main floral designer and it's the holidays. So we're on our own.

"Gracie..." Huston begins, looking up from the Sorry! game we've stopped playing. Leo takes a drink of his milk, annoyed with our chronic bickering intermissions. It's a testament to not being allowed to watch television that we're still playing these afternoon Sorry! games at ages ranging from Huston's sixteen years old to Leo's arguably more age-appropriate eleven. I'm always yellow. Huston is always blue. Abigail is red. Leaving Leo with green. He *says* it's his favorite color, but once I caught him playing Sorry! with a group of neighborhood kids. He snatched up the red pieces like they were gold...well, *red* doubloons.

"I don't have to do laundry if I don't want to! Leo doesn't have to do his laundry!" I retort.

"Leo only wears underpants and capes!" Abigail protests.

"So!?!"

"I swear to God, if you touch my stuff," Abigail warns.

Unable to control my compulsion to do the opposite of anything Abigail tells me to, I bolt over to her neatly folded basket of clean laundry and sit directly on top of it, praying to any god that will listen to please...please let me fart. I dig my narrow thirteen-year-old ass deeper and deeper into the recesses of the laundry, past tiny rainbow T-shirts, Day-Glo sweatshirts and Jordache jeans.

"I'm going to killllll you!!!" Abigail screams, charging at me.

"Huuuuusttooonnnnnnnnnn!" I scream, raising my hands defensively as Abigail and I both topple over the basket, her clean laundry spilling everywhere. Huston gets up from the dining room table and starts toward us. Leo lets out a weary sigh and focuses back on his ever-present puzzle book. He always has a Plan B.

"Don't you help her, Huston! You are so dead!!!" Abigail squeals, tugging at my hair and clawing my face.

"I may be dead, but you still have to do your laundry all over again!!!!" I hawk a giant loogie over as many of her clothes as I can. Those Skittles I picked up after school do wonders for my Technicolor saliva production. My pinkish-red spit goes everywhere—clinging to way more garments than I ever could have hoped for. Abigail lets out a primitive howl, grabs my still-spitting mouth and pins me to the living room floor. Leo meanders over from the dining room table.

"Stop it!!! Come on! It's your turn, Abigail," Leo demands, pointing to the unfinished game on the dining room table. He has an old towel tied around his shoulders, and is clad in under-pants and a pair of red Wellingtons. At eleven, Leo's a bit old to be running around in costumes. Mom hates to discipline him, really any of us, since she asked Dad to leave a few months ago after she caught him with another woman...*again*. We're hoping things will go back to normal soon. And not just Leo and his costumes.

"Enough! Enough!" Huston says, peeling Abigail off with the strength of the varsity quarterback he is. He holds Abigail by the upturned collar of her pink Lacoste shirt as she swats at me. At him. At everyone.

"I'm so telling Mom," Abigail fumes.

"It's still your turn, Abigail," Leo pleads, knowing the game is close to lost.

"You're still going to have to do your laundry again," I sing, wiping the last strands of pinkish-red spit from my chin.

Abigail defiantly walks back over to the dining room table, picks up the die and surveys the board. I am six spaces away from winning. Abigail blows on the die for good luck.

"You're going to do both your laundry and Abigail's, Gracie. It's only fair," Huston says, as both of us walk back over to the dining room table. Abigail rolls a five.

"Oh, yeah?" I answer, sitting. Abigail moves—one, two...

"Yeah," Huston says, leaning toward me. Abigail knocks my little yellow man off the board and onto the floor.

"Well, you're not Mom, so you can't decide..." I bluster, watching the little yellow game piece skitter across the floor.

"No, I'm your older brother, so I actually don't have to be nice to you," Huston says, scooting even closer, downright looming if you ask me. I am unimpressed... *stupid*, but unimpressed.

"Sorrrryyyyyyy," Abigail proclaims, sitting back in her chair.

"See? She apologized, now you have to redo the laundry," Huston says, picking me up and holding me upside down over the board. My tangled ponytail sweeps the game's surface and the pieces scatter.

"Yeah! Now get to it!" Abigail orders, grinning widely. Huston scoops me up and stands me upright.

"Fine," I say, steadying myself, giggling and picking my yellow man up off the floor along with a few others.

"Your turn, Huston," Leo urges, scrambling to put each piece back where it had been. Thanks to his freakish photographic memory he gets every position correct.

"Okay... okay," Huston says, laughing.

I put my yellow man back at Start and settle in.

"Grace?" Huston's voice crackles through the phone. I reorient myself. The din of Noah's Bagels zooms back. I steady myself on the counter, still clutching my empty large cup; the tea bag is now a crumpled mess.

"I'm not taking her calls because I'm not interested in what she has to say," I explain, turning away from Tim. He walks over to where the group is seated.

"It's your choice not to be a part of this," Huston says. The weight of what I did smothers me as it does every time I let myself think of my family.

I bolted.

I ran from the only people who loved me. I should have run *to* them when Mom died. But I just couldn't get away fast enough. Their love felt like a building on fire. I had to stop the burning.

Huston continues, "It's great to hear your voice again."

A flash flood of emotions begins to penetrate my carefully

constructed barriers. Panicked, I focus on Tim settling in next to Laura. He looks over at me. The divide between my two identities is comical.

"Me, too," I whisper.

Huston laughs. "You're glad to hear your own voice?"

"No, I mean...it's good to hear your voice, too." I laugh in spite of myself. I watch as Tim picks up our baskets of bagels. He settles back in, taking a huge bite of his—cream cheese everywhere.

I remember that back before Tim and I started dating I believed him to be a *monkeyhander*: a word Mom coined to describe (or poke fun at) Abigail's exceptionally long fingers and her habit of pawing at people like some kind of mutant-alien. As we grew up, *monkeyhander* evolved into an adjective we all used to describe a lover who was good on paper, but devoid of that...*spark*. So whenever I fantasized about Tim, we were always cuddling and lounging around doing crosswords on an overstuffed couch. Not struggling to get each other's clothes off in the heat of the moment. I had that once. Wasn't ready for it again. So with Tim I prudently fantasized about golden retrievers, morning cups of coffee and a retirement plan.

"Leo's coming," Huston breaks in.

"Be sure to bring some air freshener and bail money," I joke. Huston laughs.

I continue, "Well, then..."

"So, I'll see you later," Huston says, getting down to business.

"I...uh—"

"I understand this is tough, but you must know that we're looking forward to seeing you," Huston interrupts.

I am quiet.

"Then it's settled," Huston says.

"If by settled you mean that you've bullied me into going, then—"

"That's exactly what I mean," Huston says. Even twenty years later my brother is just as imposing as he was over a game of Sorry!

"Huston—" I start.

"Grace—"

I cut in, "Let me finish, *please*," still stupid enough to challenge him.

Huston is quiet.

"I'm standing in a goddamn Noah's Bagels…and…I just need to get my head together," I finally say.

"You've had five years to get your head together, Grace. You're thirty-five years old. The onus is on you to be a member of this family now whether you feel you're ready or not." Huston's voice slithers over the word *feel* as if it's the most ridiculous word in the English language.

I am quiet. Suddenly ashamed and embarrassed.

"So, it's settled," Huston repeats.

"Yes," I say, almost in a whisper.

"See you when I see you," Huston says, finally hanging up.

"See you when I see you," I say to the dial tone. I beep my BlackBerry off. What just happened? I walk outside. Run outside. Faster. Faster. Outside. Away. The rain. Close my eyes. Can I really return to this family? I don't have the heart…I mean, I literally don't.

It broke into a million pieces the day Mom died.

chapter three

I thought your dad was dead?" Tim whispers, as I pull a chair up to the group after finally filling my cup with hot water. Little Earl Grey flakes float on top like fish food.

"No, it was my mom who died," I say. So normal. Just words.

"Then where has your dad been?" Tim presses, crossing his long legs and turning his chair toward me.

"Apparently he's been in Ojai, California. Less than a hundred miles away. He left—well, he was *asked* to leave, when I was thirteen..." I trail off, having given Tim more information about my past in the last ten seconds than I have in all the months we've been together.

"So, what are you going to do now?" Laura chimes in.

"I'm going to eat my blueberry bagel," I answer, dismissing her and her ridiculous assumption that this is any of her business.

"Do you have any other family?" Laura presses. I swallow my bite of bagel with an apologetic shrug. They wait. Fantastic.

"I had two brothers and a sister," I admit, swallowing.

"Had?" Laura asks. A look of horror passes across her Botoxed face—at least I think it's horror—she could be laughing maniacally, for all I can tell.

"Have. I *have* two brothers and a sister," I say, wiping my mouth with a napkin. Laura relaxes. She must have thought I lost my whole family in some hideous accident. I laugh at the thought. But. Wait. *Wait.* The numbness I've luxuriated in for the past five years tingles like a foot that's been asleep. It wasn't a hideous accident. I walked away from my entire family voluntarily. I gulp my tea, instantaneously burning my mouth, esophagus and stomach lining. I slam the teacup down on the table, gulping for air. I pull my complimentary water out of my purse and drink the last droplets.

The table waits. I set the little water bottle down.

"And where are they now?" another woman chimes in. Do I even know her name? I know she's told it to me a thousand times. I always refer to her as Slip Is Showing.

"They're still here ... Huston's in Pacific Palisades—"

"Houston—like the city?" Slip Is Showing cuts in.

"Yeah, but it's just H-*U*-S-T-O-N, not H ..." I trail off.

"*O-U*-S-T-O-N," Slip Is Showing embarrassingly finishes.

"We all know how to spell Houston," Laura says, laughing.

"I couldn't let it just hang there." Slip Is Showing's face reddens.

"So, Huston spelled with just a *u* and not like the city, is in the Palisades—where's everyone else?" Laura urges. I thought my detour through Houston had blessedly led us away from where this conversation was going. No such luck.

"Abigail's in South Pasadena and Leo's in Pasadena ... where I am. Last I heard," I say, now taking the top off my tea and blowing on the hot water, which was apparently plumbed from the center of the earth.

"Last you heard?" Laura asks, thrusting her breasts in my direction.

"I haven't spoken to them since Mom died," I say. Tim is riveted. Whenever he's asked about my family, I've always just said it was "complicated." He never pressed further—one of the traits I appreciated most in him.

"What ... what happened to you?" Slip Is Showing asks, her face contorted in worry, her eyes looking on with wonder. I feel like a white tiger behind plate glass: one part scrutinized, the other pitied.

"What *happened* to me?" I repeat, sharpening my claws.

"So, you guys weren't close then," Laura cuts in.

"Oh, no—we were pretty much inseparable," I admit, feeling less and less confident with the choices I've made over the past five years.

The table is silent.

"So, you just walked away?" Tim finally asks, his voice heart-breakingly quiet.

"Yeah," I answer, my voice clear, but hollow.

Without missing a beat, "And they let you?" Laura asks, her voice angry.

"What?" I say, looking up and into her pooly blue eyes.

"You were obviously in some full-blown depression—why did they just let you run away like that?" Laura is angry. I feel a pang of guilt for rolling my eyes every time I saw her over the last seven years.

"I don't think I was reachable...to anyone," I say, almost into my teacup. I didn't exactly wile away my days on the couch, swathed in a blanket, weeping and watching daytime television. I had never been like that in the past and certainly wasn't going to start then. I simply decided I wasn't going to think about it. *Couldn't* think about it. All of Abigail's phone calls, Leo's e-mails, even the letters Huston sent rush back to me. I locked them all out and dove into work. It was the only way I could survive. This is the philosophy I've built my entire life around for the last five years. A philosophy that led me here: to an intervention at Noah's Bagels. I force myself back to the conversation at hand. Slip Is Showing is asking me something.

"For five years?" Slip Is Showing asks again.

"Are they older or younger?" Laura asks.

"Two older, one younger," I answer, automatically.

"How...how do you just walk away?" Slip Is Showing asks, marveling.

"It just got easier every day. For everyone, I guess," I say, now looking around the Noah's Bagels like I'm waiting for someone. A lone gunman, maybe? One who'll put us all out of our misery?

"I didn't know any of this," Tim says, his voice low.

"I know," I say, unable to look at him.

The table is quiet.

"You must have really loved her," Laura finally says.

My head jolts up and I look directly into Laura's now welling eyes. A person I've never taken seriously. A person whose last name I know only because it's in her e-mail address. A person who has taken that chink in my armor and torn it wide open— simply by asking a few basic questions.

"Yeah," I say, looking away from Laura, my voice quiet.

"I'm so sorry," Slip Is Showing says. I take a giant bite of my bagel.

"So, what's everyone doing for New Year's?" Tim throws out as the silence around the table grows awkward. He scoots his chair closer and wraps his arm around my shoulder. The group of people stumble into a lighter conversation, but I can tell they are haunted. By me. Great.

As they rattle off various parties, get-togethers and celebrations, I take a deep breath and close my eyes, retreating from the New Year's Eve talk that swirls around me. The wafting Earl Grey smell reminds me of Mom. She smells like Earl Grey and outside.

And then, she is there.

"But you mustn't forget it," Mom reads, her arm around me, our legs a tangle in my tiny twin bed. I can hear Leo's deep snores from across the bedroom. Abigail creaks on the upper bunk, settling in for the night. I try to read along with her, but she's too fast.

"You become responsible for what you've tamed. You're responsible for your rose . . ." Mom reads, closing the book.

"Mom, is the . . . is the Little Prince ever going to . . . is he scared up there?" I ask, listening to the rumbles of Mom's stomach.

"We'll find out more tomorrow night," Mom says, kissing my head.

"Just . . . is he . . . is he really a little prince?" I ask, as she crawls out of the bottom bunk.

"Sleep, little one," she says, bringing the covers up to my chin and gently kissing my cheek.

"Yeah, but—" I say, as she stands on her tippy toes to tuck in Abigail. I hear their hushed good-nights.

"You've read that book a hundred times," Abigail says from on high. Mom walks over to Leo, who's sprawled on his bed, snoring wildly. Mom pulls Leo's covers tight over him and kisses him gently on the cheek.

"I just . . . I just like asking her about it," I say, turning onto my side.

"Go to sleep and tomorrow we'll read more," Mom says, flipping off the light.

I open my eyes.

"That sounds great," Tim offers. Was I remembering out loud?

"Thanks, I love wearing red on New Year's," Laura says. Apparently she's been describing the dress she bought for her New Year's festivities. Whew.

"I need to get some fresh air," I say, looking at Tim.

"Yeah . . . sure. Why don't you start the car and I'll be there in a sec," Tim says, passing me his keys.

"Thanks," I say, taking the keys and standing. "Have a great new year," I throw out feebly, feeling naked and vulnerable. The group mumbles "Happy New Year" back to me, no doubt hoping that my New Year's celebration will include a team of psychologists.

I throw the teacup away, give the group a final wave, put my sopping wet hood up and race to Tim's car.

The silence of the car surrounds me. I know that Tim's in there apologizing for me. He does that a lot. Sure, he's all for my being who I am, but sometimes I wonder if he'd rather I were a little less...just, *less*.

As I sit fiddling with the knobs on Tim's dashboard (something I've been told several times not to do), I try to fend off the clatter of memories of Dad. So far away. I can barely...barely reach them. But, like a lost spoon in the garbage disposal, I pull one, bent and twisted, from the depths.

"And on piano—Grace Hawkes," Mrs. Callahan announces. The crowd applauds. The tiny auditorium is stuffy and smells of mildewed wood. The seats are pressed close to one another and the parents of the kids in the orchestra are packed in like sardines.

I stand and the piano bench squeaks behind me. My formal dress we found at the Junior League thrift shop crumples up in the back. I smooth it down and bow, searching the audience.

Mom, Huston, Abigail and Leo are all seated in the fourth row. Mom waves and smiles. I smile back. As I scan the row, I see an empty chair next to Abigail. Dad. I want to hit something. Thank God, we're starting with Beethoven.

The violins and violas bring their instruments up to their chins. The audience is quiet. My fingers are itching; I home in on the sheet music like a laser. Focus the anger.

With the downbeat comes the quiet. The elsewhere. No empty chair. No rage. Just Beethoven. My body curls over the keyboard, foot pumping the pedals, fingers racing across the keys.

Mrs. Callahan's guiding baton . . . and one, two, three, four . . . and five, six, seven, eight . . . and nine, ten—how hard was it to just get here?—eleven, twelve. One, two, three . . . why did I even get my hopes up? Four, five—I knew he wouldn't come—six, seven, eight. I *knew* it . . . nine, ten, eleven, twelve . . . and rest.

I sit back a bit on the bench. My shoulders have crept all the way back up to my ears. I force them down by watching the first violin move with the music. His long fingers move up and down the neck, making it look so easy. He closes his eyes for just the briefest second and I wonder what demon *he's* trying to quiet.

The crowd erupts in applause and Mrs. Callahan motions for us to stand. I find Mom in the audience once more. She's beaming. So happy. I hate myself that it isn't enough. As the concert goes on, I look at that empty seat as if I were waiting for a bus. Now? If I crane my neck, can I see it approaching from down the street? What about now? Brahms . . . Bach and Handel. What about now? Nothing. The only people looking back at me are my family—apologizing for the one person who doesn't deserve it. I decide right then that I won't ruin the night. I'll be happy.

I flip the page of music, almost tearing it. Could I be doing something to make Dad mad? I must be doing something wrong. Is my playing not good enough? I started playing to spend more time with Dad—he on his trumpet, me playing along on the piano. He and Mom found this little upright beauty for my seventh birthday at a church rummage sale. I've been playing duets with him ever since. I never took official lessons. It was just Dad and I sitting on that tiny bench, hunting and pecking our way through masterpiece after masterpiece. Those moments spent playing with him are some of the best we shared. Just me, Dad and music. The piano went from something Dad and I did together to something that takes me away from the pain of wondering where he is all the time and what I might have done wrong.

I have one great parent. That's more than most people can say. I look back down at the keys. My eyes are clear, my anger is focused, and as I pound away, the sting of Dad's absence lessens with every swallowed emotion.

I promised myself I'd never wait again. I'd never trust anyone except my family. And Dad stopped being family.

From then on.

I might have been able to handle one part of this scenario without the other. Dad's stroke or reuniting with my family. But both? Abigail sent me a save-the-date for my niece Evie's quinceañera. I was planning on going—I even RSVPed after I finished being blown away that Evie was already almost fifteen years old. Maybe that's what started this. Abigail saw an opening and using that crowbar-like determination decided now was the time.

Maybe now is the time.

I concentrate on Tim as he moves around the table, shaking hands and averting his eyes from various and sundry shelflike breasts.

Is there any way to prepare for what's going on with Dad now? Even if everything else hadn't fallen apart, would there ever have been a right time to face the man who walked away twenty-two years ago?

And like a lightning bolt just shot through the roof of Tim's car, my heart seizes.

Walked. Away.

The trapdoor blows off its hinges and splinters against a far wall. I bend forward, putting my head between my knees.

I can't breathe. I can't breathe. Why haven't I ever connected the two before?

Dad walked away. I walked away.

"Are you hiding?" Tim asks, opening the driver's side door.

chapter four

J esus, Grace...are you okay?" Tim asks, his hand on my back.
"I'm fine...I'm fine. It's the...the bagel. I shouldn't have eaten it right after the run thing," I say.

"You look like you just saw a ghost," Tim says.

"Interesting wording," I answer, as I squish my new revelation about Dad's and my bolting into an out-of-the-way, yet increasingly crowded, corner of my psyche.

"If you want me to believe this doesn't have anything to do with your family, you're going to have to be a lot more convincing," Tim says, his hand now at my shoulder pulling me up.

"Can we just go?" I plead, my head still between my knees.

"I'm not driving with you in that position," Tim says.

"Fine," I sigh, slowly sitting up.

"Are you going to talk to me?" Tim asks. Inside I can feel myself gathering up. Putting the memories back into place. The voices getting a little further away every second I catch my breath.

"I honestly don't know what I'm feeling, to tell you the truth," I begin.

"Grace—"

"I'm serious. I'm not being all mysterious—"

"That'd be a first," Tim interjects with the softest smile, an endearing attempt at diffusing the situation. It's also a gentle reminder that being with me is a testament to his character.

"Right...right," I answer, my voice deflating.

"Let's just get home and get out of these wet clothes," Tim says, starting up the car.

"If it's okay, I just want to go home. My home," I say, clicking my seat belt across my chest.

"Come on, Grace," Tim chides gently, as he maneuvers out of the Noah's parking lot. If I never come back here again, I'll be the better for it.

"I'm not being weird and moody, I swear. I just want to take a hot shower, maybe grab a yoga class." Maybe I'll change my name to Starla Nightbody, move to an art colony in Taos, New Mexico, and take up glassblowing or turquoise jewelry making. Could be anybody's guess how far I'm going to take this.

"Are you sure?" Tim asks, looking over. Imploring. Trying his hardest to understand.

"I'm sure," I say, resting my hand on his leg.

"Do you want to meet for dinner?" Tim offers, getting on the 405 freeway.

"We'll talk about it later," I answer.

Tim finally pulls onto my street. A street so tree-lined and idyllic it all but bullied me into buying seasonal wreaths and happy-go-lucky welcome mats. After scrimping and saving, I took the plunge and bought my first home last year while the market was down. It was a stretch, but the house had been in foreclosure and was a great deal. I bought the worst house in the best neighborhood...and then spent a small fortune renovating it. I never thought I'd buy a home of my own. We always rented growing up and never called one place home long enough for me to see the importance of it. But as I climb out of Tim's car, with the morning's events weighing heavily on my mind, having a home to come home to makes me want to wrap my arms around its little two-bedroom, one-and-a-half-bath heart.

I walk around my now ornament-stripped, browning Christmas tree that's awaiting trash pickup at the curb and unlock the outer gate. I still firmly believe it's bad luck for a Christmas tree to see the new year. I have just two days to get this dark harbinger of doom off my curb or else I'm taking it to the dump myself; I certainly don't need any more bad luck. I push the gate open to the inner courtyard as I wave goodbye to Tim, smiling maniacally as proof that I'm fine. I must look like a demented pageant queen.

As I close the gate behind me, I immediately calm down. I'm relieved that it's stopped raining long enough to allow me to get inside—the dark clouds above signal there's another storm coming. The fountain gurgles as I walk past it, my fingers grazing the thriving lavender. I bend down to pull a burgeoning weed from between the wet pavers—the beginnings of heat from the hesitant sun feel good on the back of my neck. My street is always so quiet. Too quiet.

I unlock the large glass kitchen door and turn off the alarm. The several large windows that frame the front of the house are still dappled with raindrops. I set my purse down on the kitchen counter and take in the blooming courtyard.

Forgoing the name change and move to Taos, I decide on a hot shower instead. I promise myself I'll think about everything later—just let me take a hot shower and get out of these wet clothes. I put the kettle on and tell myself that a cup of Tension Tamer tea will be the ideal remedy for all my problems. It's on the box. It'd be false advertising if my tension wasn't tamed right after the first sip, right? I look down at the phone.

Another message. Huston.

"Dad's in the ICU at St. Joseph's in Ojai. I'm on my way up now. I should be up there in about two hours, depending on how the 101 looks through Ventura." Huston takes a long pause. I've been within minutes of my brothers and sister for five years and yet still so far away. I press my ear closer to the phone. He breathes deeply and continues, "It's time to be a family again." My whole body deflates and I set the phone down on the kitchen counter. A wave of nausea overtakes me. I jolt up and barely make it to the kitchen sink in time. Retching into the colander I keep in the sink to wash fresh blueberries for my morning protein shakes. Oh, God. Now, that's disgusting. I turn on the water, rinse the colander and the sink clean, then pool the water in my hand and bring it to my mouth. Slurping up the cold water.

Be a family again. The last time we were a family is the worst memory of all.

"And delivering the eulogy in today's services is Evelyn's eldest son, Huston Hawkes," the rector says, stepping down from the pulpit and making room for my brother.

Huston climbs the steps determinedly, pulling a tiny piece of paper out of his inside coat pocket. I wrap my arm around Leo as he continues to sob, and look down the pew at Abigail. Her mood has been swinging wildly between rage and despondency while she tries to figure out whose fault this is and whom she needs to speak with to make this whole thing go away. She wipes her tears away with angry fists. Her husband, Manny, gently tries to soothe her. I can see her entire body stiffen. I sit back in the pew, look up at Huston and wait. Wait for him to start speaking. Wait for any of this to sink in. Wait until I stop thinking that this can't be happening. That it must be happening to someone else's family.

"Thank you so much for coming. Mom would really love...have *loved*—" Huston takes a deep breath and steadies himself. I look up at the sweeping, coffered ceiling of All Saints Church. This is all a dream.

Huston continues, "Mom would have really loved to have seen you all." He stops again, taking a step back and looking up, resting his hands at his hips. He breathes. His lips are tightly compressed as he scans the church's architecture. He breathes again. I pull Leo closer.

"I can't take...much more of this," Leo whispers through sobs.

"I know, sweetie...I know," I whisper back, smoothing my hand over his back.

Steeling himself, Huston continues, "The last words Mom said to me were in a voice mail message she left detailing the reasons why I shouldn't use real wood for the deck I was building." The large crowd sniffles a laugh, nodding in agreement. Huston doesn't look up from the paper.

"It seems so trivial, but it's in those seemingly insignificant details where I felt her love the most. Where I'll miss her the most." Huston stops, his voice is barely over a whisper. He exhales, situating the microphone, smoothing the little paper again. This can't be happening. Abigail lets out the tiniest sigh. Manny pulls her close. She lets him.

"She was interested in everything about me—from why I haven't settled down with a 'nice girl' to whether or not I'm going to plant lavender in my backyard." The crowd sniffles out another giggle. My face remains vacant. Leo softens in my arms.

"The day-to-day," Huston says. He makes eye contact with me for the first time. I allow the smallest of comforting smiles and immediately feel hypocritical and morbid. Huston gives me a quick nod. I fidget with the hem of my skirt and clear my throat. I feel a comforting hand curl around mine—calming me.

John.

The teakettle whistles, steam billowing from its curling red spout. I turn off the burner and try to catch my breath.

The rain has really started coming down again. The large windows around my house are sheeted with rain. I can smell the freshness it brings. Smells like outside. I breathe it in.

Back then, in those critical moments, it seemed easier to walk away from everyone all at once. Even John, the man I had been seeing for almost a year. The man I struggled to get my clothes off with in the heat of the moment. The man with whom I thought I would spend the rest of my life. A man who, unlike Tim, pressed everything, pushed every button (both good and bad) and challenged every aspect of my life . . . whether I liked it or not. I held that tightly to Mom once. I thought she would live forever. And I was wrong. I couldn't take losing anyone else and so . . . here I am in a relationship where my "boyfriend" didn't even know I had a family, let alone ever met them.

I look past the rain-drenched windows, drop a Tension Tamer tea bag into the awaiting mug, and add the hot water. As the minty lusciousness wafts upward, I can still see John so clearly. That brawler's body always clashed with the suit and tie he had to wear at the law firm. I love . . . God, *loved* how his thick, wavy black hair played against those black-as-pitch eyes and that olive skin.

In the beginning, I was attracted to him more for his general wariness and global distrust in humanity than anything else. It was comforting . . . *familiar* somehow. Whenever I visited Huston at his law firm (the visits tripled after I met John), I became more intrigued by John's chronic look of skepticism than his obvious physical attributes, although who am I kidding . . . they certainly helped. Everything about him was dark—bottomless. *Everything.* Glasses were always half-empty to him. No one could be trusted. We were constantly running off the rails, burning too hot—testing every wall I'd built.

I could barely handle him when Mom was alive. Once she— well, once she was gone—no chance.

The eulogy.

Huston continues, "When I think about Mom, I don't think

about the big stuff—graduations, weddings, births. I think about—" He stops and smoothes the paper once more.

He continues, "I think about the phone calls about lavender that *not even I could kill*, the reminders about building a more eco-friendly deck, the certain knowledge that she knew me best of all and—" Huston's voice involuntarily clutches to a stop. He quickly regains control.

"The knowledge that she loved me more than anything," Huston reads. His eyes are elsewhere as not one tear rolls down his face.

"I'm going to really miss her," he finishes, and folds the little slip of paper back up. Huston's words are far away as I officially decide that this is happening to someone else. Someone else's mom's ashes are in that tiny silver box on the altar. Leo lets out a mournful sob. I pull him closer. John tightens his hand around mine. For being as physically close as I am to the people around me, I couldn't feel more alone. The isolation is palpable.

Huston walks woodenly down the narrow staircase. The rector takes Huston into his arms and surrounds him. I hear him whisper something about Mom that only those in the first row can hear. Mom's in a better place, according to the rector.

"Thank you," Huston says, trying to get away from the rector and his theories about Mom and that this "better place" isn't here with us.

The rector climbs the stairs as Huston finds his seat next to Abigail. Huston's body is tense and his eyes look distant. As he settles back in, I see him drop his head to his chest for just a moment. The second Abigail reaches out to comfort him, he lifts his head. He's telling her he's fine. We're all *fine*.

"And now—as we say our goodbyes, Evelyn's youngest daughter, Grace, will play one of Evelyn's favorite songs. Grace?" The rector looks down at me as I robotically let go of John's hand, disentangle myself from Leo and approach the piano. I slide onto the bench—it scrapes on the marble floor, echoing throughout the church. I take a deep breath and lay my fingers on the cold keys. So quiet.

My fingers steady as I begin playing the first chords to Bob Dylan's "I Shall Be Released." The elsewhere. The quiet. I close my eyes as the song fills the church. I don't hear the rector leading the people out. I don't hear the shuffling feet. It feels like just another day where I'm playing piano for Mom. She's here with me. I hear the song and feel nothing.

Any day now I shall be released.

When I finish, I look up from the keyboard. There's a silence around me that's one part terrifying, one part comforting. The large wooden door that leads out onto the lawn where the rector is standing with a kind word and a shoulder to cry on shines brightly. I squeak the piano bench back and survey the empty church. I start walking toward the front door.

Stop.

Mom's picture, the one we finally decided on after much arguing, sobbing and inappropriate laughing, sits on the church's elaborate wooden railing. The silver box holding her ashes sits right behind it, almost hiding. Tucked away. I put my hand on the box ... so cold. This can't be happening. The Elsewhere is still here, encasing me in a bubble that's magically keeping the pain just out of reach. I look up. There's a little side door hidden just behind the altar. I bet there's no kindly rector waiting for me behind Door Number Two. No kind words. No shoulder to cry on. No pain? No reminders of what I've lost? No reminders at all. I can walk away now and feel...nothing. Keep this little fragile bubble intact.

I look back at the picture of Mom. She's smiling. She's alive. She's looking at me behind the camera with this stare that says

"Fine . . . *for you. For you*, I'll smile." I take my hand off the shiny silver box and grab her picture.

And then, the picture, my bubble and I head out the side door.

I can still hear the distant chords of "I Shall Be Released" as I walk through my newly renovated house. I pass the picture of Mom I stole the day of her funeral. It sits proudly in the hallway niche I had specially designed for it. I peel off my wet running clothes and flip my shoes off. I walk into the bathroom and turn on the shower. I unsnap my sports bra and throw it in the dirty clothes hamper, the same with my panties.

Any day now I shall be released.

I put my hand under the hot water, trying to get it just right. I step in and let it spill all around me. It pours over my head and slides down my face.

That mystifying "exact science" of compartmentalizing all the pain, sectioning off whole eras of my life, rumbles back like stampeding cattle. I'm powerless over it. As I feared I would be. I'd hoped I could postpone this day indefinitely. Live in this nothingness forever. So I'd be more ready when the magician waved his wand and the two halves of me were rolled back together with an elegant "Ta-da!!!"

chapter five

I walk out to the living room and sit on the bench of my rented piano, my damp body feeling a combination of slippery and sticky—in all the wrong places. I tighten the towel under my arms and settle my fingers on the keys.

Any day now I shall be released...

My voice is whispery quiet.

Trapdoors and bubbles. Chutes and Ladders. All a minefield.

Any day now...

The funny thing is I'd managed to convince myself that the calm I'd felt since then was some sort of evolution. Instead I'd just grown comfortably numb.

I shall be released...

I play the song over and over and over and over again. My fingers pound the keys. My towel hangs on for dear life. The house vibrates around me.

I close my eyes and a slideshow of memories and snapshots speeds past my consciousness like brake lights on a rainy night. The good with the bad. My playing speeds. The rain pummels the windows. I've worked so hard to keep these memories and feelings at bay. Amazingly, I've only had one slipup in the last five years. And that one wasn't even my fault.

I just showed up for a root canal.

The receptionist had led unsuspecting me through a dental office decorated with photographs of all of Dr. Waxman's celebrity patients.

"Grace..." The dentist rounds the corner just as I'm settling into the chair.

"Hi," I answer, putting my purse on the counter next to countless instruments of torture.

"Dr. Reilly talked to me a little bit about your *situation*," Dr. Waxman starts, flipping through my file, putting up little X-rays of my molars and flipping on the backlight. I contort myself in the chair, looking at my teeth, the roots, the gums... the *problem*.

Dr. Waxman continues, "I'd like to talk to you about the use of nitrous oxide. Dr. Reilly told me that you were a more anxious patient. We can go over the—"

"I'm in," I interrupt.

"Good decision," Dr. Waxman says, resting his hand on my arm gently. He motions to the assistant to wheel over the Canister o' Good Times while I try to make myself more comfortable.

"This is going to take about four hours—two hours for each root canal. Do you have someone picking you up, Grace?" Dr. Waxman asks, pulling over the mask for the nitrous.

"Uh... no. I don't have anyone," I say, looking up at him.

"Oh, okay. Well, not a problem. Nitrous oxide wears off rather quickly, so you can drive yourself home as long as you wait about thirty minutes," Dr. Waxman says, bringing the little pink mask to rest on my nose. It smells like bubble gum. I'm positive I look like a warped version of Mrs. Potato Head.

The nitrous begins to flow. I don't really feel different. I'm not even sure it's working.

"Grace? How are you feeling?" Dr. Waxman asks, pulling his chair close.

"Triangles," I answer.

"Okay...we're ready," Dr. Waxman says to his assistant, who passes him the tongue guard. I stare at the lit panels of fish on the ceiling and wonder why that didn't make perfect sense to him. I try to focus in on the music playing over the drilling. Is that "Life in a Northern Town"? Wait...how did it get to be "Fragile" by Sting so quickly...wait, what happened to the... who...where's everyone going...are we done...wait...why am I sitting up straight now...when did that happen...am I...how did I get back down...wait...who's that...is that George Michael...wait...I can feel...no, I mean *really feel*...choking, wrenching, burning...sadness...loss...emptiness...

"I've made you cry," Dr. Waxman says, gently wiping a tear away.

"I can feel it," I say through the nitrous haze, tongue guard and dental instruments.

"Feel the drilling?" Dr. Waxman asks, immediately stopping.

"No...*no*, my bubble is gone...no bubble..." I answer, tears streaming down my face, wondering if those are actual aquariums in the sky.

"Bubble? Grace, I don't underst—" Dr. Waxman asks, motioning for his assistant.

"Inside my body...I can feel it," I whisper, as if something almost paranormal is happening to me.

"We're almost through," Dr. Waxman assures me. The walls are down. No armor.

"Oh my God, it happened to us. It happened to me," I urgently confess.

"It's okay, Grace...we're almost done. Turn up the nitrous," Dr. Waxman instructs his assistant.

More bubble gum...more lit fish...in and...out...how did I get...*Sweeeeet Caroline, BUM, bum, bum*...wait...there it is... no...choking, wrenching, burning...I miss you...please...

don't leave me . . . I . . . I'm nothing . . . I've got no one . . . please . . . please . . . please . . . I'm all alone.

"Mommmmmmmm," I call out, as the assistants try to calm me down.

I look up from the piano keys.

My hands ache and my chest hurts. The little half breaths I've been taking, the emotion I've been swallowing, feel like the worst case of heartburn ever recorded. I look up and down the keyboard, hoping the answer lies there. As I fight to catch my breath, I can't help but realize how monumental the simple act of breathing has become. So basic. Yet as my emotions straddle that line between my being in control and my being confined to a padded room, I can't seem to master it. I am nostalgic for the days when my breath was involuntary.

I bite my lip to stop the quivering. I've feared this moment for five years. It's not the chest pain or the bitten lip I'm afraid of. It's the endlessness of the pain. The final comprehension that this *is* real. This *did* happen to our family. Those *are* Mom's ashes in that little silver box. I breathe a whole, full breath.

The blur of the last five years floats past. A life embodied by a shrug of the shoulders. Trying not to pop that bubble. The rain continues to pound. How long have I been sitting here?

Any day now I shall be released . . .

I could . . . I *should* be the better man, Charlie Brown. I should go—and be there for Dad, even if he was never there for me. I should be the person he couldn't. I'm Mom's kid. I picture Dad finally realizing . . . *knowing* he missed out.

Maybe I just can't lose another parent without saying good-bye. Maybe I just can't have another parent die alone.

I know where to start.

I am quiet. The house is quiet. No more piano. I squeak the

bench back, situating the towel once again tightly under my arms, and walk into the kitchen. I grab the phone and dial. He answers on the first ring. He hasn't changed a bit.

"Leo?" I say. Out of all four of us, Leo looks the most like Mom. He's the only one of us with light brown hair and Mom's mint ice cream eyes. The rest of look like the cast of *Children of the Corn: The Adult Years*.

"Gracie?" Leo answers, his crumbly voice always bordering on a giggle fit.

Leo was always my charge. The boy genius who graduated from a magnet high school (that none of the rest of us could get into) at fifteen. And off to Cal Tech at sixteen.

"How are you?" I ask. I feel like I should fall on a thousand swords.

"I knew you'd call. I knew it. I knew that once Abigail broke the seal with Evie's quinceañera that it'd be like this chain reaction, but not like the neutron-fission chain reaction, that'd be ridiculous. We're more of a sociological example. I'm totally bastardizing it, but you know what I'm talking about—that once Abigail reached out to you . . . wait . . . what was I talking about?" Leo speaks quickly.

"Haven't you been talking to Abigail and Huston since—" I won't say since when. I can't. Not yet. Minefield.

"Kinda, but not really. I'm busy teaching at Cal Tech. They didn't mind that I had a record, you know. You had said they wouldn't, remember? Abigail was freaking out, of course. But, come to find out they saw my little run-in with the law as kind of on-the-job training." Leo laughs and then continues, "They even finessed it so I got security clearance. Imagine that?"

"Oh, we're bragging about your little stint in the pokey now, are we?" I ask, smiling.

"C'mon, it was fifteen years ago and besides I was only in for three months, thanks to Huston and John's legal wheeling and dealing," Leo finishes. *John.*

One. Trapdoor. At. A. Time.

"They did a great job getting you out."

"*Vanity Fair* even did this whole story about the first generation of hackers. It was maybe three years ago...three or four, something like that. It was really well done, they mostly focused on Jobs and Wozniak, but there was like two paragraphs in there about me," Leo announces proudly.

"Congratulations."

"It was one of the first times the federal government's mainframe was hacked and because I was like eighteen at the time, it was a good story or whatever," Leo explains.

"Yes, editing the FBI's Most Wanted List to include the President and his cabinet was quite elegant," I say, laughing.

"Didn't keep his son from getting elected."

"Well, crime shouldn't pay, my little revolutionary."

"No, seriously. I think that's what opened the door at Cal Tech. I was finishing up my second PhD at MIT and got the call," Leo says, rattling off an educational background that still blows me away.

"How did writing an exposé on your crimes and misdemeanors land you a teaching spot at Cal Tech?" I ask.

"Because they outed me." Leo's voice is adorably conspiratorial.

"Outed you?" I ask, a smile breaking across my face.

"Yeah, nobody could figure out that I was Griffon Whitebox," Leo almost whispers.

"Ah, ye olde code name of Griffon Whitebox," I repeat, wondering why I'm now whispering as well.

"Half lion, half hawk—"

"I told you back then that a Griffon is half lion, half *eagle*," I correct.

"Close enough—come on, Leo Hawkes equaling a griffon? You have to admit that's super cool," Leo cuts in, taking a bite out of something.

"Fine. And where did Whitebox come from again?" I ask, taking a sip of my now cold Tension Tamer tea. I can't believe I am having this conversation, but then again—it's *Leo*. This is exactly the type of conversation we used to have.

"The first time the griffon was used in Dungeons & Dragons was in the white box edition. It was a highly prized monster." Leo sighs, frustrated that I don't just *know* this information.

"So, how did *Vanity Fair* figure it out?" I finally ask.

"There's been speculation for years. I still deny it, though. You know," Leo says.

"Keepin' it real."

"Exactly."

We are quiet. Actually, I'm quiet. Leo's chewing.

He continues, "Are you heading up?"

I'm quiet. Oddly stunned. Wrenched out of my delusion that everything hadn't been reset to normal. Mom isn't going to take the phone from Leo and tell me to bring chocolate over stat and make a joke about his lack of a sweet tooth.

He continues, "That's why you called, right? To tell me you're heading up? I mean, it'd be weird to call and tell me you're not going to show up. You're not calling to tell me that, are you— Gracie?" Leo's mouth is full and his words are quick. I imagine chunks of food falling.

"No, of course not," I sigh.

"Oh...okay. Phew! If you were leaving now, we could have carpooled. Are you leaving now? Hey, wait, are you still in that apartment on Raymond?" Leo takes another bite.

"No, I'm on California Terrace. Over by the Rose Bowl? I bought a house," I admit.

"You bought a house? Man, that's the big leagues. I'm still in that duplex—the one with the smell?" Leo says.

"Ah, yes." I remember.

"I like the neighborhood, you know?"

"When are you heading up?" I ask.

"I'm just out the door. Abigail called me about an hour ago, I packed a bag and now I'm on my way out. Hopefully, I can find a place to stay once I get up there," Leo rattles off.

"Just like that?" I blurt, unable to control it.

"Just like what?" Leo asks.

"Dad's been gone for twenty-two years and now we're all running back to his bedside just because Abigail says so?" I say.

I feel bad the minute I say it.

"I don't know about Dad, I just know Abigail said to come," Leo says, his voice stilted as he tries to work it out. My head drops to my chest. I feel like I just kicked a puppy. But . . .

"Why don't we just get together for Evie's quinceañera?" I try.

"I don't know, Gracie," Leo answers, his voice hesitant.

"I don't understand why we're all flocking to him after he walked away," I protest, all my earlier epiphanies and lightning bolts now negated.

Leo is quiet.

"I mean, it's Dad. We don't even know the man," I offer.

"For not knowing him, you've sure been acting a whole lot like him for the past however many years," Leo blurts.

"It's not th—" I begin to argue. Leo interrupts.

"You walked away, but I still picked up the phone."

"I . . ." I stutter.

"I knew it was you. However mad I was or am or I don't even know anymore, however mad I was—I picked up the phone," Leo explains.

I am quiet. Ashamed.

Leo continues, "I'd flock to you, if you needed me." He doesn't sound angry, not exactly. It's worse. He's crushed. Disappointed.

"I'm so sorry," I say, my head in my hands.

"I don't want to fight," Leo pleads.

"No, you're right. You're right. I'm sorry."

"Don't be sorry."

"I can be sorry if I want to."

"Okay, then, be sorry."

"I will."

We're quiet. Bursting bubbles.

I continue, "I'll pack a bag and head up."

"Good," Leo answers.

"See you when I see you," I say.

"See you when I see you," Leo says at the exact same time.

"JINX!" we both say, quickly counting to ten.

"You owe me a Coke," Leo blurts first.

"Fine," I say.

"In Ojai, okay? You'll get me the Coke in Ojai."

"Okay."

"Promise?"

"Yes."

"Okay."

"Bye, Leo."

"Good night, Gracie."

I beep the phone off, still sitting on the granite counter, and look at the clock on the wall.

It's nine o'clock in the morning.

chapter six

I roll out the suitcase I've dubbed "the Pumpkin" and throw my cashmere hoodie into the big orange piece of luggage to get the packing going. Luggage this big scares me. I absently hold a handful of panties while I try to figure out what I should bring. I spot an old backpack at the bottom of the closet. I take the hoodie out of the Pumpkin, grab the backpack and throw the panties into the bottom. Better.

I stand in my kitchen, backpack over both shoulders, and look around my house one more time. I'll have to use my vacation days. I have seventeen. I think about buying a last-minute ticket to . . . Tuscany. Call Tim and see if he's up for a spontaneous rendezvous. I can't help but laugh. Tim is one of the least spontaneous people I've ever known: the one time we vacationed in Hawaii for a week our itinerary would have made Julie, the cruise director, cry uncle. Okay, Australia. I could go to Australia. I don't want to go to Australia. I just don't want to be here. Anywhere but here. No. It's time to be a family again, whether I like it or not. Sealing the deal, I pick up the phone and dial.

"Hello?"

"Abigail?" I say, knowing full well who it is.

"It took you long enough to call me back."

"I was in the middle of a 5K when you called," I say, wanting it to not sound so ridiculous. At least I didn't call it a fun run.

"Are you on your way?" Abigail presses.

"I have to stop by the office first."

"No rush."

"I have to pick up a few files, leave a note for my assistant...that kind of thing."

"It's just a stroke. Take your time," Abigail sighs.

"Wow, this has been such a pleasure. It makes me wonder why I haven't spoken to you in—"

"Five years."

"I'd better get going, then. Wouldn't want to be any later," I say, fidgeting with my keys.

"Yeah, wouldn't want that."

"Do you want to tar and feather me now or can you wait until I get up there?"

"I'll wait until you get up here." I'm caught off guard.

"Oh...okay. Tell Huston I'm on my way?" I ask, not able to face him quite yet.

"Yeah, okay. Drive safe. I wouldn't want you getting injured before I get my hands on you," Abigail says. Is that humor?

"Okay...see you when I see you," I say.

"See you when I see you," Abigail says, one second after me.

We're quiet. Counting to ten. I'm biting my tongue.

"You owe me a Coke," Abigail finally says.

Damn, that's two Cokes. I hate losing, whatever the circumstances. I beep the phone off and set it back into its cradle. I grab my purse and turn the kitchen light off.

I'll call Tim once I get to the office. I'm going to need the next... wait...how long *am* I going to be gone? Do I ask someone to pick up the mail for me? I've got a couple of days' leeway because of the holiday. I'm literally pacing back and forth, about to walk out, then walking back in, about to walk out and then back in. I hold my car keys in one hand and a commuter mug of Earl Grey tea in the other.

I shut and lock the door behind me and walk through the court-yard, breathing in the smell of lavender and fresh air as the sky thinks about raining again. I open the gate and walk two houses down, backpack still on, purse hitched at my shoulder, keys held tightly in my hand. I walk up the impeccable pathway, past color-coded perennials and little crafty signs welcoming me, letting me know that what happens at Grandma's stays at Grandma's, and that I should, above all, have a happy new year. I approach the red glossy door and hope these people will recognize me from the insignificant waves I begrudgingly throw their way each morning. I knock on the door. And wait. The door whips open.

"Hahahahahahaha!" A little boy maniacally laughs. I take a step back.

"Um...I...uh..." I stutter.

"Owen, dear. Owen? Honey, who is it?" a voice calls from the depths of the house. The little boy gives me the once-over—taking my measure. He's unimpressed.

"Some blonde lady selling coffee," Owen yells. I look at the commuter mug in my hand. Jesus.

"Blonde lady selling coffee? Well, Owen, dear, I've nev—" The gray-haired woman walks down the long hallway, trying to work out the ridiculous description. She stops once she sees me.

"Hi," I manage.

"Oh, selling coffee! Oh—Owen, this is our neighbor. Grace Hawkes, right?" the gray-haired woman asks. I'm stunned she knows my name.

"Yes, ma'am," I answer.

"Ma'am nothing. I'm Louise. Won't you come in?" She opens the door as Owen skips down the long hallway.

"Oh, no thank you...Louise. I wanted to ask you a favor. I know I don't know you very well, I'm not a big...I'm not a big waver," I say, holding my non-waving hand up as proof.

"Oh, don't be silly. What can I help you with?" Louise asks.

"Grammy!!!!! They're showing how they build the floats!!! They're showing how they build the floats!!!" Owen screams from the back of the house.

"We're going to the Rose Parade—it's his first time. He's quite excited. What can I do for you, dear?" Louise asks.

"I have to go out of town and I really don't know for how long. My dad has had a stroke—I don't really know him that well, so it's not like . . . He left when I was thirteen. Well, he was asked to leave. He had a thing for other women . . . a lot of other women. He just never looked back, though. You can not be a good husband, but why does that mean you have to be a bad dad? I don't know . . . so now I have to head up to Ojai and . . . well, see how he's doing and see my family and I haven't seen them for around five years, you know? Ever since my mom died . . . It's been five years since she died and I kind of flipped out and just walked away . . . ran away, really. From everyone. Like he did. I didn't put that together until this morning. Weird, huh? Yeah . . . I had this great guy, too. Pitch-black eyes and he was just this . . . Anyway, I have a new boyfriend now. He's kind of a monkeyhander—"

Louise cuts in, "Monkey what?"

"A monkeyh—ugh, never mind. It's too hard to explain. So . . . now . . . I'm uh . . . I'm driving right up there and I just wanted to know if you could pick up my mail . . . or something," I finish, my hands wound around the backpack straps.

Louise looks stunned.

"Grammy, the floats!!!!" Owen's voice wafts down the hallway.

"So your mail?" Louise concludes.

"Yes," I answer.

"I can do that," Louise warily says.

"Thank you. I really appreciate it," I say, taking her hand and shaking it.

"Take care, now," Louise says, taking her hand back.

"I will. I will. Thank you," I say, breathing easier. Louise walks back into her house. I turn to walk back down the pathway.

I hear the door slam behind me.

And then there's no looking back.

"Ray Hawkes. He's in the ICU." I put my hands on the elementary-school-style lectern in the minuscule lobby of St. Joseph's Hospital. Our family always goes to the Huntington Hospital in Pasadena, otherwise known as the Caesars Palace of hospitals. If the Huntington Hospital is Caesars Palace, then St. Joseph's is the 7-Eleven with a couple of slot machines just across the Nevada state line.

Tucked away in the rolling countryside northeast of Los Angeles, dotted with oak trees and babbling brooks, Ojai is downright idyllic. An ironic setting for such a reunion. I remember being shocked to find out it was spelled Ojai, thinking, it was spelled: Oh, hi. Like a casual greeting. Oh, hi. Certainly not its beautiful Chumash Indian meaning: "valley of the moon."

Two candy stripers stand behind the lectern.

"Ray Hawkes?" I repeat again. One candy striper picks up a plastic clipboard and flips through the pages.

"He's in the ICU," the other candy striper says. I breathe deeply and stare at the two girls, hoping they'll figure out from my silence—and the fact that I just *said* that—that they're not really helping. I'm just asking for directions to the ICU. I stare. And wait. They stare back. I finally have to give up and admit I can't win this staring contest. They're probably both thinking about the color yellow right now.

"And where might that be?" I ask.

"Fourth floor. Take the elevator, make a right, two quick lefts and then another right," one of the candy stripers instructs. I do the math in my head. Have they just told me to go on a wild-goose chase by directing me to walk in a perfect circle? I catch myself doing some odd half-hokey-pokey-like movement as I try to work out the whole right, left, left, right thing. I hitch my purse tightly on my shoulder and head for the elevator, repeating right, left, left, right . . . right, left, left, right . . .

As I walk toward the elevator, it finally dawns on me where I am. The chaos of the morning has slowed down and I find myself here—zombielike in the lobby of St. Joseph's Hospital in Ojai, California. What's waiting for me at the other end of these rights and lefts?

A harried blonde lady and a young boy stand next to the elevator. She's rolling a child-sized piece of luggage behind her. They both look at the elevator button, then at me, then back at the elevator button. It's that awkward moment where you ask yourself, has the other person actually pushed the call button—or are we all just standing here waiting for nothing? There's no light on the button indicating that it's been pushed. Is she running through the possibilities? If she walks up and presses it and the light is broken—then she's insinuating that I'm the type of person who stands in front of elevators willing them to open with my mind. The little boy jabs the button with a whirlwind of energy. He can't help himself.

"Alec, I'm sure the lady—" The elevator door dings open. They seem startled and no longer make eye contact with me as they step into the elevator. The woman holds her arm in front of the elevator door, holding it open for me.

"Oh, yeah—sorry. Sorry," I say, stepping into the elevator.

"Which floor? Alec likes to push the buttons," the woman says, eyeing my outstretched arm.

"Four, please. Thanks," I say, bringing my arm back down to my side. The woman and boy step to the far side of the elevator. Away from me. I'm relieved when I feel the buzz of my Black-Berry saying that I've got a message. It's from Tim.

Good luck today. Call when you get a chance.

The door dings open and they rush out. My stomach lurches as the elevator climbs.

Thanks. I'll call when I get to the B&B, I type. I booked a room at a little bed-and-breakfast I found on the Internet when I stopped by the office to pick up some files.

The elevator dings open on the fourth floor. I hit send and pocket my BlackBerry.

I'm immediately hit with that unmistakable hospital smell. My entire body convulses. I can't do this. I need a bathroom. Not again, Jesus—not again. I'm unable to cry, but apparently I've now started vomiting like a kitten with a hairball every time an emotional situation arises. Good to know.

I close and lock the door to the bathroom. Why are all hospital bathrooms so depressing? I'm forced to stop taking in my surroundings so I can retch into the toilet. I try to keep my hands behind my back while holding my breath. My purse slides down my arm and touches the floor—I'll have to burn that later. I quickly grab some paper towels and put them just under my hands.

The smell of the hospital permeates the bathroom. Flashing, shooting images of long hallways and a doctor walking toward me. Wringing her hands, approaching families—hopeful families. Families that are about to be broken.

"Evelyn Hawkes, please...she would have been brought in about fifteen minutes ago?" I ask, breathless.

"Hawkes?" the woman behind the bulletproof glass asks.

"Yes, Hawkes, with an *e*. Evelyn Hawkes? Car accident," I say, looking around the waiting room for the rest of my family.

"Come on through," the woman says, buzzing the large double doors open.

I walk through and am hit with that smell: sickness they try to cover up with cleaning products. Bustling nurses and doctors zip from one room to another, gurneys line the halls, and everyone not in scrubs seems confused...lost somehow. We shouldn't be here. No one should be here.

"Grace!?" Leo calls from the far end of the long hallway. He slips and slides down in blue paper booties, no doubt provided by the hospital, because I'm sure Leo showed up barefoot. I catch his full weight and prop him back up.

"Hey...hey...it's going to be fine. It was just a car. She was in that giant flower truck, Leo. She's going to be—" I soothe, rocking him back and forth.

"She's their floral designer, why was she even driving that thing?" Leo asks, before I can finish my speech. I'm sure she is going to be rolled out in a little wheelchair with a sling around her arm and a "How do you like that?" look on her face any minute.

"Maybe someone didn't come in to work. She'll tell us when we're allowed to see her," I answer, looking down the long hallway.

"I'm so glad you're here," Leo sighs.

"Hey," Abigail says, walking down the long hallway with Manny and Evie: the namesake. At just ten, she's barely even allowed to be back here. The detached preteen is doing her best to not look scared. Manny is wearing a company polo tucked into dress slacks. Abigail's loafers squeak on the hospital's clean floor as she walks toward us. I can see Abigail caressing Evie's hand as she gets closer. Evie's eyes dart from one room to another. She holds on to Abigail's hand tightly.

"They haven't come out yet," Leo says, his voice tight. I am calm.

"Okay...okay...we're all here. Huston is out front filling

out some paperwork. It was just a car and she was in that giant flower truck," Abigail asserts, playfully shaking Evie's hand around. Evie's face remains creased with worry.

"Why was she even driving that thing?" Leo asks again.

"Did anyone talk to her yet?" I ask, hopeful.

"I talked to her this morning," Abigail says. We all nod. We've all talked to her this morning. We all talk every morning. We all talk every day.

"Have you heard anything yet?" Huston asks, emerging through the double doors. Huston's frame takes up the long, sterile hallway. He immediately walks over to me.

"No, nothing," I answer, Leo still curled into every nook and cranny.

"She was in that giant flower truck. She's gonna be fine," Leo adds. I smile again. This is nothing.

"The woman at the front desk didn't say anything?" Abigail asks. Evie is biting her fingernails, plunging her entire hand into her mouth. Deeper and deeper in. Manny gently pulls Evie's hand out of her mouth and gives it a tender kiss. Evie smiles, embarrassed. Manny holds her hand in his.

"She was in that giant flower truck," Huston says.

"That's what I said," I say, smiling. Huston averts his eyes and I can see his jaw clenching . . . over and over. I pull Leo close.

"Why was she even driving that thing?" Leo's voice is growing panicked.

"She was in that giant flower truck," Huston says again, still nodding.

A doctor turns the corner . . . walking down that long hallway. She's wringing her hands.

There's no sound, just muffled voices and distant beeping. I can feel my family tighten around me. Leo folds into me even more as Abigail holds on to Manny and Evie. Huston calmly walks forward to meet the doctor, extending his hand in introduction.

"Are you Evelyn Hawkes' family?" the doctor starts. Huston nods.

Oh God.

"They did everything they could. Evelyn . . . your mom? Your mom died at the scene. I'm so sorry," the doctor says.

Everything goes black.

The next thing you know, you're dry-heaving into a hospital toilet five years later.

chapter seven

I can't hide out in this bathroom forever. I came up here to show Dad that I'm Mom's kid; I have to get myself together. I douse my face with water, slurping up handfuls. I pull my BlackBerry out of my pocket and dial. Straight to voice mail.

"This is Tim Barnes of Marovish, Marino and Barnes. I'm unable to take your call; please leave your name and number and I'll return your call as soon as I am able." I wait for the beep.

"Hey...it's me. I'm at the hospital, well in the bathroom...haven't gone in yet. Haven't seen anyone yet. I have thrown up, though. So, there's that. Okay...I'd better get out there. I'll talk to you soon. Bye," I say, hanging up. I pocket the BlackBerry. With no further tasks before me, in or around this bathroom, I have no choice but to exit.

I open the bathroom door and look out into a maze of long hallways. More goddamn hallways. Each one dotted with door after door of suffering.

I make a right.

I try not to look into the rooms as I walk by, but I can't seem to help myself. Bed after bed filled with people desperate to be out of there, to not be in pain anymore. Families clustered around the beds, trying to act lighthearted and unworried. But even from the hallway I can see their hushed conversations and hidden side glances to one another, signaling a bad turn.

I make a left.

I pass a bustling nurse's station. They don't bother looking up as I pass. Clipboards, monitors and the business of healing have their full attention.

"Gracie?" The man's voice behind me is unmistakable. That giggly crumble. Funny, I don't smell marijuana or body odor. I must have gotten him on "Shower Day." Maybe that air freshener isn't needed after all.

"Grace?" Leo repeats. I turn around slowly, twisting my mouth into a smile, trying, imploring my face to take its horrified look somewhere else.

"Leo?" I manage. The man who stands before me now ... well, is simply not my brother. Is it?

"I thought that was you! I saw you run into that bathroom, so I waited. Thought I heard you kind of talking to yourself, but ... you know—who doesn't? Hey, you made it up here in great time. God, you haven't changed a bit!" he says, lunging toward me for a one-armed hug—the ever-present laptop held in the other. The fact that Leo looks like a fresh-faced ex–fraternity boy instead of someone who'd ask you for change on a street corner is mind-blowing. He still has the posture of someone who's uncomfortable with his height. Taller than Huston, Leo constantly looks like he's dipping down to fit into a shortened doorway, seemingly guilt-ridden for looking down on everyone both physically and intellectually. I've been looking up to both of my brothers since puberty.

Leo's traded his light brown mud-soaked dreadlocks for a pleasingly shaggy muss. His eyes ... they're the same. Mom's. I look away and take in his outfit. It's amazingly put-together. No tie-dye, dancing bears or hemp accessories to be found. A charcoal-gray sweater falls over his jeans and rather than having blackened bare feet he's wearing a pair of actual shoes—sure, they're Vans, but at least they're shoes. At thirty-three, Leo still looks like he could easily be in his early twenties.

"You look...Jesus...you look," I stutter, pulling back from him.

Leo laughs. "Like a grown-up?"

"A *clean* grown-up," I correct.

"It's a trip, huh? Thought I'd get a fresh start for the new job." Leo giggles.

"You ain't just whistling 'Dixie,' " I say for the first time in my entire life.

"And apparently you're now an old Southern lady. It's hot here, huh? I mean, it's late December and it's not even sweater weather. I didn't have any New Year's plans...did you? I said it wasn't sweater weather and I'm wearing a sweater! Hilarious," Leo quickly says.

"No, I didn't have any New Year's plans," I answer one part of Leo's impassioned Q&A.

"Ha, sweater weather," Leo says.

"Oh...brought you this," I say, pulling a can of Coke I got at a gas station on the 101 out of my purse.

"Aww, thanks," Leo says, taking the soda, lunging in for another hug. God, I've missed him.

"I promised," I say, mid-hug.

"We're down here," Leo says, pulling out of the hug and taking my hand. He guides me down a hallway toward...I'm not ready. I'm...*no*, Huston's speech about me locking it up and being part of this family speeds back. I squeeze Leo's hand and give him a quick smile.

We make a left and come to a far more official-looking nurse's station and a pair of double doors. Leo sets his laptop and the can of Coke down and begins signing in.

"We have to sign in for the ICU," Leo says over his shoulder as he hunches over the clipboard on the counter. The nurse hands him a name tag with HAWKES scrawled across it. Leo hands me the pen and I fill out the necessary information:

12/29
Grace Baker Hawkes
Daughter
Yes, I'm over the age of twelve
Ray Hawkes

The nurse hands me my own name tag, once again with HAWKES scrawled on it. I peel off the tag and press the paper against my sweater. I hitch my purse tighter on my shoulder.

We enter through the double doors to the right.

The buzzing of the door ushers in a symphony of beeps, blips and urgent voices. This little community hospital has quite an impressive ICU. At its center is yet another nurse's station. Around the station are four rooms, all with glass doors and windows. A sort of warped theater of sickness.

"Over here," Leo says. The room is empty. I can't see Dad yet, but I do see the outline of his body in the hospital bed. I steady myself on the nurse's station and swallow. Hard. I focus my eyes and follow Leo.

I walk past the nurse sitting sentry in a rolling office chair just outside Dad's room. She nods and smiles. How thankful she must be that this isn't her family. I look up and into the room and my eyes come to rest on the hospital bed once again.

Dad.

I hold on to my purse for dear life. Leo folds into a hospital chair with a black motorcycle helmet beneath it. He boots up his laptop. I walk forward. I can't hear anything but the sound of my own breathing. Where is the giant I remember?

This is an old man.

Dad's face is turned away from me. His eyes are closed, his body seems calm. His breathing is labored. My eyes trace his body—past his once wide chest. His arms are covered in a now graying wheat field of hair. Just underneath his once tanned skin are purplish bruises and browning liver spots. When did he get so old? My stomach turns and my face gets hot and clammy again. I try to find a point on the horizon to steady my stomach, like Mom used to tell me to do when I got carsick. All I see are machines, more tubes, more, more, more. I can't focus. I look back over at Leo.

"How old is he now?" I ask.

"Sixty-eight," Leo says, not looking up from his laptop. I place my hand on the metal bar on the side of his bed. Sixty-eight. With my bubble already popped and the trapdoor splintered, the sight of Dad's feeble body hits me like a ton of bricks. I've been so focused on reuniting with my family and starting to deal with Mom's death, or trying *not* to deal with it, that I haven't readied myself for this. Dad. Twenty-two years. I bet I *do* look like I've seen a ghost . . . for real this time. Too real. Where is the Dad I knew?

"Okay, Gracie—you start on the . . . see? Right there—" Dad is standing by my piano. Thick blond hair tousles and flips, making him look like he's being followed around by a gentle breeze. Rough features, ice-blue eyes and a build that seems best suited for pillaging. He moves with the music. Miles Davis. Again. Always. I'm supposed to come in on the downbeat.

"Yeah, on the . . . one, two, three . . . there—" I say, curling over the keys, playing my part. Dad sways, closing his eyes, listening to me play, tapping the top of the piano in time.

Dad blows the spit out of his trumpet, his knees bend, and he lifts the horn to his lips. And . . . I close my eyes.

Our music wafts through our little apartment. I don't open my eyes. I don't have to. I know what everyone is doing right now.

Dad and I were the soundtrack to our family's lives.

"Glad you could make it." I jolt out of my reverie, look up from Dad and see—

Abigail.

I automatically check to make sure I'm not wearing a piece of her clothing.

"I found her out in the hall," Leo says.

Abigail looks like she could be the PTA president of any school in any suburb—and probably is. I imagine her bringing tuppers filled with cupcakes—possibly tuppers made expressly for bringing cupcakes—to the local bake sale, to raise money for a new library. Her blonde hair is a waterfall of straw-colored wisps that fall just past her shoulders. A pink Barbie jeweled barrette keeps the hair out of her face. Abigail's ice-blue eyes are now encased in the parentheses of crow's-feet. She wears the same uniform she always has—khaki pants, a pastel sweater set, and loafers. At least someone's had the decency to stay the same. After the whole Leo debacle, I imagined walking in here only to find Abigail wearing a bustier and latex skirt while brandishing a riding crop. Abigail's sweater set means some things never change.

I marvel at how normal we look. I catch a reflection of myself in the far window, just over Leo's shoulder. The same blonde hair, except mine is longer than Abigail's and is highlighted to be more white-blonde than sun-kissed. It falls past my shoulders in a cut that's supposed to look effortless, but costs a small fortune to keep up. I'm blessed with Mom's upturned mouth. I love that about my face . . . in the right light I can see Mom in it.

"Hiya," I manage, thinking that maybe I broke the ice with the phone call. Maybe she'll . . . maybe she'll—what? Let me off the hook? I stand there awkwardly, wondering what the proper greeting is after five years with threats of a tarring and feathering hanging in the air. Hug her? Slap her on the mouth? Revert to prior performance and hawk a giant loogie on her?

"Has Leo brought you up to speed?" Abigail continues, walking straight past me without so much as a nod. Mystery solved.

"Dad's sick," I answer, the beeping and whirring of the machines helping me achieve the level of sarcasm I was aiming for. Abigail's entire body tightens. I don't even know why I say it. I can't seem to keep from turning into a foot-stomping brat whenever I get around Abigail. No wonder she treats me like one.

"Yes, well, it was nice of you to rush up here," Abigail begins.

"You *are* famous for your inappropriate invitations. At least I eventually show up," I say, picking at the scab of Abigail's inviting Dad to Mom's funeral—and the even bigger wound of his not bothering to show up.

"He had a right to be there and who knows wh—" Abigail whispers, still defending him/herself.

"Can we not do this? I mean, can you just...for like two seconds," Leo cuts in, motioning to Dad.

"Fine," I say, feeling guilty. I remember that at one of Abigail's slumber parties we started fighting about some insignificant slight that violated proper party etiquette. Leo got so upset he went over, unplugged the living room floor lamp and shoved the plug right in his mouth, quietly electrocuting himself as we fought. We spent the rest of the night in the emergency room while Leo told wild stories about how his vision looked like a staticky television screen.

"Fine," Abigail answers.

"Have you seen the twins yet?" Leo interrupts.

"Twins?" I ask, scanning the room for electrical sockets.

Abigail and Leo look at each other.

"Twins?" I repeat.

"We have twins. Manny and I," Abigail admits.

"And no one thought to tell me this on the phone?" I ask, my voice raspy as I try to continue whispering. Even after finding out that whole people exist that I knew nothing about.

"It just didn't seem like something to tell over the phone," Leo says.

"How old are they?" I ask.

"Four," Abigail answers, trying not to smile at the mention of them.

"Four," I repeat.

"What does Evie think about all this?" I ask.

"Inconvenienced half the time—well, really she's inconvenienced by all of us, so..." Abigail smiles.

"And the other half of the time?"

"When she thinks we're not looking, she's...she's adorable with them." Abigail beams.

"And this was...planned?" I tiptoe. Abigail is quiet.

"She did IVF," Leo jumps in.

"Leo!" Abigail says.

"IVF?" I ask.

"After Mom—" Leo starts.

"Can we talk about this later?" Abigail asks, her voice rising. We are quiet.

"Is Huston here yet?" I finally ask as the silence settles in.

"He was here earlier. He said he had some business to take care of," Abigail answers, relieved.

"The kids are out in the waiting room," Leo continues.

"Evie is watching them while I—" Abigail motions at Dad. I zoom back into the surroundings. The beeping and whirring of the machines come back up. Dad's labored breathing fills the room once again. How easily I forgot why I'm here. Dad coughs into his oxygen mask and I back away, instinctively looking to Abigail.

She comes forward and stands on the other side of his bed. Dad lifts his left arm to reveal that he's wearing a restraint around his left wrist.

"What's that?" I sputter.

"The stroke paralyzed his right side. They had to restrain his left arm. He was pulling everything out. The tubes. The catheter," Abigail explains, as she buzzes for the nurse. I step away from Dad's bedside and find a place closer to the glass wall of his room.

"Not pretty," Leo adds.

"Haven't seen my father in twenty-two years and the first glance I get is of his—" Abigail trails off, motioning to the more nether regions of our father. I wince. Dad wheezes again into the oxygen mask.

"He's sedated, right? He's on pain meds?" I ask, my voice rising.

"Yeah . . . he shouldn't be feeling any pain. But they tell me that it's uncomfortable, you know . . . all the tubes," Abigail explains, looking up as the nurse comes in the room.

"Everything okay?" the nurse asks, immediately walking over to Dad's side.

"He's trying to pull the tubes out again," Abigail explains, as she takes Dad's restrained hand in hers. He grips her hand tightly. Find a point on the horizon. Find a point on the horizon. He knows what's going on. He's in there somewhere. I look up at the ceiling of the hospital room.

"Now, Mr. Hawkes—just calm down. Everything's okay," the nurse says.

"This is Grace. My sister," Abigail says to the nurse.

The nurse laughs. "How many of you *are* there?"

"Just the four of us." Abigail's voice is tight.

"You're like those Narnia kids."

"Those Narnia kids?" Abigail asks, as politely as she can.

"I just saw that movie with my kids. They loved it," the nurse oozes.

"It's actually a book—a series of books," I say.

"Four of them, four of you," the nurse adds.

"Do we also remind you of the Beatles?" I ask.

"*Grace*," Abigail warns. The nurse turns away, doing her best to ignore me.

"Four of them, four of us," I add, under my breath. The nurse trades an empty bag of clear fluid for a full one.

"You'd be the Edmund," says Leo, snickering. Abigail smiles as we watch the nurse.

"What?" I ask.

"Huston is the Peter, Abigail is the Susan…that makes you the Edmund," Leo says.

"And *you* the Lucy," I point out.

"I'd rather be the Lucy than the Edmund," Leo whispers.

Abigail titters. "Didn't Edmund betray everyone?"

"I'm not the Edmund," I sigh breezily, trying to seem as un-Edmundlike as I can. Abigail harrumphs over in the corner.

"Your mom was here earlier," the nurse says. She nonchalantly checks Dad's oxygen mask, re-situating it on his nose.

"I'm sorry?" I ask, my heart skipping a beat.

"Our mom died," Leo says, almost in apology.

"Oh, I'm sorry. She said she was Mr. Hawkes' wife. I assumed—"

"No—Connie is Dad's second wife," Abigail explains.

"Connie? Connie who?" I whisper. What. Is. Going. On?

"Later," Abigail warns.

"Right…then, Mr. Hawkes is fine, he's settled," the nurse

continues, patting Dad's restrained hand. The nurse turns on her squeaky white heel and heads out of Dad's room. "Oh, well, here she is now! One big happy family!" she announces, scooting past what must be this Connie person and another man as they sweep into Dad's hospital room.

Abigail, Leo and I turn to face the woman.

"So good you could all be here for Ray," Connie says, approaching Abigail and taking her hand. This woman looks like everyone's grandmother—stark white hair, dressed in resort wear, impossibly frail.

"We're so sorry," Abigail says, consoling Connie.

"There are more of you than before," Connie notes, her voice quivering.

"This is Grace, my younger sister," Abigail says.

"The *Edmund*," Leo jokes, under his breath.

"Shut up, Lucy," I whisper back, shooting him a look as I approach Connie and extend my hand.

"Grace. Sure. You still play piano?" Connie asks, her hand tiny in mine.

"Yes, ma'am," I answer.

"Ray talked about you guys all the time," Connie says. I steal a glance at Dad. In the bed. So weak. So...old.

"He'll love that you guys made it," the other man offers.

Abigail, Leo and I look at the man. Uh...and who might you be? I don't say this out loud. I'm positive I can feel Abigail relax because she thought I would.

He continues, "Oh! Silly me, I'm Dennis Noonan, Connie's son. From her first marriage—obviously!" He extends his hand to each of us.

"Your mother was a lovely woman," Connie adds.

"Thank you," we all mutter.

Was.

"There are so many of you," Dennis exclaims. Leo sits back down in the chair by the window and looks straight ahead, leaving the laptop on the floor.

There is an awkward silence. There are three of us in the room. *Three.* First we're the Narnia kids and now this. It's not like there are so many of us we could be the road company of *Seven Brides for Seven Brothers.* You can count us on one hand. With fingers left over.

"Yes, we're quite a brood. And Huston's still to come—" Abigail concedes, offering Connie a chair next to Dad's bedside.

"Oh, thank you, dear," Connie says and sits, reaching over to grab and clutch at Dad's hand. Dennis stands on the other side of Dad's bed.

Abigail finds a seat next to Leo. None of us look at each other. Could this Dennis guy be more of a child to Dad than we got to be?

I stand next to the glass wall, crossing and re-crossing my arms over my chest. Connie is his wife now. Dennis has been in his life for years. And yet...

I can't help imagining Dad taking a middle-aged Dennis out for ice cream. They're having a heartfelt discussion about how Dennis should call him Dad. Middle-aged Dennis is licking his ice cream cone—mint chip, I think—saying something like, "Aw shucks, Ray...you ain't foolin', are you?" And with that, Ray musses up the boy's graying red hair and says, "Naw, *son.* I ain't foolin'." And then they throw a ball around until Connie calls them in for dinner. Meat loaf. Her grandmother's recipe.

I shift my weight onto the other foot and notice that Leo has focused back on his laptop while Abigail is typing something out on her cell phone...painstakingly slowly. Adults attempting to keep up with modern technology always look so bewildered. I rest my hand on the metal pane of the glass wall. The cold metal feels good under my fingers as I start to tap out "Head Over Heels" by the Go-Go's. Mom used to bribe me with sheet music from the hits of the time to get me to practice. Therefore, my piano training is heavily based on the hits of the 1980s. I try to get lost in the beat and the intricacies of the melody. It's not working. I pull my other hand back and play the harmony, going so far as to tap out the big climax. Abigail narrows her eyes at me from across the room. I clear my throat and try to act as if I had been about to stop on my own...at just that moment. The room zooms back.

Watching Dad fight for every breath sends a chill down my spine. Not because I think he might die, but, frankly, because over the years I *wished* he'd die. Standing here in the same room with his rumbling coughs, those thoughts haunt me...shame me. It's not like I really wished on him something like this.

For once, there'd be a good reason why we never heard from him.

We stand at the perimeter of the room like visiting, friendly neighbors making way for the real family.

"Where's his wedding ring?" Dennis asks. I look past Connie's frail body and spy Dad's left hand. Nothing.

"I took it off when we got here. I just didn't want to take the chance," Connie explains.

"Where is it now?" Dennis asks. I look over at Abigail and Leo. They're riveted.

"I gave it to the head nurse to put with all his other belongings. Wallet, keys..." Connie says, her voice cracking. They've forgotten we're in the room. The conversation isn't meant for us.

Wait a minute—why *are* we here?

Connie turns to us. "It's so funny how every little thing becomes important," she says, her voice cracking. We all nod.

How did Abigail even find out about this? I thought maybe

Connie called her, but now I'm positive that Connie didn't call anyone. She's far too upset. I try to catch Leo's eye. The weak link. Always the weak link. I don't know exactly how to get his attention...throw a bag of blood at him?

"Leo?" I say, as quietly as I possibly can. He looks up, as does Abigail.

I continue, "Weren't we going to go out and see the twins and Evie?" I ask. Abigail studies me. It is weird, I admit...I'm asking Leo to introduce Abigail's children to me. Well, because I can crack Leo. Abigail? *Never.*

"Oh, sure. Sure," he says, shutting down his laptop. He stands, putting it on his chair, saving it. Abigail's eyes narrow as she watches this unfold. *She knows I'm up to no good.*

Connie doesn't look up from Dad as Dennis checks the monitors. Abigail stays put, concentrating on Dad, trying not to stare. I look up at the clock just over the door outside Dad's hospital room. It's not even noon yet. Wait, what? It was 11:37 when I signed in—I remember the time exactly. It hasn't even been half an hour? Leo walks out of the room and into the ICU nurse's station. I follow. I've got to act fast.

"Second wife?" I ask.

"Apparently, Dad married her pretty much days after Mom died," Leo says, as we wait for the buzzing door. I marvel at the ways we've all dealt with Mom's death: the twins, remarrying, teaching jobs and second PhDs, drowning in nothingness. Have we all been so lost? Why couldn't we turn to each other?

"Who is she?" I ask.

"Abigail talked to her for a bit this morning. She's from here, works as a receptionist at the elementary school where Dad teaches band. Seems nice enough. I just feel bad for her, you know?" Leo says.

"Dad teaches band?" I ask. I have so many questions.

"I know," Leo says, smiling to himself.

"She seems pretty upset," I say, as we finally pass through the double doors and out into the main hospital.

"Yeah, must be tough for her," Leo answers.

"Was she upset when she called Abigail? You know, to get us to come up here?" I ask, looking off—trying to seem nonchalant.

"Connie didn't call Abigail," Leo says, opening the door to the waiting room.

Three of the most adorable children I've ever seen are scattered around the room. They all look up at the same time. Evie has grown into a young woman in the five years since I've seen her. She looks even more like Mom than I remember. I mean, to the point where I just may lose it. The light brown hair, the giant green eyes.

Two children I can only assume are Abigail's and Manny's twins are sprawled on the floor. They're surrounded by coloring books and picture books, but both are glued to a television that's showing some animated movie.

"Guys? This is your aunt Gracie. She's been, well . . . she's been on a *trip* for a while, but she's back!" Leo announces.

"Really?" I say, to his ridiculous lie about my whereabouts. But what was he supposed to say?

"A trip?" Evie drawls, looking up from her book. Her light brown hair is long and straight. Why am I relieved that her haircut is still appropriate for a young girl? She folds her body in an impossible tangle of coltish limbs, ballet flats and leggings under miniskirts.

"It's good to see you again," I say and smile, walking over to Evie.

"Mom said you were just being difficult," Evie says, not standing as I approach her. I've lost her trust. I can see it in her eyes. The irony of this moment is jarring. I've been so selfish.

"Yeah, that's closer to the truth," I say, holding out my arms with an expectant look. She stands like she's waiting for the hangman to place a noose around her neck. I pull her in for a long hug. At first she stands stick-straight, her arms at her sides. I can sense her eyes rolling and feel her inconvenienced sighs. I know one thing that'll crack that indifferent demeanor. Or at least it cracked it for the first ten years of her life.

"Washing machine...washing machine..." I joke, twisting and turning her lanky body around in my arms as if she were a load of laundry.

"You...*you*...hahahahaha." Evie finally succumbs and laughs.

"It's good to see you again," I say, pulling her in for a hug again. Evie wraps her arms around me and pulls me close. I breathe her in. I won't let this second chance slip away.

"You, too," she says, her head tucked into the crook of my neck. A baby girl I saw ten seconds after she was born and I walked away. Never again. I pull her tighter. She'll be lucky if I ever let her go.

"You're weirdies," a tiny voice shrieks.

Evie and I break from our hug. I look over my shoulder. A little boy with a tangle of dark brown hair, giant apple cheeks and that perfect little kid skin stands with his arms akimbo. He's wearing a tiny pair of glasses that are secured to his head with a neoprene strap. I can see splotches of dirt and spit on his lenses from here. I wonder if he can actually see through them. As we take him in, he unsheathes a plastic sword that's tucked into the side of his pants.

"Weirdies?" I ask, stepping toward the little boy. Evie gathers herself, meaning that she tries to appear as apathetic as possible, and settles back on the couch with a book.

"That's Mateo," Leo says, pointing to the boy.

"Mateo, huh? I come in peace," I say, extending my hand.

"We hate peas," the little girl says from the floor.

"That's Emilygrae," Leo adds.

Emilygrae is the mirror image of the little boy—well, they *are* twins. Her dark brown hair is in pigtails that are squished and lank—obviously from lying on the floor. Her huge brown eyes are accented by eyelashes I swear I can feel on my face from across the room. She's wearing a pink shirtdress with candy cane tights and Mary Jane shoes. She is also sporting two little twin casts right at her wrists. One hot pink. The other black.

"Tio Leo!" Emilygrae says, pronouncing his name *Lay*-o. She rushes over and immediately hugs Leo's legs.

Evie remains on the couch, trying to act like she's reading whatever book rests on her lap. But I can see she's watching me. Wary.

"What happened to your arms?" I continue, knowing kids appreciate a certain directness.

"Fell on the zipper," Emilygrae answers, holding up her casts for my perusal. Are they Bedazzled?

"You fell on your zipper?" I repeat. That can't be right.

"It's a playground thing. Like a zip line?" Evie mumbles, as if I'm the dumbest person in the world.

"Oh . . . right. Thanks," I respond, shooting her a wide grin. Evie looks back down at her book. Baby steps.

"Has Huston come in here yet?" Leo asks, gently pulling Emilygrae up so he can hold her. Her little legs wrap around Leo's middle. She rests her elbow on Leo's shoulder and just stares at me. No shame in her game. But Mateo has grown weary of our conversation and doesn't answer Leo as he re-situates himself in front of the TV—following much sword-adjusting.

"That's who called the house," Evie says, looking up from her book. I look over to her on the couch.

"What?" I ask.

"He told Mom about what happened to . . ." Evie trails off. Not knowing what to call Dad.

"Huston called Abigail?" I ask Leo.

"Hyooooston cawed Abigaayo . . . Hyooooston cawed Abigaayo . . ." Emilygrae chants, not quite solid with her *l*s yet.

"Who's Abigaayo?" Mateo asks, still enthralled with the television.

"That's our mami, Matty," Evie explains. Mateo looks at Evie with a look of pure awe.

"Abigaayo is Mami?" Mateo mulls to himself.

"Dad's lawyer called Huston when Dad had the stroke. That's where he's been all morning. At the lawyer's . . ." Leo explains, finally putting Emilygrae back down. She stands right in front of me. Like alarmingly close. I can feel her breath on my knees.

"Why did the lawyer call Huston?" I ask, stealing a glance at the now looming toddler.

"Huston has Dad's power of attorney," Leo answers.

Find a point on the horizon. Find a point on the horizon.

After twenty-two years of nothing, Dad has the audacity to demand that Huston handle his estate?

"Hi, kiddos."

I turn toward the door of the waiting room, my head still spinning.

"Tio Huston!"

chapter eight

Huston's hair is a darker blond, what would probably be the natural hair color for Abigail and me without the help of a colorist. He still has that air of authority he's always had. His powerful six-four frame looms large. I realize Huston looks as I remember Dad looking. Like a Norse god capable of swashbuckling whole townships in a single plunder. Now Dad looks like a sliver of that memory.

"Can I see you two out in the hall?" Huston commands. Leo disentangles himself from Emilygrae as I take in my older brother. Leo and I walk out into the hall obediently.

"I'm so glad you came," Huston says, pulling me in for a hug. It catches me off guard, so I'm uncomfortably tucked in sideways. I don't want the hug to stop, so I do my best to hug back. I breathe in. Leo latches on to Huston and me for a group hug and . . . is he humming? Huston and I both stop hugging and stare at Leo.

"Are you . . . singing?" Huston asks, still holding on to me.

"Is that 'We Are Family'?" I laugh, looking up at Leo.

"I'm happy. I'm happy and I'm singing," Leo explains, his face reddening. We unravel ourselves out of the hug.

"So, you're up to speed?" Huston says, getting down to business.

"Dad's had a stroke, he looks like an old man, there are two little kids in there that didn't exist five years ago, Dad's apparently married one of the Golden Girls, and we have a new stepbrother who I'm betting works at a used car lot somewhere nearby. That about right?" I say, looking up at Huston.

"That about sums it up," Huston says, smiling.

"Oh, and Dad gave you his power of attorney?" I announce, my face showing my disbelief.

"We're trying to figure out the legal angle on this thing," Huston says.

"The legal angle? What about the moral angle?" I blurt.

"The moral angle? Jesus, Grace—I haven't seen you in years, can you lay off the cross-examination for five minutes?"

"I liked it when we were hugging. Let's do that again," Leo says, pulling us in for another group hug. Still unable to say no to or otherwise discipline Leo, we oblige—awkwardly clustering for another hug.

"I'm not crazy," I mumble, my face shoved against Huston's chest.

"Shhh, we're hugging," Leo says.

"Moral angle," Huston says.

"WE'RE HUGGING," Leo says.

"Okay...okay," Huston and I say. Huston tightens his arms around us. I feel Leo inhale deeply. Through my one squished open eye I can see him smiling. Maybe I'm smiling a little, too. A *little*. Then...

I feel him before I see him. As if the air has stopped moving. The black suit, the black hair, the black eyes—bottomless.

John.

With my one squished eye I sneak a glance past Leo and see him standing there. He lazily watches us with his hands in his pockets. His head tilted just so. His tie loosened around his neck. Watching. Saying nothing. As Leo hums "We Are Family," I run the last conversation through in my head. "We're trying to figure out the legal angle on this thing." *We're*. The same crack legal team that freed Griffon Whitebox has apparently reunited to handle Dad's power of attorney.

I feel Huston shift his body and look over at John. He gives us one last squeeze and lets go. The guilt of what I did makes me want to grab Mateo's little plastic sword and give myself a frontal lobotomy right here. Can't it be something that someone else did, just once?

"It's time to deal with this," Huston says, his voice a deep whisper. Of course...Huston played cleanup. He and John still worked together after Mom died; they were friends before and stayed friends after. So when I walked/ran away from John, Huston probably had some explaining to do.

As I stand in this hallway staring at the man I walked away from five years ago without any explanation, I grow irrationally angry. I feel like a wounded animal that's been backed into a corner. I have no right at all, but my instinct is to come out swinging. What a shock.

It's high noon at the O.K. Corral.

"Hey, it's John," Leo announces, his arm in a supermodel-like position, presenting John like he's the star of the fall line.

"You remember John," Huston says. I take a deep breath, hoping to calm myself. My traitorous body reacts to John the way it always has. My legs feel like they're about to give out. My heart feels like it's about to burst out of my chest. My breath quickens. I feel a pang of guilt for reacting this way to John. I'm with Tim now. Tim the Monkeyhander. Ugh.

John says nothing.

"So, you're in Ojai?" I mumble.

"Obviously," John answers. This is going *really* well.

Leo and Huston are as quiet as church mice.

"Okay, well—better get back," I force out, nodding to Leo and

Huston as I start to walk back down the hallway toward the ICU, past John.

John says nothing.

I keep walking, desperately trying not to say or do something I'll regret. Say or do something *else* I'll regret. John's hands are still in his pockets. His head is still tilted just so. His tie still loosened around his neck. He appears completely unaffected. As I get closer to him, my eyes move up that brick wall of a body and meet his. His eyebrow is arched—waiting. We lock eyes. Just as our shoulders touch, brushing past each other in this impossibly narrowing hallway, he speaks. His voice a low burr. I feel it reverberate *everywhere*.

"Walking away? How revolutionary," John drawls. I force myself to continue walking down the hallway. He hates me. The man I thought could defy mortality hates me. And I deserve it.

We all walk back down the maze of hallways. As we wait to get through the double doors, I try to cope with John's dismissal. Instead, I'm dangerously close to actually remembering what it was like to be with him. To be loved by him. As I watch John bend over the sign-in sheet, my mind rockets through the razed amusement park of broken-down Chutes and Ladders, trapdoors and blown-apart compartments containing every memory I've tried to erase. I watch him tighten his tie and collect himself as Huston signs in next. As I look at John, at that body I once knew so well, the memories will not be denied.

"What's this one?" I ask, running my hands over John's naked back.

"That was during my poker phase," he says, of the ace of spades tattoo. One of several tattoos all over his body.

"I don't think that's what it means," I whisper, centimeters from his ear.

"Maybe not," he admits.

"And this one?" I ask, my fingers brushing the nape of his neck, his black, wavy hair at my fingertips.

"That's kind of self-explanatory," he says, turned away from me—flashing me the tattoo on the back of his neck that he got in his early delinquent days when he was in and out of foster homes. Expunging a juvenile record can sure brighten a future. That and a stint in the Marine Corps.

"*Never Trust a Soul*," I read, his bare skin goose-pimpling under my touch.

"Quite the icebreaker at firm Christmas parties," he says, turning onto his back. The candle on his nightstand flickers with the movement.

"Do you still believe that?" I ask, lying on my side, tracing his every sinew with my fingers. I can see the dark angles of his body in the shadows. He turns his head and the pillow crumples under him.

"Sometimes," he admits, turning on his side.

"Me, too," I sigh, facing him.

"And this...this is new. What happened? Did you hurt yourself?" I ask, running my hand over a bandage on John's bare chest. Right over his heart. The light from the candle on his bedside table flickers.

"No," John answers, kissing my forehead.

"Are you going to tell me what happened?" I press, knowing that he's quite capable of fighting whenever, wherever. I'm not sure knowing someone's checkered past helps or hurts at times like this.

John shifts his body to the side, facing me—the flickering candle now backlighting the silhouette of his body. His black hair looks somehow shinier when there's no light at all. He begins to take off the bandage.

"Is it gross? Don't show me if it's gross," I cut in, covering my eyes.

"It's not gross," John says. I can hear the tiny ripping of the medical tape from his chest. I lower my hand and open my eyes.

"Oh, John . . . it's . . ." I trail off. My fingers run along the bumpy lines of my own name tattooed over John's heart. *GRACE*.

"Do you like it?" John asks, replacing the bandage over the new addition.

"Like it? I . . ." I lean in and kiss him. He pulls me closer. The permanence of the tattoo moves me.

"You . . ." John urges, turning over to blow out the candle. He turns back over as the dark envelops us.

"You . . ." he leads again.

"Love it," I finish, taking his face in my hands.

"I'm glad," John says, watching me. His mouth curling into a smile.

"And love you," I add. John pulls me in for a kiss.

"Grace?" Leo repeats. My mind lingers around the softness of John's lips.

"Are you going in?" the nurse asks again. Gone. John's lips are gone and I'm being told to exit to my right. I purse my own lips together as I hear the door buzzing. Leo is holding it open.

"Grace?" Leo asks again. I refocus. The ICU. Huston and John are already in a deep discussion with the head nurse. I can't help but look at John's chest. I wonder if it's still there. My own heart clenches.

"Oh yeah . . . sorry. I'm sorry," I say, putting one foot in front of the other. Focus.

"You okay?" Leo whispers.

"Not sure," I answer, giving him a beleaguered smile.

"Kind of a lot to handle," Leo says.

"For all of us," I say, softening.

"Yeah," Leo says, looking into Dad's hospital room at Connie, Dennis and Abigail. The outline of Dad's body is unbearably small.

Leo heads over to Dad's hospital room. He nods to Dennis as he picks up his laptop and sits back down in the chair he saved. He leans over to Abigail, whispering something. Abigail looks toward us as Leo shifts in his chair. I focus back on Huston and John and away from the omniscient gaze of my older sister. I approach them at the nurse's station.

"Do you have the original? We'll just need a copy," the head nurse is saying to Huston. I only catch the tail end of their conversation. Her tone is eerily similar to a high school principal's. John ignores me as I approach.

"Yes, ma'am. Right here." John hands Huston the original and a copy of the durable power of attorney for health care from a file folder labeled HAWKES, RAYMOND / ESTATE PLAN. Huston hands them to the head nurse. Inside the file folder is a stack of copies of the durable power of attorney for health care and some other legal-looking documents. How many times do they think they're going to have to present these documents to people?

When did this happen?

Sometime in the last few years, Dad would have had to sit down with his attorney and tell him he wanted Huston to have his power of attorney, over both his health care and his finances. Giving someone that kind of power means you trust that person over everyone else. He must have known Mom would raise a man Dad could believe in.

"And are you Huston Raymond Hawkes? I'm going to need some ID." The head nurse scours the documents, officiously flipping them over and over again.

"Is ID really necessary?" I ask, stepping into the fray uninvited. Huston looks from me to the head nurse awaiting an answer.

"Hospital policy," the head nurse explains.

"Do you find a high percentage of people lie about their identities in times like these?" John asks.

"Hospital policy," the head nurse repeats.

"Here you go," Huston says, pulling his driver's license out from his wallet. Abigail appears at my side.

"And the alternate? Abigail Evelyn Hawkes? Is that you?" The head nurse looks to me.

"No, ma'am—I'm Grace," I say, quickly glancing over at John. He's staring right at me. I tighten my hands in fists and try to forget what his skin felt like on my fingertips. Jesus.

"I'm Abigail Hawkes-Rodriguez," Abigail says, passing the woman her driver's license.

"I'm going to need to make a quick phone call. Please excuse me." The head nurse squeaks her way into a tiny office, taking both forms of ID and the documents with her.

"I had it handled, Grace," Huston scolds, his face studying mine.

"I know...I know," I answer. Always the same reprimand, always the same act of contrition.

The four of us stand in silence. No one checks the time. No one tries to eavesdrop on another conversation. I take in a breath as if I'm going to speak. Abigail whips her head around and glares at me. *Behave*, she lasers into my brain. The office door opens and the head nurse squeaks her way back over to us.

"Mr. Hawkes—" the head nurse begins, handing the original back to Huston. Now, I know very little about the law, but I do know that those documents should give Huston, and Abigail as the alternate, the ultimate right to do anything Dad could do. Decision-making. Finances. Medical information. The works. Why they want it is beyond me...but legally they have that right.

"I just got off the phone with the legal department. I apolo-gize. It's rare that the spouse isn't given...well, I won't bore you with the details," the head nurse starts.

"We're lawyers, Nurse Miller. Details are our business," John says, attempting a bit of humor.

The head nurse ignores him and bends over to open a drawer behind the nurse's station. John and Huston share a look of concern.

She continues, "These are yours, I suppose," slamming the drawer shut. She hands Huston a large ziplock bag containing Dad's wallet, his wedding ring and a set of keys. Huston takes the bag from the woman and hands it to Abigail. She looks inside the bag briefly, shakes her head and lets her arms fall to her sides.

"Thank you," Huston says.

"And the IDs?" I demand.

"Oh . . . right. *Right*," the head nurse absently says, taking them out of her pocket and handing them both to me. I hand them back to my two older, frustrated siblings.

"Follow me, please," the head nurse says, turning her back on us and walking back toward Dad's hospital room. We follow.

She walks into Dad's hospital room. Connie is still sitting sentry by Dad's side—clutching his hand.

"Mrs. Hawkes?" the head nurse says, stepping next to Connie, gently resting her hand on her back.

"Yes?" Connie briefly looks up at her.

I look around the room at the five of us, together for the first time since Mom's funeral five years ago. Huston, Abigail, John and I are pressed against the glass wall of Dad's hospital room. Leo is sitting in a chair on the opposite wall next to the large window. We're all frantically trying to stay in control: arms held tightly across chests, clenched jaws, deep breaths.

I look at Connie as another nurse checks Dad's monitors. She probably just saw the man she loves suffer a stroke right in front of her. The man she found after so many years of being alone.

The man she thought she was going to grow old, well *older*, with. Then we come barreling in here like a stampede of feral, bickering bulls. It must be the last thing in the world she wants to deal with right now.

"Mrs. Hawkes . . . I wanted to—" the head nurse starts. The other nurse quickly exits the hospital room. The sound of Dad's labored breathing fills the room. His eyes remain closed. The machines click and whirr on. The monitors display numbers that dance and change more often than on a roulette wheel. I recross my arms across my chest and hold tightly on to myself. John steps closer.

"Oh . . . Nurse . . . thank you so much. Did you find Ray's wedding ring? I'll put it in my purse . . . to take home," Connie says, without looking up from Dad.

"That's part of what I've come to talk to you about, Mrs. Hawkes," the head nurse starts. And stops.

The room is silent. Jesus, lady—hurry up or I'm going to tell her, for crissakes.

Connie panics. "The wedding ring? There's a problem with the wedding ring?"

"I'm sure there's no problem," Dennis says soothingly.

"Mr. Hawkes named his son as his power of attorney," the head nurse blurts. Dennis beams.

"The *other* son," the head nurse clarifies, motioning over her shoulder to where Huston stands.

The room is eerily quiet in those milliseconds. None of us move.

"I don't understand," Connie begins, her frail voice cracking. I feel so bad for Connie. Dad's let her down, too. Made her feel second best.

"Yes, Mr. Hawkes has named Mr. Hawkes—*Huston* Hawkes—as his power of attorney," the head nurse explains. All eyes now turn to the fringes.

"So...so what does this mean? What does that have to do with the wedding ring?" Dennis asks.

"All of Mr. Hawkes' possessions are now the responsibility of the holder of the power of attorney. So, Mr. Hawkes' wedding ring is now in *his* possession," the head nurse explains, eyeing John, making sure she's getting all the legalese correct. His face is hard, impassive. Dennis' eyes narrow and home in on the plastic bag in Abigail's hand. Huston steps forward, unblinking.

Huston turns around and motions for Abigail to hand him the ziplock bag. "Connie, I have no intention of keep—"

"Sons of bitches!" Connie shrieks.

chapter nine

Abigail snaps her arm back to her side. The entire room screeches to a halt. Huston slowly turns back around, now with the ziplock bag in his hands. John steps forward. As do I. Leo takes his usual place in the background.

"I've got it," Huston quickly whispers as I approach the fray. I settle in next to him.

"Mrs. Hawkes, I'm sure this is not going to be a problem—" the head nurse says, trying to comfort her.

"I'm his wife!" Connie screams, her feeble voice making it sound like a broken promise. Dennis scrambles to Connie's side. Leo sets his laptop on the floor, stands up and settles in next to Dad. He reaches out and caresses his shoulder. So gentle. Almost like a little "hang in there." I'm sure he doesn't think anyone is watching. I shouldn't be—I feel like I'm violating his privacy.

"I know, Mrs. Hawkes. It's highly unusual that the spouse—" the head nurse starts again.

"Surely, just because my father has chosen to give his power of attorney to this...*this* man doesn't change anything. Surely," Dennis says. *My* father? *This* man? If I tried to speak right now I'd resemble a human flamethrower.

"Huston is his eldest *biological* son," I say. I don't know how I feel about Dad at this moment, but I do know that no one, *no one*, talks to my brother like that.

"*Grace*," Huston growls. I back off.

Dad lets out a deep cough into his oxygen mask. Leo lays a hand on his right shoulder. It pains me to think he can't feel it because it's his right side that's paralyzed from the stroke.

"This is upsetting him! *You're* upsetting him!" Connie screams.

"I think you people need to give us a moment," Dennis says, opening his arms out like a great net, hoping to ensnare as many interlopers as possible. Dennis' hand falls on John's arm. I can see John's entire body tense up.

"I'm representing the Hawkes children. Obviously I'll be staying," John says, eyeing Dennis' hand. Dennis whips his hand off, smiling at John apologetically. John looks away and sniffs.

"Fine . . . fine, but the rest of you . . ." Dennis trails off. He successfully herds the rest of us (who don't look like we could snap his neck) out into the ICU. He closes the glass door, leaving Connie, the head nurse John, and himself inside. And Dad.

We stand on the other side of the glass wall watching every move they make. There's comforting. There's pointing out at us. There's pacing. There's Dad in the middle, his body looking limp and small. Do they think we can't see them? I let out the smallest, most nervous of laughs, shaking my head and looking at the floor.

"That went well," Abigail says. A nurse whizzes past. She says, "Excuse me."

"What happened in there?" I almost whisper. Another nurse whizzes past me. I say, "Excuse me."

"I wish we knew more," Abigail says.

"That hospital room went from a quilting bee to the World Wrestling Federation's *SmackDown* in two seconds flat," Leo chimes in, moving and re-situating himself to get out of the way of a passing gurney.

"Is it wrong that I . . . kind of love that Dad gave us his power of attorney?" Abigail adds.

"Even though we don't know why," I whisper, stepping aside and away from the gurney.

"No, we don't," Huston answers, giving Leo a quick comforting smile. He watches the gurney pass, squeezing his body into the doorjamb of a supply closet.

"What happens now?" Leo asks, as Abigail guides our little powwow into a small pocket of space by the double doors. Huston looks into Dad's hospital room. John has the file open and is producing document after document.

"You know...you don't have to," I whisper, choking on my words.

"What do you mean? You mean, we should just—" Abigail starts, her voice a building whisper.

"Yeah, we could just...walk away," I say. A nurse in pink scrubs looks over at us. I take a deep breath.

"Well, that's what you're good at," Abigail spits.

"Like father, like daughter," I parry. Abigail's face flushes as she zeroes in on me.

Huston seems not to notice. "This is probably a shock for her. Her reaction is normal," he says, trying to work out the logic behind Dad's choice. He looks at Abigail.

"Have you spoken to him since...?" Leo asks.

"No," Huston quickly answers.

"Just because he gave you the power of attorney doesn't mean you have to take it," I press.

"Just drop it," Abigail says.

"Am I the only one who remembers that he left? That he ran back to his rich mommy in Ojai while we survived on food stamps? No child support, no support of any kind. I mean, I understand that marriages don't work out, but to leave your kids like that...and not even make sure they're taken care of?" My voice is a rasping whisper. The nurses stare at us again as we move out of the way of a pack of doctors headed over to another glass room.

"We all remember," Huston finally says.

"He knew Mom had it handled," Abigail offers.

"Did she?" I blurt, without even thinking. "She never remarried, she never..." I trail off, not knowing where I'm going.

"Moved on," Leo finishes.

"It just seemed like we were drowning, and Dad—" I start again, looking back into the hospital room.

"Didn't care," Leo finishes.

We're quiet. I feel like a volcano...about to...

"I know I walked away from you, but trying to forget you guys was like swallowing poison every morning," I whisper, finally trying to come clean.

Abigail smiles. "You're such a drama queen."

"Swallowing poison," Leo trills, the back of his hand at his forehead as if he's in dire need of a fainting couch. I have to laugh at myself. We fall into silence.

"Doesn't that give you some insight, then?" Abigail asks, her face open and vulnerable. We all want answers.

"Maybe," I say, meaning it.

"But when you sign on to be a parent, don't you make a pact with your children to be held to a higher standard? I mean, Grace is our sister, not our father," Leo says, his mind a blur of equations and theory. I nod...wanting it to be true. Abigail lets out a weary sigh.

"Held to a higher standard," I repeat.

"Like Mom," we all say at almost the same time.

We're all quiet.

"Jinx," Leo mumbles. We all try to offer him a smile.

"Dad wanted us here," Abigail says, trying to get back on point.

"I know, but does that mean that he just gets us?" I ask, struggling to keep the pouty preteen snark out of my voice.

"Who would it help to walk away now?" Huston asks. Why do all of Huston's questions sound like statements? How does he *do* that? Abigail opens her mouth to say something, but . . . nothing. Her face reddens and her eyes dart around the ICU.

"Does he automatically get another chance after he's already had a lifetime of them?" I ask, putting my mathematical brain to work.

Huston, Abigail and Leo look at me. Pointedly.

I continue, "I know, consider the source. I'm sorry," I say.

"You're sorry for what?" Abigail leads. Leo represses the smallest smile.

"This should be good," Huston says, crossing his arms across his chest, a smile curling across his face.

"Saying sorry—" Leo begins.

Abigail cuts him off, "Or just admitting she's wrong."

"Was always hard for me," I finish in a humiliated whisper.

They wait.

"I'm sorry," I say, through gritted teeth.

"For what?" Huston leads.

"For freaking out and running away," I finish.

"And who does that remind us of?" Abigail leads once again.

"Dad," I answer, like a child getting caught for pulling someone's pigtails.

"Now, that wasn't so hard," Huston says, clapping his hand on my shoulder.

We all stand in silence, looking back into the hospital room, looking at the bustling nurses, looking at our watches. Looking everywhere but at each other. An orderly wheels an elderly man past us and out the double doors. We're in everyone's way. We're not supposed to be here. No one wants us here.

"Huston, how did you find out about all this?" I ask, trying to pull the focus away from me. Leo looks from Abigail to Huston and back to Abigail. Huston settles into his stance.

"Dad's lawyer called me last night. Connie called him about medical insurance and then told him what happened," Huston says.

"Why does Dad have a lawyer?" Leo asks.

"Do you remember Nana Marina? Dad's 'rich mommy,' as you so colorfully put it? She had that big, blue house—the house that Dad—well, Dad and *Connie*—are living in now. I guess when Nana Marina died and Dad inherited the house, he hired this guy to handle her estate. He must've then rehired him to handle his own estate planning, well...a year ago when he drew these up," Huston says, holding up the file folder.

My entire body is tight. I'm holding back every single instinct I'm having. It's like some new version of Pilates that's centered on repressing all your emotions for a count of ten, while focusing on your pelvic floor.

"Didn't we spend a summer at that house?" Abigail asks absently.

"The summer Mom and Dad went to New York," Huston says.

"So he could make it in the jazz scene," Leo adds, his voice dripping with sarcasm, the words *jazz scene* in giant air quotes.

"I was...what, fifteen?" Abigail asks.

"It was the summer before Dad left, so I was sixteen, you were fourteen," Huston says, looking at Abigail. She nods. We all nod. The summer before Dad left. We move again as the double doors swing open, letting in another worried family.

The summer before Dad left.

I look away from them and turn back to Dad's hospital room. Connie, Dennis and the head nurse are conferring. The head nurse is going over Dad's chart as Connie clutches at Dad's hand

and Dennis simpers at his bedside. John is respectful of their space, but I can see him inch closer.

"But, you could sign the power of attorney over to Connie, right?" I ask, treading lightly.

"No," Huston answers. Clear. Concise. Definite.

"Why not?" I ask.

"Grace, enough. It's not your name on that document," Huston says.

"Huston—" I start.

"It must be nice to never have to make a decision." Huston's voice is low and downright ominous.

"Huston," Leo eases.

Huston cuts him off. "This is my decision and, as always, you can resent me for making it, but at the same time, you're all looking to me for direction. Same as always." Leo recoils. Huston's eyes dart over to Leo with remorse.

"No one asked you to make this decision," I argue.

"He did!!" Huston yells, pointing into Dad's hospital room. The entire ICU turns to our little corner.

"Okay...okay...I'm sorry," I say. Huston rests his hands on his hips, hanging his head. He regains control quickly.

"Two apologies in one day—call the *Guinness Book of World Records*," Huston sighs, attempting a smile.

"I called them once. Thought I could get the record for—you know how you stack a bunch of quarters on your elbow and then you flip them, flip them over and catch them?" Leo says, excitedly miming the whole business.

We are all quiet.

"It was a bananas number of quarters you had to flip, so I just stuck to collecting lost or left-behind grocery lists," he says, as if this were completely normal.

We are quiet, lost in our own little worlds. And then we truly process what batshit-crazy thing Leo just said.

"*What?*" We all ask one after another. Leo doesn't miss a beat.

"Whenever I go to the store, I always look for lost or left-behind grocery lists. There have been some great ones."

"Great ones?" Abigail laughs.

"What constitutes a 'great one'?" I ask.

"I like trying to figure out what people are making, what kind of lives they have . . . who they're cooking for. I'm incredibly jealous of people who buy kale," Leo explains.

"Kale," I repeat. Huston smiles, finally calming down.

"You have to really know what you're doing in the kitchen to buy kale," Leo says dreamily.

"A kitchen . . . isn't that where the doggie bags from business dinners go?" Huston asks, yielding.

"I haven't made something without a hot dog in it for years," Abigail sighs. I laugh. Abigail sneaks a quick glance at me, smiling.

"John's waving me in," Huston says, walking toward the hospital room. Abigail follows at his heels.

"You're such a weird kid," I whisper to Leo, as we trail.

"It was either that or growing my fingernails to like twenty feet or something," Leo says, opening the door to Dad's hospital room for me. "I would think you'd prefer the grocery lists." I shoot him a quick look and focus in on the scene already in progress.

"—Our privacy," Dennis finishes. I only catch the tail end of his request, but I can certainly guess how it began.

"Mr. Hawkes—" The head nurse looks to Dennis.

"Noonan. Mr. *Noonan*," Dennis corrects her.

"Mr. Noonan, once again, I'm afraid Mr. Hawkes has a right

to know what's going on with his father's health. He has his power of attorney. I know this is going to be a difficult transition, but I'm sure—" Connie clutches at Dad's hand, never turning around. No longer even noting our presence.

"Ms—" Dennis begins.

"*Nurse* Miller," she answers.

"Nurse Miller, this man has no right to any information, I assure you. He was no son to Ray. He left you . . . he left all of them . . . when?" Dennis stutters.

"Twenty-two years ago," Huston finishes. His voice is steady and low. My heart breaks into a million pieces. *Again*.

"Twenty-two years ago! He wasn't a father to them at all!" Dennis announces.

"Whatever our relationship, it's simply not pertinent to the power of attorney, Mr. Noonan," Huston explains.

"Not pertinent! Get a load of this guy," Dennis guffaws.

"Then why did he put his name on the document, Mr. Noonan?" Abigail asks, her voice calm, but climbing.

"I don't know . . . you could have, you could have made him," Dennis answers.

"He could have just as easily put your name on there," I say. Huston looks from me to Dennis. Abigail does not shoot me a look. We all wait for an answer.

"This isn't helping," John whispers, looking mostly at me.

"You don't even know the man," Dennis argues, using the same reasoning I did just this morning.

"My name is on that document, Mr. Noonan. I intend to see that Dad's estate is handled the way he wants. The way the power of attorney legally allows," Huston says, his voice clear and calm.

"You're going to take our house away," Connie sobs.

"I don't intend to do any such thing," Huston answers.

"All of our belongings are going to be put out on the street," Connie sobs again.

"I don't intend to do any such thing," Huston says again.

"Then why do you even want the power of attorney?" Dennis questions again.

"Because my father wanted me to have it," Huston answers.

"Why do *you* want Dad's power of attorney?" I ask, stepping to Dennis. The room stops. Everyone turns to Dennis. Silence. Waiting.

"Isn't one of you a criminal?" Dennis blurts, looking at the head nurse. All eyes shoot to Leo: the doe-eyed boy genius standing in the background. He looks like he might start to cry.

"Don't you dare—" I bark. Leo wipes at his eyes and looks away. Huston steps forward. Abigail walks over and stands close to Leo.

"Why don't we all just take some time to cool off?" John cuts in, eyeing both Huston and me. We both stop. Abigail wraps her arm around Leo. He melts into her.

The head nurse takes this opportunity. "Why don't we all give Mr. Hawkes some time to rest. He's stable and it would do him some good to have a little quiet. Do you all mind?" Nurse Miller asks. Dennis stands on the other side of Dad's bed awaiting the answer. I gather myself, unable to look at John, and step back. Despite how conflicted I am about Dad and this whole arrangement, I know this isn't right. We *do* have a right to be here. For whatever reason, Dad wants us here.

That power of attorney is an engraved invitation to Dad's deathbed.

Huston shifts his weight. "I just want what's best for Dad." He tries to get Connie's attention. She doesn't look up or make eye contact. He lets out a long sigh. Oh, Huston.

"We'll need you to set up a meeting with the finance department, the legal department and Mr. Hawkes' primary care doctor—so we can all get up to speed," John adds, looking at the nurse.

"I'll arrange that for first thing tomorrow morning," Nurse Miller says, throwing us a bone.

"He's...he's stable?" Abigail asks.

"He's gotten through the worst. He had the clot blaster shot within an hour of the stroke and now we're just waiting on the neurologist. He's a fighter," Nurse Miller adds. Find a point on the horizon. Find a point on the horizon.

"We'll be back at seven a.m.," Huston says.

"Mr. Noonan?" Nurse Miller asks.

"We'll wait for them to leave, so we can have a moment alone with Dad, then we'll head home. Let Dad rest," Dennis says.

"That'll be fine. Thank you, Mr. Hawkes. Mrs. Hawkes-Rodriguez, Ms. Haw—well, just... there's so many of you...thank you...*all* of you." Nurse Miller breathes a little easier and ushers Huston out into the ICU. Leo grabs his laptop and the motorcycle helmet that's been underneath his chair and follows us out, his eyes welling up and red. Abigail takes her purse off the chair, hitches it over her shoulder, and walks out as well. John waits. Watching. Wary.

"Please give us some privacy," Dennis instructs us. Once again, my compulsion to do exactly the opposite of what people tell me to do flares. Dennis eyes me, waiting for me to leave. I grab my purse, pull it up on my shoulder. I need to touch Dad, to see if he's real, I need to let him know I'm here. That I was raised right. That I'm strong.

I push off the glass wall and in a fugue state walk up to Dad's bedside. I see John reach out his hand to stop me, but he quickly pulls it back. He helplessly looks on. Connie looks up, but I keep

my eyes on Dad. I reach out and touch his knee, the left knee—
so he can feel it. My hand closes around him, warming him. I
look up at his face. From this angle all I can see is the oxygen
mask and the shock of gray-blond hair.

"It's Grace. We're all here," I say, holding his knee and touching my father for the first time in twenty-two years.

chapter ten

M y arms itch, Mami," Emilygrae says, presenting her twin casts to Abigail as we walk out of the hospital. To say I'm shocked—to say *we're* shocked—would be the understatement of the century. I wait for Leo, holding out my hand. He shifts his helmet to the other hand, his laptop now safely inside his messenger bag, and takes my hand. He brushes at his eyes with his fist and gives me a little smile.

"Where's Papi? Where's Papi? Where's Papi?" Mateo sings.

"Working," Evie sighs.

"My arms itch!" Emilygrae says again.

"I know, mija. Let me just—" Abigail stops, reaches into her huge purse, and pulls a decorative chopstick from its depths.

"Where's Papi? Where's Papi? Where's Papi?" Mateo sings again.

"Honey, he's holding down the fort," Abigail says, holding up the chopstick.

"You said fart," Emilygrae trills, immediately plugging her nose.

"Fort, mija," Abigail says, pulling Emilygrae's hand away from her nose and plunging the chopstick deep into the casts, one at a time. Emilygrae looks like a puppy getting her tummy rubbed. Huston pulls his cell phone out of his coat pocket, checks the screen, and slides it back.

"You know, your mom once broke her leg so badly that she

had to wear a cast, too," Huston says, finally calming down. Mateo presses the button for the elevator.

"You broke your leg?" Evie asks.

"I fell down some stairs," Abigail says, shaking off the conversation.

"You fell off the *couch*," I correct. Leo giggles. The entire group smiles and breathes a little easier. Our little Leo is giggling again.

"You broke your leg falling off a couch?!" John laughs. I try not to stare at him. I try to think about Tim. Thinking about Tim brings back the nothingness. I wonder whether all that nothingness is such a good thing. I shake my head and refocus.

"Where did you get that couch?" Mateo asks.

"The couch has been gone a long time now," Abigail explains. We all load into the elevator. All eight of us.

"Was it a giant's couch?" Emilygrae asks, doing a little twirl—knocking into Huston. He lovingly steadies her.

"You'd think," I answer. The elevator sags and descends.

"No, Em, just a regular couch," Abigail explains. We stop on the third floor. No one gets on. It seems Mateo has gotten a tad overeager with the elevator buttons.

"A couch is just a big chair," Evie adds. The twins are awe-struck by this new information. Evie is now Stephen Hawking in their eyes.

"But that's not even the funny part," Huston begins, settling into prime storytelling mode. Mateo turns his attention away from the now lit panel of elevator buttons.

"Huston, please." Abigail laughs.

"Your mom thought that her cast was waterproof. And when I tried to tell her that the doctor only meant that if a little water splashed on it, it'd be okay—" We stop at the second floor. The door opens.

"No water can go on my cast, Mami says! I have to take baths with samwich bags on them," Emilygrae interrupts, urgently holding up her little casted wrists. The elevator door closes.

"Well, you're super smarter than your mom was, honey," Huston explains.

"You were quote-unquote babysitting me and Leo while we went swimming at the Woods'. Remember?" I add.

"Of course I remember, I almost died that day," Abigail says.

"She was convinced it was waterproof, so she went right over to the deep end and jumped in. Cast and all," Huston says, his eyes wide.

"Mami jumped in the pool?" Mateo yells.

"With a broken leg?" Evie adds. The elevator door opens on the ground floor.

"With no samwich bag on it?" Emilygrae's face is contorted with worry. We pour out of the elevator.

"That's bonkers," Evie droopily sighs.

"I sank to the bottom of that pool so fast. I could see your two goofy faces at the ladder, just looking down at me. Laughing hysterically, while I slowly drowned," Abigail says, slowing her pace as we walk toward the doors.

Leo laughs. "I'd forgotten about that!"

"Uncle Huston had to dive in and pull me out," Abigail says, taking Mateo's hand. Evie grabs Emilygrae. I hold on to Leo. I glance back at John, with his hands still in his pockets. Our eyes meet again. My adulterous body reacts and it takes everything I have to look away.

"You must have weighed close to seven hundred pounds with that cast hanging off your leg," Huston says.

"You never told us you broke your leg, Mami," Evie says, forgetting for just a moment that she's supposed to be unimpressed with everything and everyone.

"Well, now you know why," Abigail says, laughing.

"Mom was so mad at you," Huston says.

"Yeah…she…" Abigail trails off.

The laughter subsides and a hush falls over the group as we open the doors to the parking lot. One by one our smiles evaporate. *Mom.* I let out a small residual sigh, swing my purse forward and begin the excavation for my car keys. Leo smiles at me. I wiggle his hand around in mine and smile back. Abigail brushes Mateo's wild curls out of his eyes. Huston's cell phone rings again. He quickly answers it.

"Huston Hawkes? Yes, sir. Just a second." Huston puts his cell phone down, "It's Dad's lawyer. See you here at seven?" he asks the now dispersing group. Everyone nods. Everyone deflates. Abigail and the kids wave their goodbyes and head over to their awaiting minivan. John stands next to Huston while he finishes talking to the lawyer. I motion to Leo to hang on a second and run after Abigail.

"For you," I say, passing her a can of Coke from my purse.

"Thanks," she says, hesitantly taking it.

"See you tomorrow?" I ask.

"Seven a.m.," Abigail answers. I give a quick wave to the restless natives just inside the minivan. Abigail climbs into the driver's side. She puts the Coke in the cup holder.

"For later," she says, and backs out of the parking space. I watch them leave and walk back over to Leo.

"You okay?" I ask.

"Yeah," Leo sighs, looking off into the distance.

"It was a shitty thing he said," I say, trying to get him to look at me.

"Shitty, but true," Leo says, his eyes welling up again. I take a deep breath.

"We all make mistakes. Do things we regret," I say. Leo finally looks at me.

"It wasn't a mistake and I don't regret it," Leo says, a smile breaking across his tearstained face.

"Well, maybe I'm the only one who regrets things," I say, noticing that Huston has finished his phone call and that he and John are now in deep discussion.

"Yeah, but I get it," Leo says, working it out in his head. I can feel my BlackBerry vibrating in my pocket. I ignore it.

"*You* didn't walk away," I say . . . just barely.

"No," Leo agrees, still working it out. I can see the wheels turning.

"So," I say, eyeing Huston and John once more.

"We all died that day," Leo starts, his theory now complete.

"Who's the drama queen now?" I joke, trying to lighten the mood.

Leo continues unmoved, "It's not like anyone actually dealt with it," he says, finally finishing his equation. I look at him putting together all the factors and creating a working theory. My shoulders relax a little. Leo shakes his head and puts on his motorcycle helmet. His face squishes up as he flips up the glass visor.

He continues, "See you tomorrow? Seven?"

"Seven," I agree, reaching through the open visor and pinching his cheek. He smiles, which looks hilarious, and walks to his motorcycle. I begin walking over to my car. I look over to where Huston and John were talking.

Gone.

My BlackBerry vibrates again. As I stand alone in the middle of the parking lot, a new rain just starting to fall, I pull the phone out of my pocket, see that it's Tim, and send the call to voice mail as I walk to my car. I toss my BlackBerry on the passenger seat, start up my ancient BMW, press the clutch in and put the car in reverse. I look in the rearview mirror as a precaution.

John.

My foot quickly hops off the gas pedal and the car stalls in an elaborate symphony of backfires and rumbles. I unbuckle my seat belt and leap out of the car.

"I could have killed you," I say, slamming my car door. The rain mists around us.

"You can't keep arguing with everyone like that. It's going to make this harder if you keep coming at people like you want to rip their throats out," John says, his voice urgent.

"What are you talking about?" I ask, trying to get my bearings.

"Right, I need to be far more specific, I forgot," John says, settling into his stance. I flinch, stunned. John's mouth opens to say something, and then closes. Why I expect him to forgive me so easily is laughable, and yet I can't help but want it more than anything right now.

"Don't hate me. I can't have you hating me," I say, looking down.

John says nothing. I look up, not sure I can handle seeing anger in his eyes still. Our eyes meet and I see a flash of something. A hint of something. And then...it's gone.

"I'm here as your family's attorney. I no longer have any personal feelings about you one way or another. But as your attorney I am telling you, you *have* to control your temper," John advises, his voice clear, his eyes cold. Whatever hope I had, whatever I thought that flash meant, slips away.

"Control my temper," I repeat, nodding.

"That's all."

"Consider me advised," I answer, shutting down, back to the Nothing. I look down at the ground, trying to catch my breath. I feel John hesitate. I look up, that nagging hope makes me look at his chest, to see if my name is still engraved over his heart. I can almost feel his skin under my hands, his black, wavy hair at my fingertips. His soft lips on mine. I move my gaze up his body and we lock eyes again. I can't breathe. He holds my stare.

"Grace?" a voice calls. Who dares to call my name right now? I resolve to punch whoever it is smack in the face. The residue of John's warnings about controlling my temper hangs in the air as I tighten my fist. I turn, my eyes wild, and see Tim casually ambling across the parking lot. I loosen my fist...a *bit*.

No. Please. No.

I see John steel himself, the vulnerability of the last moment completely gone, as he looks from me to Tim and back again.

"Grace," Tim says again. This time it's more of an exasperated statement. I can't look at John. I step toward Tim, hoping somehow that John will simply not notice. Maybe he'll think Tim is a kindly salesman who's offering me a snazzy new vacuum. If only Tim would have brought a vacuum. A Dirt Devil, even. No such luck. John stuffs his hands back in his pockets and just...takes in the scene. *He knows*.

And suddenly, I know.

As Tim walks over to me, what I know for sure is that I never loved him. In reality, love wasn't even on the table. He was the polar opposite of John, and I wanted to be anyone but me. The rain mists around us and I can't seem to get a breath.

"Tim," I say, hoping he'll just drive back down to LA and forget he ever knew me. He doesn't.

"I just called you. It went straight to voice mail," Tim

announces. I look guiltily at my BlackBerry on the passenger seat. *Bad* BlackBerry.

The three of us stand in silence for several seconds. Awkward.

"Tim Barnes," Tim finally says, extending his hand to John. Doesn't he know that men have lost limbs for less? I eye John. His face is completely unreadable.

"John Moss," John says, pulling his hand from his pocket and extending it toward Tim. They shake hands. During this exchange I think I'm having a small stroke. Maybe this is just another thing Dad and I share.

"Are you one of the siblings?" Tim asks, looking from me to John.

"My name would probably be Hawkes if I were," John answers, his face showing his amusement.

"Ah," Tim answers, fully picking up on John's tone.

"John is our attorney," I cut in. I let my hand fall on John's arm as I formally introduce him. I can feel the curve of his bicep through his suit jacket. His muscle twitches under my hand. Heat surges through my body and as if I'm being electrocuted, I tighten my grip. This time, he doesn't pull away.

"Attorney? Why do you need an attorney?" Tim asks, as the mist begins to morph into droplets of rain.

"People usually call an attorney when they have a legal issue," John explains mockingly. Tim's entire body stiffens. He glares at me.

"You ready to go?" Tim asks, eyeing his car.

"We needed an attorney because Dad gave Huston his power of attorney and not the second wife," I explain, finally easing my death grip on John's arm. He shifts his weight and moves a few inches closer to me. I feel my blood pressure rise. My heart beats faster. I...*feel*. Dangerous...dangerous.

"That's bizarre," Tim says.

"My Dad's bizarre," I joke, trying to lighten the mood.

"Oh, so you know him now?" Tim asks, chuckling. I know he's trying to be funny, but making a joke about my strained, yet budding, relationship with my father stings.

"Wow," I hear John huff.

We fall into an uncomfortable silence once again.

"So, I'll just wait in my car and you can…I'll just follow you to the…Just let me know when you're done here," Tim stutters, turning and walking quickly toward his car through the now falling rain.

"Pleasure meeting you," John calls after him.

Tim turns around, briefly thinks about coming back. I'm willing him, *willing him* to just walk away. John looks unaffected, downright *relaxed*, as he watches Tim. I can't help but imagine Tim as a young man, his underpants pulled up somewhere around his shoulders, having this same internal battle. He tightens his fists, his face tense, and looks from me to John and back again. The rain falls.

"You, too," Tim finally manages, his entire body deflating. He turns and walks to his car, beaten. A wide smile breaks across John's face as he turns to me.

"A proud moment," I say, turning to him.

"For both of us," John says, stepping closer.

"He's a…it's a…" I stutter.

"It's a little late for explanations," John finishes, his head tilting just so.

I have a vision of a tiny pinprick of light miles above this prison floor. Tilting my head back, the rain falling on my face, I take the deepest of breaths.

A way out.

"It's not too late," I say, looking John in the eye. Straight.

Shooting right through those black-as-pitch eyes and diving, body and soul, down to where the memories of me . . . the memories of *us* live.

Tim honks the horn off in the distance. Ah, yes—please make me break up with you faster than I was already going to. We won't even make it out of this parking lot as a couple now.

John rips his gaze from mine. I take pleasure in noting it was difficult for him.

"You'd better get going," John finally says, his voice low.

"John—" I start, my hand outstretched.

John cuts in, "I trusted you and you broke my heart." His mouth tight, his eyes focused. I recoil, my stomach churning, my legs about to give way. I open my mouth to say something.

John holds up his hand, stopping me, and continues, "I'm going to take a page out of your book and just . . ."

And he walks away.

I watch him retreat to his car as the rain starts to really fall around me.

"Who is he?" Tim asks, as I fold into his car seconds later.

"My ex," I say. I'm so tired of lying.

"Is he even your family's attorney?" Tim asks, clicking the indicator right . . . left . . . right . . . left.

"Yes," I say, my purse on my lap, my seat belt unbuckled.

We are silent, save for the clicks of the indicator.

"So . . . dinner?" Tim offers, looking over at me.

I am silent. The words I need are stuck in all the broken-down architecture of the last five years. But they *are* coming.

"Grace?" Tim asks again.

"I need some time," I start.

"To get ready . . . take a shower?" Tim says, starting his car up.

"To myself. Alone," I say, hating that I sound all cryptic and mysterious.

"I wasn't insinuating we shower together. I know you aren't into that," Tim says, trying—once more—to defuse the situation.

"You're the perfect guy," I start.

Tim reacts. His face flushes.

I continue, "Just not for me."

Tim turns the car off. I shift my body in the passenger seat and grab the door handle.

"Look, you're going through a really difficult time. You're going to need someone," Tim offers. I pull the handle and the door clicks open.

"I already have someone," I say. I push open the door and climb out into the fresh, cold air.

"Grace?" Tim calls.

"I'll see you back at the office," I say, slamming the door.

I tilt my head back. That pinprick of light that was so far away from the prison floor is now within reach.

chapter eleven

Y ou from around here?" a soft, gooey lady asks me as we stand in line at the B&B's breakfast buffet the next morning.

"Pasadena," I say, putting on my best early-morning etiquette. The woman puts a luscious-looking blueberry scone on her plate, adding a dollop of clotted cream for good measure.

"Up here for the holidays?" she asks. Flashes of the ICU, Dad's rumbling cough, being herded out of his hospital room like interloping trash, Tim's surprise visit. *I trusted you and you broke my heart...*

"Absolutely," I lie.

"Are you here with your husband?" the woman asks, now eyeing the array of fresh fruit. I stare at her. My night of panic-stricken sobbing, chocolate and *Frasier* reruns looms large.

"It's more of a family vacation," I say, spooning a big helping of oatmeal into my bowl.

"Isn't it just..." The woman trails off as I grab an Earl Grey tea bag and pour myself a mug of hot water. I smile and put what I hope to be an insurmountable, yet polite, distance between us. It's probably only about a foot—but in breakfast buffet yardage it should be equal to the Serengeti Plain.

She scoops up some fresh strawberries and piles them next to the scone and clotted cream. Only in California. Fresh strawberries in the dead of winter. I spy a small Adirondack chair just outside on the veranda. One chair. The gooey lady is still talking. Apparently, she and her husband are from somewhere in Minnesota and just love coming out here every year. She says something about the weather.

"Have a great morning!" I manage, walking out onto the veranda with my breakfast and fresh mug of tea.

"Happy almost new year!" the woman replies, waving wildly as I walk through the French doors to freedom.

I set my mug of tea on the ground next to me, balancing the plate of fruit and yogurt on my knees, along with the overloaded bowl of oatmeal. The fresh, cool air blows my still wet hair. I breathe in deeply. I pick up my mug of tea, taking a long sip.

Am I here with my husband? I repeat. The breakup scene with Tim flashes in my head. I can't help but feel relief. I know I did the right thing. Staying with Tim was a sham. One of many.

I'm in love with someone else.

I look back at the gooey lady as she settles into her table, blissfully unaware of the furor her simple question has caused. *Husband.* How do perfect strangers always seem to ask the exact question that makes you feel terrible about yourself? Because they don't know not to ask it, I suppose. I set my mug back down on the ground. You have most people in your life trained to behave a certain way and then along comes a blundering stranger and whammo . . . are you here with your husband? Why don't you ask me if I'm pregnant—that question always goes over well with women you don't know.

I dig into my oatmeal. *Husband.* The idea that there could be such a union between two people where one isn't compelled to flee always baffled me. Just because you have a piece of paper doesn't mean anything. Mom and Dad never divorced. He just walked away. Back to that again. I take another sip of my tea and set my mug back down on the ground.

Trust.

Such a giant concept for something you can't touch. I take another bite of my oatmeal. *I trusted you and you broke my heart.* It was always about trust with John. With me, for that matter, as well. And even when we danced around spending our lives together, there was still this escape hatch we each kept in some part of our hearts. As a crisp breeze blows across the blooming gardens of the B&B, I can no longer fend off the memory of the last time I tried to escape the terror that being in a real relationship caused.

"John?"

"Grace . . . *Grace?*"

Leo and I are standing at the end of a row at the Ahmanson Theatre trying to find our seats. Instead we find John, *my boy-friend*, sitting in the middle of the row with a tiny blonde woman who, I hardly need to point out, isn't me. His black wavy hair is carefully combed and he's wearing a suit and tie.

"What's going on?" I ask, my tiny lamé evening bag a tragic prop to this turn of events.

"Nothing much, what's going on with you?" John says, standing. Blocking?

"That wasn't actually a casual greeting, John. I mean, literally, what's going on—*here*," I ask again, motioning to the confused woman just behind him.

"Hey, if it isn't Griffon Whitebox," John says, extending his hand to Leo.

"Not in public, man. Not in public," Leo warns, sneaking glances around the Ahmanson for possible hacker fan boys or Feds.

"Oh, right . . . *right*," John says, shaking my younger brother's hand.

"Did you want to introduce us to *your* friend?" I ask, motioning to the woman.

"I'm going to go find our seats . . . good seeing you again," Leo says, taking the tickets and waving goodbye to John.

"This isn't what you think it is, Grace," John starts. He bends just that much closer. The black eyes. The heavy-lidded black eyes that made me—*compelled* me—to write startlingly bad poetry.

"Really?" I ask.

"No . . . it's not."

"Oh . . . okay. Um . . . Miss?" I say, craning past John.

"Tammi," John says.

"Tamm . . . Are you kidding me?" I say, leaning back to John.

"She's a paralegal over at O'Melve—"

"Hey, *Tammi*?" I say, easily moving past John—our bodies so used to each other. Being close . . . curving, bending.

"Yes?" Tammi answers, confused.

"So, what do *you* think this is?" I ask. I can feel John just behind me.

"It's a . . . He asked if I wanted to see a play. I said . . . I said yes," Tammi stutters.

"And what do most people call that?" I ask.

"A . . . a date," Tammi confesses.

"Which, for the record, is what I thought this was," I say, bending back toward John.

John laughs. "Are you sure *you're* not the lawyer?"

"This isn't funny," I say, finally starting to walk out of the row of seats toward Leo.

"Grace . . . Gracie?!" John calls after me.

"No...seriously...a play? You hate plays. But...have at. She seems nice," I say, my voice flat. I scan the theater for Leo. John takes my arm and stops me.

"Grace...this is just a casual date." John's voice is quiet.

"Yeah, that seems to be the consensus," I say, tugging my arm away. John takes my arm again and pulls me in. Close. So strong, yet so gentle.

"I was the one who tried to have a conversation with you about—" John starts.

"So, this is how you react when I tell you I'm confused about what 'getting serious' means," I add, my lamé bag jumping around as I do giant air quotes around "getting serious." I've been waiting for the other shoe to drop for months.

"Confused? You refused to even talk about it," John says. True, but I thought if we talked about it, he would say he wasn't ready. That he didn't love me back. If we didn't talk about it, we could just keep going on as we were.

John continues, pulling me even closer as people continue to head to their seats, "I thought that meant you didn't want to get serious," John whispers, his mouth tight.

"And now I know why," I say, motioning at Tammi. Am I relieved? Why am I relieved?

"It's not like I'm fucking her!" John yells.

And the entire theater screeches to a halt.

"Well...I'm glad we cleared that up," I say, tucking my little bag under my arm. I see Leo stand up in the far corner of the theater.

"Grace..." John says...his voice quiet...pleading...

"Have a nice life," I say, turning to leave.

"Have a nice life? All your shit is at my apartment! You going to walk away from your toothbrush? Your clothes? Your laptop?" John's face is stunned, hoping this is all a joke. I tug him up the aisle and into the Ahmanson lobby. He allows me to.

"You don't get the answer you want, so you start seeing other people? You couldn't wait for me to figure it out?" I blurt, as I find an unpopulated corner down a long hallway.

"I thought you didn't want to talk about it, because you didn't want to get serious," John says.

"And *this* is your solution?" I ask, pointing back to What's-Her-Name.

"It just kind of happened," John sighs.

I stop. Stunned. Nothing to respond with. Too angry to be broken. I'm sure it will set in soon.

"I don't know how to do this," he says, looking at the ground.

"This...what?" I answer, trying to steady my breathing. The lights in the lobby flicker—on and off, on and off. The play is starting.

John hesitates. I can see his face moving and contorting with a conversation in his mind. The lobby is clearing out, our little corner becomes more and more private.

"Take too long to decide and I just might walk over to that usher and ask if he wants to get lucky," I crack.

John jolts up, looks at me, then the usher, and just...laughs. I can't help but laugh. The usher I've pointed to looks like Burl Ives.

As Burl Ives closes the house doors behind him, John takes a step closer. He looks at the ground for the briefest of seconds, takes my hand and looks up. We lock eyes.

"When you didn't want to talk about..." John trails off.

"Getting serious," I finish.

"Spending the rest of our lives together," John corrects. I recoil, John pulls me closer, his other hand tucks a piece of hair behind my ear. His hand lingers at my cheek, so soft. His face is inches from mine. His breath hot and quickening.

"Is that what that conversation was about?" I mumble, my hand now at his belt, pulling him closer.

"Yeah. So when you changed the subject…" John starts, his eyes closing just a bit as I undo his belt.

"It was imperative I ask you what you wanted in your coffee," I say, my hand now sliding down the front of his pants.

"Black. You know I like it black," John says, his eyes scanning the dark hallway as I kiss his neck.

"Maybe I was trying to change the subject," I whisper, centimeters from his ear, my breath ruffling the flips of his black hair.

"Maybe," John repeats, his hand at my waist. He pushes open a small door, revealing some kind of janitorial closet. He whips me around, his hand on the small of my back, and leads me into the small room.

"I hope Tammi doesn't mind that you didn't come back," I mock, as John lifts me onto some kind of stack of crates. I steady myself—grasping his shoulders. I'm overcome with the feeling that I could hold on to John in a hurricane and yet stay firmly on the ground. I pull him even closer. John slams the door behind him with his foot.

"Who?" John says, pulling up my dress, my little lamé bag falling to the floor.

Five years later I can still feel the heat of his body. I sip my tea to calm down and can't help but smile. I lost all thought when I was with John. But it wasn't the nothingness I feel with Tim. I was free. No niggling voices of doubt and insecurity that plagued all my other relationships. Relationships built on the sturdy foundation that unavailability meant love. My relationship with Tim now seems like a giant middle finger to real love and intimacy. I know that now. Who am I kidding…I always knew that.

If Dad, the one man bound to me by biology, could leave, why wouldn't every man after?

As I gather my mug and now empty oatmeal bowl, I wonder if I'll ever learn that lesson. Will I ever give someone a chance to prove my theory wrong?

"Are you wearing the same thing you wore yesterday?" Abigail asks, as we climb out of our cars in the hospital parking lot later that morning. I look down at my outfit: jeans, white T-shirt and camel-colored cashmere hoodie. It's all I could fit into that damn backpack.

"It's not anything of yours, if that's what you're insinuating."

"Ha ha," Abigail allows.

"I changed my panties," I say, blowing on the tea I bought at the organic market across the street from the bed-and-breakfast. I slam the door of my car.

"Charming," Abigail says, zooming the minivan door open to reveal Emilygrae and Mateo both elbow-deep in their mini plastic baggies filled with Cheerios. Emilygrae kicks her feet wildly as Mateo leans forward against his car seat restraint. Freedom is nigh. Evie slides out of the front seat.

"Not until I say so, you two," Abigail warns. The twins' fingers are pulsating at their booster seat latches.

"I brought you...well, I didn't know what kind of day it was going to be," Abigail says, passing me a little paper bag. I peek inside: a water bottle, two protein bars and some dinosaur-shaped gummies.

"Thank you," I say, looking up at Abigail. Aww. I tuck the paper bag into my oversized purse.

"No problem," Abigail says, pulling Emilygrae out of her kid seat. She breaks free and rushes over to me while Abigail gives Mateo the high sign. He leaps from his kid seat.

"Hey, Evie," I say, giving her a little wave. She ekes out a smile for me as she leans against the minivan, smoothing her hair behind her ears. I'm determined to erode her suspicions and re-earn her trust. She looks away with a sigh. Touché.

"We stayed at a hotel last night!" Emilygrae says, looking up at me.

"First time ever!" Mateo announces.

"I'm seriously rethinking the two queen beds versus a suite," Abigail sighs.

"They need their own wing," Evie says.

"By morning we were pretty much all in the same bed," Abigail says.

"Kickie and Punchie over there slept just fine," Evie says, yawning. The twins do their best to look like little angels.

Abigail laughs. "For little kids they take up an alarming amount of space."

"Do you know what's really awesome?" I say, picking Emilygrae up, making sure I'm careful with her little wrists. She rests her elbow on my shoulder, zipping and unzipping my hoodie.

"What?" she asks, exploring my collarbones and flipping my gold owl necklace up and down, up and down. The gnarled plaster of her little hot pink cast is rough on my skin.

"When you go back to that hotel everything's going to be clean—your beds will be made . . . the works," I announce. Mateo ambles over to Emilygrae and me, hitching his Batman backpack over his shoulders and resituating his sword in the belt loop of his tiny corduroy pants.

"How does it get clean?" Mateo asks, as Abigail slides the minivan door closed again. She bends back into the front, grabs her purse and a monogrammed canvas bag from between the seats, and whirls back around, closing the driver's side door.

"The hotel hires people to clean the room while you're gone,"

I say to Mateo, flipping the strap of his backpack right side out. He eyes me suspiciously.

"You should have said fairies," Evie says, looking up from her book.

"I should have what?" I say, laughing. C'mon kiddo, give me a smile.

"It would have been cooler if they thought it was fairies," Evie repeats flatly.

"Pretty big fairies," Mateo says, holding his arm up so Abigail can take his hand as we begin our trek through the hospital's parking lot. Abigail blows an errant tress of blonde hair out of her face and takes the little boy's hand. Evie falls in beside her.

"Pretty big fairies," Emilygrae whispers, her chubby, Cheerio-bedecked hand absently patting the nape of my neck, smoothing my hair. Her face is centimeters from mine. I can't help but smile. Abigail's a lot more bearable with her whole little comedy troupe around.

Mateo races over to the elevator and pushes the call button. Abigail soothes Emilygrae with promises of pushing the button for the fourth floor once the elevator comes. I set Emilygrae down just as the elevator door dings open. Mateo races inside the elevator and it's all anyone can do to stop him from pushing the inside button. I don't even think he wants to push it...he just wants Emilygrae to think he does. To know he could—but that he's *letting* her.

The elevator lurches upward as my stomach sours once again. Find a point on the horizon. I try to get lost in the kids' three-ring circus as they argue about button-pushing, their little faces dead serious. Abigail plays judge and jury. Mateo's hand rests on her knee. Emilygrae points and argues with the fervor of a latter-day Clarence Darrow. Evie smirks and brushes Mateo's curls out of his glasses.

As we chime past the third floor, I have to admit to myself that Abigail is a really good mom. Despite her hero worship of Dad, she absorbed more of Mom than I would have expected. Quietly directing, but not controlling. Supporting, but not coddling. Loving, but not suffocating. The elevator door dings open and the kids run pell-mell down the hallway to the waiting room—the only people in the world to be excited about coming here today.

"They really are adorable," I say, trying to make small talk. I watch Emilygrae wedge herself into the door of the waiting room milliseconds before Mateo can. Fighting ensues. Abigail weighs whether she should intervene or let this be one of those blessed "teaching opportunities" where the twins police themselves. Abigail is on edge as Evie walks a few paces in front of us, almost to the waiting room. What'll she find when she turns that last corner: Emilygrae being threatened by an unsheathed plastic sword at the hands of her bespectacled doppelgänger? Evie looks back just as I form the question. Abigail's eyes dart from Evie to the closed door of the waiting room door and back to me. Evie slouches into the waiting room and Abigail and I follow.

"Evie's talking about wanting to do a summer abroad in the next couple of years. Oxford," Abigail says, her face creased with concern.

"Oxford, as in England-Oxford?" I ask.

"The very one."

"That's amazing . . . far, but amazing," I allow.

"I'm kind of stuck on the far part," Abigail says.

"Makes sense," I say.

"We have to get past the quinceañera first, though," Abigail says, smiling.

"I can't believe she's almost fifteen."

"Okay, guys...be good. We'll be right down the hall," Abigail says, collecting herself.

"When's Papi coming?" Mateo asks as he plops down in the middle of the floor with various books, forgetting his earlier Battle of Who Could Enter the Waiting Room First. It'll soon be eclipsed by ten thousand other little battles, I'm sure.

"He should be here later this afternoon, mijo," Abigail says, leaning over the boy and giving him a kiss on the forehead.

"Papi makes lights go on," Emilygrae announces to me. Abigail bends over and gives her a little peck on the forehead too.

"Electrical engineer and yet can't replace a lightbulb in the guest bathroom," Abigail sighs, winking at Emilygrae. Evie was a bit of a surprise, so Abigail had to scrap her big college plans early on. As Abigail stayed at home with Evie, she earned money by watching neighborhood kids in their tiny apartment. Manny continued with college and then went on to become an electrical engineer for a small consulting firm in Los Angeles. It's a testament to their marriage that they made it through...well, that they simply made it. Abigail and Manny's happy marriage threw a wrench into my convenient "unavailable dad equals unavailable lovers" theory.

"Papi wears a tie," Mateo announces. He pours the entire canvas bag of Legos onto the waiting room floor.

"Plph," Emilygrae spits, kneeling next to the Legos.

"Don't touch them! I'm waiting for Tio Leo. He said he could build the Def Star," Mateo decrees. I wonder if the Def Star is a version of the Death Star, but with LL Cool J at the helm. Emilygrae immediately bursts into tears.

"Mateo," Abigail warns.

"You...you can play with the...*those*," Mateo says, pushing a pile of giant oversized Legos toward Emilygrae.

"Those are for babies," Emilygrae huffs.

"You got this?" Abigail asks Evie.

"Same ole, same ole," Evie says, yawning.

"Thanks for watching them. I'll check back soon," Abigail says to Evie, giving her a quick peck on the cheek. Evie tries to act like she's bothered by her mother's affection, but I can see that she leans into the kiss—despite her show of attitude.

The kids barely notice that we leave. As we close the door to the waiting room, Leo emerges from the elevator. He rests his hand lazily on the strap of the messenger bag slung across his chest. His other hand is wound through the open visor of his motorcycle helmet.

"Hiya," I say, smiling at him.

"Hey," Leo answers, his eyes bloodshot.

"You okay?" I ask, as we continue down the hallway.

"Whose idea was it that we all go to our hotel rooms last night by ourselves? I must have spent a million dollars on tiny bottles of booze from the minibar," Leo says, running his hand through his light brown tangle of hair.

"I ate a pint of Häagen-Dazs. Not pretty," Abigail says, over her shoulder.

"York Peppermint Patties, *Frasier* reruns, and I broke up with the guy I was seeing," I say.

"What?" Abigail says, stopping.

"York Peppermint Patties?" I ask, looking down the hallway.

"The other part." Abigail narrows her eyes.

"You were seeing someone?" Leo asks.

"*Was* being the operative word," Abigail adds.

"You *was* seeing someone?" Leo asks.

Abigail lasers in. "What's the problem?" No matter how much time has passed, my love life is still fair game.

"He was a monkeyhander," I confess, my expression dire.

Abigail and Leo shrink back. Stunned.

"A *monkeyhander*?" Abigail blurts, like I've confessed to dating a serial killer.

"How did you even date him in the first place? Where do you even meet monkeyhanders anymore?" Leo yelps. We continue walking down the hallway.

"I think it was his monkeyhandedness that attracted me," I admit. Abigail's mouth drops open. She's quieted. A first.

"Didn't you and John…" Leo trails off, his face flushing. Abigail nods.

"Yes," I say, sighing. An *audible* sigh.

We are silent.

"Definitely *not* a monkeyhander," Abigail mutters, her eyebrows raised.

"Definitely not," I say, envisioning that janitor's closet and the decidedly non-monkeyhanded events that took place within. We all sign in to the ICU, each receiving a name badge.

"Okay, enough. This is getting gross," Leo says. It's odd how normal all of these rights and lefts seem after just one day.

"Definitely *not* a monkeyhander," I repeat.

We stand shoulder to shoulder at the door, girding ourselves for what's behind it. The door opens. We are hit with the buzzing, whirring inner workings of the ICU. It takes me a second to recalibrate.

Dad's hospital room looks empty. We stop at the nurse's station. Nurse Miller, from the night before, gives Abigail the international sign for "wait a sec."

We cluster around the nurse's station. We try not to look at each other or into Dad's hospital room. I choose my shoes. I'll look at my shoes.

"Mrs. Hawkes-Rodriguez? Ms. Hawkes? Mr. Hawkes. Good to see you," Nurse Miller begins. We wait. She doesn't elaborate.

We are obviously all questioning why we were asked to "wait a sec."

"How did Dad do last night?" Abigail asks when Nurse Miller falls silent.

"The same . . . the same." Nurse Miller nods. I look to Abigail, then to Leo.

"Well, that's good news," Abigail says, knocking on the counter as a kind of exclamation. She smiles politely and turns toward Dad's hospital room. As she turns, Abigail gives me the smallest eye-roll.

"We're going to go in," I announce to the Wonder Nurse.

"Mrs. Hawkes wanted me to tell you she would be in at eight-thirty," Nurse Miller blurts. Ahh, there's the reason for the "wait a sec." We all turn around and wait to hear what this has to do with us.

"And?" I ask.

"I just thought—" Nurse Miller starts.

"Thought what?" I interrupt.

"Connie had a really rough day yesterday after leaving Ray's bedside," Nurse Miller says. Connie? It's Connie now?

"We all did," Abigail says democratically.

"She explained that you kids never had much of a relationship with your father," Nurse Miller says.

"Wow, where was that question on the hospital intake?" I ask.

"I've got this," Abigail says, holding up her hand. I pull back. Leo pulls his messenger bag around, nervously tugging on it.

"I would appreciate it—" Abigail starts, her face bright red.

"Connie's right about the age my mom was when we lost Father. We had some stepbrothers and -sisters that just came in at the end and made everything difficult—" Nurse Miller says.

"You are aware that Dennis is the stepbrother," I explain. I hear Leo sniffle in the background. I pull my hand back, grab his and hold tight. Stay with us, little brother. He holds my hand in return, stepping a bit forward.

"It would just make things easier," Nurse Miller starts.

"For whom, Nurse Miller? It might make things easier for whom?" Abigail says, stepping in closer to the nurse's station. I love how, even when she's pissed off, her grammar is perfect.

"I know this is difficult, Mrs.—" Nurse Miller starts.

"Yes, having a parent who's suffered a stroke can be very difficult," I say.

"That *would* be difficult," Nurse Miller concedes.

"We'll need to get in there, then," Abigail finishes, turning on her loafer heel. Nurse Miller looks like she has something else to say, but looks down at her clipboard instead. Smart. Smart move.

We walk into Dad's hospital room and are surprised to see a very alert patient. Dad's eyes are open, and when we walk in, his whole face reacts. We stop dead in our tracks.

This just got really real, really fast.

"Morning." A disembodied voice from the corner scares the shit out of us. Abigail instinctively puts her arm across my body, the way she used to when we came to an abrupt stop in the car or when we crossed the street. She seems almost embarrassed by the gesture now.

"Huston, Jesus...you scared us to death," Abigail says. I get my bearings. My eyes focus. The hospital room is dimly lit. Huston sits in the darkest corner. His suit jacket open, his shirt neatly tucked in.

"I'm sorry," Huston says, standing. He gestures for us to go outside with him. Dad's eyes scan the room. The fear he must be feeling. When he was unconscious it made it easier for me to dehumanize him. But now, seeing his darting eyes, his restrained hand flailing for something to hold on to—my heart wrenches.

The fear. The knowing that . . . well, just the *knowing*. I am pulled toward Dad. Pulled toward that panic. Pulled toward the need to comfort.

No thought. No flashbacks of piano recitals, graduations or a seat empty at dinners bought with food stamps. No judgment.

Huston walks out into the ICU. Abigail and Leo follow.

"Just a second," I say. They walk out and huddle just outside the door, already speaking in hushed tones. Dad's eyes immediately fall on me. He raises his hand . . . it stops short, the restraint.

"It's Grace," I whisper, trying to stay cheerful for him. I take his hand in mine. His grip is surprisingly strong. He squeezes tightly, letting me know he's still in there. Still strong. Still fighting. Whatever our history is . . . in this moment, in this room— there is the most basic, most visceral of connections. Dad shrugs his left shoulder—I imagine he thinks he's shrugging both shoulders. He keeps rolling his eyes. He looks like he's trying to convey that either he's embarrassed or . . . *sorry*? I'm totally projecting. I'm a walking Psych 101 textbook right now.

Dad's rumbling voice winds through a sentence of pure gibberish. I can kind of make out some words by the inflection and vowel placement.

"Really? Wow," I answer. Trying to be an active listener. Dad shrugs his shoulder and rolls his eyes again. He tightens his grip and kind of shakes my hand around. He's so strong. He rattles off several sentences, very passionately, trying hard to enunciate and be heard. By me. It sounds like he's talking underwater . . . but worse. I can't understand it. And he knows it. He's getting more and more frustrated.

"Huston, Abigail and Leo are just outside. They want to talk to me about something," I say, hitting every consonant and vowel clearly. Dad's not deaf. He's probably sick of people yelling at him as if he were. He rolls his eyes and shrugs again, bends his left leg and shifts his weight. He grips my hand and shakes it around with a little half smile. I smile back, trying to look breezy. Does he think he's dying? Does he know he's dying? Does he think he's going to get better? Does he know that...Jesus, all of the sudden there are no words.

Who could stay mad at someone in this state?

I get it now. I get the power of attorney. I get the engraved invitation. It's a dirty trick, for sure. But I get it now.

"Grace?" Abigail calls from outside Dad's hospital room. I turn around and gesture to her to give me a second. She smiles and falls back into hushed conversation with Huston and Leo.

"Still bossy," I whisper down to Dad. He laughs a rumbly, heartbreaking crack of a laugh, gripping my hand tightly. His eyes blink, longer and longer. He's getting tired. I take his hand in both of mine. "I'll be right back," I say, as his eyes flicker closed and he lets go of my hand. My eyes dart to his chest. Up. Down. Okay...okay, he's okay. I smooth out his hospital gown and make sure he's asleep. When I'm sure, I turn toward the hallway and try to compose myself by the time I reach the others. I exhale deeply and stand next to Huston.

"I talked to the neurologist this morning," Huston starts. Leo is already crying. I take his hand. He desperately grips it back.

"And?" I ask, looking at Abigail. Her face is blotchy and intense.

"Dad's prognosis is...not good," Huston says.

chapter twelve

But he's so strong," I say, remembering Dad's grip.

"I know," Huston answers. He doesn't make eye contact as he crosses his arms across his chest.

My eyes dart around the ICU. I'm panicking. I realize my ridiculous bubble has long since popped. The Chutes and Ladders are firewood at this point. But how deep will it go? There are untouched memories still hidden, emotions muffled by layers of armor. Despite whatever change I'm trying to muster, I'm still holding on to a sliver of the life I've cobbled together for myself in the five years since Mom died. That sliver being the possibility that I won't have to hurt anymore. What's happening right now threatens what little control I have left.

"Dad had the clot buster within an hour of the stroke, but it didn't work. It was a massive stroke. His right side is affected, which means he's lost most of his speech," Huston starts, his demeanor strained, but even.

"Didn't work," Leo mumbles. I wrap my arm around him. He mumbles it again.

Huston powers on, "She said that patients who have suffered the kind of stroke Dad had aren't cognizant of what's going on around them. They often answer yes to anything they're asked. We have to be ready for there to be a level of..." Huston stops, looking at Leo and weighing whether or not he can bear to hear what follows. Can any of us?

"Brain damage," Abigail whispers. Huston nods, studying Leo's reaction. Leo drops his head to his chest and covers his face with his hands. Huston, Abigail and I share a look of concern as I pull Leo closer. I wonder what I'm supposed to do with this new information. I didn't want Dad to be trapped in there with all of his faculties, but hearing this certainly doesn't make me feel any better. There's got to be a way to fix this. This can't be final.

I come out swinging. "They have speech therapists and physical therapists and...I mean, he's so strong. The brain can be brought back, it's definitely not...he's only sixty-eight. It's just about finding the right combination of...the right doctors." Huston clenches his jaw as his face reddens. Abigail looks away, her face wistful...empty. Leo looks up and wipes his tears away. I can see Nurse Miller out of the corner of my eye. Yes, this is the behavior of a family who doesn't care.

"That's all true, but Dad's decline isn't in relation to any of that. Dad has a feeding tube and yet he's still not absorbing any nutrients. His body is rejecting everything," Huston explains.

"So he has a fight in front of him. He's a fighter. Nurse Miller said he's a fighter," I say, using the word *fighter* too many times.

"Grace," Huston starts.

"No...*no!*" I blurt. I feel the anger building in my chest and shoulders. I need to hit something. Where's Dennis when you need him?

"Gracie," Huston starts again. The softness of his voice breaks me.

"Don't say it," I plead, my stomach churning. Leo wipes at his tears. Huston takes a deep breath and studies me. Find a point on the horizon. I look up and make eye contact with Huston. I breathe deeply as my stomach calms. Calms.

We are quiet.

"What happens now?" Leo finally asks.

"Since he's stabilized, Dad will move to a regular room and out of the ICU," Huston says, looking at Leo.

"None of this makes any sense," Abigail says, growing angry.

"He's going to need skilled nursing care. Until he...well, for the rest of his life." Huston's voice is detached.

"Is that like a full-time nurse?" Leo asks.

"They were talking about a more specialized facility, because of the feeding tube," Huston says.

"We have to move him? While he's this...sick?" I ask, searching for the right words.

"The worst part is going to be transferring him to a gurney, after that the ambulance drive can be fifteen minutes or two hours. It won't matter," Huston says, his eyes elsewhere. Leo stares at Huston. His wheels turning. Equations and theory being formulated.

"When...how much time have we got?" I ask, not knowing really to what I'm referring. Time here in the ICU or time in general.

"They'll move him to a regular room in the next day or so and we'll find a place for him straightaway," Huston says.

"Wait...we have to find a place in the next couple of days?" I ask.

"What about Connie?" Abigail adds.

"Was she at the meeting this morning?" Leo asks.

"No, just John and I," Huston answers. Leo nods, figuring out another integer in his equation.

We are silent.

"So—did they give us a list of facilities in the area?" I ask. Huston is quiet...watching, observing.

"That would be a good first step," Abigail adds, pulling her organizer from her purse, slipping the pen out of its holder and waiting. At the ready.

"We'll have to look into insurance and all that. I imagine there's going to be a lot of red tape and weird hoops to jump through," I say to Abigail. She adds INSURANCE under TO DO RE: DAD.

"Maybe Connie knows, we can ask her or the lawyer about all that," Abigail says absently, pen flying over the paper. Leo is quiet. Studying Huston.

"We're going to have to tread lightly—not seem pushy," I add. Abigail nods.

I continue, "We can just offer to do some of the busywork, so she can be here with Dad." I want all the bad blood of yesterday to be gone. Abigail nods yes, still madly writing.

We are quiet—the buzzing of the ICU, the scrawl of Abigail's writing.

"You're going to take him back down to LA, aren't you?" Leo asks, his eyes focused on Huston. Abigail's head jolts up from her organizer. I look at Huston. His face gives nothing away.

"I have his power of attorney," Huston says.

"*Huston*," Leo pleads, his hands now at his hips.

"I have to be close so I can carry out the terms of the document," Huston adds.

"You . . . you want to move a sixty-eight-year-old stroke patient away from his wife and home?" Abigail asks.

"Have you even thought this through?" I chime in.

"It's what he wants. Why else would he have given me—" Huston starts, his voice smooth. His eyes are icy.

I interrupt, "What about Connie, Huston? You can't just take Dad down to LA and leave her here! She may have issues with us, but she's still his wife. Or are you going to move her, too? Why don't you move Dennis the Menace while you're at it?

Maybe they have a cat—you can throw it in a pillowcase and pack it all up in a rented van!"

Huston is quiet.

"What are you thinking?" I press.

"It's my name on that document," Huston says, his voice defiant.

"This *can't* be about you swooping in and—" I start. John emerges through the buzzing doors looking like he's just in time for a bar brawl. He pushes his shirtsleeves to his elbows and quickens his pace.

"I'm not swooping in, Grace!" Huston's voice rises just enough to be terrifying. Leo and Abigail are quiet, shocked, and utterly without words. John takes his place next to Huston.

"Bullshit!" I challenge.

"What's going on?" John asks, looking from one of us to the other.

"Mr. Knight in Shining Armor here wants to move a sixty-eight-year-old man away from everything and everyone he knows and loves," I explain. The stab of me not being one of those things or people is all too painful.

"Hust—" John starts, the look on his face a combination of pity and confusion.

"He knows and loves us. That's what the power of attorney means. That he loves us. Loves...*me*," Huston argues, his eyes now rimmed in red. He drops his head and rests his hands on his hips.

And there it is. No more safe zones, no more distant emotions. We are here. That little pinprick of light is within reach. I push off the prison floor and burst through the surface of the water, gulping for breath. Treading water in the middle of this unknown sea, I take in my surroundings. I immediately set my sights on the fray. Mine to jump in.

"Huston—" I start.

"I wasn't there when Mom got hurt and look what happened," Huston says, valiantly trying to regain control. His eyes dry as he looks up.

"She was hit head-on by a drunk driver," I say.

"If I had been there—" Huston starts. He takes a long, deep breath and settles back into his stance. I lock eyes with Abigail— the tiniest of side glances. She's just as haunted as I am. We both look to Leo. Same. John looks studied . . . the calm at the eye of the storm.

"We're going to do everything we can to handle your dad's estate the way he wanted. We're going to do right by him, Hus," John says, his voice strong. Huston looks to him. Another deep breath. His jaw impossibly clenched. His lips compressed tightly. Nodding. Nodding.

"Mr. Hawkes?" Nurse Miller warily approaches our group. Abigail is the only one who tries to compose herself.

"Yes?" Huston answers, stepping forward. Always the first to step forward.

"We're missing some of Mr. Hawkes' personal papers to complete his file: a Medicare bill, medical insurance card, and we're going to need his Social Security card. It wasn't in his wallet. Men his age don't usually, well—no matter. I'm sure they're at his home. Mrs. Hawkes will be here within the hour. This might be the perfect opportunity for you to go and get them?" Nurse Miller asks, holding out Dad's chart as proof of something. I don't know what we did to this lady, but she couldn't want us around less.

"We're here—" I stop before I give in to the *we're here, we're queer, get used to it* begging to come out of my mouth.

John jumps in, "We've established that my clients have a right to be here, Nurse Miller."

"I left a message for Connie. I just thought...it would make things easier if—" Nurse Miller answers.

Abigail interrupts, "I think we can work together here. If we leave now, maybe Connie will still be at the house and we can just ask her where the documents are," Abigail says.

"That would work," says Nurse Miller, breathing more easily. She hands Abigail the list of things we need from Connie. Abigail scans it.

"This might be a good opportunity to mend some fences," Abigail adds, looking at me. I nod.

"I'm staying," Huston announces.

"We'll be back as soon as we can," Abigail says, ignoring him.

"Thank you," Nurse Miller sighs.

"Leo? Grace?" Abigail says.

We jump in line and follow Abigail out of the buzzing ICU doors and down the long hallway. We don't say anything and none of us look back at Huston. I do sneak a look at John in those last buzzing seconds—he looks away. As we walk through doors and down long hallways, I can't shake this fog of disbelief. Whenever tragedy strikes, you ready yourself for the worst, never really thinking it's going to happen. And when it actually does, the shock of it is half the haze of the grief that follows. We've been here before and the familiarity haunts me with an eerie sense of déjà vu.

We finally get to the waiting room and Abigail takes a beat. Her hand rests on the doorknob for just a few seconds. In those quick moments, I see her gather herself. Abigail clicks open the door, never looking at me or Leo, and enters the waiting room to a resounding "Moooommmmmmmmm!" We follow her in.

"We have to go to Dad and Connie's house to get some documents," Abigail announces.

"What about the Def Star," Mateo asks, looking at Leo.

"That's apparently where we're heading," I say, under my breath.

"We'll build it when we get back, Matty," Leo assures him, plopping the motorcycle helmet down over the little boy's head. He looks like a pint-sized bobblehead.

Mateo can barely control himself as he starts loading piles of Legos back into the monogrammed canvas bag from this morning. Emilygrae gathers all the books into her backpack, all the while asking Leo when it will be her turn to wear the helmet. Evie looks up from her book. Abigail nods to the angst-ridden teen that yes—this means her, as well. There is much eye-rolling.

"We'll be quick," Abigail says as the kids run down the hall-way toward the elevator—in search of another button-pushing title. Evie sighs down the hall after them.

"Connie wouldn't even take the ziplock bag," Abigail says, motioning to her purse, where the plastic bag filled with Dad's personal effects rests.

"What?" I ask, watching Mateo push every elevator call button.

"Why do they hate us so much?" Leo asks as we lurch down-ward. Leo transfers the motorcycle helmet from Mateo to Emily-grae. Mateo looks lost without it. Emilygrae's squeals of delight fill the elevator.

"It's that son and plus we're . . ." Abigail trails off.

"Either being portrayed as gold diggers or good-for-nothing kids," I finish.

"We don't want or need any of Dad's money," Abigail says, her voice defiant.

"Maybe we need to make that more clear," Leo says.

"If we talk about money, even by denying our need for any of it, we make ourselves look like gold diggers. It's a catch-22," I say.

"That's just weird," Evie says, as the elevator doors open on the first floor.

"It *is* weird," I answer, placing a hand on her arm. She doesn't pull away. A baby step forward.

The elevator dings open and all six of us traipse through the hospital lobby. Leo pulls the helmet off Emilygrae's head and takes her hand. Her face falls; Leo's hand is clearly a distant second to the helmet. Mateo is holding Abigail's hand while his other hand holds up his pants. They're weighted down with pockets filled with who knows what along with an assortment of swords tucked into tiny belt loops. His Batman backpack toddles along, bouncing with his every step. I take Evie's hand as we step down from the curb and into the parking lot. Her fingers unconsciously curl around my hand. I swallow a smile—don't want to jinx my progress.

Abigail opens the minivan door. Mateo and Emilygrae climb into their respective kids' seats, seats encrusted with crumbs, action figures and random torn pieces of colorful, shiny paper. Evie sneaks into the third row as Abigail latches the twins in.

"You can sit in front," Leo offers. My car sickness is legendary. I nod to Leo's ass as he bends and contorts into the back with Evie. I climb into the front seat just as Abigail is inputting Dad and Connie's address into her GPS system. I click my seat belt. The system bells in and tells us that we should go right in one hundred yards.

"Where are we going?" Emilygrae finally asks, after we've properly turned right.

"We have to go to Ray and Connie's house. The hospital needs some papers," Abigail repeats, looking in her rearview mirror. I look back into the minivan. A sea of faces looks back at me. Leo and Evie a million miles away in the third row, Leo reading over Evie's shoulder. I see Evie bend her body to give him a better view. Emilygrae and Mateo are front row center—wiggling and fussing. Mateo is digging his tiny hand into the sides of his seat, no doubt looking for some old cracker crumbs to nosh on. Emily-grae kicks her feet back and forth as she listens intently to where the GPS system says we're going. Abigail reaches back and gently quiets Emilygrae's feet.

I fight every urge to start singing "The Wheels on the Bus."

"I still don't understand why we're doing this," Evie asks from the way back. Abigail glares at her in the rearview mirror.

"They'd left a message for her, but we thought we could help things along by . . ." Abigail trails off.

"A little olive branch," I add, trying to think of something metaphorical that would fly over the little kids' heads.

"You didn't tell me Connie was going to be there," Evie whines.

"It'll be fine," Abigail says.

"Why didn't Tio Huston just do it?" Evie asks as we turn up a more residential street of Ojai. The houses are mostly ranch-style with large plots of land. The mountains loom over the neighborhood as we are told to head due north. Right up into the mountains of Ojai. I wait for something to look familiar. I did stay an entire summer at this house.

"Tio Huston wanted to stay with Dad . . . well, my dad your grandfather," Abigail answers, her narrowed eyes letting Evie know the question-and-answer portion of this show is now over. Evie sinks back into her book. Leo leans over and once again reads over her shoulder, as Evie softens just a bit.

"We're looking for nine twenty-four, guys. Can you guys see the numbers on the houses?" I ask. Emilygrae leans forward.

"One, two, free, ten, w, firtyleven," Emilygrae announces.

"They don't quite know numbers yet," Abigail explains.

"Well, what about colors? Can you guys tell me the colors on the houses?" I ask, turning around in my seat, the car sickness flirting with me.

The kids are quiet.

"They're awwl white," Mateo answers.

"Not all of them," I say, turning to look out the window. Wow, weird, the entire street is filled with white houses. Abigail merges left and the GPS system tells us we're getting close.

"Blue! There's a big, blue one!" Emilygrae screams, pointing at a big, beautiful prairie-style house that sits right up against the mountains themselves.

"Nine twenty-four," Evie says, from the way back.

"That's it. That's it," Abigail says, parking the car right in front. Abigail, Leo and I notice the car in the driveway at once. Dad's ancient pickup truck. The last time I saw that truck, it was driving away from our house packed full of Dad's belongings twenty-two years ago. I look at Abigail.

"I can't believe he still has that old truck," Abigail sighs, putting the car in park and turning off the ignition.

"He still has that old truck?" Leo asks from the third row.

"We were just saying that," I say, turning around.

"So, did the last two decades not really happen?" Leo jokes.

"Hey, at least I have a new car," Abigail says, eyeing me and my inability to get rid of my ancient BMW.

We all wait. Like we've been invited to a party and just noticed we're the first ones here. It doesn't look like anyone's home.

"It doesn't look like she's here." Leo always had a gift for the obvious.

"We must have just missed her," Abigail says, pulling the keys from the ignition. The kids are quiet. Waiting. We all watch the Big Blue House for signs of life.

"What should we do?" I finally ask.

"Well—" Abigail starts, looking into her purse at the ziplock bag: wallet, keys and wedding ring. I follow her stare toward the bag.

"You can't be serious," I say. Abigail shrugs her shoulders.

"Let's go in," Leo blurts, undoing his seat belt and beginning the contortions necessary to get out of the third row.

"Are you two nuts? We can't just go in," I say, unbuckling my seat belt and turning around. Leo kneels between Mateo and the sliding door of the minivan. Mateo stares at him as his little hand rests gently on Leo's.

"Look, she's not here. She's already at the hospital. We have the keys," Leo answers, with that shoulder shrug that is supposed to make *me* feel like the crazy one. The crazy one who doesn't want to break and enter. I raise up my armrest and turn my body all the way around.

"Are you trying to get three strikes?" I ask, my mouth tight.

"Very funny," Leo says blithely, still completely unused to anyone telling him no.

"We can't go inside someone else's house just because we have the key," I argue.

"It's not *someone's* house. It's Dad's house," Leo says, Mateo's hand still on his.

"And Connie's. A woman who…well, let's face it, we're not her favorite people right now. What if she's just at the corner market getting some, I don't know—orangey lipstick and hard candies? She comes back only to find us rummaging through the house she thinks we're going to kick her out of? I can't see that going over very well," I argue. Abigail is oddly quiet.

"She's definitely on her way to the hospital," Leo answers.

"You can't know that," I say.

"We need the documents," Abigail reasons.

"And I need a million dollars, but I'm not going to break into Donald Trump's penthouse to get it," I say.

"It's not there anyway...it's tied up in real estate," Leo says.

"Well, why don't you just hack his computer and find out," I mutter.

"Already have...that's how I know," Leo says, casing the joint.

"Look, Griffon Whitebox—" I start. Leo immediately ducks and looks around furtively. Convinced no Feds are tailing him, he looks back at the house and then at me.

"It's not breaking in," he argues.

"When we have the key," Abigail finishes, holding up the de-bagged keys. Dad's keys. The keys are anchored with a worn leather fob. Dad has a keychain? I guess he would have to. It's weird to think about how many things he must have that I'd have no guess about. I shake my head and return to the crime at hand.

"Fine, but you're the one who's going to have to explain to your husband why your kids have a criminal record," I say, opening my door and stepping out of the minivan. Leo follows.

"You are such a drama queen," Abigail sighs again, stepping out of the driver's side.

"*I'm* a drama queen. We need those documents *stat*! Let's break into the old lady's house *stat*!" I scoff, stepping aside as Mateo and Emilygrae unlatch themselves and start climbing out of the minivan. I take Mateo in my arms and put him down on the patch of grass next to his Tio Sticky Fingers. Mateo unsheathes his little plastic sword and stands at the ready. Leo starts to sing the theme song to *Mission: Impossible* under his breath.

"This is not funny," I say.

"Loosen up," Leo says. He looks back and mimes holding a gun, darting along the pathway like an international spy. I imagine Connie in some upstairs bedroom watching all of this unfold. What a bunch of idiots we must look. Evie stands next to me watching Leo and Mateo as they head toward that long porch. Abigail and Emilygrae walk around from the other side of the car.

"She's totally not home," Evie says.

"Et tu, Brute?" I say, smiling just a little.

"What?" Evie asks, focusing fully on me for the first time.

"Julius Caesar," I say, placing my hand on her shoulder.

"Latin?" she asks, starting up the pathway. Leo and Mateo are waiting by the door.

"It's Latin, he's Roman. Very good," I say, noticing that Leo has rung the doorbell. Mateo looks around wildly, whipping his little sword to and fro. Unbelievable.

"Et tu? Brute?" Evie asks. Doesn't say two words to me all morning and now she wants to make conversation about Roman emperors? I'll take what I can get, I guess. My mouth is dry. I keep checking the street for cars. I have no idea what kind of car Connie drives, so every car is a possible heart attack.

"What it means is 'Even you?' or 'You, too, Brutus?' When Julius Caesar was murdered, those were allegedly his last words. Brutus was his friend, well up until he stabbed him to death, I guess. So people tend to say it when they feel betrayed by a close friend," I explain, wondering if Abigail is going to call me out for scaring the children . . . you know, in the midst of the already-in-progress felony.

"Well, you are the Edmund. You'd know a thing or two about betrayal," Abigail says as we all walk up the long pathway.

"Shh, we're busy breaking into someone's house," I snap back. Abigail exhales deeply, pats Evie on the back and gives her what I can only describe as a "knowing smile." As if she's had to tolerate my brand of crazy far longer than poor Evie could ever understand. Abigail might as well be laying a duct tape boundary down the center of our room. *Again.*

"Hello? Connie?" Leo calls, knocking on the heavy wooden door. Emilygrae and Mateo peer through the long side panel windows that frame the door.

Leo looks back at all of us with a "Well?" kind of look on his face. Like he's tried reasoning with the castle folk, but we're going to need that battering ram after all. Abigail steps forward holding Dad's keychain. I lunge at the doorbell once more and ring it. And ring it. And ring it.

"She's not home. I told you she wasn't home," Leo says as Abigail tries the first key. No go. She flips through the keychain, trying key after key like Russian roulette.

Click.

Abigail looks over at us as she pushes the heavy wooden door open with a loud creeeakkkkkk.

"This is ridiculous," I say, hoping it hides my terror. This is how a billion horror movies start, after all. Creepy door creak and everything.

"Connie? It's Abigail—Ray's daughter?" Abigail announces, once we're all inside. The heavy wood-paneled foyer is impressive. So impressive it can harbor six interloping criminals in total comfort before they meet their certain doom.

We all stand in utter silence. My heart is beating a mile a minute. I look around at our little ragtag group. Hilarious.

"This is nice," Leo says, looking up the sweeping staircase.

"Looks exactly the same," Abigail whispers, looking my way.

"Why are you whispering if no one's home?" I ask.

"LOOKS EXACTLY THE SAME," Abigail almost yells.

I wince. "Jesus."

"Not in front of the kids," Abigail warns.

"You mean, while we're breaking and entering there can be no taking the Lord's name in vain...yeah, that makes sense," I say, following Leo, the twins and Evie into the living room.

I stop. Just as they did. All of us staring at the same thing. I choke back the emotion and look back at Abigail. She looks as stunned as I feel.

A large marble fireplace takes up most of the far wall of the living room. Sitting on the fireplace mantel are . . . pictures of us. All of us.

I approach the fireplace, all fear of Connie forgotten, as I try to understand what exactly I'm seeing.

The picture frames are worn and the glass is smudged, making the pictures beneath barely visible. They obviously haven't been dusted in some time, but that doesn't take away the enormity of what we've stumbled upon.

Our entire childhood. Just slightly different. We had similar pictures in our house, and while these look like they are from the same rolls, each portrays a different moment from the same day. The shot *after* the shot. Like seeing our memories from another vantage point. An idea so radical it takes me a second to really mourn what having two parents would have been like. I am speechless.

I reach up and touch the top part of a frame. Just checking—it's real. The room is so quiet. All I can hear is the creaking of the hardwood floors as we take in the . . . well, the *shrine*. I had always secretly hoped something like this existed, but I was sure he'd forgotten us. I'd have staked my life on it. I'm overcome with sadness and, startlingly, with sympathy. For *Dad*.

I walked away from this family for five years. At the end of that time I was a shell of the person I used to be. Dad was gone for twenty-two years and chose to look at those he abandoned every morning before he took on his day. How hollow must he have been? Or am I just . . . Could he not have been affected? How do you just walk away . . . and *stay* away? What could that do to a person? I shudder at the person I was becoming: the haze of numbness that was taking over my life, the loveless relationships...wait...*wait*...my heart clenches. Loveless relationships? Dad married Connie days after Mom died. I ran to Tim because he was nothing like John. The growing similarities between my father and me have begun to make me hyperventilate. I breathe in and close my eyes for the briefest of seconds. The smell of dust and...his trumpets.

And there they are. Standing in the corner of the living room, looking like some elaborate Dr. Seussian pipe organ. That smell—like a cork-spit-and-brass combo, unmistakable. I'm immediately zoomed back. I look away. I...I just can't take it all in.

I turn away from the trumpets and face the shrine once more. The six of us move around the room as if it were the Louvre. We keep a safe distance from the masterpieces, our hands safely in pockets or clasped behind our backs. We look at these pictures with an awe usually saved for the masters.

Baby pictures. Huston in his Little League uniform. Leo in floaties in some backyard pool. Me at the piano, curling over the keys, unaware my picture is being taken. Abigail at a tea party surrounded by her dolls. The entire family—even Mom—in the middle of some hike, all of us in hiking boots and shorts. I've never seen that one before. I go in closer. Abigail moves on to the next one, making room for me. Mom and Dad must have asked someone else to take it, because there's Dad, with Leo on his lap, looking out from behind his golden curls. Mom is standing with her arm around Huston, Abigail and I standing in front of them. God, we look happy.

There's one of Mom and Dad sitting on some batik-slipcovered couch. Mom's languidly resting her legs over Dad's lap as he does his best to entangle himself in her. They smile wide at the camera.

"They used to sit like that all the time. Remember?" Abigail whispers, staring at the picture.

"Yeah," I say, nodding. I had forgotten, but when we were young, there was never a time when they weren't touching, hugging or caressing each other. It was, of course, humiliating as a kid to have parents who were so "gross" with each other, but now? Their love continues to confound me with its mixture of utter tragedy and quieting beauty.

Propped against the framed photos are new pictures of Abigail's kids. Evie's school pictures. The twins' pictures from when they were born. Abigail's wedding photo. More proof of Abigail's fascination with Dad through the years. But proof it might not have been as unrequited as we all thought. Abigail takes her wedding photo down from the mantel and brings it closer. She lowers it so the twins can get a look.

Leo moves in behind me to stare at the hiking picture. I see him touch the frame as well. We're so sure this isn't real. So sure we've somehow stumbled upon an elaborate fantasyland where Dad...remembered us.

I can't take any more in. I turn away from the pictures and face the other side of the living room. I clap my hand over my mouth.

A large brown mohair couch sits under the front window of the house. The curtains are drawn and they've definitely seen better days. A patterned chenille wingback chair sits with its back to us. Right next to it are two pairs of shoes. Worn-out loafers. Slung over the back of the wingback chair is a grayish Members Only jacket. I didn't know they even made those anymore. On the coffee table is a stack of magazines, mostly car and airplane stuff. Next to the magazines is a little rubber-banded pile of business cards—at the top: an optometrist. All around the magazines are various glasses, bifocals, trifocals and even a magnifying glass, which is resting on a car magazine. It looks like he must have started sleeping down here, maybe the stairs got to be too much for him. That must have been hard on Connie.

There's a little blanket and sheet along with a couch pillow stuffed into the creases, like it's been slept on. Another pair of loafers sits on the floor next to the couch. The giant television sits on the other side of the living room, the focus of all of the remote controls—lined up neatly next to all the various glasses. Abigail and Leo have both turned around. We all just stand there. Taking it in. Letting it wash over us.

There is a smallness to this life. To the person who lives here. Everything contained in one little part of such a huge house. It kills me. My enormous, larger-than-life father living in this tiny space.

"The documents," Abigail says quietly, finally breaking her gaze away from the couch.

"He must have an office or something," I say, looking up the stairs, wanting to get away from here. Not look at it anymore. It's all so wasted. So much time wasted.

"Leo, can you watch the kids while Grace and I see if we can find the office?" Abigail asks, heading up the stairs.

"Yeah, sure. We'll do a little exploring of our own," Leo says, heading into the dining room, with its dusty, heavy furniture. I start up the creaky stairs behind Abigail and pass the crucifix— the frightening staircase guardian from my childhood.

"That thing stills scares me," I say, climbing the stairs.

"It *is* a tad gory," Abigail concedes.

As we climb the stairs to the second floor, I notice a mahogany sculpture of the Madonna and Child hanging on the wall of the landing next to the crucifix. A little spot on the Madonna's forehead has been worn off, along with a matching spot on the child's forehead.

"I didn't know Dad was religious?" I observe, pointing at the Madonna and Child.

"Sure, he was always Catholic," Abigail says, coming up behind me.

"What happened here?" I ask, pointing at the two spots that are worn off.

"That used to be in the hallway of the old apartment, the one right outside Mom and Dad's bedroom? He used to rub it every morning," Abigail explains, now standing next to me.

"Why?" I asked. Mom and Dad only baptized Huston. Looking back, it may have been more Dad's doing than Mom's. After that she took a stand: if/when the rest of us should want to explore religion, it should be our choice. Abigail chose Episcopalian aka Catholic Lite in her teens and has never looked back. She still wears a tasteful silver cross around her neck even today. Leo dabbled in the usual carousel of Hollywood religions: Kabbalism, Scientology, Tibetan Buddhism, Vedantism and Wicca—finally settling on admitting that he simply believes in a "higher power." Before Mom died, Huston described himself as agnostic. By the time of her funeral, the only baptized Catholic in the bunch had denounced God altogether. My relationship with spirituality boils down to a hope that there's something out there that unites us all. I'm basically a believer in the Force from *Star Wars*.

"It was part of his prayers, Grace," Abigail says, staring over at me with disdain, her little silver cross shining.

"I get the distinct impression you're judging me," I say.

"I *am* judging you," Abigail shoots back as she continues on.

We reach the top floor and walk through what was probably Dad and Connie's bedroom at one point. The bed looks tired and wan with a faded comforter lying flat over the bed. The pillows are depressingly thin. There is a thick layer of dust over everything. Abigail moves on to the next room.

"Grace? In here," she calls from another room.

I walk down the long hallway and into one of the rooms at the front of the house.

Abigail is bending over the large wooden desk.

"I can't take much more of this," she says, holding up a picture of Mom. It's an older picture taken when Mom was probably in college. It looks professionally done. She looks so retro 1960s in it: Peter Pan collar, helmet hair and dainty closed-mouth smile. Not the woman I remember. But probably the woman Dad fell in love with.

"Where was this?" I ask, entering Dad's office and taking the picture in hand.

"Right here," Abigail says, pointing to a prominent space on his desktop.

"That must be a little awkward for Connie," I say, setting the picture back down right where it was.

"You think?" Abigail says, opening up the top right-hand drawer.

"Any luck?" I ask, looking into the drawer. It's filled with stacks and stacks of steno note pads, each page containing a list of some sort. Abigail takes the top one out and hands it to me while she searches for the stuff we actually came for.

"This is definitely the place," Abigail says, opening up another side drawer. I flip open the steno pad and it reveals a list written in spidery handwriting of what looks to be Dad's monthly bills. Telephone, water and power, mortgage . . . The list is neat. A $19.47 telephone bill pulls at me. I close the steno pad and just stop. I stare at the old picture of Mom.

My entire personal family history is being ripped apart stitch by stitch. We were the first thing Dad woke up to and the last thing he went to bed thinking about? Why didn't he just pick up the phone? What made him want only photographs of us and not the real us? I know the answer all too well. Real love means getting hurt and sometimes it's easier to just *like* people. When they leave, you don't want to rip your heart out or wish they'd had the courtesy to do the honors before leaving.

Oh wait . . . they do.

My chest clenches as I remember.

I am standing outside of All Saints Church.

"You have to go in, Gracie. Your family needs you," John whispers. I'm clutching the "program" for my own mother's funeral. *IN MEMORIAM: EVELYN BONITA HAWKES. AUGUST 11, 1948–AUGUST 29, 2004.*

"It's a beautiful day," I say, my eyes closed as I luxuriate in the wind on my face.

John waits. I don't move. I don't do anything. He probably doesn't know that this isn't happening. This is all a dream. This is where the entire world morphs into a roller coaster ride and we all realize we've showed up to work without our pants on.

"Grace . . ." John soothes, coming up beside me. His hair smells of the shower, his black-as-pitch eyes are rimmed in red, his just-shaved face is soft and inviting.

"I've had some time to think about it," I start.

John is quiet. Cautious.

"It's not real," I say, distant and unaffected.

"What?" John asks, his face worried.

"A dream," I clarify, breathing in.

"Grace—" John says.

"We're going to wake up any minute," I say, sure of myself. John pulls me in for a hug. My arms are lifeless at my sides.

"Gracie . . ." John whispers, his mouth so close to my ear, our bodies knotted in a black-clad tangle. This can't be happening.

"Any minute now," I repeat, my head on his chest. John takes a big breath and squeezes me tighter.

"John . . . Grace, we have to go in," Huston says, appearing in the gray, arched doorway, his face expressionless. His suit is perfectly pressed. John warily lets go of me and turns to Huston.

"You...you okay?" John asks.

"I'm fine," Huston answers, his voice detached and lifeless. John helplessly stuffs his hands into his pockets. We're all fine.

"I'm on my way," I say, my voice coming from some other body. Huston walks into the church, a tiny slip of paper in his hand. I can literally hear the world stop turning. The wind stops blowing. No birds. No leaves rustling.

"The wind stopped," I note, my voice now a distant rumble.

"Grace, we have to go in," John urges, taking my hand. I can't feel it. I can't feel anything.

"Oh, sure...sure..." I dreamily answer, straightening my dress. John tightens his grip around my hand, his brow furrowed. We climb the stairs to the church as I anticipate the alarm clock buzzer that will surely awaken me from this nightmare.

And I wait.

My heart seemed to simply stop serving as anything but a vital organ. No emotion seeped in or out of its sealed chambers the day Mom died. I suppose that made it easier to walk away...from Huston, Abigail and Leo. From Evie. From John: a man who demanded my whole heart. After that day, I simply had nothing to give.

I look up to see Abigail. She is still. Her shoulders hunched over...exhausted. She's looking at a pile of letters that are strewn on Dad's desk.

"What...what is it?" I ask, stepping closer.

"Letters. Unopened and returned. Addressed to Mom," Abigail says, flipping through the pile of letters on the desk.

"How many?" I say, unable to fully grasp what I'm seeing. What exactly happened between Mom and Dad? And were we just the collateral damage of their star-crossed love affair?

"Tons," Abigail answers, carefully sifting through the letters.

"Open one," I say, quiet. Unable to touch them.

Abigail picks one up that has come open from being in the drawer so long. She slips her fingers inside the envelope and delicately unfolds the piece of paper within. She reads. I'm not breathing. Abigail flips the letter around revealing two words.

I'm sorry.

Abigail opens another letter: *I'm sorry.* Another: *I'm sorry.* Another: *I'm sorry. I'm sorry. I'm sorry. I'm sorry.* A thousand times...*I'm sorry.*

"She never read them," Abigail sighs, holding one in her hand. The paper wrinkles and sags like a little dead body.

"How many times can you say you're sorry and still cheat?" I ask, remembering the women who called the house and hung up whenever we answered. The women Dad brought home to "jam with." The women Dad got caught with at various hotels/coffeehouses/bars. The women he prized more than Mom. The women he prized more than us.

"I know." Abigail nods.

"What was she supposed to do? What would you have done?" I ask. How was it possible that two people who loved each other just simply couldn't live with each other?

"I would have done the same thing," Abigail confesses, putting the letter back down on the desk. She sifts through the wreckage and pulls a single piece of paper off the desk. I shuffle through the letters, trying not to think about the choices I've made. The shortsighted choices that felt good at the time. I can easily envision a future that has me writing a thousand letters with the same two words. Abigail's entire body sags as she reads the sheet of paper she's unearthed.

"He was there," she sighs, cradling the paper.

"There? Where? What...what are you talking about?" I ask,

reaching for the paper in her hand. The program. *IN MEMORIAM: EVELYN BONITA HAWKES. AUGUST 11, 1948–AUGUST 29, 2004.*

"He was there," Abigail says again. She is growing angry. She wants answers. We all do.

"You didn't mail him this?" I ask, holding the program carefully.

"No!" Abigail insists, some of that anger being funneled my way. I back off.

"Okay," I soothe, secretly flipping the program around, looking for proof it wasn't mailed. Abigail narrows her eyes at me.

"Jesus, Grace—he was there," Abigail yelps, snatching back the program.

"None of this makes any sense," I mumble, shaking my head.

"We'll figure it out later. Let's just get the documents we need and get the hell out of this haunted house," Abigail says, her voice dipping when she says the word *hell*. She collects herself once and for all.

"Right...right," I agree, taking a deep breath. Abigail sets the program aside, stacks all the letters and robotically gets back to the job at hand.

"Okay—here's his Social Security card. That's one," Abigail says, laying the tattered blue piece of paper on the desktop. Raymond Mateo Hawkes.

"You named Mateo after Dad?" I ask, holding up the evidence.

"I liked the name," Abigail says, over her shoulder.

"Ah, you liked the name," I repeat with disdain.

"Later...remember?" she warns, pulling out file after old file. I open the steno notepad back up and flip through the pages while Abigail shuffles through the old file folders. I scan the entries.

"Dad must have a rental," I say, noticing there's another address that he seems to be paying the mortgage on.

"Oh yeah?" Abigail says, pulling out an old Medicare bill.

That's two out of three. All we need now is his medical insurance card. I flip the pages of the steno notepad some more.

"He pays the utilities there, too. Sweet deal. Remember that apartment over Top's Burgers where the utilities were paid?" I ask.

"We should probably let the tenant know what's going on, just in case there are any problems," Abigail says, sifting through papers and files deep in the desk.

"We can add it to the list of things we're not going to be pushy about," I say, still flipping the pages of the steno. Abigail gives me a little smile as she continues to search for the final document.

"Nana Marina must have been loaded," Abigail says, flipping through Dad's banking records.

"And Dad got everything," I say, flipping another page.

"Aha!" Abigail says, holding up the medical insurance card victoriously.

"Abigail?! Abigail?!" Leo calls, bounding up the stairs. It sounds as if a herd of buffalo are following him.

My stomach drops. Oh, shit. Connie's back. Connie's back?!

"In here," Abigail says, closing the drawer and stacking the necessary documents to take to Nurse Miller. She's trying to act calm and collected, but I notice her hands are shaking as she piles the documents and starts for the door.

"I told you she was coming back," I say, feeling nauseated.

"We'll just explain to her that we needed the documents. Nurse Miller will have to back us up, she knows we need—" Abigail is cut off by Leo breathlessly approaching the office door. The twins are right on his tail. Evie is just next to him, ready to burst. I close the steno pad as I formulate a plan to duck out the back.

"Is she in the house already, or did you just spot the car?" I blurt, not able to help myself.

"I'm sure it'll be fine—" Abigail says, herding everyone out of the office. Leo stops us.

"No . . . no. It's not that," Leo says, stopping us cold.

"Not what?" I need clarification.

"Connie's not here," Leo quickly replies.

"Then is the house on fire, because that's the only other reason you should have come barreling up here like th—" I start.

"No woman lives here, Gracie. No woman has lived here for a very long time. Like since Nana Marina," Leo interrupts.

chapter thirteen

What are you talking about?" I say.

"No pwetty soaps," Emilygrae offers.

"Just because there are no pretty soaps, mija, doesn't mean—" Abigail begins.

"There aren't any woman's clothes," Evie adds.

"Are you proud of yourselves? I believe there's a grassy knoll out back, maybe the women live there?" I say, eyeing Leo.

"It's not a conspiracy theory. Where are Connie's clothes? Where is all the ... girl stuff?" Leo stutters.

"What are you trying to find? Tampax? I think Connie's a little long in the tooth for that," I say, shutting the desk drawer and looking to Abigail.

"Leo, Connie and Ray are married. They live in this house. Now, we need to get back with these documents," Abigail says, herding the children out of the office.

"Will you just come look?!" Leo shouts.

We are all silent. Shocked. Emilygrae and Mateo move closer to Abigail. Evie looks uncomfortable at Leo's tone. Even Leo looks a little taken aback.

"I'm sorry ... I'm sorry," Leo says, taking Abigail's hand, and as is always the way—no one can tell Leo no.

"You have five minutes," Abigail says.

Leo leads us into the first bedroom that Abigail and I walked into. The depressing worn-out comforter and the half pillows are just as dismal the second time around. Leo goes over to the closet door and opens it wide.

"Well?" he says, standing back so that Abigail and I can see inside. It's one of those older-home closets—small and cramped. It is packed with men's clothes: jackets, slacks, shirts, all in some shade of navy, black or gray. The floor of the closet is littered with luggage and a couple of random pair of shoes. All men's.

"Honey, a lot of couples spread their clothes out over several closets. Women tend to have more clothes than men," Abigail says. Leo shuts the closet door.

"That's what we thought, too," Leo says.

"But we checked all the closets and nothing. No girl clothes," Evie adds.

"No gore cloves," Emilygrae repeats quietly.

"Not even on the floor," says Evie.

"Not even in the washa-machine," Mateo says.

"We need to get back to the hospital with these documents. It's a proud moment for everyone. We should really consider writing *Parenting* magazine," I say. Leo sighs loudly and looks at Evie.

"What . . ." Abigail says absently, obviously not listening.

"We should probably get back before Leo recruits the kids as drug mules," I say. Leo crosses his arms across his chest.

"What were you saying about that other property?" Abigail starts. Leo perks up.

"That Dad had a rental?" I say, lifting up the steno pad. Leo glares at me.

"How do we know it's a rental?" Abigail asks. Leo steps forward.

"We don't . . . I guess," I say.

"No, we don't. Two pieces of property for two different people," Abigail says, walking out of the bedroom and back into the office.

"This isn't an episode of *Law and Order*," I argue, following Abigail into the office.

"We can't dismiss the whole 'sons of bitches' thing," Leo whispers, just out of kid earshot.

"I'm certainly not defending what she said, I swear. But can we just take a second here? Grief makes you do and say some crazy stuff. Trust me...I know," I plead. Leo darts around me and joins Abigail by Dad's desk. He sees the program.

"What's this?" Leo asks, holding up the program.

"The program to Mom's funeral," I say, promising myself that we're not trying to figure that out just yet.

"Did you mail it to him?" Leo asks Abigail.

"Why do people keep asking me that?" Abigail exclaims.

"We think he was there," I say quietly.

"And those?" he asks, pointing to the stack of letters.

"Unopened letters from Dad to Mom saying *I'm sorry*...over and over again," I say, mechanically.

"Awesome," Leo mumbles. He shakes his head. My thoughts exactly.

"A haunted house," I say.

"We need to get out of here," Leo agrees, opening a drawer in a small file cabinet just to the side of Dad's desk.

"I never wanted to come in here in the first place," I say.

"Then let's find what we're looking for," Abigail says. The kids are riveted.

"Here we go," Leo says, pulling out a file filled with bills.

"Anything?" Abigail asks, looking over Leo's shoulder.

"This is marked November 2005. It's all of the paid bills for that month," Leo explains, flipping through the bills in the file. We all watch. And wait.

"There! There!" Abigail blurts, pointing inside the file folder.

"It's the water and power bill for 1375 Daly Street. Constance Noonan," Leo proclaims, holding up the bill.

None of us knows what to do. We just stand there and stare at one another. Even the kids are silent.

"We're driving by," Abigail says, looking at her watch and heading out of Dad's little haunted office.

"Wait, what?" I say, following her out.

"If Connie's living at this Daly house, she's just about to leave for the hospital. We can catch her coming out," Abigail says, hopping down the stairs. I race down after her, carefully avoiding eye contact with Nana Marina's crucifix. Old habits. Leo, the damning water bill and the kids are behind me.

"And do what? Tackle her? Ask her to go on *Judge Judy*? Will you just be rational," I plead, whirling her around at the bottom of the stairs.

"She's been lying to us, Grace. Lying! She's been making us feel like second-class citizens while our father is dying. I'm not going to tackle her, but I sure as hell want to," Abigail says, wriggling her arm free and walking out, the word *hell* not whispered in the least.

"Listen, will you? Abigail!?" I yell, following her. Leo stands on the porch with the kids safely behind him as Abigail strides down the front walk, opens the minivan door and waits. Leo looks down at the kids and then to me.

"There's no harm in driving by. Evie, close the door," Leo says, stepping down off the porch with the twins on either side. I finally catch up to Abigail.

"Are you actually thinking about this? Do you think maybe stalking a senior citizen with your children in tow might be a bad idea?" I say.

"She doesn't know what kind of car we drive, besides what's worse? Figuring out that she doesn't live there or finding out that she does?" Abigail says, latching Emilygrae into her car seat as I latch in Mateo. Evie climbs into the third row with Leo.

"You know, it could just be Dennis who lives there. Sure, it's not exactly a good thing that a billion-year-old man is mooching off his stepfather, but that could explain all of this," I say, climbing into the front seat. I look back at Leo. His face is resolute. Scary, even.

"Could be," Abigail says, inputting the Daly house into her GPS. The machine bells on and tells us to flip around and head back the way we came. The directions are brief: this other house is apparently within walking distance.

I sit back in my chair and stay quiet. I can't believe this. We're stalking an old lady. Stalking. Old lady. A soccer mom, her jailbird brother, the AWOL sister and a pack of kids. In a minivan. Are stalking Everyone's Nana. This is the worst cloak-and-dagger shit I've ever seen.

If we get caught...if Connie, *wait*...if Connie sees us, that means she's coming out of the Daly house. Which means she doesn't live at Dad's house. Which means that...she lied to us. She made us feel unwelcome at our own father's bedside. I buckle my seat belt across my chest just as the GPS unit tells us we're arriving. Not quite the gesture of unification I was hoping it would be.

"Okay, there it is. It's a town house, that one...the beigey one on the corner," Abigail says, pointing at a very modest town house that looks kind of new compared to the other houses in the neighborhood.

"If you pull over on the other street we might not be quite as visible," Leo says, leaning forward and pointing to a much busier street where our car might not stand out as much. I don't bother reminding Leo that our stalkee is an old lady and not Henry Hill from *Goodfellas* and therefore probably not scanning the streets for our impromptu stakeout.

Abigail makes a quick U-turn and parks on the north side of the cross street. All of us fight the urge to duck down. Or at least I do. As I turn around and look at the back of the minivan, I see Emilygrae and Mateo have unlatched themselves and are now crouching on the floor along with Leo and Evie.

"She'll see you!" Emilygrae giggles. I crawl back into the minivan and crouch down by the door, where Leo had crouched earlier this morning. Abigail squats down between the two front seats, poking her head up now and again to get a better look. Leo comes up and squats next to me. The minutes pass. It's nearly eight-thirty a.m.

"This is ridiculous," I whisper.

"Shh," Leo scolds. Mateo lets out a giant fart just behind me. He collapses into a fit of giggles.

"Mattayyyyyyooooooooo!" erupts the entire minivan.

"Wait! Wait, shhhhh," Abigail says, from the front seat. We are all instantly quiet, the smell of little boy fart wafting in the air. We take our spots by a window and watch as an old Honda Accord pulls up in front of the beigey town house on the corner. A red-haired gentleman is behind the wheel.

Dennis.

I'm not breathing. I look at Leo just as he's turning to look at me. He shakes his head in disgust and turns back to the window. The minutes pass as the Honda sits idling at the curb. Abigail remains crouched at the front of the minivan, looking crisp and efficient in her little sweater set.

"That's that guy from the hospital," Evie says. We all nod in agreement, but still don't speak. Our eyes are all trained on the front door of the town house. As we wait, I wonder what would be worse: seeing Connie walk out that front door or having Dennis pull out and continue on to the hospital. Ojai is a very small town, it could happen. He could just have pulled over to make a quick phone call.

"There she is," Leo whispers. Sure enough, Connie in all of her white-panted glory steps out of the front door, checking to make sure it's locked, and heads down the front pathway and right into Dennis' waiting car. We all watch them pull away as they head toward the hospital.

"Well, I think we just figured out who the White Witch is," Leo says, taking way too much pleasure in the Narnia theme.

"How long? How long has she lived here?" Abigail whispers.

"Are they even still married?" I add. I think about the picture shrine back at Dad's house. Why couldn't he just tell us all this, instead of playing mind games by giving Huston the power of attorney. Wait . . . *wait*. The power of attorney. The skilled nursing facility.

"We have to get back to the hospital. Huston," I say, latching Mateo back into his car seat.

"I know, but we need something. If we're going to—" Abigail can't finish the sentence. What is it we're going to start here? What are we getting ourselves into?

"We're going to need more proof," Leo says from the way back.

"I have to go pee-pee, Mami," Emilygrae announces, standing over her still crouching mom. Abigail slides Emilygrae into her kid seat, latches her in and sits back down in the driver's seat.

"The steno pads. There were tons. A whole drawerful. We might be able to figure out how far back this goes. Maybe even find a deed," I say, getting back into the front seat and into work mode.

"Mija, you can use the potty back at the Big Blue House, okay?" Abigail says, putting the minivan in drive and pulling back onto Dad's street.

We drive the short distance back to the Blue House in silence.

chapter fourteen

Just throw it all in," Abigail says, grabbing an old cardboard box from the closet. Leo opens up drawer after drawer and empties the contents into the awaiting box. Abigail made sure to separate the three documents Nurse Miller had asked for—the three documents that seem completely insignificant now. I find a bag of rubber bands in an upper drawer and take handful after handful of Dad's spidery-written steno pads, band them together and put them into Mateo's Batman backpack, which he let me borrow. But just for today.

Abigail is putting stacks of file folders into the canvas bags from her car. Evie and the twins are playing in the front yard. Some kind of tag where everyone's pissed that they're It and the entire game is spent disciplining and fighting. You know, normal tag.

I get to the bottom of the second steno pad drawer and pull out what I think is the oldest one. I flip it open as Leo and Abigail sift through the other desk drawers. I read the date written on the top line in writing much more assured, much less spidery.

3/26/05—1375 Daly Street, Mortgage Payment—$779.00

"When was the wedding? When was Connie and Dad's wedding?" I ask, unable to quite understand what I'm reading.

"It was right after Mom . . ." Leo trails off.

"So, about a month after that?" Abigail says, walking over to me.

"September something," Leo says, throwing a pile of files into the now overloaded box.

"He was paying the mortgage on the Daly house by March of '05," I say.

"What? That can't be right," Abigail says, taking the steno pad from me. Leo walks over to us. Abigail flips the pages back and forth. Back and forth. Each time growing angrier. Each time becoming more violent.

"Six months?!" Abigail says, shoving the steno pad back at me.

"*No*," Leo says, taking the steno pad.

Abigail paces. "They were together six months?"

"How long did they even know each other before they got married?" I ask.

"If Dad came to Mom's funeral after all . . ." Leo says. I grab the steno pad. Flipping pages, doing math and trying to understand what all of this means.

"He freaked out," I say, dropping the steno pad to my side.

"Just like the rest of us," Abigail sighs. *Us.* I look up . . . directly into her eyes. Soft. Wrenching. Confused. I hope that instead of the haze my eyes have displayed for the last five years, I have the good sense to look horrified.

We stand in silence.

"I should have believed you," I say to Leo, feeling horrible.

"I didn't want to believe me either," Leo answers.

"I'm sorry about the drug mule line," I say, ashamed.

"No, it was funny. It took me everything not to laugh," Leo says. I give him a quick smile as he lets out a crackling giggle.

"Huston was right. He knew that power of attorney meant something," Abigail says.

"How were we supposed to know any of this?" Leo implores.

"Regardless, we have to get back. Do we have enough?" Abigail asks, eyeing the canvas bags, the Batman backpack and the overloaded cardboard box.

"I'll see if I can find something more in the documents on the drive back," I say, hitching Mateo's backpack over my shoulder and taking Mom's picture off the desk. I have a habit of taking pictures of Mom when I shouldn't. This time, however, I envision that bulletin board in Dad's hospital room. It really does need a bit more color.

"I think I should stay," Leo says. Abigail and I turn to him.

"Why?" I ask, stopping in the doorway.

"I think we should change the locks. I can call a locksmith. They can usually be here within an hour," Leo says.

"I don't think we have anything to worry about. If she had any interest in the house, she would have come in last night," I say, Mateo's backpack digging into my shoulder.

"She's about to find out that we know she's been lying. And everything that proves it is right here in this house," Leo points out. Abigail sets down the two canvas bags.

"Can we do that?" Abigail asks.

"Huston has the power of attorney. He can do anything Dad can do. Dad has the right to change his own locks. So Huston does, too," Leo argues.

"But we're not Huston," I say, finally setting down the Batman backpack.

"He'll okay it later," Leo says, picking a phone book up off a stack of them in the corner. We don't stop him.

"How will you get back to the hospital?" Abigail asks.

"I'll figure it out," Leo says, opening the phone book to the locksmith section. Baby step by baby step this family has gone from slightly dysfunctional suburbia all the way to Mafia.

"We'll call and keep you updated," Abigail says, picking the canvas bags back up. I hitch Mateo's backpack over my shoulder. The giant overloaded cardboard box sits in the middle of the office. Awesome. I grunt my goodbyes as I bend over and heave up the box. The tiny backpack slides down my arm, cutting off my circulation as I trudge down the stairs, Abigail just behind me. We shift and maneuver the various canvas bags, backpacks and boxes into the minivan as the kids settle in.

I buckle myself into the third row, the cardboard box at my feet, and begin sifting through. Carsickness be damned.

Evie asks if she can help, so I pass her a stack of documents. I tell her to look for legal-looking stuff. We might find the deed to the Daly place or maybe even some divorce papers—*one can only hope*. We stack the papers we've already seen in front of Evie, tightly wedging them so they won't slip under my seat. Evie may not know what she's looking for, but she sure looks like she does. She shows me a few bills and a couple of insurance booklets, which might be useful for figuring out what type of coverage Dad has. Jesus. Coverage. Skilled nursing care for the rest of his life. The rest of his life. Down the rabbit hole. Wait, I can't think about this now. Lock it up. Just sift. I find bank records for his primary bank account.

"Dad has about $612,000 left in the bank—that must be from what he inherited from Nana Marina," I announce from the third row.

"So he bought the Daly house with the inheritance money?" Abigail asks, making a turn onto the main Ojai drag.

"I would assume. I mean, where else would he get that kind of money?" I ask, flipping the pages of Dad's bank records. Failed jazz man turned elementary school band instructor in Ojai, California, doesn't really equal a $612,000 nest egg.

"Yeah, you're right," Abigail agrees. I set the bank records between Evie and me, as she leans down in front of me to pick up another stack of papers. We make the final turn into the hospital and Abigail begins to search for a parking space.

"What about this?" Evie asks, passing me a stapled-together document. It doesn't look like anything legal, but I take it anyway, not wanting to hurt her feelings.

THE LAST WILL AND TESTAMENT OF
RAYMOND MATEO HAWKES

Holy. Shit.

"It's his will. Evie found his will," I proclaim, beaming at my niece. She doesn't know how to react and finally allows a wide smile to break across her face. My elation at this connection is short-lived. Do I want to read this document? Do I want to know who Dad left his estate to? Do I want to not see my name in these bequests? Abigail finally pulls into a parking space. I flip the pages randomly, my hands shaking.

Abigail zooms the minivan door open and the sun streams in. I take a deep breath and flip Dad's will to the front.

MY NAME IS RAYMOND MATEO HAWKES (3/17/1931) AND THIS IS MY LAST WILL AND TESTAMENT.

I WAS MARRIED TO EVELYN BONITA HAWKES: DECEASED AUGUST 29, 2004.

I HAVE FOUR LIVING CHILDREN: HUSTON RAYMOND HAWKES (02/16/1971), ABIGAIL EVELYN HAWKES (05/26/1973), GRACE BAKER HAWKES (04/18/1974), and LEOPOLD MILES HAWKES (06/19/1976).

I AM MARRIED TO CONSTANCE LEE NOONAN. I MARRIED CONSTANCE LEE NOONAN ON 9/16/2004. I SEPARATED FROM CONSTANCE LEE NOONAN ON 4/9/2005.

"It says he separated from Connie on April 9, 2005," I read, as Abigail leans into the door, deciding not to unleash the hounds just yet. Emilygrae and Mateo are growing ever more impatient. I keep going.

"Why didn't he just divorce her?" Evie asks. Her frankness startles me. I look at Abigail.

"The Catholic thing," Abigail says, beaten. I look up from the document.

"Are you kidding me?" I ask.

"Well, he didn't marry Connie until after Mom died. It's not like Mom and Dad ever got divorced," Abigail explains. I look back down at the document. One hurricane at a time, please.

"Huston's the executor, and you're the alternate," I say, flipping the page.

"What does *omit* mean?" Evie asks.

"What, sweetie?" I absently ask. Evie is reading the page I've already flipped past.

"Omit, what does it mean?" Evie asks, pressing the page in question back down. She points to the word. Omit. OMIT. I read along where her little bitten-down blue fingernail rests.

I INTENTIONALLY OMIT TO PROVIDE FOR CONSTANCE LEE NOONAN IN THIS WILL.

I INTENTIONALLY OMIT TO PROVIDE FOR DENNIS BRUCE NOONAN, THE BIOLOGICAL SON OF CONSTANCE LEE NOONAN, IN THIS WILL.

"Omit means to leave out," I sigh. I reread the sentences.

"Who's getting omitted?" Abigail blurts.

"Connie and Dennis," I say, looking up at her.

"Connie and Dennis?" she repeats.

"Yeah, he intentionally omits them from his estate. Names

them. And omits them," I say, looking up from the will. I look back down at Dad's will.

I LEAVE, BEQUEATH AND GIVE MY WHOLE ESTATE, WHETHER REAL OR PERSONAL, TO MY FOUR BIOLOGICAL CHILDREN IN EQUAL SHARES.

"He's . . . he's left everything he has to us," I say. Abigail stands just outside of the minivan with her arm propped against the doorjamb.

It should be a moment of empowerment or inspiration, I mean, our Dad *chose* us. But all I can feel, and from the look on Abigail's face she's on the same roller coaster, is sadness. I close my eyes. Our pictures on the mantel. The unopened letters and the program from Mom's funeral lovingly saved. The sad little couch campsite with the rows of glasses, rubber-banded business cards and old shoes. A man who chose to be alone because it was easier to love from afar snaps before my wrenched closed eyes. Did he even know he was doing it? And in that moment, all the adrenaline finally dulling a bit, I am completely overtaken by grief.

My dad is dying.

I open my eyes and look up at Abigail: tears are streaming down her face. She tries to turn away from the kids, but they see. Emilygrae and Mateo sit in their little kid seats and watch as Abigail wipes at her eyes like a child herself. Evie watches me. The last will and testament of my father is crumpling in my sweaty hands.

"Not again," Mateo sighs, seeing Abigail sniffle back tears.

"She was crying last night in the hotel room, too," Evie confides.

"She was?" I ask. Evie nods. I look back over to Abigail.

"We should go. Bring that," Abigail commands finally. She

leans over and gives Emilygrae the high sign that means she can get out of her booster. Emilygrae brings her tiny hand up to Abigail's face and strokes her cheek. Just once. Her little hot pink cast leaves a giant scratch on Abigail's face, but it's the gentlest thing I've ever seen. Abigail kisses Emilygrae softly on the forehead and sets her down on the pavement next to the minivan.

"Touch the car, mija. Remember, we touch the car in parking lots," Abigail instructs, wiping away the last of her tears. Emilygrae lays a single hand against the minivan. Abigail leans into the driver's side and grabs her purse. She double-checks to be sure it contains the original three documents that Nurse Miller asked us to retrieve. Nurse Miller. Everything about her offends me now.

I push the box forward and climb out of the third row, clutching the steno pad from 2005, Dad's last will and testament and the original deed to the Daly house I found in the bottom of the old cardboard box. Evie crawls out just behind me and Mateo follows. Evie beeps the minivan door closed and we set off across the parking lot: Mateo holds his hand up to me and I take it, Evie falls in beside me with Emilygrae holding her hand, and Abigail brings up the rear. I feel like we're the slow motion iconic shot of *Reservoir Dogs* . . . but the Disney version, where no one cuts anyone's ear off to "Stuck in the Middle With You."

Yet.

The twins run through the tiny lobby of the hospital and once again Mateo pushes the outside call button. The elevator door dings open and we all walk inside. Abigail motions for me to pass her the stack of papers. I do. There's only one person Huston can hear this from. We pass the second floor. My breathing steadies as I roll out the knots in my neck. We pass the third floor. Mateo unsheathes his sword. Abigail and I share a quick smile as the elevator door opens.

We make a right.

Emilygrae and Mateo run pell-mell down the hallway as usual

and on into the waiting room. Evie walks with us down the hall-way until she has to, once again, turn into the Twin Watcher. She opens the door and we already hear fighting coming from within. About firsties. Evie rolls her eyes.

"I'll tell you what happens," Abigail says, kissing Evie.

"You can't forget anything either," Evie says, finally push-ing open the door and heading inside. Abigail and I continue walking.

We make a left.

My mind is running through the events of the morning as we walk toward the nurse's station just outside the ICU. They should really have an open bar in hospitals.

We make a left.

Abigail signs in. She is handed a name tag with HAWKES writ-ten on it. I follow. Sign in. I get a name tag. We're buzzed in.

For half a second, Abigail and I stand shoulder to shoulder at the door. Abigail reaches the inch that separates us and takes my hand. I curl my fingers around hers as she squeezes tightly. The door opens and we are hit with the buzzing, whirring and urgent voices of the ICU. One last squeeze and we let go. I scan the room and see Huston standing in the corner of the ICU talk-ing to John. Huston is imposing enough, but the addition of John makes it look like the hospital is in some kind of FBI lockdown.

Connie and Dennis stand at Dad's bedside. Connie is doing the usual clutching, gripping, hand-holding thing while Dennis stands idly by, gazing adoringly at a man who was his daddy for only six months. When he was fifty years old. What a bottom-feeder. Huston sees us and gets the attention of John, and they walk over to us.

"Do you have the documents?" Huston asks, approaching us.

"We need to talk," Abigail says, holding up the stack of papers from Dad's office.

chapter fifteen

H uston's mouth drops open.

I can see him having a whole conversation in his head. He's trying to work this out. Understand it. I want to tell him to quit while he's ahead—that there is no understanding it. No answers...just questions. Questions, I might add, that'll remain unanswered. Mom is gone. Dad's unable to speak for himself. We'll never know for sure whether or not he came to Mom's funeral. We'll never know why Mom never opened those letters or, for that matter, why Dad kept sending them. We'll never know why he married Connie. We'll never know why he decided that love was best experienced from a distance.

We are quiet. The hospital cafeteria bustles around us. None of us touch the cursory items we bought on arrival.

I sneak a glance at John. He's trying to process the information, but his expression is different from Huston's look of stunned confusion. John looks like he wants to kill somebody. That's my boy.

"Huston..." Abigail starts. He looks away from her, shaking his head.

"What proof do you have?" John asks, his face now resolved.

"We've got Dad's will, bank records, steno pads and bills dating back to 2005," I rattle off.

"That's not enough," John argues.

"What more proof do you need?" Abigail asks.

"Connie can argue that she and Ray had a certain under-standing. She can say they may have lived apart, but they still loved each other and spent every waking moment together," John argues.

"Then why would he leave her out of his will?" Abigail asks.

"Several reasons actually: mental incapacity, undue influence, or that it's an out-and-out forgery."

"Well, how would she—" Abigail starts.

"Regardless, can you state with one hundred percent certainty that their relationship isn't like that? That they didn't spend every waking moment together?" John asks.

We don't know our father at all.

"No," Huston finally says.

"And that's what they're going to exploit," John finishes.

"So what do we do?" Abigail asks.

It finally dawns on me: "We act like we don't know," I say. John nods in agreement.

"Why would we do that?" Abigail frowns, realizing she's not going to get to walk into the ICU and drag Connie out by her lit-tle white pants.

"We need to get all our ducks in a row," I say.

"He can't stay here. We need to find a facility near Los Ange-les," Huston says.

"And the minute you tip Connie off that you know anything, she'll get a lawyer and start telling anyone who'll listen that she's a little old lady who's the love of Ray's life. And you'll all be labeled the gold-digging ne'er-do-well children who never came to see him. Can you even prove that he abandoned you? She could argue that he tried to get in contact with you all these years, to have a relationship, and you had no interest in seeing him," John says. His voice is confident.

"Enough," I say. I haven't been able to come up with a

satisfactory explanation for why Dad abandoned us over the last twenty-two years; I certainly couldn't do it in a courtroom. And the more I find out the less I understand. It was almost easier when I thought he didn't love us.

How do you prove love anyway?

"John's right," Huston says, his head bowed. The table falls into silence.

"The power of attorney is the key," John adds, shifting in his plastic chair. We all look up.

"It can hold up?" I ask.

"Unless Connie is appointed your dad's conservator, and by her chronic absence at all the meetings pertaining to his care, I don't think that's what she wants. No, that power of attorney means Huston gets to make all the decisions regarding your father's care and finances," John says.

"It seems like there are an awful lot of variables," I say.

"But why can't we—" Abigail tries to cut in. John stops her.

"This isn't going to be easy," John finally says.

Abigail laughs mirthlessly. "Ya think?"

"I've been here for twenty-four hours and I already want to kill myself," I say, looking from Abigail to John, the smallest of smiles offering to defuse the moment.

"God, twenty-four hours . . . is that all?" Huston sighs, softening just a bit.

"It's like time has stopped," I answer.

"Do you remember when Mom died?" Abigail asks.

A chill passes over the table. We all remember the worst day of our lives.

Abigail continues, "That day went on forever."

"Literally," I say, realizing that I'm still reliving that day even after all these years. Maybe it's about time I stopped.

"The kids haven't even missed any school," Abigail mutters.

"Not a day of work," I say, my seventeen vacation days still untouched.

"It's not even New Year's Eve," Huston adds.

"It's so bizarre to think that other people are just going about their business. Going to work, buying groceries or whatever," I say.

"And we're here," Abigail says, her head dipping, her eyes closing.

We fall silent again as we yearn for the little, quiet lives that seem so very far away.

"Why didn't he just pick up the phone?" Abigail sighs. We are quiet. I take a deep breath.

"Because every day that goes by, it gets a little bit harder," I mumble, the words coming from deep below the surface.

"Harder for whom?" Huston asks.

"Harder to admit you're wrong. Harder to admit that the people you left behind aren't actually better off without you." I can't look at him. Any of them.

"Better off without you," Huston repeats, his voice challenging. I sneak a glance at John. His eyes meet mine and I will myself not to look away.

"Every day erodes away at the person you are, and it's not too long before you begin to forget you were ever a part of anything at all," I explain, my voice just over a whisper. Everyone is quiet.

I continue, "I think that's where the whole Connie thing comes in. Love becomes company and company becomes something you do just to pass the time. So you won't be alone." John looks away. My face flushes.

"All of those pictures," Abigail says.

"Not one of Connie. That's got to count for something," I say, hoping this will get us back on track.

"This is not about Connie," John says, his voice solemn.

"How is this not about Connie?" I ask.

"This is going to be about you. The four of you."

"But we didn't do anything."

"If you fight back, you have to get ready to be dragged through the mud by someone who doesn't give a shit about the truth, doesn't give a shit about ruining your lives. Obviously. She sat in a hospital room holding the hand of a dying man who left her years ago. She turned an entire nursing staff against you and, while she was at it, made all of you believe she was the grieving wife. So...this is not about her. She's a monster," John says.

"It's about more than that," Huston argues.

"Not for them. They're going to make it as basic as possible, you're the ones who are trying to evict a little old lady at a time when the husband she loves is dying," John says, scooting in his chair even more.

"Allegedly," Huston adds.

"It's not fair," Abigail says. She sounds so much like Emilygrae I have to swallow a smile.

"No, it's not. But, bottom line—you have to ask yourselves if you want to go forward. Forget that it's unfair, evil and deceitful. Is your Dad worth it?" John says, his hands tight in fists.

We are quiet.

John's words hang in the air. Why are we here if not to finish what we started—what Dad started?

"I'm in," I say.

"Me, too," Abigail says.

"What do we do first?" Huston asks.

"Like Grace said, we get our ducks in a row," John says. His voice saying my name is a speck of light in the darkness. It just rolls off his tongue.

"I'll start making some calls about facilities. There are quite a few around where I live," Abigail says, gathering herself, taking out her organizer once again.

Something has begun that we can't stop. Dad's too sick. Connie's too vile.

The only way out...is through.

"Where do you live?" John asks Abigail, his pencil hovering over the legal pad.

"South Pasadena. It's just south of Pasadena...kind of by—" Abigail says, writing in her organizer.

"Right by where Grace lives," John says, writing something down on his legal pad.

"I bought a new house on California Terrace last year," I say, for no apparent reason.

"I know," John says absently. I stare at him. He shifts in his chair...not looking at me. You *know*?

"So..." John begins again, his voice cracking. Please look at me. He does. Quick. A flash. A glance. He knew I'd bought a new house.

Huston clears his throat and continues. "So, South Pasadena it is, then."

"As soon as Leo gets back, we'll head back down to LA with the kids," Abigail says.

"Where's Leo?" Huston asks, standing.

"He's at Dad's. Changing the locks," I say absently.

"He's what?" John blurts. Abigail and I immediately see the problem.

"It's not a problem," I start.

"She's going to know," Abigail yelps, terrified we've already screwed this up.

"No, she won't. She has to act like she has the keys, like it's her house. How can she ask us for the keys to her own house? And even if she does go to the house and try to get in, who's to say Dad didn't change the locks years ago? She doesn't know. No, we're good," I work out.

"You have to run that shit by me," John "advises." Abigail and I nod.

"I'll call Manny and tell him not to come up after all. You guys can hold down the fort while we're gone?" Abigail asks, looking up. Huston, John and I just look at each other. We know we've gotten the short end of the stick. Staying up here means keeping up the Big Lie. It also means spending more time with Dad.

I'm not sure which one will be more difficult.

chapter sixteen

She's not ready to have you come in just yet," Nurse Miller advises, as we step back into the ICU after Abigail puts in her call to Manny. We look into Dad's hospital room, where Connie is standing by Dad's bedside. Dennis is sitting in one of several chairs in the room, reading a magazine. He looks up as we enter the ICU. I wish we didn't know about Connie. I genuinely wish she just wanted what's best for Dad. I try to look and see if Dad's awake, as he was earlier this morning. It looks like he's sleeping. That gives me some solace. Dennis approaches our little huddle in the corner like a prince approaching a gaggle of servants.

"Hey, man," Dennis says, patting Huston on the shoulder in a bizarre hypermasculine move that's supposed to pass for brotherly.

"Dennis," Huston answers.

"Dennis Noonan," he says, reaching his hand across to John.

"We've met," John says, his hands at his sides. His eyes distant. Dennis' hand hangs in the air between the two men.

"Oh...right. Moss. The attorney," Dennis says, his hand sagging back to his side.

John looks at his watch.

Dennis turns to Abigail and gets down to business. "Mom was wondering if you guys could do her a favor and return Ray's possessions to her. It'd be a big help."

"I'm so sorry, Dennis—I left the ziplock bag back at the hotel," Abigail says, so genuine.

"Oh, no worries," Dennis lies.

"Do you need it right away?" I ask.

"Mom's just worrying. I'm sure it's all the—" Dennis motions around at the ICU. Yes, this has been really hard on Connie, we all nod in agreement.

"Well, we'll get it to you just as soon as we can," Abigail assures him, placing a hand on his shoulder in concern. She's good.

Dennis walks back into the hospital room. We watch. He doesn't tell her that their plan didn't work. He just sits in one of the hospital chairs and picks up his magazine. Connie doesn't even bother to look up. Maybe he put her up to this? Or did she put *him* up to it? I have to snap out of this . . . it's ridiculous. I feel like Harriet the Spy. Every second we waste on Connie is time not spent with Dad. A chill passes over me as it dawns on me that I honestly don't know how many seconds we have left with him. This situation needs to be remedied. And fast.

"When can we visit with our father?" I ask Nurse Miller, breaking away from the group. Does she work here all day, every day, for crissakes? Couldn't we catch a break and have someone in charge besides her? The rest of the group looks on.

"Connie says she'll be leaving within the hour. I gave her a list of excellent facilities in the area that would be capable of handling Ray's . . . situation," Nurse Miller says, looking at another clipboard. Huston walks over midway through Nurse Miller's confession that she's usurped the power of attorney. *Again*. Abigail and John follow.

"Nurse Miller, I think it's time you and I met with the legal department together. I don't think you understand what a power of attorney means. Can you get them on the phone and set something up. *Now*. I'll wait." Huston speaks quickly and clearly, but I can see that his ears are bright red and his entire body is tense.

"I understand, Mr. Hawkes—" Nurse Miller starts.

"I'll wait," Huston interrupts, raising his voice. We are silent. Waiting. Nurse Miller turns on her little squeaky white heel, goes back behind the nurse's station and dials the phone.

"Hi, Frank, it's Nurse Miller in the ICU. I have Mr. Huston Hawkes here and he'd like the three of us to meet regarding some confusion with the power of attorney," Nurse Miller starts. She waits as "Frank" talks.

"There shouldn't be any confusion. That's probably what he's telling her now," John leans over and whispers to Abigail and me. I nod up at him, trying not to—well, it's a toss-up: do I straight inhale him or grab his face and start making out with him just to feel something good? Apparently, I've signed on to feel again. Pain seems to be the primary emotion that's come flooding back during the last twenty-four hours. But with it comes an almost overwhelming urge to feel good again. Being here with my family feels like wrapping up in a snuggly blanket as the chill creeps into a drafty cabin. But what I crave from John? That'd set the entire cabin on fire.

"I understand, Frank. I was simply—" Nurse Miller is cut off. John raises an eyebrow and gives Abigail and me the smallest of "I told you so" looks. I smile back at him, hoping I don't look like the twitching mess I feel like.

"We'll be there in five minutes, then. Thank you, Fr—" Nurse Miller looks at the phone like something completely alien has caused the line to go dead. No, dearie. He hung up on you. Nurse Miller looks up at Huston with such…disgust. Wow. John's speech about this being about us comes screaming back. Connie *has* fooled everyone. I can't wait until we get Dad out of here and into a regular room. Until we can take him all the way home.

"We'll be right back," Huston says, as he follows an enraged Nurse Miller out of the ICU. Abigail, John and I stand there for a moment in awkward silence.

"I'm going to check on the kids, see where Leo is and start calling around to facilities near us." Abigail whispers "near us." Adorable.

"If Leo needs a ride, just let me know and I can swing by and get him," I say to Abigail, as she pulls the organizer out of her purse once again.

"I will. I will. I'll let you know if I find anything," Abigail says. And then she does the strangest thing. She leans in and gives me a quick kiss on the cheek. Really fast, like she realized what she'd done too late. She stops for a quick millisecond and then gives John a wave and heads out of the ICU. She raises her eyebrows the slightest bit as she looks from John to me. Always the yenta.

John and I fall silent.

John rolls an office chair over and motions for me to sit down. I do and watch as he rounds up another chair for himself. In the aftermath of the morning's events I feel exhausted, but somehow invigorated.

Maybe I'm just punch-drunk from seeing all those pictures in Dad's house. A lifetime of wondering and now I finally have some proof that he loved us...that he loved me. I'm not forgettable. Without the ballast of Dad's indifference, how high can I fly?

I watch as John pulls a chair from an empty ICU room. I look into Dad's room. He's still asleep and Connie's at his bedside. I look away. There are a thousand Connies and Tims out there just waiting to fill the void. But there's only one Evelyn. Only one John. One shot at true love.

"How are you holding up?" John finally asks.

"I'm good," I say, fighting the urge to stand atop this chair and proclaim John as my one true love. Huzzah! Probably not the time.

"You sure?" John presses. I turn and look at him. We lock eyes.

Black as pitch. I mean—no difference in color from the pupil to the iris. Pure black. I've never seen anything like it. John waits patiently as I assess the rarity of his eye color. Epiphanies seem to not understand that there is a proper time and place for enlightenment. I look away.

"It's just a lot," I finally allow.

"That's the understatement of the century," John says.

"It's just..." I spin around in my little office chair, rolling over toward him, overshooting a bit and bumping into his leg.

"Just what," he says, steadying my knee. His hand lingers.

"It's one thing after another. This house of cards where nothing is solid and yet we keep building, building, building," I say, gesturing wildly with every "building."

"You're way out of your comfort zone on this one," John says gently.

"That's your big pep talk?" I ask, smiling a bit.

"No! God, no...I was just saying I understand why it would be daunting."

"You never think this kind of stuff is going to happen to you."

"I know," John agrees.

We are silent.

"We never talked about him," I finally say, looking into Dad's hospital room.

"Your dad?" John asks, following my gaze.

"Yeah," I answer, trailing off.

"You can only say so much."

"He wrote letters," I admit.

"Letters?"

"With just two words. *I'm sorry.*"

John looks away with a cynical laugh.

"What?" I ask. John shrugs me off, looking anywhere but at me.

"What?" I press again.

"It was about him. *He's* sorry?" John asks.

"Right, *he's* sorry."

"So what?" John asks, his face reddening.

"So what?" I ask, growing angry.

"You write to the love of your life over and over again and all you can say is *you're* sorry?" John says.

"He's the one who screwed up," I say, trying to figure out where John's going with this.

"I get that," he says.

"What would you have said?"

Without missing a beat, "I love you."

I shrink back. The words. The eyes. The man. John looks away.

We are silent.

"Do you think about your biological parents at all?" I am panicking, trying to derail the conversation completely.

"What's to think about? They left me at a firehouse when I was nine hours old. End of thought," John says, shifting in his chair.

"The why," I say, my voice soft.

"That way lies madness," John says.

"But if you don't think about it, you bury it and you find yourself five years later dating guys named Tim," I ramble on.

"No, *you* found yourself dating guys named Tim," John says, his eyes steely.

"Not anymore," I say, looking away.

John is quiet.

"Some people just go to therapy," he finally says with the slightest laugh.

We're quiet. I think about the letters. What would I have said? My breath quickens. I look up and see John as if for the first time. Whenever I looked at him in the past, I would find myself trying to memorize the lines of his body so I could remember him when he left. I couldn't help committing him to memory. As I take him in now, my breathing slows. Instead of tracing and retracing the lines and sinews of his body like multiplication tables, I allow him to make an impression on me at a cellular level. As his DNA absorbs into mine, I finally understand that people can be permanent if you let them. I take in a full, whole breath and exhale.

"I love you," I say, clear as a bell.

John turns his head and meets my gaze.

"I love you," I say again, a little louder.

I can see him yielding, his shoulders lower, his face softens.

"I love you," I say again, inching closer.

I watch as he steels himself, building the walls once more. I strike before he can finish the job.

"I love you," I say again, reaching out my hand, across what once felt like a great divide, and placing it on his.

John is quiet. Hesitating.

"Where's Huston?" Leo breathlessly asks, appearing out of nowhere next to John.

"What?" I ask. John stands. Clearly I'm going to have to kill Leo.

"Huston? Where's Huston?" Leo asks again, his messenger bag slung across his chest.

"He's in with Nurse Miller and the legal department. *Again*," I say, standing.

"What's going on?" I ask. What I want to say is "Any last words?"

"I brought th—" Leo starts, opening his messenger bag.

"Abigail, right?" Dennis approaches our group once again. Saved by the...well, saved by the bottom-feeding grifter. Not quite a bell, but a close second.

"I'm Grace," I correct. My voice flat. My eyes dead. Leo turns around, sees who it is and immediately backs up.

"We're going to take a break. Maybe head down to the cafeteria. You're welcome to go in," Dennis offers. How generous.

"Thanks," I say, coolly.

Connie walks out of Dad's hospital room, passing right in front of us.

"Did you ask him if he had the keys?" Connie calls to Dennis.

"They'll get them to us as soon as they can," Dennis answers, smiling benignly at us—letting us know what's expected of us.

"He's right there. Can't you just ask him?" Connie motions at Leo.

"Mother, that's not Huston." Dennis laughs, walking over closer to her.

"Course it is."

"That's...Sir, what's your name again?" Dennis quickly asks.

"Leo. Leopold Hawkes," Leo answers, his face red.

"That's the little one, Mother," Dennis oozes.

"The little one?" Connie sniffs, looking up at Leo, the giant of a man.

"The youngest one. The—" Dennis cuts off, raising his eyebrows. Leo shrinks back as it becomes clear that Dennis is trying to jog Connie's memory about Leo being the "criminal" he told her about.

"Oh...that's right," Connie says, as they quickly exit the ICU.

"Takes one to know one," Leo says, his voice tight. John and I try to offer Leo a smile.

"Sweetie...you're nothi—" I start.

"I know . . . I know," Leo quickly agrees.

"I'll leave you to it," John says, sitting back down.

"You'll be here . . . when I get back?" I ask, turning around, as Leo continues on into the hospital room.

"I'll be here," John answers. Not going anywhere.

"Okay," I say almost to myself. As I walk away, John sits back down in the office chair, bending over slightly with his elbows on his knees. I look back to see that he's dropped his head into his hands.

When I get to Dad's hospital room, I wonder if he'd understand if we told him we figured out his puzzle. Maybe it wasn't a puzzle at all. Dad probably didn't plan on having a stroke. He probably thought he'd die suddenly, not linger, like we all wish we would. He set this whole thing up, so after he died we'd get everything.

Except him.

I meet Leo in Dad's room. Dad seems to be sleeping pretty soundly, so we sit down in the two hospital chairs against the far wall under the big window. Leo digs in his messenger bag and pulls out the mahogany sculpture of the Madonna and Child.

"What? Wait . . . why?" I stutter, watching him pull the giant wooden face of the Virgin Mary out of his bag. Leo stands up, holding the Madonna and Child, as he looks for a place to hang her.

"I just thought . . . you know, it might help," Leo says, his voice quiet, his eyes darting. I don't know what to say. I'm not sure how much of a believer I am, especially since Mom died. But knowing that Dad is devout in his beliefs is helping me. Knowing his fear is being diluted just a bit by his belief in the afterlife, or Heaven, or whatever, has calmed me somewhat.

"Heyyy," Leo says, noticing that Dad is watching him.

"He's up?" I ask, standing up and moving to Dad's right side. I lay my hand on his shoulder, knowing full well he can't feel it.

"I brought this from your house," Leo says, holding up the Madonna.

Dad raises his still-restrained hand and lifts two fingers up. Two.

"Two?" I ask. Dad struggles to look over at me.

"Two?" Leo asks.

Dad raises his arm again and once again lifts two fingers. My mind races. Two. Two. Two. The Madonna and Child and...

"The crucifix," I blurt, seeing the landing of the staircase at Nana Marina's house clearly in my mind. "Two. Two. They're together. They're always together," I say to Leo.

I rush over to the other side of the bed and ask it again, "The crucifix?" I ask Dad, remembering Huston said he answers yes to everything. I just...I think I'm right. John comes over and stands in the doorway to Dad's room. Watching.

"The crucifix?" Leo asks. Dad watches Leo intently. I dig wildly in my purse and pull out a black pen and draw a large cross on the back of my hand.

"The crucifix?" I ask, holding up my hand. Dad raises his restrained hand and pulls mine close to his face.

Dad nods yes. Yes. Yes. Yes.

"Yeah?" I say, knowing it's not a real yes, but, for the first time in twenty-two years, I feel like I'm talking to my dad. We're connecting about something. I'm back at the piano, looking up to him for the downbeat. I have to do this for him.

"I can go get it," I say to Leo.

"Yeah, yeah...I'll stay here," Leo answers, taking Dad's hand.

I dig into Leo's messenger bag and find the newly minted set of Dad's keys. I grab my purse and walk out of Dad's hospital room, ready to speed over to Nana Marina's house, grab that creepy crucifix right off the wall and bring it back. John shifts his body so I can pass and looks down at me.

"I know it's not real. I know he says yes to everything. I just..." I admit.

"I'll come with you. Maybe see if we can gather up some more documents," John offers.

"You'll drive?" I ask, continuing out of the ICU.

"I'm sure as hell not driving in that buckboard you call a car," John says.

"Thank you...thank you—not about calling my car shitty, but you know—" I say, opening the door to the ICU and heading out into the maze of the hospital. John keeps up with me while we make the various lefts and rights that have burned them- selves into my brain.

The elevator dings open and Huston looks up from inside.

"I think Frank from Legal finally set Nurse Miller straight," he says, stepping out into the hall.

"I'll draft a letter on the firm's letterhead confirming the con- versation," John says, his arm blocking the door from closing.

"Thanks. Where are you guys off to?" Huston asks, as the ele- vator door bangs against John's arm.

"Leo brought the Madonna from Dad's house and Dad said there were two," I explain, pressing the one button.

"Dad said there were two?" Huston asks, stepping back into the elevator.

"He held up his fingers. Two fingers," I explain, holding my fingers up as proof.

"I thought I might be able to find some more documents," John adds.

"I can't believe he did the two-finger thing," Huston says, almost to himself. He rides down in the elevator with us.

"I asked him if he wanted me to get the crucifix, you know— they're always together. Two..." I explain, as the floors ding by.

Huston nods. "And he said yes...that that's what he wanted." The door dings open on the ground floor.

"But, Grace, you know—" Huston starts.

"I know it's not real. I know he says yes to everything. I just...thought it could help," I say, finally finishing the original sentence.

"It's a good idea, Gracie," Huston says, his voice softening.

"Thanks," I say, starting out through the lobby, the tears clogging my throat. The bizarre zigzaggian reality of my grief is still a mystery to me. One minute I'm fine and the next I feel like screaming. One minute I'm okay and the next I feel the pain is never going to end. The last time I had these feelings I shut them down. I can't let myself do that this time...however tempting it is.

"I have a meeting with Dad's lawyer in twenty minutes. I'm going to make sure he's up to speed on what's been going on. Hopefully you guys can find some more documents," Huston says, walking us on out into the parking lot. I'm on a mission.

"We'll do our best," I say, keeping pace to John's car. Huston falls back as John and I continue.

"I'll have my cell phone on," Huston yells.

"Okay!" I say, over my shoulder.

"John?" Huston calls. John turns around and walks over to Huston, while I continue. I don't know what they say to each other, probably some "Take care of the overly emotional girl" kind of shit. Emotional, my ass—I just don't want to dilly-dally in the parking lot any longer than I have to. If that makes me "emotional," well, so be it.

"You coming?" I yell to John over my shoulder. He quickens his gait and falls in next to me.

"Do you even know what I drive?" John asks.

"Uh...you were driving that—" I shift around in the parking lot.

"It's this one," John says, beeping a shiny black Cadillac Escalade unlocked.

"It's not ostentatious or anything," I say, climbing into the immaculate front seat.

"Hey, I'm a poor foster kid from the projects...allow me my little luxuries," John says, starting up the engine. He revs it for effect. We both laugh, then stop, self-conscious.

We are silent as we wind through the streets of Ojai—a city whose natural beauty is completely lost on us. I look over at John with his left arm curling over the steering wheel, his body leaning as he drives. I think about his hand curling over mine.

"Thanks for doing this," I say, crossing my right leg over my left. Closer. I want to be closer to him.

"No problem," he says, glancing quickly over at me.

We are quiet again.

"Here it is," I say, pointing to the Blue House.

"Okay...just wait...let me stop the car first, Gracie," John says, putting his arm across me—holding me back from leaping out of the moving SUV. Now I get why Abigail does it.

We walk up the pathway. I'm still nervous about going in, thinking that Connie and Dennis are hiding in the bushes somewhere ready to jump out and accuse us of breaking and entering. At least the kids aren't with us this time.

I try the keys in the door one by one. John peers in the side panel windows and walks the full length of the porch, taking in each side of the house. Then I realize, like an idiot, it's probably the newest key on the chain.

Click.

I push the door open as John walks back over and follows me inside. I quickly close the door behind us and John checks to make sure it is locked—just in case Connie and Dennis stop by.

"The office is up the stairs," I say, walking through the foyer and on up the stairs. John stops in the foyer and takes in the living room. The room I can't even look at. He stands there, almost stepping in, but not. I see him scanning the entire room: the picture-shrine mantel, the coffee table filled with bifocals, magazines and rubber-banded business cards. The sad little couch bed with the pair of old shoes at the foot.

"The office is up here," I say again.

"There are no pictures of Connie," John says, still looking into the living room.

"That's what we were saying," I say, peering in from the foot of the stairs.

"It's just so wrong," John says, shaking his head.

"I know . . . The office is up here," I repeat again.

"Yeah . . . yeah, right behind you," John answers, finally turning away from the living room, looking sad.

I stop at the landing and take down the crucifix. It's surprisingly heavy. A lot heavier than I thought. And older. This has definitely been in the family for a long time. John passes me and heads up to the office. I hold on to the crucifix and go up the stairs behind him.

"In here?" John asks, motioning down the hallway.

"Yeah," I answer, walking to the office. Two. Dad told me two. That's not a yes. But it's not nonsense. It's a clear sign that there's someone in there. He knows he can't speak and he's devised another way to get across that he wants both pieces of iconography. There's someone in there. This doesn't have to end . . . we might be able to save him.

"Your dad has a pretty impressive portfolio," John says, kneeling on the floor. He's digging deep into a file cabinet that's inside the closet.

"We need to hurry up," I say, standing at the door.

"Brokerage accounts . . . Oh, holy shit, he's got a Fidelity mutual fund, you couldn't even get into one of those for a few years," John says, flipping through file after file.

"Are you serious?" I say, taking the piece of paper.

"Did you know your dad came from money?" John asks, looking up from the page after page of assets.

"Yeah, I guess," I say, grabbing a canvas tote bag from the closet and kneeling down. I set the crucifix down and stack huge piles of papers in the bag.

"But you said you guys were on welfare growing up," John says, looking up.

"We were," I say.

"Ah," John answers.

"Yeah," I cluck, fighting off emotions I still don't know what to do with.

"Here," John says, holding the tote bag a little wider.

"Thanks," I say, looking up from the closet floor. He kneels down next to me.

"You okay?" he asks, the bag getting fuller.

"No," I say, tears starting to well up. I can't stop them this time. I've been numb for so long that this pain is bubbling up through every new crack in my foundation. The walls are down, and like an angry mob with torches and pitchforks, my emotions are getting ready to storm the castle whether I like it or not.

"Okay...okay...just..." John takes the bag and leans it up against the closet door. I sit back on my haunches, my head in my hands.

"I'll...just give me...shit...I'll get it together," I plead, wiping away the rebellious tears.

"No one is asking you to get it together," John soothes, moving closer.

"We don't have time for this, we have a job to do."

"Okay, let's make a deal," John says, brushing the hair out

of my face—strands getting caught on my now wet cheeks. He spends time swiping them back behind my ear.

"What?" I ask, snot bubbling out of my nose. John wipes my nose with the sleeve of his coat.

"I think you're right in a really shitty way. There isn't time for this and it sucks. This whole thing...all of this with your dad has been hijacked—and it's not your fault," John says gently, keeping his hands on the sides of my face.

"What can I do?" I ask, sniffling.

"Okay, here's what we do. We get the crucifix back to your dad, the documents back to Huston, and get ready for whatever happens at the hospital." John stops, lifts my face up and looks me right in the eye.

"Okay...okay, I can do that," I say, gathering myself. Breathing. Breathing.

"Okay," John says, wiping the last of my tears away. So soft.

"I can do this," I say again, focusing in.

"I know," John says, pulling me closer.

"I know you know," I say. Ugh. I KNOW YOU KNOW?!

"I know you know I know," John laughs, just inches from me now. The quiet of Dad's office is all but gone.

"I know you know I kn—" I can't help but attempt a joke. John stops me with the gentlest kiss. Light. Warmth. Comfort.

"I'm sorry," he says, pulling back.

"Didn't you say that you would have said 'I love you—'" I point out.

"I love you," John says, without hesitation. I brush his lips with the tips of my fingers. I can't help myself. He watches me intently.

"I know," I answer.

"So you're Han Solo now?" John laughs. Right. I unwittingly

called up Han Solo's nonchalant response to Princess Leia's declaration of undying love in *The Empire Strikes Back*.

"No . . . *right?*" I babble. John helps me up off the floor of Dad's office.

"No, right?" John repeats.

"I always thought that was an asshole line, too. But now I think I get it."

"Are we honestly talking about *Star Wars* right now?" John asks, his head tilted.

"No, well, yes—but no."

"You sound like Leo."

"I always knew I loved you, but I never really believed you loved me. That I . . ." I trail off. Where I'm going with this sounds pathetic.

"That you?" John presses.

"That I deserved to be loved back," I finish, my stomach turning. My brutal honesty is working as a sort of organic ipecac, ensuring that I will most certainly vomit again if I insist on voicing my innermost thoughts further.

"Yeah, I can understand that," John agrees. I breathe deep.

"I guess I wasn't the only one who was abandoned," I say, pulling him close.

"Nope," John answers, his eyes darting around Dad's office.

"I'll never walk away from you again," I promise, steadying his body.

John takes a deep breath, his eyes averted and searching. He lets out a wry laugh, but finally allows his gaze to rest on me again. His head tilts as his eyes lock on to mine.

I let my hand fall onto his chest, his crisp oxford-cloth shirt just underneath. I unbutton the top button of his shirt. Then the next. Then the next. John's breath quickens. I open the top of his shirt, my hands moving eagerly over his now bare chest. His gaping shirt barely hangs on to his broad shoulders.

Then my eyes fall on my own name. Engraved across his heart. He notices and starts to raise his arms to protect himself. I gently ease his arms back down to his sides and look up at him. He looks anywhere but at me, panicked and vulnerable. I run my fingers over my name as his skin goose-pimples underneath. He flinches. My deliberate, almost intrusive exploration of him goes against every fiber of his being. I can feel his heart beating. Quick, strong thumps under my hand. Under my name. John reaches his hand up and takes mine in his.

"You go any further and I'm not going to be able to stop," John says, a roguish curl to his mouth. I look up at him.

"Right," I agree, my hands now hovering just above his naked skin.

"This isn't quite where I envisioned our big reunion," John says. Dad's haunted office comes zooming back and immediately my face flushes. I feel monumentally embarrassed.

He leans back, buttoning up his shirt, and continues, "Let's just call this intermission."

"Intermission," I repeat, tightening my hands in fists, hoping it'll somehow trap the heat from John's body.

"Get the crucifix. I'll get the bag," John says.

chapter seventeen

I'm running down the hallway of the hospital with a giant crucifix in my hand. I must look like some kind of crazy, jogging exorcist.

"Grace—slow down," John says, his heavy footsteps just behind me as we make the final turn before the ICU nurse's station. He's acting like he can't move faster than me, but I can see he's hardly trying. And without the giant crucifix in his hand, he doesn't pack quite the same visual punch as I do.

"Almost there," I say, my back to him.

"We're making quite an entrance," John says as I set the giant crucifix on the counter of the final nurse's station.

I sign my name. The nurse passes me my name tag. I pat the HAWKES sticker onto the same hoodie I'm apparently going to die in and watch as John leans over and signs in after me. The bend of his back. The black hair cut sharply at the nape of his neck. The hint of the tattoo that looms just underneath his starched collar. Mine for the unearthing. I force myself to shake it off. *Intermission.* I pick up the crucifix and wait by the door. John pats his MOSS name tag onto the lapel of the custom-tailored suit jacket he put back on after almost being mauled by me in Dad's office and apparently again right here at the nurse's station.

We walk into the sound of buzzing, whirring and urgent voices, and instead of my heart rate climbing, I calm down just a bit, knowing I've brought Dad something he wanted. I've done something useful. Leo and Huston are standing at Dad's bedside while Abigail sits in the hospital chair against the far wall under the window. I like it like this. No Connie and Dennis. Just us. Offering Dad some sense of peace.

I walk over to Dad's bedside, next to Huston, and show Dad the crucifix.

"Two. Two?" I ask, holding the crucifix so Dad can see it.

Dad's face immediately lights up. He raises his restrained hand and gives me a big thumbs-up.

"Ha!" Huston laughs, clapping Dad on the shoulder. Dad barks out a cracking laugh and shrugs his shoulder for Huston.

"I got it," I say, still holding the cross over him. From the outside, it must look like some weird religious rite is going on in here.

Dad gives me another thumbs-up and holds his hand out for me. I hand the crucifix to Huston as he steps aside to make room for me. Huston and John stand just behind me.

"I got it," I whisper again. Dad grabs my hand and tightens his grip, shaking my hand around a little. He launches into sentence after sentence of gibberish, which causes the whole room to go quiet. We had convinced ourselves he was getting better. But this torrent of nonsense reminds us that he's still a stroke victim. He's still sick. I smile down at Dad as he tightens his grip.

"You said two. I understood," I say, feeling bad. I don't mean to be talking down to him, I just want to answer as broadly as I can, hoping he'll know I heard. Dad stares up at me. The ice-blue eyes that I inherited. The face . . . that face. His face. I tilt my head and just take him in. He allows a wide, crooked smile. I inhale, taking in with the breath the stream of tears I've promised will stay away until later. It's not the time.

Say something, I think to myself. Stop talking about the damn crucifix and tell my dad I love him. Or I forgive him. Or I know

he'll pull through. Or something meaningful. A beautiful solilo-
quy that neatly conveys all my emotions. I open my mouth and
take a breath, getting ready to say something meaningful, but
then I stop. I don't want him to think...I don't want him to
think he's dying.

"We were talking last night about when Abigail broke her leg,"
I blurt. Huston perks up behind me as Abigail rolls her eyes.

"She loves telling this story, Dad," Abigail says, from the hospital chair against the far wall.

"She hates when I tell it," I say, winking down at Dad. "So
Abigail is convinced that the cast is waterproof."

Abigail laughs. "The doctor told me it was!" Dad barks out
another rumbly laugh and tightens his grip on my hand. I
breathe in. Dad laughs again...rumbly and low. That cracking
laugh I remember. Breathe.

"The doctor said you could *splash* it by accident," Huston adds,
his face becoming blotchier.

"So, we're all swimming in the neighbors' pool. The Woods',
you remember?" I ask. Dad nods yes. He nods yes to everything.
Leo sniffles and Abigail hands him a tissue.

"And she jumps in!" Huston says, coming up beside me, resting his hand on mine. Dad smiles wide and tries to turn his head
to where Abigail is. She gathers herself, smiles wide and stands,
joining Huston and me on Dad's good side. Keep it together.
For Dad.

"Cast and all," I add, my face as animated as if I were reading
The Very Hungry Caterpillar to the twins.

"I thought it was waterproof!" Abigail says, her brow furrowed. Dad is watching us all. Taking us all in, smiling wide and
laughing. Tightening my grip on his hand, I keep leaning over
and smiling.

I love you, I say inside my head. *A thousand times, I love you.*

"She sunk right to the bottom," I say, bringing my other hand from under Huston's to mime *right on down.*

"Right to the bottom," Abigail adds, turning away for the briefest of seconds. She collects herself and turns back around.

"Huston had to dive in and save her," Leo adds, finally able to speak. He stands at the foot of Dad's bed. Dad makes eye contact with him. The eleven-year-old boy he left. How grown-up Dad must think he is now. Leo smiles back at Dad. I see him make the effort to keep smiling and not crack. He stares at me and I offer him an easy smile. It soothes him and I see him take a deep breath.

"She must have weighed close to seven hundred pounds," Huston adds, his face reddening further.

"I don't think you've ever admitted you were wrong," I say, laughing over at Abigail. She contorts a smile back.

"Because I wasn't wrong! My doctor said it was waterproof," Abigail says, deftly wiping her nose on her sweater set.

Dad shakes my hand around a bit and then lets go, reaching for Huston. I take a step back and focus on Huston as he steps in. I reach for John's hand like I'm falling off a cliff. He takes it—closing his hand tightly around mine.

"Can you believe that, Dad?" Huston says down to Dad, his voice singsongy and light, but I can see his entire body is tight and restrained. Focus. Dad reaches out for Abigail as Huston steps back next to me. He wraps his arm around me and brings me in close. His jaw clenches as he lets his head fall to his chest for the briefest of seconds. He squeezes my waist tightly as he looks back up, his eyes rimmed in red. Not a single tear. We're here to make Dad feel better, not burden him with our sadness.

"You had it handled, I know," I whisper.

"You did a good thing," he whispers, as he pats my back.

"He's really laughing," I say, trying to just get one deep breath. To my surprise, it works—I breathe, deeply. I look back down just as Dad reaches out for Leo. Abigail steps back. There is an awkward moment between Abigail and Huston. They don't know quite how to comfort each other. They reach for each other's hand, then shoulder, then waist. They know they need to hold each other, but they just don't know how. In the end, Abigail lets herself fold into Huston and allows him to hold her. Leo takes Dad's hand and comes in close to his face.

"Jumped right in! Cast and all!" Leo laughs, his free hand a contorted mess just below the hospital bed. I can see Leo's teardrops hit the metal safety bar on Dad's bed, but his entire body is easy and his smile is clear and bright. Dad shakes his hand back and forth and speaks sentence after sentence of gibberish, his face animated and alive with determination. Leo hangs in there, trying to understand him, trying to answer back. But in the end he simply repeats, "I know...I know..." Over and over again. Dad calms down and his eyes begin to blink slowly. Tired again. Leo keeps saying "I know...I know..." as Dad slowly fades into sleep, finally letting go of Leo's hand. Leo steadies himself on the now damp metal safety bar and turns around. Huston takes his arms from around Abigail and catches Leo as he falls into his arms, quietly crying.

"I know...shhhhh...shhhh," Huston whispers, patting his back.

Leo quietly sniffles. "We really got him going, didn't we?"

"He was really laughing," Huston soothes, pulling Leo close.

The room falls silent as we all try to compose ourselves. Abigail is the first to speak. She has lists that need checking off.

"We have to go," she says, looking at Leo. I look past Huston and see Abigail and Leo make eye contact. She raises her eyebrows expectantly at him as if to imply, "Wrap this up." We have work to do. We must take care of Dad, not sit around crying. Find a proper facility for him back in LA.

"Okay…okay…" Leo says, wiping his face again. Abigail nods and takes his hand, giving him a quick squeeze.

"I've made appointments at five places for this afternoon. We can get back down the 101 and at our first stop by eleven-thirty," Abigail says, gathering her belongings. All business. Leo follows, sniffling and swiping at his face, holding Abigail's hand like one of the twins. Dad's rumbling breathing fills the room.

"Are they all in South Pas?" Huston asks, smoothing his coat.

"Three are in South Pas, one is in Pasadena and one is in Alhambra," Abigail says.

"And you'll call when you've found a place?" Huston asks, turning to Abigail.

"I'll call when our first duck is officially in a row," Abigail says, shifting up onto her tiptoes to give Huston a quick peck on the cheek as she walks out of Dad's hospital room with Leo in tow.

"Now, let's get to those documents," Huston says, turning to a very uncomfortable-looking John, who's still holding my hand. Huston looks at us. Looks down at our hands and then back up at us. His face registers a flash of embarrassment, but then he just takes a deep breath as a smile breaks across his face.

"They're in John's car," I say, my face flushing.

"Let's get to it," John says, squeezing my hand tighter.

chapter eighteen

D id you want the coffee with soy?" the woman behind the counter of the organic market asks John. We've just finished having dinner served up with a side of stilted, yet slightly suggestive, conversation.

Where do we start? The beginning? All over again? Just after *intermission*?

"Just black will be fine," John answers, turning back to me, getting ready to speak.

"Black?" The woman is confused. John turns back to her.

"Plain. Black." John's voice rises just a bit.

"Skim? Two percent? Whole? Raw?" the woman asks, becoming annoyed.

"Black." The woman begins to scrawl on John's cup. He continues, "No milk. Just coffee." The woman scratches out what she wrote. We both stifle a smile at her passion for dairy products.

"And for you?" the woman asks me, noticeably annoyed.

"Earl Grey?" I ask, scanning the menu.

"We have chamomile, red rooibos and a really fantastic house tea called Eve's Revenge," the woman impatiently relays. John rolls his eyes, passes me a twenty and walks away.

"I'll have the chamomile," I say, handing her the twenty.

The woman hands me the change as I scan the market for the one person who doesn't fit. Amidst the hemp-panted, Birkenstock-wearing clientele I find the one lone business suit, perusing an entire endcap loaded with hundreds of types of raw sugar.

"Here you go," the woman says, passing me the drinks. I take them and make my way back over to John.

"I feel like some crotchety old square in here," John says, taking the coffee.

"I think using the word *square* suggests that you are," I say.

"Ten minutes to order a black coffee," he mutters, taking a sip.

"It's a very complicated process," I say, happy to be away from the hospital.

"So . . ." John trails off as we walk out the automatic doors and onto the beautiful streets of Ojai.

"So . . ." I repeat.

"What's Huston doing tonight?"

"He said he was going to try and get some sleep. Big day tomorrow," I say, feeling a pang of guilt that Huston's by himself.

"He can be such an old man sometimes."

"A square, if you will."

"Oh, you know I will." John laughs. My face flushes.

"Is Huston seeing anyone?" I pry, as I've done my whole life. Huston has always been a vault when it comes to his love life. Leo and I were notorious for whipping open Huston's bedroom door at odd times, hoping to catch him "in the act" with whatever girl he had over at the time. We never caught him "in the act," but we did get more Indian burns and noogies than were really deserved, in my opinion.

"He was seeing this actress for a while," John answers.

"An actress?"

"And then a few others. There was a vet." John trails off.

"Like a Vietnam vet?" I ask, crossing the street. John takes my hand as we navigate the traffic, nodding thank-you to a woman who allows us to cross. So normal.

"Yeah, it was kind of a May/December thing," John says, laughing. We stand in front of my bed-and-breakfast. He doesn't let go of my hand.

"You're not going to tell me any hard facts, are you?" I ask.

"No," John answers simply, facing me.

"You're a good friend," I say, looking up into the bed-and-breakfast.

We are quiet. An elderly couple nods hello as they walk up the steps.

"Is intermission over?" I blurt.

"Hell yes," John says, tugging on my hand as we climb the stairs.

"This is the worst tea I've ever tasted," I say, tossing my cup into the trash bin just inside the lobby.

"I wasn't going to say anything, but *Jesus*," John says, tossing his cup in as well.

"I'm up here," I say, nervous and jittery.

"Yeah, I got that," John says, climbing the rickety staircase behind me.

"Is...is this wrong?" I ask. John climbs the two steps that separate us. He backs me up against the railing. I can feel my face begin to redden—what would that elderly couple think of us now?

"No," John says, just before coming in for a deep, beautiful, warm, long kiss. Goodness.

I curl my fingers around the wooden railing, trying to keep my balance, getting lost in him, in the jolt of comfort he offers. His body is hard against mine, his arm pressed against the wall just behind me, his leg now in between mine. I uncurl my fingers from around the wooden railing and wrap my arm around his waist, pulling him closer. Closer. I inch my hand up to his neck, his jaw, his face, his hair, and back around his head...closer, closer, closer.

"Where's your room again?" John breathlessly asks.

"Here. This...just..." I stutter, taking his hand once again and leading him down the narrow hallway to my room. As I fiddle with the old-fashioned key that was probably adorable to the innkeepers, but just serves as a temporary chastity belt for me, John kisses the back of my neck. The key finally clicks over and I push the door open.

I slam the door behind us.

Quiet.

And then we're on each other again. Untucking shirts. Kissing. Kicking off shoes. My hands in that thick, black hair. Unbuttoning shirts. His mouth. Opening his shirt, pulling it off. I close my eyes as my shirt is pulled up and off and we fall back on the bed.

"If you ever pull that shit again," John says, his voice low.

"What shit?" I ask breathlessly, my brain rifling through a legion of lists of "shit" I've pulled.

"Don't leave me. Don't walk away from me again," he says, his eyes pleading, yet steely.

"Never," I say.

As the warmth of his body covers mine, I feel a terror gripping me. I'm soaring with nothing holding me down. No numbness to keep me safe and protected. No battlements. No ballasts. I thought I'd taken down all my walls for John five years ago. But as I fight to catch my breath I know I've never felt anything like this. This kind of freedom. This kind of openness. Almost like I'm back in that dentist's chair—though that's not really a fair comparison. Still, the same panic. The same terror. No walls. No armor.

We're on the bed. Naked. Vulnerable. And I'm racing through the sky with no parachute. My brain is trying to claw at something that will stop me from falling. Nothing. There's nothing keeping me tethered to this world. I can't catch my breath. I can't breathe. I...I...

"I love you," John whispers, his mouth centimeters from my ear.

The parachute snaps open. And we soar.

We soar and soar.

"I love you," I whisper back.

Free.

chapter nineteen

Where is it?" Huston asks Abigail, standing just outside the hospital the next day. I can't believe I'm back here. After a night so good, it is inconceivable that I return to all the hell within these doors, but it is real. My night with John will just have to be an oasis I can revisit when I need to get away from all this. A light in the darkness.

It's New Year's Eve.

I'm sitting on a stone bench, listening as Huston takes the phone call he's been waiting for. The hospital has decorated its more public areas with sparkling streamers and signs. The cafeteria has a big HAPPY NEW YEAR banner stretching across its entrance. Perspective, anyone?

John is poring over the documents from Dad's office as Huston and I endure another day of the Big Lie. Dad was moved to a regular room early this morning. At least we no longer have to deal with Nurse Miller.

It's oddly fascinating to watch as Connie's lies get more and more elaborate. There have been trips abroad, apparently. The house she and Dad share is a "sanctuary." Connie can't stop talking about the hundreds of greeting cards and floral arrangements she's received from her devoted husband over the years. She's saved everything Ray gave her, she weeps to an orderly. In truth, everything Dad gave Connie could easily fit into the back pocket of those white pants she insists on wearing every day.

Earlier, while Dad's linens were being changed, and much more disturbingly while *he* was being changed, I ran out to a little thrift store in town and bought an old Casio keyboard that was made for kids. The keys are ridiculously small. But it does the job. I thought it might keep my mind occupied and maybe I could play for Dad. Like before. He loved when I played. I tap out Miles Davis' "So What," remembering bit by bit as I go along.

"Okay…so, this Sister Marjorie Pauline person is going to call—" Huston stops, listening to Abigail explain exactly how transporting Dad is going to work. His lips compress as he listens. He looks off into the distance. He's tuned out my playing—as he always did—and yet every once in a while I can see him tapping his foot or moving to the music.

Huston's dark suit is wrinkled just a bit. His crisp white shirt is open at the collar. Apparently he decided against a tie this morning. I, of course, am wearing the same thing I've been wearing for going on three days.

"She should talk to Frank from Legal. He's the guy I talked to—" Huston stops again, listening to Abigail. I look down at my keyboard. *Ba-dup. Ba-dup.* My entire body is curled over the tiny keyboard as the crisp morning air moves around me. I zip my hoodie up all the way.

"So, we'll pay their ambulance driver in cash. Yes, Dad's ready now," Huston says, pushing his hand down into his pocket.

And that's where the trumpet comes in. *Ba-dup. Ba-dup*, looking up at Huston as I hunt and peck.

"Okay, I'll go talk to Frank, let him know we're ready to transport Dad," Huston says, nodding, nodding, nodding as Abigail talks. This is all happening so fast.

"Right. Right. Okay, I'll call you once I get out of my meeting with Frank and let you know what to tell—" Huston stops again. I look back down at the keyboard. I tap a few notes of Pachelbel's

Canon. As the cold settles in, I take a quick sip of my tea and look up at Huston. I set the cup back down on the stone bench.

"Okay, let me know. Great work. Right . . . right. Okay, Abby . . . See you soon," Huston says, flipping his cell phone closed. Moonlight Sonata.

"That's a bit depressing," Huston sighs, walking over to where I am seated on the bench. I lift my fingers from the keys and take another sip of my tea.

"She found a place?" I ask, scooting over just a bit so Huston can sit on the bench next to me.

"St. Teresa's in South Pas. She says they have an opening. Apparently finding a private room for a man is really difficult—" Huston starts. He looks tired. His night of sleep doesn't look like it went all that well.

"And this is a good place?" I ask, thinking about all the horror stories I've heard about skilled nursing facilities. I can't even . . . I hope Abigail hasn't chosen a place like that. Of course she hasn't.

"What about something a little more upbeat," Huston says, eyeing my keyboard.

"What?" I ask, following his gaze.

"Something upbeat," Huston says again. I look down at the tiny keyboard. Not much to work with. Nonetheless, I start to play "Linus and Lucy" from the Peanuts sound track.

Huston sighs.

"So, what happens now?" I ask, between notes.

"Sister Marjorie Pauline is going to call Frank from Legal here and set up the transport. I talked to Frank at length yesterday about what's been going on and what we plan to do. He seemed understanding," Huston explains, his face expressionless. Frank seemed "understanding"? I can't wait to get out of here. Back through the wardrobe. I want out of Narnia once and for all.

"When is this all going to happen?" I ask, looking from the keyboard to Huston. The music stopping.

"Sister Marjorie Pauline says she's going to put in a call to their ambulance company now. By the time we get clearance from Frank, they'll already be halfway up the 101 freeway," Huston explains, his voice flat. I am quiet. I don't know what to say. Is this where we talk about what hell we're in for in the next few hours? Connie is not going to stand by and let us take Dad out of this hospital without a fight. She's also made it very clear that she has no qualms about yelling and carrying on in front of Dad, hence the earlier "sons of bitches" episode.

"How are we going to do this?" I finally ask.

"*Play*," Huston says. This time I decide on something a bit more . . . modern. I begin playing.

Huston laughs. "Is that 'Bette Davis Eyes'?" He scoots a bit closer to me on the bench.

"Right up there with *Moonlight Sonata*, wouldn't you say?" I joke. I play as Huston leans back on the cold concrete façade of the hospital. He closes his eyes as the brisk morning settles in around us.

He turns to look at me, his face wan. I breathe in. He takes my hand from the keyboard and holds it tight. I stop playing.

"This is going to be one of the hardest things we are going to have to do," Huston says, staring off once again into the distance, his dark blond hair fluttering in the morning air.

"I know," I say, looking down at the keyboard.

"Once she finds out what we're doing, she's going to pull out all the stops," Huston says, his ice-blue eyes focused elsewhere.

"Then we shouldn't do anything until the transport actually gets here," I offer. Huston turns to look at me. "Why give her any more time to whip everyone into a frenzy? We should go talk to Frank from Legal, tell him what's going on. He'll have talked to that Sister Marjorie Pauline person by then. We can tell him we want his assurance that this information is to be kept confidential," I argue, starting to sound like John.

"They're going to have to get Dad ready for transport. You know, medically," Huston points out.

"They can do all the necessary things under the guise of moving him to that new room. This is the only way we've got a chance at getting him out of here without a huge scene," I say, knowing I might have made it sound too ominous—but in a way, it *is* life or death.

"You're right." Huston nods, gazing back down at the keyboard.

"It's the only way," I say again, my fingers curling over the keys once again.

I start again: "Her hair is Harlow gold." Huston smiles, his eyes crinkling. I give him a quick wink and keep playing. The morning settles around us.

A few minutes later, Huston and I wait just outside Frank's office, ready to go in and plead our case. Abigail just called Huston to let him know that the ambulance is on its way up the 101 freeway. We have two hours.

No turning back.

I look up from my mini-keyboard to see John walking down the hallway toward Huston and me. My entire body softens.

"John." Huston stands as the men shake hands. Huston seems genuinely happy to see him.

"Hey," John offers, giving me a little smile. I smile back, checking to see if Huston notices I'm blushing. He does. I clear my throat and look away.

"I went through your father's bank records this morning," John starts, taking the seat next to Huston.

"I've already added Dad to my medical insurance, so there's

no sense of urgency. We just need to make sure that the banks have a copy of the power of at—"

John cuts in, "Your dad has a joint account with Connie. She's never made any deposits or written any checks on it. It's an older account. That's the only thing that might be characterized as community property. He owns the house and the condo outright. He inherited all his money from his mother. All of his holdings can be traced back to his inheritance, which, by California law, is his separate property. So, besides that one joint account, there's no other community property that I can find."

"So, Dad's protected," Huston finishes.

"I went on the bank's website to take a look at any recent activity on the account," John says.

"And?" Huston urges.

"Connie cleaned out that joint account yesterday," John says, his face serious, his voice low.

"What?" I ask, my keyboard falling to the floor. I bend over and quickly scoop it up. Huston shakes his head and looks away. His jaw tight.

"She cleaned it out," John says again.

"How can she do that?" I ask, sitting back up.

"It was a joint account, legally she had the right," Huston explains, still shaking his head.

"She'd never withdrawn any money from it before? Or deposited anything?" My voice rising.

"No," John answers. We're all afraid to ask the obvious question. John waits.

"How much?" Huston finally asks.

"One hundred and thirteen thousand dollars," John confesses. I suck in a gasp of air. Huston just stares at John. Not saying anything. Studying him.

"Does Dad have anything left for when he gets out of—" Huston cuts himself off. He may be comfortable with secretly thinking Dad's going to get better, but he's obviously uneasy with saying it out loud. Or maybe that's just how I feel.

"There's plenty left, don't worry about that," John answers.

"I'm not worried, more pissed off. If she needed money, she could have spoken to me," Huston says angrily.

"Why would she need $113,000? Was there some fire sale on little white pants we didn't know about?" I ask, horrified.

Huston is quiet, searching. John looks from me to Huston.

I continue, "This isn't good."

"This actually works to our advantage. We can tell Frank this new information and it helps to prove our point," Huston argues.

"So, what? She can just...steal it?" I ask, enraged.

"It's not stealing. It was a joint account. The only one, thank God. She can't get to anything else of Dad's," Huston says, looking at his watch.

"So she can live out her days in that town house forever?" I ask.

"Well, that's a little trickier." John's voice becomes a bit lighter.

"How trickier?" I ask.

"Ray bought that town house after they separated with his inheritance. It's not community property, and with power of attorney..." John trails off.

"We can evict her," Huston says.

"Obviously the timing would have to be right, keeping in mind that she still looks like that little old lady Boy Scouts would trip over themselves to help across the street," John adds.

"She's repellent," I say.

"Absolutely, but just because we know her to be Satan's nana doesn't mean that everyone else won't sympathize with her," John says.

"First things first. We have to get Dad out of here," Huston says.

"Mr. Hawkes?" The mythical "Frank from Legal" appears through an office door. He looks exactly as a "Frank from Legal" should look. Ruddy face. Balding. Light blue, short-sleeved oxford. Polyester pants hitched up just under his rapidly increasing belly.

"Thank you for seeing me," Huston says, standing and extending his hand. The two shake hands. John and I stand.

"Please come in. Let's see what we can do about getting your dad discharged," Frank says, leading Huston through the office door.

John and I sit down in the hallway.

"One hundred and thirteen thousand dollars?" I repeat, my voice urgent.

"Yeah," John says, rubbing his face.

"She reminds me of a cockroach—surviving and evolving no matter what. Relentless. Single-minded. Heartless."

"We're going to get through this," John says again, bending his head to make eye contact with me. He waits. And waits. I stare at the wall. Enraged. Without my usual armor, I feel this anger with an acute clarity I haven't entertained in years.

"Why does she have to be so cartoonish?" I whisper, finally looking at him.

"I don't know."

"As if this wasn't hard enough," I say, looking around.

John is quiet.

I continue, "She's hated us since the moment we met. All the 'honeys' and 'dears' and the whole time she hated us."

"You've got to hand it to her," John sighs.

"Yes, she's truly a marvel," I say, looking away.

"Grace," John says, taking my hand.

"What?" I say, shaken.

"This is about your dad," John repeats.

"I know," I say, letting my head fall onto my chest.

"We have to focus," John says, pulling my chin up and toward him.

"I know," I say, tears crowding behind my eyes.

"Good," he says, scooting closer.

"She's not going to like this one bit," I say, shaking my head.

"Connie?" Huston asks, approaching her at Dad's bedside.

"Yes?" Connie turns around to face Huston. Her voice sounds feeble. Her body looks so tiny next to Huston. Next to anyone.

The ambulance is five minutes out.

Dad's ready to go. All the discharge papers have been signed. We've all checked out of our respective hotels. Our bags are packed away in our already gassed-up cars. All we have to do is get Dad on a gurney, roll him out of this hospital and into the waiting ambulance. Down the 101 freeway—away from here. Away from the sad little couch bed. Away from the six-month marriage he couldn't break free of. Away from the loneliness. Back to his family. Back home.

"I'd like to talk about Dad's care," Huston starts.

"Sure..." Connie answers, turning around. Dennis watches the exchange with interest. I stand just outside the room. John stands beside me. We didn't want it to seem like we were ganging up on Connie. I cross my arms and step forward just a bit. Closer.

"If we could speak out in the hall?" Huston asks, motioning to Dad, who has just fallen back to sleep.

"Denny?" Connie calls to Dennis as she inches toward Huston. Not far enough. She's not far enough away from Dad. He can still hear. He can still be upset. Dennis stands and joins his mother.

"I think it would be best if we transferred Dad to a facility in Los Angeles for his skilled nursing care," Huston says, his voice unwavering, his gaze steadfast. Connie and Dennis recoil from Huston's words. They manage to look offended and confused. But mostly, they look as if they can't quite figure out how this happened.

"*You* think it's best?" Dennis answers. I step forward. John eases me back.

Four minutes.

"I have to sit down. Dennis, go out in the hall and see if the nurse can get me a glass of water. I'm feeling faint," Connie calmly says, walking back over to Dad's bedside and dropping feebly into the chair. Dennis scrambles past the bathroom, with its cups and running water, and out to the nurse's station.

"It's my decision to make," Huston says to Connie's back.

"My heart," Connie whimpers, her liver-spotted hand at her chest. I look back and see Dennis talking to the nurses. They are staring at Huston, John and me like *we're* the monsters.

"Do you need to take a moment? Maybe we can go into the lounge and talk," Huston says, his voice low.

"I have to be here for my husband," Connie clucks, her eyes fixing on the nurses as she swoons. Dennis is beside himself with worry, yet no glass of water in sight. I look from Connie to the nurses. A direct line of sight. My stomach drops as I realize that she's playing to them. This is all a show and we're the villains with the handlebar mustaches tying the damsel in distress to the train tracks.

"Go stand in the doorway," I whisper to John, motioning at the gossiping nurses behind us taking in the show. John doesn't ask any questions, sneaking a glance at the nurses as he settles into the doorway. Connie's eyes narrow as her audience's view is obstructed.

"Dad gave me his power of attorney, it's my decision to move him to Los Angeles where I can properly oversee his care. Just as he wanted," Huston says, looking over at the bed. I follow his gaze. We both notice simultaneously that Dad's awake and following this conversation closely, or as closely as he can given his condition. Dad's face is twisted with concern, his restrained arm flailing. Huston watches Dad, torn between making a move to comfort him and standing his ground and getting him safely out of this hospital for good. Huston stands his ground.

Three minutes.

"I can't breathe," Connie whimpers.

"We want to make this as easy a transition as possible for everyone," Huston eases, still trying not to make a scene.

"I'm his wife," Connie sobs.

"I understand that you were Dad's wife at one time."

"At one time?" Connie snivels.

"You were separated in 2005."

"We are the loves of each other's lives," Connie sobs.

"You were separated in 2005," he repeats.

"We spend every waking moment together," Connie insists.

"We know you live in a town house at 1375 Daly Street."

Connie stands abruptly, teetering. Huston and I rush over to help her. Her tiny body completely surrounded by ours. Connie suddenly clutches at Huston's arm, pulling him down toward her. It looks like she may faint.

"Are you feeling oka—" Huston starts.

Connie cuts in, in a voice only Huston, John and I hear, "Do whatever you want with Ray. I just want what's mine."

Stunned, we fall back, letting go of Connie.

Huston's face drains of color as we back away. John steadies himself in the doorway. Connie takes a deep breath, gets back into character and begins to walk feebly toward the door of the hospital room . . . and toward her adoring audience. But she has to get through John first. Huston and I immediately go to Dad.

Two minutes.

John puts his hand gently on Connie's tiny shoulder, appearing to assist her out the door. John the Lawyer fades into the background as John the Juvenile Delinquent steps forward. His face hard. His eyes narrowed, looking directly into Connie's rheumy red eyes. He's downright terrifying as he leans in and whispers, "You better watch your back, because *I* might just give you what's yours." I see her eyes dart wildly behind him as she sees the ambulance driver rolling the gurney down the hallway toward Dad's hospital room.

"Now? You're doing this now? You're disgusting, Mr. Hawkes," Dennis accuses from the nurse's station. The nurses gasp and point. I walk past John and into the hallway to flag the ambulance driver down. We're all focused on one thing.

Get. Dad. Out.

The ambulance driver, thank God, is a beefy young kid. He rolls the gurney into the hospital room past John.

"Denny? Denny, do something!" Connie sobs, the nurses scrambling around her.

"Can't anyone do something?" Dennis wails, looking to the heavens and yet not entering the hospital room.

I look away from The Connie and Dennis Show and watch as Huston leans over Dad's bed, finally taking his hand. He whispers something in Dad's ear and I can see the tears streaming down Dad's face. My heart tightens. John helps the ambulance driver shift all of Dad's medical equipment around. Two nurses have braved the front lines and are helping to get Dad on the gurney. This is the hardest part. Once we get him in the ambulance, he's in the clear. We're in the clear.

I focus on the Madonna and the crucifix. They're hanging on the bulletin board next to some of the twins' drawings and the picture of Mom I stole from Dad's office. Dad's finally all settled on the gurney. I breathe deeply. Almost there.

John has been holding Dad's feeding tube delicately throughout the exchange, careful that it doesn't pull or tug on Dad. Dad's face is worried, he's staring up at Huston. Focusing on him. Focusing on the calm in the storm.

Connie's and Dennis' sobs and protestations fade into the background as the ambulance driver starts to wheel Dad out of the room. Connie collapses into Dennis' arms.

"Look what you've done to my mother!" Dennis wails. Huston simply walks past them. His pace never falters, his focus never wavering from Dad, their hands never letting go.

I can see the gurney finally disappearing behind the closed elevator doors. I remember I have a part in The Connie and Dennis Show. I hitch my purse over my shoulder, heavy with the Madonna and Child and the crucifix. I tuck Mom's picture and the twins' drawings into an outside pocket of my purse and grab my Casio. I start out of the hospital room.

"We've left directions and contact numbers for St. Teresa Manor with Nurse Miller, along with a copy of Dad's medical file for you," I say, delivering my one line before they have time to respond.

I walk down the long hallway toward the elevator. It dings open and I step in. As the doors close, I catch a final shot of Connie and Dennis lurching back toward the nurse's station in search of Nurse Miller, Dad's medical file and directions to Dad's new facility.

The elevator doors close.

My body convulses forward. I try to steady my breathing, steady my body. The walls close in on me as I bend forward, put my hands on my knees and close my eyes. I've got four short floors to get this under control.

I'm afraid this is just the beginning. We've seen what they're capable of. Knowing Connie and Dennis will stop at nothing scares the shit out of me.

The elevator door dings open. I stand up straight, breathe in and walk.

Out. Out. Out.

Home.

chapter twenty

Excuse me?" I ask a woman whose all-white nun's habit hits her about mid-calf—cocktail length. It's like a beginner's habit. She's probably the nun equivalent of a Webelos to an Eagle Scout.

I made it down the 101. Two hours of urgent phone calls, status reports, hoping that Dad was doing okay on the trip down.

"Yes?" The Webelos nun turns around, her round face tightly framed by the habit.

"My dad is going to be checked in today and I was just wondering—"

"Raymond Hawkes?" the Webelos nun interrupts.

"Yes, Ray Hawkes."

"Your family is in the sunroom. They're waiting to meet with Sister Marjorie Pauline," she says, walking out from the nurse's station and into the hall.

"Am I supposed to follow you?" I ask, not knowing whether to stay or go.

"Yes, please," the Webelos nun answers. "Are those yours?" she asks, motioning to the Madonna and Child and crucifix in my hand.

"They're my dad's." She smiles and continues down the hallway.

We walk in silence down the hallway past doors and doors of sick old people. I know this is a good place, but even the most skilled nursing homes seem like haunted houses with rooms populated by the ghosts of people who once existed. If they would have had an open room for the last five years, I would have fit right in. I try to steady my breathing and focus back on the little Webelos nun.

"Thank you," I say, as she leads me into a large sunroom. I blink my eyes and the room comes into focus.

"Tia Gwacie!!" Emilygrae runs over, her little casts banging into my knees. I quickly set the Madonna and Child and the crucifix on a chair along with my purse.

"Hey, sweetie," I say, looking down at her and scanning the room for the other little ones. I nod a quick hello to Evie, she's in her usual position: curled up in a chair, reading a novel. Mateo is flipping through a giant pirate book at Evie's feet, taking out moving parts and looking at a bit of text with a decoder lens. All very interactive. He is riveted. Leo is standing by the doors that lead outside.

"How'd it go?" Abigail asks, approaching me. I look down at Emilygrae and smooth her long, tangled hair, tucking a bit of it behind her ear. She leans into my touch.

"We got him out. That's all that matters," I say, meeting Abigail's gaze, not wanting to go into it now. Maybe never wanting to go into it.

Abigail listens absently. "Good . . . good . . ."

"Grace? It's been a while." Manny approaches me. I reach out to shake his hand, but he envelops me in a huge bear hug. I pat at his back, but can't make my body relax. I pull away and smile awkwardly. He smiles back and walks over next to Abigail. Emilygrae shifts over and starts hugging her father's legs. He rests his hand on the top of her head as she gazes up at him. Manny's freshly pressed polo shirt is tucked neatly into his equally pressed dress pants. He's started to lose his hair, but he otherwise looks just as I remember him.

"How far behind were they?" Leo asks, waiting at the door, biting his fingernails.

"Not far," I answer, walking over to him. I pull his hand out of his mouth and smile. Leo softens.

"Have you gone home yet?"

"Do I look like I've gone home yet?" I smile, motioning to the same outfit I've been wearing for going on what feels like three months.

Leo looks out the automatic door, his mouth forcing back a smile.

"What?" I ask.

"Well . . ."

"What?" I ask.

"While we were making keys."

"We?"

"Abigail told me to," Leo blurts.

"Told you to what?"

"We copied your house key, too," Leo confesses.

"Why?"

"Yours, Huston's. Mine . . . even John's."

"How?" I ask.

"You know how kids love to play with real keys." Leo laughs, eyeing the sticky-fingered twins.

"Why, though?" I press.

"Abigail has a surprise for you," Leo whispers.

"For me?"

"The other keys were just a cover."

"Why?" I ask again.

"She hired movers to deliver your old piano to surprise you, for when you got home," Leo whispers. I look from Leo to Abigail.

"My old piano?" I gasp.

Leo beams. "That old upright Mom and Dad found."

"She's had it this whole time?" I ask, having to look away and out the automatic doors.

"When we cleaned out Mom's house, she thought you might want it someday. When you came back," Leo says, biting his nails again.

"How did she know . . . I would . . ."

"Come back?" Leo finishes. I nod. "She just did, I guess."

"They'll come through that door," Abigail announces, pointing at where Leo and I are standing. I give her a ridiculously out-of-proportion smile. She immediately looks confused and sits back down next to Evie. Manny lifts Emilygrae up and bounces her around. Her giggles fill the room. I hold firm near Leo and we watch the door. *She knew I'd come back.*

We wait. The minutes pass.

"There . . . there they are!" Leo shouts, his arm shooting out. Pointing. He presses the button that opens the automatic doors to the pathway just outside.

Dad made it.

We all stand and watch as the same beefy ambulance driver pushes Dad in on the gurney. Dad is propped up and has a bright yellow blanket over him. His hospital gown is listing slightly off his left shoulder as he comes up the pathway. Huston and John follow behind the gurney, looking like Secret Service men, talking quietly, making sure the final step is successful. Dad turns the last corner and enters the sunroom.

"Daaaaaddddddd!" we all say, waving and smiling. Dad's eyes set on one face after another. He raises his now unrestrained arm high in the air, smiling crookedly. The ambulance driver stops right in the middle of all of us. We converge on Dad, offering pats, smiles, waves, caresses . . . whatever we feel we can do to let him know that he's safe. We did it. We got him out.

His idea worked.

"Hey," John says, sliding his arm around my waist. Abigail notices instantly. So does Evie. Abigail beams at us. Evie's face turns bright red.

"Hey," I say, leaning into him.

"Okay . . . let's get your dad set up in his new digs," the ambulance driver says, wheeling Dad out of the sunroom and into the hall. Dad beams at all of us as he's wheeled down the hall. We watch him go.

The entire room breathes a sigh of relief.

"We did it," Huston sighs, his body tense, yet somehow relaxed. Leo bounds up to Huston and hugs him. Huston immediately starts to comfort him.

"You did so great," I say, smiling at Huston.

"You . . . man, that was . . . They surpassed even *my* expectations," Huston admits, with his arm around Leo's shoulder. Leo wipes at his eyes and looks over at me, making "I'm okay" faces.

"This place is perfect, peaceful, kind of," I say to Abigail.

"Thanks . . . Leo actually found it," Abigail says, motioning to Leo.

"Internet," Leo admits.

"Finally, something you won't get thrown in lockup for." Huston laughs, pulling Leo close.

I lean against the wall just outside Dad's room, still holding on to John. Abigail's already noticed. Dad's safe, that's all that matters.

I scan the hallway. A bunch of old ladies in wheelchairs have begun moving down the hallway—like an even creepier version of Alfred Hitchcock's *The Birds*. One minute there was only the one old lady dressed in all red, now there's like ten of them. They're all shuffling around in their wheelchairs, using their feet to zip and zoom in and out of traffic. They finally settle in just below the statue of the Virgin Mary. A destination spot, I take it.

I'm taking in the birds on the wire when a nun all decked out in a brown-and-white habit turns the corner in one of those electric mobility scooters. *Red.* She's speeding along at quite a clip as she approaches our little hallway grouping.

"You must be the Hawkes clan," the nun announces, screeching to a halt mere centimeters from Abigail.

"We're Ray Hawkes' kids," Abigail announces, extending her hand to the nun, whose round face is tightly framed in the brown habit.

"Sister Marjorie Pauline, I'm the one who signs your dad into St. Teresa—the welcoming committee," she responds. For a nun, Sister Marjorie Pauline seems a tad rough around the edges. I like her immediately. Sister Marjorie Pauline scoots past Abigail and heads down the hallway, toward Huston.

"Huston Hawkes. Thank you so much for making room for us," Huston starts, holding out his hand.

"Heard you had a rough time of it up there, Huston," Sister Marjorie Pauline jolts to a stop right in front of him. Her speech is kind of blue-collar, like she could be taking your breakfast order at the local greasy spoon. Calling you "hon."

"We did," Huston answers. The rest of the family is craning to hear the conversation.

"Well, you're here now. Your dad's here now. Safe," Sister Marjorie Pauline says, staring him down. I can see his jaw clenching, his eyes focusing anywhere but at the little nun. Sister Marjorie Pauline breaks eye contact, zooms her little red scooter forward and takes his hand. Huston looks horrified.

"Thank you," Huston answers, never looking at her.

"This has been weighing on you." Sister Marjorie Pauline keeps hold of Huston's hand.

"It's been weighing on all of us."

Sister Marjorie Pauline brings her other hand across and takes both of his hands. His eyes dart around as he becomes more and more panicked.

I don't want her to tell him the worst is over, because it isn't. I don't want her to tell him he can relax now, because he can't.

Sister Marjorie Pauline holds Huston's hands for several more seconds. I realize she's saying a prayer for him: the atheist. He bows his head and closes his eyes.

"Amen," Sister Marjorie Pauline finally says, letting Huston's hands go. He opens his eyes and looks around awkwardly, clearing his throat and looking at his watch.

"He's all ready," a Webelos nun tells Abigail as she finally exits Dad's room.

Sister Marjorie Pauline reverses her little red scooter, almost mowing down one, if not both, of the twins. They loooooove it.

We all stream into Dad's room.

He looks exhausted, but rested, somehow. He acknowledges each one of us as we fall in around the hospital bed. Countless tubes still crawl around his body, the numbers on the monitors continue to dance. I see the kids cling to their parents, not knowing what to make of all this. They were banished to the waiting room while we were in Ojai, so this is the first time they've been able to visit him. I imagine it's a pretty scary sight for them.

Sister Marjorie Pauline scoots in behind John and Manny, parking just behind the privacy curtain. She carefully stands, grabs her cane in the little rear basket of her scooter and walks the few steps over to Dad's bedside. We all watch as she approaches him.

"So, you finally made it, Ray," Sister Marjorie Pauline barks over the metal safety bar, coming right up close to Dad's face.

His entire face lights up. In a way I've never seen. I look at Leo and mouth, "Great place." He nods back with a look of huge relief.

"You've got quite a family," Sister Marjorie Pauline says, lean-ing over Dad. Dad gives Sister a big, crooked grin. This one statement sends a shock wave through the room. The awkward throat-clearing is almost instantaneous.

"Okay, you've had a big day, I bet you're exhausted," Sister continues. Dad shakes his head yes. He says yes to everything. He says yes to everything.

I don't want to leave him. I don't want him to be here alone. I'm not factoring in how sick he is. Dad is...well, right now Dad *needs* his rest. Sister Marjorie Pauline understands this. She dips in close to Dad one more time, whispers something that no one but he can hear. Dad is quiet, his eyes closed. They both nod at the same time. We all look on. Sister Marjorie Pauline hobbles back to her little red scooter and makes it clear that we're supposed to follow.

One by one, we say goodbye to Dad, and stream out into the hallway after Sister Marjorie Pauline. When it's my turn, John quickly exits the room, indicating he'll be just outside. I approach Dad, he raises his arm, and I take his hand in mine.

"I'm so sorry about before," I say, smiling into his eyes. "I'm glad you're here now." Dad's face lights up and he tightens his grip on my hand. I nod and pass his hand over to Leo, who crumbles into tears the minute they make eye contact.

"—handling all this?" Sister Marjorie Pauline is saying to John, as I catch only the tail end. I settle in next to him.

"I'm an old friend of the family who just happens to be a law-yer," John says, his smile easy. Sister Marjorie Pauline looks from John to me and back again.

"Nice coincidence," Sister Marjorie Pauline chuckles, inching the scooter closer to John. He backs up and apologizes.

"We're thinking they're probably going to make quite a scene," Huston says.

"We've seen it all," Sister Marjorie Pauline says, making googly faces at Emilygrae and Mateo. They squeal with delight. Evie narrows her eyes...intrigued.

"We have quite a fight ahead of us," Huston presses. We all wait. Listen.

"But you're up to it," Sister Marjorie Pauline answers.

"Yes," Huston answers.

"Ray knew you were up for it," Sister Marjorie Pauline says. Huston nods, his entire face tight.

She continues, "He knew all of you could." She scans the entire group and peels off down the hallway. No one makes eye contact with anyone else.

"How did that lady know all those things?" Emilygrae asks Abigail as we all shuffle toward the exit. Abigail looks over at Manny. He scoops up Mateo and makes it clear that this question is for Abigail to field...alone.

"She knows people," Abigail vaguely answers. Emilygrae immediately looks over to Manny with an expression of "That's it?"

"You're making it sound like she's connected, Abby," Huston reproaches gently.

"Not knows people, like knows people who know people. I meant that she knows people, like *understands* people," Abigail explains, her voice quick, yet exhausted.

"Because you're making it sound like Sister is somehow connected to the Corleone family," Leo says as the automatic door slides open. Abigail rolls her eyes.

"Aha! In the Corleone family, I'd be the Michael!" I proclaim.

"What?" John asks.

"Before I was the Edmund, but now I'd be the Michael. And *you'd* be the Fredo," I declare, eyeing Abigail. She shakes her head, smiling.

"Before?" John asks, as you would.

"When we were in Narnia," I say easily.

"Narnia," John repeats. A nervous energy buzzes around our group, as around a table of little kids at a birthday party just after cake.

"Why am I always a girl? First Lucy and now Connie," Leo muses.

"You do have a tendency to…" Abigail trails off, pulling Leo close.

"Be a crybaby," Mateo finishes.

"I'm gonna make him an offer he can't refuse," Leo cracks. The fresh air feels good. Huston laughs. It's good to see him smile.

"That's the worst Marlon Brando impersonation I've ever heard," I say, laughing.

The cool air wafts over us as we walk through the St. Teresa's parking lot in search of our various cars. I feel the most tenuous of threads linking us, albeit a bit worse for the wear.

"Is Gus' Barbeque still on Fair Oaks in South Pas?" Leo asks, his hand woven through his motorcycle helmet.

"It's still there, but it's been completely remodeled, I hear the food is great, though," Abigail says, holding hands with Manny as they herd the kids between them.

"Do you want to try it anyway?" Leo suggests. We were high on all the emotion, but there's an awkwardness now that that we're not with Dad or surrounded by all of the hospital drama.

"It's New Year's Eve. I'm sure it's either closed or packed," Huston says, beeping his car unlocked in the distance.

"New Year's Eve is just the night before New Year's Day," Evie offers. Mateo's mouth falls open. Un-believ-able.

"We could do a little potluck thing at our house?" Abigail suggests, her voice sounding hopeful.

"Can we stay up past midnight?" Mateo asks. Oh my God, this is going to be the world's longest potluck.

"I have to get out of these clothes," I say, pleading with Abigail. She looks at John, raises an eyebrow and then looks back at me. I immediately blush.

"Let's say seven, then?" Abigail proposes. Huston walks in front of us all, not looking back.

"Huston?" I call after him. He looks back at me. At all of us.

"I'm exhausted, guys. I'm afraid to think what's waiting for me back at the office," Huston says, stopping at the back of his car.

"Nothing's waiting for you back at the office," John says. Huston tilts his head slightly, eyes narrowing.

"Et tu, Brute?" Huston sighs. Evie and I immediately lock eyes. She can't help but point at Huston and smile knowingly back. Ha! If she's a Shakespearean scholar one day, she'll have me to thank.

"It's the week between Christmas and New Year's," Leo offers. I think to myself that nothing is waiting for me, either. After I e-mailed all my end-of-the-year reports to Tim's assistant, I officially began my seventeen days of vacation. Tim was very understanding.

"Huston?" Abigail presses.

Manny leads the twins and Evie over to their minivan. He swoops up Emilygrae and bets Mateo he can touch the car first. Of course, Mateo takes that bet. Evie glances back over her shoulder at the group of us.

"I think it'd be nice for us not to be in a hospital for once," I add.

"We need to...We did a good thing here and we should...we should be together tonight," Leo rambles. Huston shifts his weight.

"So it's settled?" Abigail presses.

"We're all going to worry about Dad tonight...we might as well do it together," Leo says, across the parking lot. Huston's shoulders lower. He lets out a long sigh. No one lets him off the hook. We all wait.

"Fine. Seven," Huston agrees.

"We'll do burgers and hot dogs. Grace, you and John bring some kind of dessert, Leo you bring buns, and Huston—why don't you bring the beverages," Abigail says.

John and I watch as Huston pulls out of the St. Teresa's parking lot, followed by the packed minivan and Leo's motorcycle that sounds like a jet engine. The dusk zooms up around me. It smells like rain.

"So we just got assigned a dessert," John says, flipping his keys around.

"We, huh?" I say. John turns around in the empty parking lot. Serious.

"Yep," he says, standing in front of me.

"Wait . . . are you seriously equating getting back together with committing to bringing dessert to a potluck?" I say, tilting my head, smiling. Dad's safe. Dad's safe.

"It does make it sound a little . . ." John trails off, pulling me close.

"If you say sweet, I swear to God," I say, kissing him. And kissing him.

"I wasn't going to say sweet, because in my mind we were bringing some kind of cobbler," John says, taking my hand.

"Yes, that could have been misleading," I say, walking to my car.

"So, I'll meet you at your house?"

"Well, with the whole romantic dessert commitment, how can a girl refuse?" I say, unlocking my car.

"See you there," he says, closing the door behind me.

"Remember—we have to take the southern route because of parade traffic," I say, as he begins to walk away.

"Right . . ." he answers, giving a quick nod.

I smile and watch as he walks to his car. The red lights flash in the distance as he beeps it unlocked. He climbs in and waits.

I put my car in reverse and head out of the parking lot, just as night settles in around me.

John follows.

"No, just the hot dog. No bun. No . . . no ketchup or anything." I can hear Manny bringing Huston up to speed on Mateo's Spartan eating habits over by the grill. Mateo is trying desperately to keep the required distance between himself and the grill. This is a feat of great strength and control; the grill pulls men of all ages toward it. John and Leo have already succumbed to the tractor beam and stand idly by as Manny scans the yard. Mateo is going to make a run for it. I walk inside to the kitchen and find Abigail and Evie bustling around the kitchen. I spy a bowl of chips and can't help but partake.

"So?" Abigail asks, as she pulls a bottle of sparkling water out of the fridge.

"No, but I knit a little," I say, popping a corn chip into my mouth.

Abigail sniffs. Waits.

"You and John?" Abigail begins.

"He's hot, Aunt Gracie," Evie offers.

"Evelyn Grace Rodriguez," Abigail warns.

"Well, he is," she says, smirking. I can't help but smile back. Evie gives me a little peck on the cheek, the look of distrust in her eyes gone. I got another chance. She heads outside unaware that she just made my night.

"Didn't you guys break up?" Abigail presses.

"Yeah," I say, dipping another chip into the guacamole.

"What changed?" Abigail asks, carrying the bottle of sparkling water out onto the deck.

"I don't know," I answer. Abigail turns around, blocking me.

"You don't know?" Her voice is dripping with contempt.

"No, I mean—I did, I guess."

"Well, *you'd* better not mess it up this time," Abigail finally says, her body stiffening as she awaits my comeback. I think of my old upright piano now sitting in my living room and don't say a thing. Abigail looks back confused, waits a beat, shakes her head, smiles and continues out onto the deck.

"We've got hamburgers, hot dogs, grilled chicken, and one gross veggie blob," Huston announces, setting a tray of barbeque fare down in the center of the table. I grab my gross veggie blob and wave off the cries of disgust from the table.

Abigail has set a silvery runner down the center of the table, dotted with candle-filled hurricane lamps. The brisk night air has kept us all bundled up throughout the evening, but not quite enough to take this little party inside.

"Mateo, get away from the grill!" we hear in the distance.

"Thank you all for coming over tonight." Manny smiles, lifting Emilygrae up into her seat. He tucks a napkin into the collar of her shirt and begins to cut her hamburger into tiny pieces. Her little face glows in the candlelight as she looks around at everyone.

"John?" Abigail says, motioning at the tray, pushing Mateo's seat under the table. Mateo eyes my gross veggie blob. John grabs a burger.

"It's vegetables smushed up into a blob," I whisper to Mateo.

"Ewwwwww." He laughs, watching as Manny sets one single hot dog on his plate. The tiny bespectacled superhero tilts his head, scouring the hot dog for absolutely any unfamiliar hangers-on. A speck of relish? A crumb from a nearby bun? He's vigilant.

"Have a seat, Huston," Manny calls from the head of the table. Huston climbs the stairs to the deck and tucks in next to John.

"You know that took the longest to cook, right?" Huston announces, eyeing my gross veggie blob.

"It's very dense," I explain, whipping my napkin into my lap.

"Insert dense joke here, just about any one will apply," Leo cracks, reaching into the center of the table for a hamburger. The table erupts in laughter.

"Evie, mija, did you get your hot dog?" Abigail asks, as Evie holds up her plate. Satisfied, Abigail squeezes in next to Manny and reaches into the center of the table for a chicken breast. Leo picks up the pasta salad.

"Who's hungry?" Huston and Abigail both say at the exact same time. The four of us share a moment. Just like in the old days. I sigh. I'm part of something. Again.

"Before we go on... here's to a new year," Manny toasts, raising his glass. We all follow Manny's lead. The center of the table is crowded with jelly jars, sippy cups, wineglasses, and two pint glasses.

"To a new year." We all toast. Huston keeps his glass up.

"To Dad," Huston adds, lifting his glass just that much higher.

"To Dad," we repeat, lifting our glasses. The flickering candlelight reveals glimmers of smiles, welling eyes and worried looks. But underneath is the most unbelievable thing—we just toasted our father. This is unprecedented. We are silent. Awkwardly silent. I cut into my gross veggie blob and stuff it into my mouth.

"Mmmmmm," I coo. The entire table cringes, but everyone is glad for the distraction. Those few quiet seconds brought flashes of Dad in the hospital, Connie screaming at the top of her lungs, and pain. Leo passes the pasta salad to Huston. He scoops out a generous helping and waits as he watches me overact swallowing.

"She ate it!" Emilygrae screeches with her mouth full, pointing her fork across the table at me.

"Em," Abigail warns, her smile negating her scolding tone. Emilygrae giggles into her plate. Huston passes the pasta salad to John, shaking his head. John scoops out a helping and passes it over to me. In his struggle to make sure the bowl, as well as its contents, doesn't touch his hot dog, Mateo chokes, hacking up the tiny morsel of chewed "meat" onto his plate. Manny pats his back and holds out a glass of water (no ice) for him to take. Abigail watches intently. Emilygrae shoves a forkful of pasta salad into her mouth, seemingly unfazed by her fallen comrade.

"Drink this, Matty," Manny says, sweeping Mateo's mouth with his finger. Mateo hacks again, takes the glass and drinks in. He coughs a bit and hands the glass back to Manny.

"There was sumfin on it," Mateo declares, wiping his mouth of any disgusting remnants. We all relax.

"Phew," I say, shoving a giant bite of gross veggie blob into my mouth. He scrunches up his face and re-situates his glasses in response. I make a silly face at him, wobbling my head around. Mateo just stares. Quiet. Disgusted.

Visions of Connie and Dennis are thankfully far away.

For now.

I awake the next morning to the sound of a B-2 stealth bomber and two F-22 fighter jets flying overhead. The Rose Parade. I check the time. Just before eight a.m. Visiting hours start at ten a.m. Two hours until . . . well, just two hours.

It's New Year's Day.

I rub my eyes and stretch my arm across the impression John's body left in my bed. I let my eyes get accustomed to the sunlight and whip the covers off to go investigate. I am unreasonably proud of myself that my initial thought wasn't that John fled sometime during the night.

Stepping out into the chilly hallway, I am forced to pull my
robe tightly around my pajama-less body to keep warm. I walk
past Mom's picture in its little niche. I have a flash of regret that I
didn't make the niche bigger—am I going to have to add another
picture soon? I cinch my robe tighter as the chill settles in.

I smell coffee.

I am just about to walk into the kitchen when I spot John
out in the backyard. At least I hope it's John—either that or I'm
being burgled by the most lackadaisical criminal in history. I
am about to open the French doors, but find myself just staring at him through the wavy glass. He's bending down to test
the temperature of the pool in the backyard. He's wearing the
same suit as yesterday, but now it's being worn in a far more
intimate, early-morning deconstruction. The pants are loose and
hang just above his bare feet. The crisp white oxford-cloth shirt
hangs open and unbuttoned. His thick black hair is a ruffling
muss in the early-morning chill. He whips the water off his hand
and stands, finally catching sight of me through the French
doors. A smile breaks across his face as I approach. A light in the
darkness.

"Surprisingly warm," he says, pulling me in for a long kiss. I
breathe him in with unending pleasure.

"Me or the water?" I say, my lips centimeters from his.

"Both," he answers, pulling me in again.

"I forgot how much I love having an outside," he finally says.

"You're still in that downtown loft?" I ask, remembering and
remembering.

"Go ahead and say it."

"The Furnished Downtown Loft with No Soul," I rattle off.

"Yes, I'm still in the Furnished Downtown Loft with No Soul,"
John admits.

"Before I saw it, I would never have believed in the devastating power of an all-black leather décor," I joke.

"Well, then see—right there, you learn something new every day."

"And all those Lichtenstein prints really warmed the place up." I twist the knife further.

"I don't even notice them anymore," John argues.

"Yes, well—that's really the purpose of art: to not notice it after a while."

"I didn't know you swam," John says, motioning to the dark blue pool in the middle of the backyard.

"It was just a concrete slab when I moved in. I redid all of this about a year ago. I wanted it to feel private and away from everything," I say, surveying the blooming lavender, the outside dining area with real, working fireplace, and the pool I *had* to have, but have yet to swim in.

"It doesn't even feel like we're in the city at all," John adds, taking in the skyscraping Carolina cherries that surround the entire property.

"That's what I was going for," I answer.

"So, you swim?"

"Well..."

"You have got to be kidding me." John is genuinely shocked.

"I just never had the time," I admit.

"We have time right now," John says, checking his watch.

"To what?"

John eyes the pool again.

"I was thinking more along the lines of breakfast," I say, starting back into the house.

"All you have in there is some bullshit kefir and blueberries. Not quite the breakfast that's going to tempt me," he says. I turn back around and find John half-naked, his shirt in a puddle next to the patio table I've never sat at once.

"What are you doing?!" I blurt, unable to wipe the smile off my face.

"I'm going swimming," he says, shedding his pants one leg at a time.

"I have neighbors," I say, staring. Staring. Staring.

"You said yourself that you built this with privacy in mind," he says, now pulling his boxers down. He's enjoying this far too much. Shit, I'm enjoying this far too much.

"Not *naked* privacy," I say.

"*Naked* privacy?" John laughs, kicking his boxers into the perfectly tended lavender.

"It's a valid concern." I laugh, unable to stop myself. John gives me one last look and launches into the pool with what can only be described as a "hoot and a holler." I immediately look over at the neighboring houses. Not one peeping neighbor aghast at my . . . *naked* privacy. John bursts through the water's surface, his black hair wet and slick.

"You coming in?" he says, dipping under again. I clutch at my robe, my eyes dart around the backyard. I start for the pool house.

"Let me just get my bathing suit," I try, running along the pavers to the small cabana I've never been in that holds the bathing suit I've never worn.

"Gracie, I've already seen you naked. The jig is up," John yells from the pool.

"Yes, you've seen me naked, but Owen and his grandmother haven't, so . . ." I trail off, my hand on the door to the pool house. John goes underwater again, I can see him swimming toward me. My hand stops. He's almost here. One more stroke and he'll break the surface. I breathe in the crisp air. Time slows. I watch John under the water and I'm overtaken with an overpowering

need to feel alive. *I am alive.* I yank my robe off and launch myself
into the pool, cannonballing just next to the love of my life.

"It's about damn time," John says, laughing, as we both come
up for air. The water feels amazing. This pool has been here for a
year and I've never gone in. The overarching metaphor of this is
not lost on me at all.

"You're a naked pool bully," I say, swimming over to him.

"Naked pool bully?" John repeats, laughing. John easily envelops me as I float into him. He steadies himself against the tiled
wall and holds me close. I wrap my everything around him as I
try to stabilize myself.

"So, you in need of a pool boy?" John says, as the water laps
around us.

"I'm being serviced by a nice gentleman already but thank
you," I say, kissing him.

"How else am I going to earn my keep around here?"

"I'm sure we'll find another way," I answer, fervently hoping
Owen and his grandmother can't see what John does next.

"Any sign of Connie and Dennis?" I ask, setting my purse next
to the folding chair in Dad's room at St. Teresa's. I'm holding my
Casio keyboard and a cup of tea. My hair is still wet from this
morning's pool rendezvous. I feel like I've just gone from fifth
gear on the Autobahn to a crashing halt. But, strangely, both are
equally life-affirming.

Dad's dressed in a striped polo and sweatpants and seems to
be sleeping soundly. His color looks better, but he's definitely
losing weight. I don't want to ask if he's getting better. I don't
want to ask if his body is finally absorbing the nutrients that are
being pumped into that ever-present feeding tube.

"No, no sign of them," Abigail answers, taking a sip of her
coffee.

"Where are the kids?" I ask, thinking the room feels a little stuffy. I begin to tap out the first notes of Miles Davis' "So What." *Ba-dum...Ba-dum.*

"Manny took them all to the Rose Parade," Abigail answers, her foot tapping.

"Why haven't Connie and Dennis come to see Dad?" Leo asks, flipping the page of his *Wired* magazine.

"They're not interested in Dad. She made that perfectly clear," I whisper, not wanting Dad to hear. I continue playing.

"What was he thinking?" Leo whispers, violently flipping a magazine page.

"I wanted to make sure he has these," Abigail says, rummaging through her purse. She pulls out the ziplock bag from the hospital with Dad's wallet and his wedding ring. Abigail takes Dad's wallet out of the bag and sets it in the drawer of his bedside table. Right next to the Bible. We probably don't have to worry that these cloistered nuns are going to skip off with Dad's wallet. Abigail digs deep into the ziplock bag and pulls out the wedding ring. She holds it out with a look of repulsion.

"What should we do with this?" Abigail says, dangling the ring on her finger.

"Have Frodo take it back to Mount Doom," I say, picking my tea up off the ground and taking a sip. Abigail whips the ring around, throwing it to Leo.

"'I will take the ring, though I do not know the way,'" Leo recites, holding the ring.

"First *The Godfather* and now Frodo? Who's the nerd now?" I ask, setting my tea back on the ground.

"Oh, my God," Leo yells.

"What? What?" we say, immediately jumping up to Dad's bedside.

"No . . . *no* . . . the ring," Leo says, examining the inside of the band.

"Jesus H. Christ, you scared the shit out of us," I say. "I thought for sure he saw Dad convulsing or something." Abigail walks over to Leo.

"What about it?" Abigail asks, now standing over Leo.

"*RAYMOND AND EVELYN HAWKES: MAY 26, 1968*," Leo reads. Abigail puts her hand over her mouth. Abigail has had to share her birthday with Mom and Dad's anniversary her entire life. Needless to say, it's been a difficult affiliation.

"Oh my God," I whisper, my Casio keyboard almost falling to the ground.

"He's wearing . . ." Leo says, almost to himself, lovingly closing his hand around the ring.

Each day, another piece.

"Good morning!" A nun buzzes into Dad's room. She's so tiny her brown habit seems to swallow her whole. Her olive skin and dark features are framed by the stark white band of her headpiece.

"Good morning," we all respond.

"I'm Sister Carmella, I'm Raymond's day nurse," she announces, her Spanish accent lilting, so Dad's name sounds like *Ray-mawnd*, stressing the second syllable. She makes his name sound so lovely, I can't bear to tell her he always liked to be called Ray.

"Nice to meet you," Abigail responds. Leo and I nod hellos.

"How's our patient?" she asks, checking all of Dad's machines. He rouses, opening his eyes and taking in the room.

It's surreal to look at Mom's and Dad's love affair from this vantage point. Epiphanies come fast and hard when you're watching someone fight for his life. Someone you love.

And he loved me.

I began this journey wanting to convince Dad I didn't need

him. That I was Mom's kid. Now I know that because I'm Mom's kid—because I'm *their* kid—I'll honor them by never walking away from great love ever again.

"If you could please wait outside, I'm going to change your father's linens and diaper," Sister Carmella asks. My *father's* diaper.

And just like that, epiphany time is up.

I stand. Leo, with Dad's wedding ring still in his closed hand, follows Abigail out into the hall.

I walk into the hallway. The Lady in Red is sitting beneath the statue of the Virgin Mary. She waves. I smile back. I crane my neck to see if her old-lady posse is assembling. Not yet.

The glass doors open at the entrance and Huston walks toward us down the long hallway. He's wearing a pair of pressed jeans, a crisp white T-shirt and a navy blue cashmere sweater over the top. Even his casual dress is contained and efficient. His LA Dodgers baseball cap is pulled low. He notices us and gives a quick wave. He slows his pace as he approaches.

"Any sign of Connie or Dennis?" Huston asks.

"No," I say. Abigail and Leo are shaking their heads no.

"So they kept to their word," Huston says to himself.

We are silent.

"Dad's wedding ring? We should send that back to Connie." Huston eyes Leo's now open hand.

"It's *Mom* and Dad's," Leo says, letting Huston read the inscription.

"Ray and Evelyn," Huston reads. We all nod. Huston hands the ring back to Leo, takes a long, slow breath and takes off his baseball cap. He runs his hand through his mussed hair and replaces the cap. He's been doing that his whole life. It's amazing how little we change.

"Ray and Evelyn," Abigail repeats.

"Why didn't they just ... They should have just stayed together," I sigh. Quiet.

"Okay, he's all ready," Sister Carmella says, sweeping out of the room with a plastic bag filled with ... well, filled.

We all anxiously stream back into Dad's room, away from the oppressive quiet of the hallway. Dad's awake and watching the pre–Rose Bowl game specials on a small staticky television. He looks happy. Like this is what he'd be doing if he were home. Just sitting around watching football.

"Watching the game, huh?" Huston says, taking Dad's outstretched hand. Dad nods yes. He does say yes to everything. I notice that Sister Carmella has hung the crucifix over Dad's bed and the Madonna is within reach on the bedside table. So he can touch it, continue his ritual. We're in the right place.

"What do you think?" Huston asks, motioning around the room. Dad gives him a big thumbs-up. Huston's entire face lights up.

"Good ... good," Huston answers, squeezing his lips tightly together.

"Knock, knock." An older gentleman in a doctor's coat walks into Dad's room a bit later. His stark white hair is clean-cut. He's wearing a plaid shirt and dress pants underneath the doctor's coat. He's holding a chart and has his pen at the ready.

"Hi," we all say in unison.

"Happy New Year," the doctor says, walking over to Dad.

"Huston Hawkes," Huston says, extending his hand to the doctor.

"Dr. O'Rourke."

"Dr. O'Rourke," Huston repeats, and then goes around the room introducing us all. Dr. O'Rourke shakes hands with each of us. He seems like a genuine kind of guy. A real old-school doctor.

"Ray, you've got the game on, I see," Dr. O'Rourke says, walking back over to Dad's bedside and flipping the pages on Dad's chart.

"Pregame," Leo corrects, unable to stop himself. Abigail narrows her eyes at him. Leo clears his throat.

"It looks like you're having a hard time keeping stuff in, Ray," Dr. O'Rourke reports. Dad nods yes. Of course.

"Is there anything we can do about that?" Huston asks.

"We can try a couple of other formulas, but this is definitely something we have to watch. The threat of dehydration concerns me," Dr. O'Rourke says, focusing on Huston. Awesome. Let's jot down "dehydration" on the ever-growing list of threats to Dad's life. Down the list from "massive stroke." Just a bit.

"Dehydration," Huston repeats.

"Let's go talk in the hall, let Ray watch the game in peace," Dr. O'Rourke says, smiling at Dad. Dad nods yes. Leo controls himself and doesn't correct Dr. O'Rourke again. Dr. O'Rourke looks at Huston and then at the rest of us. He wants all of us.

"Sure . . . sure," we all mumble.

"Ray, I'm going to steal your kids for a second," Dr. O'Rourke says, putting his hand on Dad's shoulder. Dad shrugs his shoulders. We all shuffle into the hallway. I don't know where to look. I lock eyes with Abigail. She looks just as confused as I do. Leo's eyes have already begun to well up. I take his hand. Huston's arms are wound tightly across his chest.

"You have concerns?" Huston starts.

"I just wanted a chance to speak more frankly," Dr. O'Rourke says, tucking Dad's chart under his arm.

"Thank you for your discretion," Huston says.

"Your father has suffered a massive stroke, as you know. It looks like his body is still rejecting any nourishment."

"Yes, we're aware of that," Huston answers. Leo flips Dad's wedding ring onto his thumb and slides it all the way down. I sneak a peek at the Lady in Red under the statue of the Virgin Mary. Still there. Staring right at me.

"St. Joe's up in Ojai also noted a severe drop-off in your father's urine output," Dr. O'Rourke offers.

"His urine output?" Huston asks.

"His body isn't releasing enough fluid," Dr. O'Rourke explains. Dad's sitting up in his bed breathing, thinking, and waiting for us to come back in. Dad's going to get better. He's watching football in a little striped polo. It's New Year's Day, for Christ's sake.

"We just got him here," I say, my voice barely a whisper. I look over at Huston. His face is in a battle to stay expressionless. Why did we move heaven and earth to get him here if...if...I can't say it.

"Hospitals aren't equipped to handle long-term care," Dr. O'Rourke answers.

"We had to move him," Huston whispers.

"Your father's situation is dire. I must prepare you," Dr. O'Rourke says, his voice soft, but authoritative.

"Prepare us?" Huston presses. Abigail claps her hand over her mouth. I squeeze Leo's hand, tighter and tighter.

"St. Joe's indicated that you should think about a hospice program for your father. I agree that it's the best option for Ray, given his decline," Dr. O'Rourke says. He takes Dad's chart from under his arm, opens it up, and hands Huston a pamphlet. That pamphlet was like a ticking time bomb just waiting in there for us.

"Wait...*wait*...what are we talking about here?" I eke out.

"Hospice?" Abigail interrupts, watching as Huston opens the pamphlet and begins to read. His baseball cap low, his eyes hidden.

"Why did we drag Dad all the way down here?" Leo almost whispers to himself.

"The philosophy of hospice is more about making the patient comfortable, rather than imposing harsh treatments that might be painful," Dr. O'Rourke explains.

"And fruitless. Painful and *fruitless*, right?" I ask. Dr. O'Rourke nods in agreement.

Huston looks over at me. We've brought him all this way. Doesn't Dr. O'Rourke know what we had to do to get him here? I shake my head again. I knew it. I knew Dad was...well, I just *knew*. He's just sitting in there watching football, though. I take in a deep breath, trying to breathe. I breathe out.

We are all quiet. No one dares say it. No one dares ask it. We don't want clarity. We want to stay in the dark. Seconds...minutes pass.

"Dad's not going to get better?" Leo finally asks.

"I'm so sorry," Dr. O'Rourke says, resting a hand on Leo's shoulder.

chapter twenty-one

T his is bullshit," Leo says once we're safely outside in the little picnic area just off the St. Teresa's cafeteria. He slumps over the table.

"Why did we come all the way down here when he could have just stayed up in Ojai?" Abigail asks, bending into a small picnic table bench.

"Hospitals take care of the sick," I say, sitting next to Leo. My anger is rising.

"Not the dying," Huston finishes.

We are quiet. Two nuns walk by with an older woman in a wheelchair. We all smile and greet the women. We remain quiet long after they've passed.

"We didn't get enough time with him," Leo says, looking down, not daring to look at anyone.

"The ring thing…we just now figured out the ring…" Abigail trails off, pointing to the wedding band on Leo's thumb. The wedding band that proves Dad always loved Mom even if we—even if she—didn't know it.

"Goddamn it," I say, the pressure in my shoulders and chest rising.

"I don't think I can sit there and watch him die," Leo says, his voice cracking.

"It's why we're here," I say, his face becoming more and more red and blotchy.

"I can't do it. I can't go back in there and smile and hold his hand and talk about waterproof casts and football games...when... when...How am I supposed to do that?" Leo asks.

"You just are," Huston answers.

"Historians say that how a culture of people takes care of their sick and...*dying* is a sign of being civilized. It shows a level of humanity...a level of evolution," I ramble, wanting to talk about something academic. Skirt the emotion as long as I can.

"I can't...I can't..." Leo crumbles. I shift over and sit closer to him, wrapping my arm around his convulsing shoulders. He leans into me and I can feel him sobbing uncontrollably. I'm terrified of that kind of crying. We fall silent once again.

"He's wanted out since Mom died," Huston finally whispers, glancing at the ring.

"I don't want him out...I want him here," Leo sobs. I pull him close. Abigail is quiet.

"He doesn't want to be here," Huston answers. He is stoic and decided in his theory. He has to be. Abigail is just nodding, nodding, nodding—formulating theories and trying to believe in them.

"No one *wants* to die," Leo chokes. My body is numb. I don't know what terrifies me more: the pain that awaits me or the ability I have to completely shut down emotionally.

"Huston's right—Dad wants out," I finally say.

"Once again, we're not enough. He doesn't want to stay with us," Abigail yells as she slams her hand on the table. We all jump back.

"That's not it, Abby," Huston soothes, not thrown at all.

"Yes, it is! We're never enough! Never!" Abigail screams. Her voice echoes throughout the entire picnic area.

"He's dying, Abs. He can't stop—" Huston says.

"Yes, he could! He could *try* to get better! He needs to try harder...please...he can't leave us, again...he can't leave us again," Abigail says, her voice finally crumbling into sobs.

"Abby," Huston says, pulling her close. She fights him like a child being put on time-out—her body squirming, her cries of protest empty and pained. She finally allows Huston to pull her in as she collapses. Her sobs are a torrent of anger, frustration and unadulterated pain. I've never seen her like this. Leo and I sit back...helplessly watching and trying to compartmentalize our own pain.

"Shhh...shhhh..." Huston eases.

"People aren't supposed to die! God...do you know what the last words I said to Mom were?" Abigail wails into Huston's chest. We all wait.

Abigail continues, "Talk to you later." Her head sags, convulsing, shuddering...finally letting go.

"Okay, Abby...okay," Huston soothes.

"We were good...we were being good..." Abigail sobs.

"We need to let him be with Mom," Huston finally says.

"What about us? What are we going to do?" Abigail flares, her mood swinging from utter despair to anger once more.

"I don't know," Huston answers.

"We're all alone," Abigail gasps.

"We're not alone," Huston soothes, smoothing her hair.

"How do we go back in there?"

"We just do," Huston answers. Leo sniffles and wipes his nose on his sleeve.

"If he dies, the answers die with him," Abigail sniffles. Huston takes a deep breath. So many questions left unanswered that we now know will stay that way.

"We need you," Huston says, his voice just over a whisper.

"I can't," Abigail sobs. Leo sniffles.

"*I* need you," Huston says.

"How...how do...how can we..."

"You have to ask yourself what you'd want if you were..." Huston trails off.

"Dying," I finish, looking up at Huston. Huston nods. His eyes clear.

"*Who* would you want?" Huston asks again. Abigail looks up at him. Then at Leo. Then at me.

We all come up with the same answer.

"We'd better get back in there, then," I say, keeping my eyes locked with Abigail's. I take a deep breath and unfold from the picnic table. Standing.

"Okay...okay," Abigail says, gently disentangling herself from Huston. He watches her, making sure she's okay. She can't look at him. She's more than a little embarrassed for her show of...*emotion*. Huston takes his baseball cap off, runs his hand through his hair and replaces the cap. Leo wipes and wipes at his face as he unfolds himself from the picnic table.

"That's what I'd want, too," Huston says, standing. Abigail picks a white thread off Huston's navy blue sweater and gently smoothes her hand over his shoulder. He waits. She sags her head slightly, tears welling once more, her hand still resting on him. He pulls her in for an enveloping hug. Leo and I wait. Shoring ourselves up. Processing what's happening. Abigail never cried when Mom died...at least not in front any of us. Abigail takes one deep breath after another, trying to regain control. I hold Leo close, knowing he could go at any time. He seems almost spellbound by Abigail—studying her like a chemical reaction. I don't say a word. I don't talk at her or insert myself into the fray. For Abigail, this is a monumental act of kindness on my part. She decisively unravels from Huston once and for all. They have a whispering back-and-forth that no one else is privy to and we finally start back into Saint Teresa's.

Our eyes are unfocused and darting. Our minds all running through the possible scenarios the next few days—weeks? months?—will hold. None of them are good and all of them suggest an anguish that none of us can yet fathom. It's what civilized people do. It's what you do for the people you love. You comfort when you have everything to lose.

Them.

We didn't have this opportunity with Mom. She was ripped from us without as much as a wave goodbye. We were stunned into numbness. I now know her death was merciful. The automatic doors open and a Webelos nun bustles by us, jogging us out of our hazes.

"I'll take the morning shift," Huston says, motioning into Dad's room.

"I'll join you," Leo and I add simultaneously.

"I'll bring the kids by after they're done at the parade," Abigail says, reaching in her purse for her keys.

"We'll be here," Huston sighs.

"I know." Abigail smiles, giving Huston a quick hug. He walks into Dad's room and settles in at his bedside. This is what civilized people do.

"Can you bring back some sandwiches?" Leo asks, running his hands through his uncombed hair.

"Sure. Tuna?" Abigail offers, knowing it's his favorite.

"Barbeque potato chips and a real Coke. You put the chips inside the sandwich," Leo adds, flipping Dad's wedding ring from one finger to the next.

"A *real* Coke?" I ask, taking his hand in mine. Calming him.

"Everyone drinks diet these days—you have to specify," Leo

explains, nodding that he understands he's supposed to calm down. Just like when we were kids. Abigail hitches her purse back over her shoulder.

"Caprese sandwich and a sparkling water?" Abigail asks me.

"Sounds perfect," I answer, smiling. *Sigh*. Abigail starts down the hall, and then stops. She turns around.

"Evie's Girl Scout troop has their robotics qualifying round this weekend. Leo's their mentor. You want to come, too?"

"Robotics?" I ask.

"With Legos. It's really fun," Leo answers immediately.

"Absolutely," I agree, feeling hypocritical for planning anything fun-sounding.

"Perfect, I'll let her know you're coming. I'm going to try and get Huston there, too. Bring John." Abigail winks, leaning in to hug Leo and me.

"John?" Leo asks, his nose pink. I can't help but smile.

"I'll see you in a few hours," Abigail says.

"With sandwiches," Leo presses.

"And real Cokes. Yes, I know," Abigail answers, turning again toward the automatic door. Abigail walks out into the sunlight. Leo and I look at one another and then into Dad's room. In that quick second I feel both of us brace ourselves as if we're wading into the ocean and a big wave is cresting large over us. Turning our backs and closing our eyes, we let it crash down, just trying to withstand its power and keep standing. As we settle into Dad's room, the most implausible thing of all happens, life goes on.

Huston checks in with work and talks football with Dad. Sandwiches and real Cokes are delivered. The kids stand uncomfortably on the fringes of Dad's room, presenting him with drawings and then nervously asking when they'll be able to go home. John calls and asks about dinner. I suggest a vat of vodka. He suggests Indian food. Huston goes in to work for a quick meeting and Leo and I get a mean game of Boggle going as the sun sinks low. Leo peels off to teach a night class in a subject I can't even pronounce and I'm left alone for the first time.

As I sit by Dad's bedside, I think about what Abigail said around the picnic table this morning. *If he dies, the answers die with him.* I fight the urge to ply Dad with questions. I think about driving back up to Ojai and searching high and low for a journal, no—a trunk *filled* with journals. What does he think of us? What did he think of Mom when they met for the first time in that jazz club in San Diego? Whom did he vote for in the last election? What does he want to be when he grows up? Why did he marry Connie? Was he lonely? Did he ever want to come back? What did he think of his parents? I suddenly want to know what he thinks of everything. Instead I sit in an uncomfortable chair at Dad's bedside and play the hits of the 1980s on a tiny Casio keyboard as Dad falls in and out of sleep.

"Thought I'd stop by and maybe spend some time with Ray," Manny announces as he strolls into the room, a cup of coffee in one hand and a *Los Angeles Times* in the other.

"Hey," I say, looking behind him to see if Abigail is trailing.

"How are you holding up?" Manny asks, walking over to me, no Abigail in sight. He envelops me in a big bear hug. He's apparently going to make me into a hugger if it's the last thing he does. I can feel the flutter of the newspaper on the side of my face as Manny squeezes me tighter.

"No Abigail?" I ask, as he crunches me in close.

"The kids are over at our neighbor's for dinner. Well, Emily-grae will eat. Mateo will pick everything off of his food and Evie will mope in some corner with a book. At home, we just call that *dinner.* Abby's making sure they're settled," Manny says, letting me go and taking in the room.

"It's awesome you came by," I say, standing awkwardly.

"What? Oh...yeah, no problem," Manny absently says, as if I've said something ridiculous. He walks over to Dad's bedside and rests his hand gently on Dad's shoulder.

Manny continues, "Did you want to go grab some dinner?" I realize I have no idea what time it is. I know I'm hungry, so it could be night-ish. I look at my watch: seven-thirty p.m. Jesus. I shake my head...how is time now going by so quickly? I want to grab the hands of my watch and hold them in place. It's going too fast. I haven't had enough time. I breathe in and realize my body is just as tight as when Leo and I braced ourselves for that great wave earlier this morning. I exhale and focus back on Manny.

"I was going to meet John for Indian food," I say, tucking my keyboard into Dad's closet and grabbing my purse off the chair.

"We'll be here. Visiting hours are almost over so I'll just make sure Ray's tucked in for the night before I head home," Manny says, pulling up another chair and settling in with his coffee and paper.

"I'll be back in the morning," I whisper, touching Dad's shoulder softly. I look down at him. He's fighting for every breath. Up. Down. Up. Down. I take a deep breath. If he's strong enough to fight, then so am I. I just may be his kid after all.

"How's he doing?" I look up. John walks into the room. He's wearing a pair of jeans, a Marine Corps T-shirt and a zip-up hoodie. Manny looks up and stands.

"Good to see you," Manny says, extending his hand to John.

"Good to see you, too," John answers. Neither of these men is related to Ray and yet they're both here.

"Hey—" I say, tugging on my purse.

"Thought I'd meet you here," John adds.

"I'm trying to get her to eat something," Manny offers, sitting.

"Me, too," John says, as Manny waves goodbye and begins

elaborately dissecting the newspaper. I look back to Dad once more. Asleep. His chest rises and falls.

"Looks like the economy is getting a bit better, Ray," Manny announces to the sleeping patient. I smile at him as he continues to read the front-page story aloud. I reach for John's hand and savor his fingers curling around mine. I feel myself relaxing. We walk out into the hall.

"I talked to Huston. No new information since this morning?" John asks, saving me from having to explain Dad's regression and the details of hospice. I thread my arm through his and lean on his brick wall of a body. He wraps his arm around my waist in response. He decides, for once, not to press the issue. We squeak down the immaculate hallway and past the sundowners who gather nightly at the feet of the Virgin Mary. The Lady in Red gives us a wave as another old woman scoots into line.

"He's still at the office?" I ask, officially changing the subject. Old habits.

"No, he's home now. Thought we'd stop by later. Maybe ask if he's up for dinner?" John answers, fishing his keys out of his pocket.

"Sounds good," I answer, the grief of the day roiling in my stomach.

"We spent some time this morning getting all of the documents together. We're definitely going to be ready," John says as we walk to his car.

"Oh, good," I say again, trying to swallow the emotion down. That vat of vodka is looking really good right about now.

"Where's everyone else?" John asks, beeping his car unlocked. He opens the passenger door for me.

"My car is over there," I say, absently pointing to the nearly empty parking lot.

"I doubt any of the cloistered nuns are going to hot-wire it," John says.

"But I have to—" I start.

"If you need a ride tomorrow, I'll give you one," John says.

"You're taking advantage of me while I'm in a weakened state," I sigh, climbing into the passenger side and pulling the seat belt across my chest.

"Yes, I am," John answers, smiling.

"Thank you, baby," I say, my face tingling from the use of the word *baby*. John shuts the door behind me.

"*Baby?*" John asks, his voice soft, as he climbs into the driver's side.

"I know," I say, smiling. John puts his keys in the ignition and starts the car.

"I thought we'd pick up some food at Holy Cow on Third and then head over to Huston's house in the Pali—" John starts.

I can't hold it in anymore. My throat feels like it's closing. My lip is quivering. I must look like a child who's just slammed her finger in a car door—right before the first scream of stunned pain is unleashed.

"Okayyy, okay," John says, reaching for me across the Escalade's embarrassingly gigantic center console.

"Did you know that Dad's still wearing his wedding ring—but not the Connie wedding ring, the Mom wedding ring? Did I tell you that?"

"Huston mentioned it at work today," John says with a gentle smile.

"Do you think he was wearing it the whole time?" I ask, wringing my hands, trying to keep it together.

"From the looks of his house it seems like he spent a pretty significant amount of his time thinking about all of you guys," John soothes.

"Sorry. Abigail lost it today. It's like we're each taking turns," I say, my voice elsewhere.

"Has it been your turn yet?" John asks, treading lightly.

"No," I answer, quickly.

"Right, that'd be lunacy," John says, the smallest smile creeping across his face.

"I mean, have you met me?" I answer, crackling out a laugh.

"So, that just leaves you and Huston, because Leo's basically been crying for the past five years."

"How do you know Huston hasn't lost it?"

"He's like the walking dead these days. Even worse than when Evelyn passed away," John says, trailing off as he says Mom's name.

"I know," I agree, remembering that Huston looked, at the very least, *affected* by Mom's death. With Dad, he's been on autopilot.

"Well..." John leads.

"What?"

"You and Huston are more alike than either one of you will admit."

"I know," I agree, too weak to keep arguing. John looks stunned that I conceded so quickly.

We are quiet. I'm lost in thought. I'm trying to process the big and small events of the last day—no, the last four days. *Four. Days.* Hard to comprehend. Down the rabbit hole, through the wardrobe—however you portray it, dealing with Dad's illness has been like traveling to an alternate universe where time is either stopped or speeding forward. Huge epiphanies combined with seemingly insignificant moments—making each moment feel like another invitation to dine with the Mad Hatter.

I begin speaking before I can edit what I say. "You think life is going to go on forever, that you're going to have all the time in the world to say you're sorry or start over. But you don't. You have hospice and not enough fluids and dusty photographs and little shoes next to the couch and rubber-banded business cards." My voice is detached.

John listens. Quiet.

"Did you know human beings are alone in their knowledge of their own mortality? You'd think knowing we only have a finite amount of time would change the way we live day in and day out...but it doesn't. So arrogant."

"You can't live in fear, Gracie," John offers.

"I wish it were fear. That would, at least, be more interesting. I live in...*feh*. Nothingness," I say, shrugging my shoulders.

"You live in...*feh*?" John repeats.

"I've always loved you...even before I had the right," I start, unable to keep from smiling. John is quiet, not knowing where this is going.

I continue, "And I just walked away." I shrug my shoulders, my eyes focused on a little Webelos nun walking into the St. Teresa's gift shop on the south side of the parking lot, her breath puffing in the cold night air.

John pulls me close. I swing my legs over and literally sit on top of him, my legs teetering on leather seats, bits of John, and some of that 5K muscle finally kicking in. John steadies me, resting his arm on my waist, looking up at me...waiting.

I continue, "I'm being allowed to see my life, that version of my life, like I skipped to the back of the book and can read the ending now."

John brings his other arm to rest on my waist. I slip down and find my knees now on either side of him. Face-to-face.

"And it's not pretty," I say, tears welling up. Finally.

"Gracie—" John tries.

"And I hate that it's happening to Dad...that it happened to

Dad. That he never got the chance to see how his life would turn out before...He should have stayed with Mom. He should have stayed with us. He would have never walked away if he could have seen...if he would have seen...how it all turned out," I say. I choke on my words. My head falls to my chest.

John waits.

I whisper, "My only consolation is that they had a great love."

"Have," John says.

"What?" I say, looking up.

"They *have* great love," John says again.

"How can they *have* it? Mom's gone and Dad's..."

"Just because someone goes away doesn't mean love stops," John says, his voice quiet.

"No?"

"No," he says. So close.

John continues, "Your mom and dad never stopped loving each other. And it's that...that's what's in his heart now."

"I want to believe you so badly."

"How can you even question it? The love you've carried for your mom is beyond belief and it certainly didn't stop the day she passed away," John says, pulling my face up.

"No, it didn't...it didn't," I say, my voice cracking. I know the feeling of being warmed from the inside by someone who's no longer here. That fire never goes out. Ever.

"Of course it didn't," John finishes.

I am quiet. Trying to catch my breath. Find a point on the horizon. Anything to stop the world from spinning.

John continues, "And I hate to break it to you, but even though Ray and Evelyn were definitely the loves of each other's lives, it was probably the four of you that made them both the most proud." His face is hesitant. He's obviously not sure I can handle what he's saying.

I can't.

The tears speed up my throat, from deep within. So deep. So buried. *Intentionally.* I knew my turn would come. I watched it happen to Abigail. I knew it wouldn't be long before I was overtaken. And now, as I finally allow myself to really feel the loss of Mom, I begin to feel this sensation of weightlessness and freedom. A glimmer that I can be whole again. That I might be able to heal. John's arms tighten around me as I begin to mourn a family I didn't know was broken, a father I wish I'd known and a future where I must now go on without parents who loved me more than anything.

"I guess it's officially your turn," John says, as my sobbing finally subsides. The windows of his Escalade are steamed up. To passersby, it probably looks a bit tawdry.

"You saw to that," I say, taking a long, slow breath. I can finally breathe deeply and grab all the air my body has to give. No more Chutes and Ladders. No more compartments and roller coasters. No more obstacles. But instead of feeling empty, I feel... hope.

"You said something about Indian food?" I ask, untangling myself from John. He nods, turning on the ignition.

I continue, "Nothing like a good tikka masala after a mini-breakdown."

chapter twenty-two

"What took you guys so long?" Huston sighs, opening the large wooden front door to his house for John and me. Without traffic, it only took us about forty minutes to get from South Pasadena to the Palisades where Huston insists on living. It's near the beach, he argues. What it's not near is any of us. I think that's probably more of a pull than its proximity to the ocean.

"I had a mini-breakdown in the parking lot," I answer, stepping into the foyer of Huston's house.

"Of the Indian place?" Huston asks, taking some of the bags of Indian food.

"St. Teresa's," I answer. The Spanish tile is buffed a beautiful orangey-red, the arches are high and solid. When I last saw this house it had been taken down to the studs and Huston was living in a tent in the backyard, aka the sandlot in the back of the "fixer-upper" he bought for a few million dollars.

"Why does it matter which parking lot it was?" John asks.

"I guess it doesn't," Huston muses, walking into the kitchen. We follow.

"No, I see where you're going with it. If the breakdown were in the Holy Cow parking lot, it would've been a lot more dramatic. Exposed, somehow," John argues, as we thread through the rooms leading into the kitchen.

"Plays to state of mind," Huston adds. He's wearing a

paint-splattered Harvard Law T-shirt and an old pair of jeans. Bruce Springsteen blares from his iPod and a bottle of Corona sits on the counter.

"Can I get off the stand now?" I sigh, taking in the kitchen. John pulls several take-out boxes and various tinfoiled batches of naan from the plastic bag. Huston turns the music down and walks over to the refrigerator.

"You brought it up," Huston says, passing John and me a couple of beers.

"Something I'll never do again," I say, cracking open the bottle and taking a swig.

Huston laughs. "Oh, please."

"This is nice," I say, looking around the almost completely renovated house. Who needs therapy when you have a kitchen that needs retiling?

"That's right—you haven't seen it since—" Huston answers.

I cut in, "There were walls."

"I burned that tent in a ritualistic pyre after I moved into the main house," Huston says, taking a long swig of his beer and eyeing the food.

"We got you the vindaloo," I say, pointing to an orange-tinged, oozing take-out box.

"I'll get plates," Huston says, reaching up into one of the cupboards.

John and I settle in around the dark wooden table tucked into a little nook in the corner of the kitchen. There are four chairs around it, but it's tucked in so tightly to the nook that only one chair is really functional. John and I wedge ourselves into the other chairs and don't say a thing.

"I had Charlotte collate all the information we were talking about today," John says, loading up his plate with rice.

"Who's Charlotte?" I ask, dumping my tikka masala onto the plate.

"My assistant," John says, tearing off a piece of naan.

"I think that's probably the key to this whole thing," Huston answers, taking a bite of his vindaloo.

"What are you two talking about?" I blurt, my mouth burning with overly spicy Indian fare.

"Whoa," Huston says.

"If you tell me not to have another mini-breakdown I'll—"

"Hawk a giant loogie on me?" Huston laughs, taking another huge bite of his vindaloo.

"I'm definitely not above that," I say, taking a long swig of my beer.

"Your dad set up a bunch of accounts for the little kids: Evie, Matty, and Emilygrae," John says, carefully watching my reaction.

"You okay?" Huston tests.

"Accounts?" I ask, feeling hungry for the answers to as many questions as possible. And with the mini-breakdown clearly in my past, I don't feel that constant threat of impending hysteria looming around every corner.

"Money for college, they were named on life insurance policies—that kind of thing," John answers.

"John thinks it establishes another layer of Dad's...involvement," Huston explains.

"Involvement," I repeat.

"They're going to come after us, but having proof that Ray also wanted to take care of the little ones..." John trails off.

"Shows a purposefulness and integrity to his actions that should stay above the fray," Huston finishes.

"Are we expecting a fray?" I ask, piling my masala and some saffron rice onto a piece of naan. I shove it into my mouth. How long has it been since I've really eaten? I just picked at the sandwich Abigail brought by this afternoon.

"I think Connie made that quite clear," John answers. We all remember the day we got Dad out of St. Joseph's in Ojai. It seems so long ago and the fact that it was just yesterday stuns me.

"I guess I thought that since she had her $113,000 and a town house that she might just slink into the background," I offer.

"She might," Huston answers, taking a swig of his Corona.

"She won't," John cuts in.

"She hasn't been to St. Teresa's. One could argue that if she had big legal plans she would want to, at least, look like she's tried visiting Dad," I argue. Huston nods.

"We were all there that day. Not one of us believes that she's done with this family," John argues, no longer eating.

"I don't know. I have to agree with Grace," Huston starts.

"You have got to be kidding me." John stops, his fork drops to his plate.

"She's all about the endgame. If she wanted to keep this circus going, she would have had to come to St. Teresa's to build the sympathy vote," Huston argues, pointing his rice-clad fork at John.

"We talked about this earlier and I didn't agree then either," John counters.

"It's just a theory."

"Call it what you want," John says, taking a swig of his beer.

"I just called it a theory, so obviously I'm referring to it as such."

"I just want you guys to be prepared," John presses, trying to sit back in his cramped chair.

I smile. "That's why we have you."

"Right," John answers, his face tense.

"We're not deluded, but maybe she's not quite the mastermind we built her up to be," Huston offers, his voice calm.

"Then how do you explain Ojai?" John argues.

"It's an upper-class enclave of about ten thousand people tucked away in the hills of Southern California," I answer, giving a small wink at Huston. He smiles.

"Very funny," John says, his expression easing.

"Let's just eat," I beg.

"Fine," John concedes.

"I'll give you the grand tour when we're done," Huston says. He motions to the rest of the house with his fork.

"I'd like that," I say, beaming at him and relishing the fact that I'm here. John picks up his fork and continues eating. He's quiet while Huston and I chatter on about light fixtures, subway tile and the lavender that's now blooming in his backyard.

"Mateo, get away from that grill!" I yell, standing in a park just down the street from St. Teresa Manor early the next morning. No sign of Connie or Dennis again this morning.

"Yeah, so I was walking in the parking lot last night and happened to see your little sex show," Leo announces, as we watch the kids play. My face flushes red and I immediately want to bury my head in the sandbox.

"We were talking," I say, watching Mateo move over to the climbing structure.

"Yeah, I talk to everyone like that." Leo laughs as Emilygrae joins Mateo on the play structure.

"I had a mini-breakdown," I confess.

"Was it anything like Abigail's?" Leo sighs, shaking his head.

"No," I answer quickly.

"Where did that *come* from?"

"Same place all of ours have come from, I guess."

"All of that...all of that was just in there," Leo theorizes, his eyes elsewhere.

"I know," I sigh.

"Mateo, don't eat the sand!" Leo yells.

Once John dropped me off at St. Teresa's this morning, I asked Abigail if she wanted to spend some time with Dad alone. She agreed, deftly skirting questions about her show of emotion yesterday. She's clearly not comfortable with our thinking she's vulnerable. She quickly jumped into issuing strict orders to wash my hands and said something about getting my taxes in on time. I just nodded and allowed her the moment.

I understand Abigail's hesitation at being alone with Dad. When we huddle in groups in Dad's room, we can hold it together and stay upbeat. But when we're alone with him, whether by accident or on purpose, everything comes crashing down. It's almost an immediate reaction. Walk into room. See you're alone with Dad. Start trying to fend off the growing torrent of sobbing as you end up mumbling something about love and forgiveness under your breath.

Leo and I walked over to the park with the twins soon after. Abigail and Manny thought Evie should go back to school when it started back up after the holiday. Evie responded to their decision by screaming, "That's FINE! It's just that everyone hates me at that GODDAMN school!" Her great moment fizzled when Mateo responded, "I don't think everyone even knows you at that goddamn school." After many stifled giggles and language warnings, Evie flounced off to her room proclaiming that no one understood her.

"Should I be doing some sort of penance? I mean, I feel weird about the whole straddling-John-in-a-Catholic-parking-lot thing," I ask, noticing Mateo in full conversation with himself on the rickety bridge between spiral slides. There's much karate-chopping.

Leo laughs. "That's the most ridiculous sentence I've ever heard."

"I know, right in the middle of it—I was like...stop, STOP, STOP!" I respond, laughing at myself.

"It's the whole life-affirmation thing," Leo argues, now lost in thought.

"I never really understood that."

"Well, it wasn't so much after Mom died, because I think we were all just...well, we all just turned off, didn't we?"

"Yeah," I sigh.

"Roller coasters and skydiving..."

"Piña coladas and getting caught in the rain?" I laugh, finishing Leo's laundry list of life-affirming activities.

"If you like." Leo smiles.

"It just seems creepy to even have these feelings with everything that's happening to...well, with just everything that's happening..." I trail off, remembering another night of passion and "life-affirming" activities with John. I can't help but feel guilty.

"No, it totally makes sense," Leo says, turning his body toward me. "Mortality gives you this bird's-eye view of how you're living your own life."

"I can't even say the word," I whisper.

"What word?" Leo asks. The word *death* stands like the Reaper himself between us.

"I say mortality, too," I say.

"Yeah, well." Leo clears his throat.

"It just seems anti-instinctual."

"Quite the opposite, in point of fact," Leo says, his voice becoming passionate.

"If you start singing 'Circle of Life,' I swear to God," I say with a weary smile.

"It's actually quite relevant," Leo agrees, his mind now lost in theory. I watch the twins go down the big spiral slide one after the other.

"And what about you? Any life-affirming relationships?" I ask, channeling Abigail.

"It's hard to get serious about anyone," Leo says, his voice distant.

"You haven't caught this whole life-affirming thing?" I ask.

"It's almost like I can't even think about it. You go on a date with someone, then there's marriage and kids and...I just don't have any models for that kind of thing," Leo says, his voice detached and cold. Always ten steps ahead, working the equation out way into the future.

"Huston," I suggest, looking at him.

"I know...I thought of that. I think of him a lot."

"A kind of 'What Would Huston Do' sort of thing," I joke.

"I've got little bracelets and everything. WWHD?" Leo laughs.

"It doesn't look like either one of you has made any big commitments, though," I say, getting a bit more serious.

"I know." Leo's voice is quiet.

"There isn't anyone?" I press. Leo looks like he's about ready to burst. He speaks quickly.

"There's this really cool physics professor from Delhi. Amazing theories on how th—" Leo stops dead as we both hear the screaming coming from the play structure. The twins.

We get up and run over to where Mateo is trapped on the spiral slide by an oversized rat of a dog. It's barking, sniffing and nipping at the terrified little boy. *Our* terrified little boy. Leo picks up Emilygrae and I swoop in and pick Mateo up from the spiral slide, nudging the dog back. Mateo's cries subside as I smooth his hair and tell him it's okay...it's okay...it's okay. The dog is nipping me as I stand there. Every time its wet nose touches my leg, I get angrier. Mateo was terrified. Mateo *is* terrified. I look around for Rat Dog's owner.

"He's friendly! He's friendly!" A woman in a flowing ensemble of scarves and linen approaches like a gypsy in an open-air market somewhere in the desert sands of Arabia.

"Come get your dog," I say, my voice loud and clear. Leo and Emilygrae walk over to the benches. I gather Mateo even closer.

"Oh, he's friendly!" the woman keeps repeating, getting closer and closer.

"Whether you think your dog is friendly or not has nothing to do with how terrified my nephew is. Just come and get him," I say, as the woman wrangles the Rat Dog at my feet. Her scarves and linen don't quite cover up the doughy roll around her midriff.

"It's okay, though. No harm done," she says, standing up, her dog still not on a leash. The dog sniffs at my feet and charges up again at Mateo. Mateo squeals and clutches my neck tighter. The woman lets out a little chuckle. I hold Mateo tighter and closer.

"Can you hold your dog? Leo, can you come get Matty?" I start, yelling over my shoulder at Leo, who's coming up fast, his arms wide, ready to engulf little Mateo. The woman pets her Rat Dog, mumbling something about it being friendly and how I need to "loosen up." I hand Mateo over to Leo and wait. Wait for them to get out of earshot.

"I'm sorry your boy doesn't like dogs," the woman finally offers as some kind of backward attempt at an apology.

"What are you thinking? This isn't your backyard, lady. This isn't even a dog park," I start, stepping toward her.

"You don't need to—" The woman's face flushes red.

"What I *need* to do is go see if that little boy is okay after your dumb-ass dog traumatized him. That's what I *need* to do," I spit.

"My dumb-a—" the woman repeats.

"Leash your dog up and get out of here. We clear?" I say, inches from her face.

"I . . . I'm sorry your boy was upset," the woman mutters.

"I'm sorry you're a shitty dog owner," I say, staring her down. Unblinking, I rest my hands at my hips and wait. The woman pulls a tiny pink leash from a quilted fanny pack pulled taut at her waist. She clips the leash on the Rat Dog's collar and starts off across the sand.

"Your language . . ." the woman starts.

"My language? Your dog mauls my nephew and you're worried about my goddamn language?!" I say, stepping forward again.

"He didn't *maul* him," the woman whispers as she hurries out of the sand pit toward the path that leads out of the park. I can see her mouthing something to Rat Dog—something about the "mean lady."

"Have a great day!!" I yell, giving a big wave to the woman. I look over at the benches where Leo and the kids are watching. I give a big smile to Mateo and he beams back at me, giving me a giant thumbs-up. My smile gets even bigger.

"You did it, Tia Gwacie!" Emilygrae yells, her arms shooting high in the air as she jumps down from the bench. Mateo gives her a triumphant high five.

"They have special parks for dogs," Mateo announces.

"This isn't one of them," I say.

"She should put that dog in the special park," Emilygrae adds.

"I'll tell that lady where she can put her dog," I mutter under my breath.

"Grace," Leo warns. The kids run back over to the play structure. I settle in next to Leo.

"'I'm sorry you're a shitty dog owner'?" Leo repeats with a smirk.

"They couldn't hear, could they?" I ask.

"No . . . I could kind of make it out, but I'm sure they don't know half the words you were using." Leo laughs. My Black-Berry rings from my jacket pocket. I pull it out and check the caller ID. Abigail.

"Hello?"

"They've called a priest."

chapter twenty-three

P lease, Gracie. Please come, hurry," Abigail chokes.

"Huston. What about Huston?" I ask, gesturing at Leo to round up the kids. He hops up and bolts over to the play structure. I can already hear their protests.

"He's already here. He's already here. Please, Gracie, we need you here," Abigail pleads.

"We're on our way. We're on our way."

Leo and I finally get to Dad's room after waiting in the sunroom for Manny's parents to take the twins. Where, I have no idea, just away from here. Far away from here. John is standing in the hallway already. The priest is just leaving. We've seen him around St. Teresa's before, roaming the halls in a hospital gown and boxers. He's a patient here, too. As he walks out of Dad's room, I notice he's added an elaborate robe and sash to his usual costume, both askew and thrown on. Just underneath? Shower sandals.

"Hey," John says, as Leo continues on into the room. John's eyes lock on mine.

"What the hell happened?" I whisper. I knew this was coming. We all knew this was coming. But it is still somehow shocking.

"I don't know...I don't know," John answers, his voice urgent and a little frustrated—as if he should have all the answers. I take his hand. I breathe in...this is what civilized people do. *Oh God*. Breathe. John and I walk in together.

"I got a call," Huston says to Leo, standing at Dad's bedside, his entire face creased in worry. Abigail is holding on to Manny as she stands on the right side of Dad's bed.

"We were here all morning," I say, taking my place at the end of Dad's bed, John at my side. Dad looks particularly gaunt today. Particularly weak. Particularly sick.

"I have the power of attorney. They had to call me first," Huston explains, stroking Dad's arm.

"What happened?" Leo blurts, staring at Abigail and Huston.

"Dr. O'Rourke noticed that he was looking bloated, so they checked his urine output and it's just . . . stopped," Huston says.

"Stopped?" I ask, taking in Dad's shrinking frame. All that talk about speech therapists and physical therapy seems so . . . naively optimistic now.

"His body is shutting down," Abigail finishes, dabbing at her eyes with a tissue. Manny pulls her close. Dad rumbles into the oxygen mask. His eyes are darting around the room, finding each one of our faces. We are each there for him.

"Is he in pain?" My voice dipping as I question Abigail, Huston . . . somebody?

"I don't know . . . Dad? Dad? Are you in much pain?" Abigail asks, leaning down.

"He answers yes to—" Huston begins, but he's stunned into silence by Dad's sudden, but very precise movements in response to Abigail's question. Dad lifts his body up, looking Abigail dead in the eye, and nods his head yes . . . yes . . . yes.

"You're in pain, Dad?" Huston presses, knowing what we all know. That if he answers yes to everything, this might be because he's suffered a stroke. Or is this the real deal? We also know, from our Hospice 101 meeting, that at this stage once Dad starts receiving morphine for his pain . . . well, it could suppress his breathing and . . . But Dad was very specific about this in his power of attorney. The plan for the next couple of days was set down years ago in a tiny lawyer's office in Ojai. None of us were invited to that meeting, but we're the ones who now have to carry it out.

The weight of what Dad is asking us to do is overwhelming.

Dad lifts himself up using Huston's hand as leverage, gets inches from his face and nods yes...yes...yes. He tries to say something, but it just comes out a rumbling line of gibberish. John's hand is closed around mine, his arm looped around me. All the emotions. God...he's pleading with us. Pleading with us to make the pain stop.

"Go get Sister Carmella," Abigail instructs Leo. Leo bolts out of the room.

"We're going to go find someone, Dad. We're going to go find someone," Huston says, leaning down next to Dad.

Dad nods, nods, nods his way back down on his pillow, closing his eyes once he lands. Like he's just expended his last burst of energy to tell us how much pain he's in. Huston looks at the door. Waiting. His eyes are steely and resolved. I watch as Abigail fusses with Dad's blanket, making sure it's perfect.

Is this it?

"Is everything okay?" Sister Carmella floats into the room, her little Webelos nun outfit clean and crisp.

"Dad's in pain. He said he's in pain," Huston says, his voice resolute.

"Raymond? Hello, my son...it's Sister Carmella. Are you hurting?" I choke out a sob. She's so gentle. So loving. Oh, God...this is it. I squeeze John's hand and turn to him. My eyes are pleading with him to answer my question. Is this it? John presses out a smile and pulls me closer. I take a long inhale and steady myself. Resolve myself.

Dad rears up once more, higher than ever, grabs onto Huston's hand, stares directly at Sister Carmella and nods, nods, nods.

Yes. Yes. Yes. And launches into a passionate tirade of nonsense. Sister Carmella gently rests one of her hands on Dad's forearm. Listening and nodding her head as he winds his way through his nonsensical speech. He finishes by pointing weakly at his body and nodding yes...yes...yes. He's hurting everywhere.

"Okay, Raymond. Okay...I'll take care of it. We'll take care of it," Sister Carmella soothes, smoothing his gray-blond hair. Dad exhales loudly, letting go of Huston's hand and lying back down. He's still nodding, nodding, nodding. He's trying to make eye contact with each of us. We all pull ourselves together and each nod back. Eyes clear, smiles easy, faces calm.

"We're all here, Dad," Huston soothes. Dad blinks his eyes closed, closed, closed.

Sister Carmella floats out of Dad's room, no doubt to return with the hospice team. With the morphine drip. How are we supposed to know how to do this? Bury our dad...bury our parents. We watched a video, read pamphlets, and were given phone numbers to call if we had further questions. They used phrases like *relief of suffering* and *dignity for the dying*. I guess it doesn't matter how prepared we thought we were. No field guide in the world could have prepared us. No field guide in the world could make it easier for sons and daughters to say goodbye to their parents.

Sister Carmella leaves us alone with Dad. We're all looking around wondering how we landed here. How we got here so quickly. It's been a little under a week and we thought...well, we thought we'd all make it out alive.

We didn't know we were going to leave a man behind.

But Dad's ready. He's ready not to be in pain anymore. He's ready to stop fighting. He's ready to be with Mom. He is quiet, seeming to sleep.

We all stand still. Holding our breath, trying to look anywhere but at each other. My hand is sweaty and clammy in John's.

"I thought he was going to make it," Huston whispers, his face blank and stunned. Abigail lets out the smallest of yelps as she swallows down her sobs. I breathe in, looking at Huston. He looks sixteen again as he clutches at Dad's hand. His eyes clear, his face almost mesmerized.

"We all did," I answer.

"You did?" Huston asks, looking up from Dad.

"Sure." Abigail's voice is just above a whisper.

"I thought we'd have at least twenty more years with him," I add.

"Maybe . . . maybe this is just. . . ." Leo trails off.

We fall into silence.

"I don't want him to be in pain anymore," Leo concedes, almost to himself, stepping closer still. The equations are just not adding up in his head.

"None of us do," I say, looking up at Leo. I hold my hand out. Leo shuffles over to me and takes it. I get a flash of Mom's funeral. Huston remains quiet and awestruck. He's clutching at Dad's hand as if that will keep him connected to the known world. We're here again. We're here again.

"Kids?" Sister Carmella floats back in to the room to sniffles, runny noses, red eyes and ragged breathing. She's followed by a young man in a pair of cargo shorts and a polo shirt with the hospice company's insignia on it.

We all look up. The hospice man takes Dad's chart and reads it carefully. I look at Dad. I just . . . I . . . I want to shout, "I LOVE YOU! I LOVE YOU!"

But as I look around at his four children, I finally get what love is. It's not a word you say or something you write in a greeting card. It's a climate-changing phenomenon. Love . . . *true* love . . . saturates. When you really feel love for someone, the last thing you need to do is say it. It's not bound by life or death.

Dad can feel it. We can feel it. Mom felt it. We don't have to say anything.

We're all covered in it.

"Do you want to say the rosary?" Sister Carmella offers. The hospice man takes the morphine drip out of a large plastic bin with HAWKES written on the side. Huston lets out a long sigh. I finally let the tears fall. And fall. Dad knows we love him. I can only hope to have this outpouring when I take my last breath. I look around the room in that instant and know that I now will.

"He'd like that," Huston answers. Sister Carmella walks up to Dad's bedside, squeezing next to Huston so she's closest to Dad's face.

"Raymond, you get to go home now. Raymond? It's okay. You get to fly up to Evelyn now," Sister Carmella says, loud and clear. She knows our time is limited with Dad and she has absolutely no qualms about being perfectly clear about what's happening. She needs him to know he's dying.

"In the name of the Father..." Sister Carmella starts, making the sign of the cross. We all bow our heads, trying to mumble along with her, sobbing and sniffling. The hospice man hooks the morphine drip onto the now empty metal stand next to Dad's bed.

"...The communion of saints." Sister Carmella's voice is calm. Dad's eyes are locked on to Sister Carmella, then over to Huston. The hospice man clips the morphine drip into Dad's already existing IV.

"...The forgiveness of sins." Huston gently holds Dad's hand, his eyes clear and bright. He stands tall as Dad focuses in on his eldest son's easy smile. Not one tear falls down Huston's unwavering face. Strong. Stalwart. Steadfast.

"...The resurrection of the body." Dad is blinking, blinking, blinking. Huston holds on as Dad's eyes close. Leo and Abigail both look up. Abigail sinks into Manny. He cries silently as Abigail pulls at him, her movements angry and violent. Letting go.

"And life everlasting." I hold on to John. His face is blotchy, his lips tight and compressed. Leo lets out a long, throaty sob as he squeezes my hand.

"Amen," Sister Carmella finishes. I take a deep breath.

"Our Father, Who art in Heaven; hallowed be Thy name." Sister Carmella's hands busily move around her rosary. Dad is quiet. Peaceful.

The hospice man checks the morphine drip, pressing on the bag, watching the drip-drip-drip, and quietly leaves.

"Hail Mary, full of grace..."

chapter twenty-four

"I t was really a beautiful service," the older man says to Abigail as he extends his hand to her.

"Thank you. Please...make yourself at home. The food and beverages are in the kitchen," Abigail answers, pointing to her kitchen like a game show presenter. The man nods and moves into Abigail's house.

"Who are these people?" I whisper.

"I think that was one of Dad's friends, played bass or something," Abigail says, smiling to a group of black-clad people coming through the front door. She says *bass* with particular contempt.

"That was actually his old boss at the newspaper," Huston says, briefly falling in beside me. He absently smiles to the older be-scarved couple who just walked in. They smile at us with concern. The percentage of "hep cats" in attendance this evening is alarmingly high. And by "hep cat," I mean an aging gentleman who fancies himself Miles Davis by night and toils in corporate America by day. We can spot these guys easily by their choice of accessories: either an ascot or a tweed fedora. Someone sporting both is an obvious slam dunk.

"Very touching funeral. The sisters did a great job," some random woman says to me as I stand next to the fireplace in Abigail's living room. I look up and see Laura and Slip Is Showing from the office standing red-eyed in front of me. What are they doing here?

"I'm so sorry for your loss," Slip Is Showing says, lunging at me for a hug. Abigail watches the exchange. I pull back from the woman as Abigail extends her hand. I panic, realizing I don't know this woman's name.

"Abigail Hawkes-Rodriguez," Abigail says, taking Slip Is Showing's hand. Laura looks on.

"Evelyn. Evelyn Connor," Slip Is Showing says. Holy shit. Doesn't take a team of psychologists—no wonder I could never remember it.

"Laura Zabala," Laura says, extending her hand to Abigail.

"Thank you so much for coming. There's food and drink in the kitchen," she says, as the women walk to the kitchen.

"Hm," I say, warming to the two women as I watch them pour themselves a glass of wine.

"Friends of yours?" Abigail asks. We are more than a little exhausted and our demeanors reflect fatigue combined with a punchiness that comes with having nothing to lose. We've been through parental loss boot camp—*twice*—and I don't know how we're going to start over, but I do know that we're going to do it together.

"Yeah, I guess they are," I answer.

"Nice rack," Leo whispers, leaning over.

"Really?" I laugh, motioning at the legion of black-clad mourners that surround us.

"Life-affirming even," Leo adds, smiling. It feels so good to smile. I hear Huston chuckle, now at the far end of the receiving line. He's been distant and zombielike since Dad passed away. We've all been concerned that he hasn't really processed what's happened. Not that we're ones to talk. I find myself laughing one minute and sobbing the next. Usually in public. Which, I've found, can be a bit off-putting to bystanders.

Huston circles back to us. "I talked to the attorney today," he starts. We all smile at a passing woman who looks very concerned for our well-being. We don't know her. We've never known her. We smile back and nod, letting her know we're fine. *Fine*.

"And?" Abigail presses.

"He's started the probate, filed the necessary papers."

"Any word from Connie?" Leo asks.

"Nothing," Huston answers in a voice as devoid of feeling as his face.

"Does she think she's going to be able to just stay in that condo forever with Dad's money?" Abigail asks, pointing out the bathroom to an ascoted gentleman with long, stringy hair drawn back into a ponytail.

"I'm thinking that it really wouldn't be that bad of a situation. I talked to the attorney today about maybe setting up a trust for her," Huston admits.

"What, why?" Leo demands, the tinkling of the ambient music in the background taking some of the edge off his harsh response.

"She's his wife, whether we like it or not," I add, not caring where she lives. Dad's gone. She can't hurt us anymore.

"So, she's rewarded for lying," Abigail says, taking a long drink of her wine.

"It's over," Huston finishes, his voice distant.

"It was a lovely ceremony," a young woman says, shaking each of our hands.

"Thank you," we each say, as she grasps our hand.

"It's just not fair," Leo fusses.

"There's food and drink in the kitchen," Abigail says, pointing the woman to where the sweets are.

"Lovely ceremony," an older couple says, lovingly shaking each one of our hands.

"Thank you," we all say, as they grasp our hands.

"There's food and drink in the kitchen," Abigail repeats, pointing the couple to the kitchen.

"Then Dad should have divorced her," I say.

"Which he didn't," Huston adds.

"So we're stuck with her?" Leo asks.

"She'll be in Ojai. We'll be down here. I don't think that's really being 'stuck' with someone," Huston says soothingly.

"Beautiful ceremony." I look up. John.

"Oh, thank you," Abigail answers as he pulls her in for a hug.

"That was a beautiful eulogy; your dad would have been proud," John says to Huston, pulling him in for a hug. Huston claps him on the back and breaks from him quickly.

"Thanks, man," Huston says, his eyes averted.

"I'm so sorry for your loss," another woman says to Huston, as John moves in front of me.

"You doing okay?" John asks, pulling me in for a hug. I tuck in and smell the starch from his shirt, breathing it in.

"I'm so glad you're here," I say, straightening his lapel. John smiles and falls in just next to me.

A young man approaches Huston. "I'm so sorry for your loss."

"Thank you," Huston says, extending his hand.

"Huston Hawkes?" the young man presses, bringing his hand around.

"Yes," Huston answers.

"You've been served," the young man says, putting a blue-backed legal document, instead of a sympathetic handshake, into Huston's hand.

"What? What did you just say?" Huston fumes, grabbing the guy's hand and pulling him back. His entire body resembles a volcano. Time stops as we are all helpless against his imminent eruption.

"You've been served," the young man repeats, his voice dripping with unfounded righteousness.

"The fuck I have," Huston yells, swinging his fist around and connecting with the young man's face. The young man is thrown back against the floor. The crowd scatters—gasps of surprise and screams of horror fill Abigail's living room.

"Whoaaa, okay...okay." I jump in between the two men as John holds Huston back. The young man wheels up, lunges at Huston and connects with the right side of my face. A flash of pain shoots through my body and I hear my voice cry out, but far away. Somewhere out there. I hit the living room floor and immediately bring my hands to my face. Wet. Something is wet.

"Get the kids out! Get the kids out!" Abigail shouts at Manny. He gathers the little ones quickly. The crowd herds into the kitchen.

"Take him. TAKE. HIM," John yells, handing Huston over to Leo and quickly "escorting" the young man outside.

"Serve me at my father's wake?! You're going to SERVE ME AT MY FATHER'S WAKE?!" Huston screams, crawling over Leo—his voice now cracking and wrenching.

As Abigail hunches down over me with a wet rag from the kitchen, I hear what sounds like someone hitting a side of beef. Over and over again. Grunts and moans from just outside. And then a slammed door.

"You okay?" John says, coming into focus.

"Something's wet. Someone spilled their drink," I say, looking at Abigail. Fix it. Fix it, Abigail.

"You're bleeding, sweetie," Abigail soothes, taking a bag of ice from Manny and putting it on my eye. I recoil.

"Yowwww," I mewl, grabbing John's hand. Pulling at him. Tugging at him.

"Okay...you're going to be okay," John soothes.

"Where's Huston?" I ask, looking around the room. Abigail presses the ice bag against my face and scans the room as well. No Huston. She motions to Manny to get things back on track. Leo is crouching on the floor, picking up the scattered papers. No Huston.

"Wine, anyone? Anyone want wine?" Manny offers, grabbing a bottle of red wine off the table. Everyone jumps at the offering. Leo passes the papers to John. He takes them and helps me off the floor as we all follow Abigail into another, more private part of the house.

"Was I just punched in the face at my father's wake?" I mumble, pulling the bag of ice off my eye. John is seething. All he can muster in response is a low growl. We file into the twins' bedroom just off the living room. I re-situate the bag of ice as Abigail closes the door behind us.

Huston is slumped against the wall, his face hidden in his now bloodied hands. His sobs are wrenching and bottomless. Abigail immediately goes to him.

"Oh, Huston..." she starts, sitting down next to him. He crumbles into her, sobbing.

"I really thought he was going to get better," Huston says, over and over again.

"We all did," Abigail says calmingly, smoothing his hair, cradling him. Huston looks up, his face wild.

"They're both gone," Huston cries. Leo claps his hand over his mouth. He's paralyzed. "We're on the front line, Abby. If she wants to come at us, we've got no one. We're it. Dad's gone," Huston wails. I set the ice bag down on the alphabet rug on the twins' bedroom floor and kneel in front of Huston. Abigail watches.

"We've got this," I say, my face close to Huston's.

"Grace . . . it's just us," Huston sobs.

"And that's plenty. We can do this," I say, pulling his face up. His tearstained face is red and blotchy. I lock eyes with him. I am focused. Resolute. And my goddamn eye is killing me.

"He didn't make it," Huston whispers.

"I know," I say, pulling him in for a hug. He envelops me. I can feel his body shuddering and convulsing, but I hold tight.

"We've got this," I whisper, over and over again in his ear. I break from Huston, sitting next to him on the floor of the bedroom. Leo hands me the ice bag and I put it back on my eye, acting like I'm not about to vomit from the pain. Huston picks up a Transformer off the floor and busily changes it from Optimus Prime to a semitruck, Optimus Prime, now back to a semitruck, and on and on. The transformations are violent and brutal. His nervous energy clicks with each and every transformation. Tears still stream down his face as I set my hand atop his. I pull Optimus Prime away from Huston and take his hand in mine. We look at John.

"It's a will contest," John reads, focusing on the papers. Huston tries to catch his breath, shaking out his fists. Each one of us was served with a subpoena by the interloping (now bloodied) party crasher—a single-page document that compels us to testify at the hearing on Connie's will contest. I can't help but think about dinner at Huston's. We were so naive. John was the only one who saw this coming. "It's in Ventura court. In less than a month."

"What . . . I don't understand," Abigail says. We all try to focus. Huston wipes at his face, taking a long deep breath, and stands. He attempts to collect himself as he walks over to John. Even his gait is modified by his anguish. Everyone takes note that Huston may have survived the Big One, but we're all in for a few more of his emotional aftershocks before the night is over. Huston settles in and scans the documents over John's shoulder. We all warily look on.

"She wants to invalidate Dad's will, so she gets everything—like there was no will at all," John says, wincing at the sight of what must be my quickly swelling face. Or it could be the stench that fills the room from a giant red-and-blue guinea pig cage, along with the squealing whistles of the furry bag of an animal now cowering within.

"What? How?" Abigail asks, now standing. She's begun picking up the twins' strewn clothes off the floor.

"She's basing her petition on the grounds that we exerted undue influence over Dad," Huston reads, his voice now steady.

"What does that mean?" Leo blurts, pacing the tiny blue-and-pink room.

"It means she's trying to say that you somehow cajoled Ray into leaving you everything. She…well, here in her declaration, she states that you threatened to withhold your love and—" John stops and shakes his head, his eyes continuing to scan the following lines.

"Withhold our love…what?" I press.

"That you basically held your love hostage until he folded and guaranteed you an inheritance," John explains.

"That's what Dennis was blathering about in the hospital room. Remember?" I say, placing the bag of ice back on my eye.

"Well, it's not true," Leo says. Thank *you*, Professor Einstein.

"Of course it's not true, but she's a little old lady and—" John explains, going into lawyer mode again.

"I know, and we're the gold-digging ne'er-do-wells," I finish for him bitterly.

"We talked about how that's how she's going to paint you," John reminds me.

"But we weren't in contact with Dad. That's so...He didn't want anything to do with us," Abigail finally admits, flipping Emilygrae's comforter up and over her unmade bed. The throng of stuffed animals, books, and action figures strewn around that tiny bed is staggering. Even a girl as tiny as my niece must have to do contortions to get a comfortable night's sleep in it. With one swoop of the comforter, though, all the child paraphernalia disappears. As we all watch Abigail fuss with Emilygrae's bed, she looks up. "I cleaned the rest of the house. I...I didn't think anyone would come in here," she apologizes, fluffing Emilygrae's pillows. Leo pats her shoulder and I shoot her what I hope is a comforting look—though with my now swelling eye, it probably missed the mark totally. I almost certainly look like Popeye the Sailor Man beseeching Abigail for a can of spinach.

"Connie doesn't know we weren't in contact with Dad," I say.

"Connie doesn't know shit," Leo spits, taking the legal document from John. He flips page after page. Huston folds his arms and watches.

"We'll call Dad's attorney. He can speak to Dad's state of mind and the whole process," I say. Huston nods.

"Can you handle this?" Huston asks John.

"Hell, yeah," John says.

We are silent except for the crowd noise from just outside the twins' bedroom door and the settling ice. Leo reads on.

"She claims we stole her money...that we broke into her home and stole property from her and changed the locks. Oh my God, she's talking about the Madonna," Leo says, looking up from the document.

"She's not talking about the Madonna. She didn't even notice the Madonna. She's talking about the documents we took from Dad's office," I answer.

"She says that we banned her from seeing Dad. That we intentionally moved him a hundred miles away so they couldn't be together," Leo reads, his voice growing more and more hysterical. Huston takes the document back.

"Don't," he urges, trying to calm Leo.

"Oh my God, that's why they never came and visited him, we should have guessed what they were up to," Leo realizes, flopping onto Emilygrae's toy-riddled bed. I sneak a look at John. He knew.

"Honey, it's all lies," Abigail soothes, sitting down next to Leo and wrapping her arm around him. Abigail's eyes implore Huston to say something.

"What do we do now?" Leo asks, his voice tiny. All eyes fall on Huston.

"We have to prove that we didn't influence Dad," I say. I look to Huston with my one good eye. He's right there with me.

"The only way we can argue we didn't exert undue influence over Dad is to prove that we weren't in each other's lives," Huston adds, still looking at me.

"We have to prove that he abandoned us," I realize, shaking my head at the terrible irony of it all. Leo whimpers on the bed.

"And that he wanted nothing to do with us while he was alive," Huston adds.

"What? Wait . . . what? We have to do what?" Abigail asks.

"How can that help?" Leo demands.

"Undue influence means that absent your taking such unfair advantage of him, Ray would have left everything to Connie, his rightful heir," John explains, taking the document from Huston and going through it.

"How can she even say that? Dad was clear that he wanted her left nothing," Leo says.

"Of course, but she's going to stick with the scenario I painted back at the hospital. They were the loves of each other's lives, spent every moment together, yet had some understanding about keeping separate residences," John explains, flipping another page of the document.

"But, what about the will, though? He *omitted* her, remember," Leo interrupts. John looks up.

"Undue influence. She'll say that Ray went into his attorney's office in a fugue state, willing to do whatever it took to woo you four back into his life. That you all conned him into drafting that will and, in so doing, cheated Connie out of her rightful inheritance as his wife," John recites automatically, his eyes trained on the document.

"Right," Huston agrees, nodding to John. "It's going to take more than that."

"We have all those documents," I say, looking at John. He nods, but . . .

"We're going to have to prove that Dad was a shitty father?" Leo asks, imploring us to shake him out of this nightmare.

We are silent until a quiet knock on the door startles us back into reality.

We're at Dad's wake.

Evie pokes her head in. "Mom?"

"Hi, mija." Abigail smiles, perfectly composed. She approaches the door.

"People are asking where you are," Evie says, her eyes falling on me and my ice–bag–covered face. Her entire face creases with worry. Abigail quickly herds Evie out into the living room. Huston is seething. His anger fills the room.

"What is it?" I finally ask.

"Probate court is a court of equity. That means the judge can do pretty much whatever he or she wants—to make it come out the way he or she wants. And Connie's a very sympathetic figure. She's going to try to drag this out as long as she can. We can't prove any of it," he says flatly.

"We have all those documents and the will. The attorney can testify to Ray's state of mind," John argues.

"Yeah, but we can't. She's right, we *don't* know him!" Huston shouts, his voice catching. His breakdown too soon in the past and this aftershock hitting sooner than anyone thought.

"Huston," I say gently. Leo quickly closes the door to the hallway.

"We barely know each other anymore," Huston adds.

"We got to know Dad...in the end," I offer.

"Yeah, and then he..." Huston stops, motioning into the living room.

"He wanted us to handle his affairs. And that's what we're going to do," Leo says.

"Then why...why did he leave us with this mess? And how are we supposed to go up there and swear under penalty of perjury that we know anything about Ray Hawkes? I don't know the first goddamn thing. Do you?!"

"Ironically that's just what we have to testify about. That we don't know anything about him and that we don't know why he left us everything. But he did." I am alone in my fearlessness of Huston. I approach him readily.

"What kind of man does that? What kind of man does that?" Huston repeats. Abigail comes bursting back into the room. John and I lock eyes—or *eye*, as the case may be.

"I can hear you out in the living room," she hisses.

"What kind of man does that?" Huston repeats. Abigail immediately softens. John gives me a quick nod and exits the twins' room, closing the door behind him.

Just. Us. Four.

"I guess we'll never know," I say. If only that mythical trunk of journals existed.

"Isn't there supposed to be some deathbed confessional? Why didn't he tell us why?" Huston erupts.

I set the bag of ice on the bedside table and approach Huston. I don't quite know how to comfort him. He's so physically large, there's no way to encircle him. I take his hand, and he grips it tightly, looking down at me, his eyes pleading with me to just leave him alone. From the other side, I see Abigail taking his other hand and looping it around her shoulder. She holds him tightly around his waist. Huston pulls her in closely. Leo walks over, wraps one arm around Abigail and the other around me, pulling me in snug. I let go of Huston's hand and thread my arm around Huston's waist, resting my head on his chest. Huston breathes deeply and gives Leo a quick kiss on the top of his head. He tightens around us all.

"My *eye*," I whimper.

"He's going to get lost, you know? The Dad we were starting to know is going to get lost in all of this," Huston whispers, his voice rumbling in his chest. We all look up from all around him and it's a race to see who can say it first.

"No, he won't," I say first.

"We won't let him," Leo adds.

"That bitch is going down," Abigail proclaims.

And Huston smiles . . . just a little.

chapter twenty-five

"Swear the witness in," the judge orders.

Connie steps into the witness box at the front of the courtroom, remains standing and raises her right hand.

"Do you swear to tell the truth, the whole truth and nothing but the truth, so help you God?" the clerk asks.

"I do," Connie answers. I half expect her to burst into flames.

"You may be seated," the judge instructs.

"State your name for the record, please. And spell it," the tightly wound clerk says.

"Constance Hawkes," Connie answers.

"Spell it, please," the clerk says. Leo shifts on the bench next to me, his foot kicking, kicking, kicking me. All the time. I see that Dennis is in the front row on the other side. I wonder what he's going to say . . . he was like a father to me?

"C-O-N-S-T-A-N-C-E. H-A-W-K-E-S," Connie rattles off. I'm surprised she can even spell it, she probably never uses it except when she thinks it'll help her case.

"You may proceed, Counsel," the judge urges, looking at Connie's attorney. I crane my neck past Abigail and Huston to get a look at the guy who filed declaration after sob-sister declaration that each sound like a spurned lover's late-night wine-soaked rant to nowhere. They're so personal, I imagine turning to the last page and finding that her attorney has scrawled, "I'm the best thing that ever happened to you!!"

"Mrs. Hawkes, where do you reside?" the attorney starts, his stark black hair unmoving, his wattle moving enough for everyone.

"Nine twenty-four Dean Street in Ojai, California," Connie answers, her voice calm.

"And are you married?" the attorney asks, leaning up against the bar that separates the courtroom from the seating for the masses.

"I was married. I'm a widow now," Connie says, moving her body forward so she can speak clearly into the microphone.

"To whom?"

"Ray Hawkes."

"How long have you been married to Ray Hawkes?"

"Almost five years," Connie answers, her voice catching.

"Were you happily married?"

"I searched my whole life for Ray, found him when I was...well, let's just say I found him when I was no spring chicken. I didn't think I'd ever find true love, but I did. We were everything to each other," Connie oozes.

"So, you've lived together all those years?"

"Yes." Liar! Ignoring my silent accusation, her lawyer continues smoothly.

"Why don't you describe a typical day for the two of you for us?"

"Well, we'd sit and have coffee and read the morning newspaper. Talk about our day, what we had planned, maybe do a little shopping. Sometimes in the late afternoons we'd play board games in front of the fire, take walks through town. Every once in a while we'd entertain, have dinner parties for our friends, go out to a movie or the playhouse. I just love the art shows, and God bless him, Ray would just let me drag him anywhere. It was idyllic. We were inseparable." Connie's voice cracks. Our four mouths drop open in unison.

"I have to ask then, why did you maintain separate residences?"

"We didn't, really. Ray bought me the town house early in our marriage. We were having a few difficulties early on. Adjustments. He bought the town house for me then," Connie answers.

"And since then?"

"Like I said, idyllic. That short time apart showed us how deep our love was for each other. It brought home how much we needed and loved each other every day from then on," Connie says. The entire courtroom sighs. The four of us are steely. I can see the back of John's head from here. He is unmoving. Solid. He told us to remain neutral. It's making the hardest thing I'm ever going to have to do that much harder.

"This must be very hard for you. Take your time," her attorney says.

"No, please. I have to do right by Ray. He would do the same for me. He was always so strong," Connie says.

"I realize this is a difficult question and I'm sorry to keep pressing it, but after your short separation, why did you two keep the town house?" the attorney asks.

"Ray said that it was a good investment and sometimes Dennis, my son, would stay there when we celebrated the holidays or when he would come up on long weekends together. Ray and I loved having people visit from out of town, and the town house worked really well as accommodations for all of our guests," Connie oozes. The four of us haven't moved. Neutral. Neutral.

"Mrs. Hawkes," the attorney starts.

"Connie, please," she demurs.

"Connie, will you let me know if you have to take a break. I know this is upsetting and tiring for you," the attorney says again.

"No, no...as I said, I've got to be strong for Ray. No one else here cares about him or what he wanted," Connie says. Breathe. Breathe.

"I realize this is difficult, but I need to ask you some hard questions, so bear with me, and again if we need a recess so you can rest, just let me know."

"Go ahead."

"Ray's children have told the court that you and Ray separated six months after you got married and haven't lived under the same roof since," the attorney says, in a voice that betrays how ridiculous he finds this notion.

Connie breaks down. "That's just not true . . . we were everything to each other. It's just not true . . . I don't know why they would tell such lies."

"Well, that's why we're here," the attorney soothes. The entire courtroom turns around and looks at us. I look straight forward.

"That was the only dark cloud over our marriage. Ray just wanted those kids to love him, to be a part of his life again. So badly . . . so badly that he'd do anything," Connie says, her eyes welling with tears.

"Anything indeed," the attorney agrees.

"And finally, the hardest question of all, after all those years of love and tenderness and togetherness, why didn't Ray choose to leave you anything in his will?" the attorney asks gently.

Connie convulses and lets her head fall into her hands. She raises a single finger, asking for the court to give her a second to collect herself. The clerk hands her a tissue. She dabs at her tears and finally raises her head to speak.

"I've thought and thought about this since my Ray passed. And I have to think that they somehow played on his guilt to the point of . . . he . . . he must have been seeing them. They must have come up here. Maybe when I was visiting Dennis in Oxnard, as I often do. Ray knew I didn't approve of those kids, they were horrible to him, already put one parent in the grave and now they were working on the other. And there was nothing Ray could do. That woman brought them up hating him, and now all they know is to hate and manipulate. But, they must have found out...that one...that oldest one is a lawyer, not the kid that's a criminal, but that one who's a lawyer probably did a search...and found out that Ray's poor mother had died. And sure enough, that's when they started rubbing their hands together and figuring out how they were going to break my poor Ray's heart and get him to leave all his money to them out of some misplaced sense of guilt and shame. They...they must have started working on him right after his mother died. Pounced on him right away. He...he never had a chance." Connie crumbles into a fit of tears.

"Your Honor, no more questions, but I'd like to take a break before Mrs. Hawkes has to endure a cross-examination. And at her age..." the attorney asks.

"Of course. We'll reconvene in fifteen minutes for cross," the judge announces, slamming the gavel down.

The attorney goes up, takes Connie's hand, and helps her down from the stand. Dennis leaps up from the front row bench, swoops in, and both of them help the poor woman outside for a drink of water. The entire courtroom empties.

"This is going *really* well," I say, my face now a lovely color of puce.

"You have to stay with me here," John says, leaning on the railing between us and the witness stand.

"She's gone completely O.J. She totally believes her shit." Leo's eyes are glazed over and he's staring at the witness stand.

"She's been well coached," John says. "But I'm pleased."

"What?!" we all sputter in unison, all except Huston, who sits stony-faced.

"They've given us the perfect setup. Seriously. It couldn't have gone better," John says, straightening up, stretching.

"Well, it's our only shot," Huston sighs. John nods. "So, you'll do cross—do you have those documents?" he asks, cracking his now scarred knuckles.

"I've got them here. I plan on using them during cross," John says.

We are silent. All four of us.

"But everybody bought it," Abigail says, her voice low and scared.

"Sure, she's a little old lady who's saying the big bad wolf, or four big bad wolves, blew her house down. But that's about to change. You need to trust me. And if you can't do that . . . trust your dad. He did everything he could to make sure that you were taken care of," John presses, in full lawyer mode.

"Except divorce her," Leo whispers.

"You know, he was a religious guy—so, okay, he didn't divorce her, but he went to exhaustive lengths to make sure every last penny he had found its way to you."

"Thanks, John. It's just been a rough couple of weeks," Huston apologizes, patting John on the arm.

"You're almost there . . . This is where things start not adding up and her histrionics will do nothing but make her look like a greedy, tantrumming two-year-old," John says, getting more and more passionate.

"We really appreciate all you've done," Abigail offers.

"No worries, really," John says, shooting a quick glance at me. I get embarrassed and check my watch. We have a little less than five minutes.

"And we go up after your cross?" I ask, fidgeting with the wristband.

"Actually, no. Connie's attorney said he was only calling Huston, who I'll then question. Then I'll put Ray's attorney on the stand to paint a picture of Ray's state of mind when he drew up this estate plan in the first place."

"Got it," I answer.

"Okay, this is very important. I need you to not react when this cross-examination is going on, as well. The judge will be watching your reactions, to see if you're getting off on this, anger, rage—what have you. So, I know it's Herculean, but just try to look neutral," John advises.

"I think shutting down emotionally will not be a big leap for this family," I say. Even Huston cracks a smile. John gives me a quick wink.

People start trickling back into the courtroom. No one looks straight at us. There are side glances and shaming stares, but no one ever stops and really takes us in. Takes in the pain and grief. People see what they want to.

"I'd better get up there," John announces, and he pushes through the bar, not looking back.

The door to the courtroom swings open once more and Connie and Dennis make their way down the center aisle. As the crowd looks reverently at her, I can see their glances sneak over to us, turn to judgment, and soften as they return to the feeble old lady who just wants to preserve the memory of her late husband.

Dennis leads Connie back through the swinging gate and back up to the witness stand. The crowd settles in.

The bailiff stands as the clerk walks hurriedly to her desk and sits down.

"All rise," the bailiff announces.

We all stand.

"The Honorable Paul Kohl presiding," the clerk announces. The judge enters and sits.

"Please be seated. Counsel?"

"John Moss on behalf of the Hawkes children."

"We'll go ahead with cross. Mrs. Hawkes, you're still under oath."

"Yes," Connie agrees. Once again, I'm expecting flames. Just engulfing flames. Maybe some smiting. A good old-fashioned smiting would be nice.

"Please begin," the judge says.

"Thank you, Your Honor. Mrs. Hawkes, if you will—please let me know if you ever need a moment or a short recess. If this all gets too emotional." John waits.

"Yes...I'm fine," Connie says, nodding her head. Her eyes steely.

"So, I just want to backtrack over a few of the questions your attorney asked earlier, is that okay?" John asks, his voice soft, like he's just sitting in a parlor somewhere with his grandmother.

"Yes, that's fine," Connie answers, on full alert.

"It won't take that long, I promise," John says, smiling.

"I'm fine."

"You stated earlier that Ray bought you the town house on Daly Street when you were having some minor difficulties in your marriage early on, is that correct?" John asks.

"Yes," Connie answers. Clear. Concise. Well rehearsed. Just answer the question, don't volunteer anything.

"But after the rough patch was over, you moved back into the house that was left to Ray by his mother," John says, reading from a legal pad. He looks up, awaiting an answer.

"Yes, that's right."

"So, from 2005 on, you lived full-time in the house left to Ray by his mother and used the Daly Street town house mostly as guest accommodations for either your son or out-of-town guests?" John asks.

"Yes, that's right," Connie answers again. She shifts in her chair—getting comfortable. She's not uneasy at all. So calm. She's so calm.

"So why are all of the utility bills for the Daly Street town house in your name only?" John asks, producing a stack of bills. "Exhibit One, Your Honor," John announces, handing them to the clerk.

"We just never changed them back, I suppose. Ray kept all the books and paid all the bills," Connie answers.

"Okay, but what about your Medicare bills, dental bills, and your phone bill? Why were those sent to the Daly Street address?" John presses. He produces another stack of mail. "Exhibits Two through Five, Your Honor." Once again, he hands the stack to the clerk.

"The town house is just down the street, so rather than going through the hassle of changing everything, we just kept it the same. Ray didn't mind," Connie explains, her voice coquettish.

"Moving on to the house Ray's mother left him, Mrs. Hawkes—you said here earlier that you've lived in that house continuously since roughly 2005?" John asks, heading back over to his files.

"Yes."

"So, where are your clothes, Mrs. Noonan? Your personal effects? Your furniture? Your Honor, Exhibit Six is date-stamped pictures of the closets in the nine twenty-four Dean Street house showing that the only clothes in the closets were those of Ray Hawkes," John finishes, handing the pictures we took on that final cleanup day to the clerk to mark and pass along to the judge. The judge flips through the pictures and looks down at Connie. Waiting.

"Well, they obviously staged these pictures. Pulled all of my clothes out and took the picture of an empty closet," Connie explains, never raising her voice.

"And the personal effects?"

"I don't...I don't understand," Connie says, recrossing her legs.

"Pictures of the two of you together, flower vases, your family heirlooms," John rattles off.

"Ray let me express my creative design sense in the Daly Street town house. He didn't like any of that woman stuff," Connie explains, sneaking a small smile. Several women in the crowd titter at Connie's assessment of men's quirky decorating tastes. She's as bad as one of those Cathy comic strips. Next thing she'll be proclaiming is that she has "catitude."

"Earlier when you testified, you said that Ray had bought you the town house on Daly Street when you were having some minor difficulties in your marriage. Isn't it true that you've been separated from Ray Hawkes since April 9, 2005?" John asks.

"No, we were the center of each other's universe," Connie protests, her eyes welling up. With fury, I knew, but would the judge ever figure it out?

"Do you need a moment, Mrs. Noonan?" John's voice is easy, his whole body soft and concerned.

"No, I'm fine," Connie says, dabbing at her eyes with a tissue.

"Well, isn't it also true that Ray Hawkes had divorce papers drawn up on April 9, 2005, which he signed? Let the record show that I'm entering these signed divorce papers in evidence as Exhibit Seven." John hands a copy of the divorce papers to Connie and the original to the clerk.

"Like I said, we had a rough patch in the beginning. As you can see, they were never filed. We worked through our problems and came out loving each other even more," Connie says, not even touching the divorce papers.

"Earlier you testified that Ray gave everything to his kids in the will because they blackmailed him emotionally and unduly influenced him to leave everything to them," John starts.

"Yes."

"So, did Ray's kids blackmail him into setting up college funds for his grandchildren: Evelyn, Mateo, and Emilygrae, and any grandchildren that might come later?" John asks, heading back to counsel table his for exhibits.

"What?" Connie blurts.

"A trust in each of Ray's grandchildren's names to be used for a college education. Exhibits Eight through Ten, Your Honor," John says, handing the documents to the clerk, who in turn hands them to the judge. This time Connie picks up one of the documents and scans the text.

"They must have. That Abigail is the worst, always trotting out those little Mexican kids. She should be ashamed of herself," Connie says, tossing the documents back down onto the banister of the witness stand. Abigail curls her fingers under the court bench.

"And do you think Ray's kids blackmailed him into making each of them beneficiaries under this one-million-dollar Metropolitan Life Insurance policy that he purchased just after your separation?" John asks, handing a copy of the document to Connie along with one to the clerk. "Exhibit Eleven, Your Honor."

"There are four kids. They were raised on hate by that woman. They got to him. My poor Ray never had a chance!" Connie breaks down.

"Ms. Noonan, do you need a minute? We can take a quick recess for you to collect yourself."

"No, I'm fine," Connie assures, once again.

"Your Honor, at this time, I'd like to enter in Exhibits Twelve through Twenty-one, which show that Ray left several other insurance policies and bank accounts solely to his children,"

John says, passing the exhibits to the clerk, then on to the judge.

"Mrs. Noonan?" the judge asks.

"They got to him—each one of them," Connie repeats.

"You testified earlier that Ray bought you the town house on Daly Street during the troubles you were having in your marriage. Your Honor, I'd like to enter the deed for the Daly Street town house as Exhibit Twenty-two into evidence. Why didn't Ray ever put you on title to the property in the years since he gave it to you?" John asks, putting a copy of the deed in front of Connie.

"He said it was some kind of tax thing. I trusted him," Connie answers.

"You testified earlier that you have lived in the nine twenty-four Dean Street house with Ray Hawkes throughout your marriage. Your Honor, I'd like to enter into evidence the deed for the residence located at nine twenty-four Dean Street, Ojai, as Exhibit Twenty-three into evidence. Why didn't Ray put you on title to this house either? The house where the two of you lived as husband and wife?" John asks, setting a copy of that deed in front of Connie as well. The clerk passes along a copy to the judge.

"He said it was a tax thing too. Ray minded the books. I trusted him," Connie answers.

"Well, okay, then why didn't he give you his power of attorney instead of Huston Hawkes, his eldest son from his first marriage? Your Honor, I'd like to enter the power of attorney and the durable power of attorney for health care as Exhibit Twenty-four and Twenty-five in evidence," John says.

"Well, that oldest one's a lawyer and the littlest one is a criminal. Those kids had him wrapped around their little finger. He would have done anything," Connie explains.

"So, all these things. Insurance policy after insurance policy. Bank account after bank account. College funds for the grandchildren. Deed after deed. Powers of attorney. Last will and testament. All of these documents done at different times, over a period of years, it is your testimony that he did these things because his own children bamboozled him, blackmailed him. But why do you think he did all this? What was he trying to do?" John asks.

"I don't know, I guess they got to him." Connie says.

"So, over a course of years, your husband basically gave away your home, your *homes*, I mean, your money, your future, everything, everything you built together, to a bunch of kids he left twenty-two years ago?" asks John.

"Objection, Your Honor, asked and answered," Connie's attorney interrupts.

"Overruled; answer the question, Mrs. Hawkes," the judge says.

"Yes, that's what happened," Connie says, shifting in her chair.

"So, are you the love of his life or not?" John asks, arms wide.

"Yes," Connie says again.

"I've got to be frank with you, Mrs. Noonan, if I were Ray and you were the love of my life, I would have taken better care of you," John says.

"Objection," Connie's attorney shouts, standing.

"Overruled," the judge says.

"Why didn't he? Why was he so worried about these ungrateful kids? There was plenty to go around. Why were you the only one who got left out?" John presses, approaching Connie.

"Because they made him," Connie says again.

"So he cared more what they thought of him. He wanted their love more?" John presses.

"Yeah . . . no . . ." Connie stutters.

"Well, which is it?" John asks.

"I was his wife!" she yells.

"Yeah, I get that. But why did he care more about his kids?"

"We were the loves of each other's lives," Connie says again.

"And yet you're left with nothing."

"It's all because of them!" Connie yells, pointing at us.

"Because he loved them more."

"Yes," Connie says, the mask slipping slightly.

"So, you're saying he loved them more," John repeats.

"Yes," Connie says, exasperated with John's inane questions.

"You're saying they're the loves of his life?" John acts confused.

"What? No..."

"So he made sure the loves of his life were taken care of," John says.

"It was supposed to be mine. All of it," Connie says, impatiently.

"But let's review, you just said they were the loves of Ray's life." Connie nods. "And what Ray wanted was to make sure that the loves of his life were taken care of."

"But he never even saw them, he left them twenty years ago. Never looked back, even," Connie argues.

"You just said that they must have been visiting Ray when you were in Oxnard—do you need the court reporter to read that back to you?" John motions for the court reporter.

"No."

"You can't have it both ways, Ms. Noonan. Did he abandon them or not?" John presses.

"It was all supposed to be mine!" Connie shouts.

"Supposed to be yours?" John quickly asks.

"Ray went and made that oldest one his power of attorney," Connie says.

"Isn't that a choice that couples usually make together?" John presses quickly.

"I hadn't seen Ray in years when he—" Connie catches herself. Her face drains of color and her eyes wildly dart from John to Dennis and back to John. The mask finally shatters completely. The crowd reacts in unison. Finally seeing what's under the mask. Recoiling from her.

"You hadn't seen Ray in years when he chose his son, Huston Hawkes, to have his power of attorney," John repeats.

"No...I...I...it didn't—" Connie flounders.

"I have nothing further," John says, walking away from her.

"She knew all along," Leo whispers, shaking his head in disbelief, as Connie stands and begins her descent from the witness stand.

"Of course she did," I whisper back.

"What kind of person does that?" Leo whispers back, trying still to figure her out. We watch Connie's attorney help her down from the witness stand. Dennis sits tightly, his arms crossed, his face crimson, and makes no effort to help his mother anywhere.

The wooden gate creaks open and Connie is led down the center aisle. The crowd whispers and stares as she passes.

Connie looks straight ahead, clutching her attorney's hand as he sits her down in the back of the courtroom.

"At this time, Your Honor, I'd like to request a dismissal of Mrs. Hawkes' will contest, as evidenced by her own admissions of malicious intent and her actual knowledge of Ray Hawkes' true objectives with his estate," John says, standing. Connie's attorney walks back down the aisle and opens the bar, taking his place once again at his podium.

"Your Honor, the only thing that was proven here today is—" Connie's attorney starts.

"Save it, Counsel. I've heard enough. I hereby deny Ms. Hawkes' motion to invalidate the last will and testament of Raymond Mateo Hawkes and hereby order Mrs. Hawkes to reimburse the Hawkes children for their attorney's fees and costs. Case dismissed," the judge announces, banging the gavel down.

The sounds of the world are muffled all around us.

John spins around and finds us, giving us a broad smile, just so we can see. He is positively beaming. I make eye contact with him.

"Thank you," I whisper, my shoulders finally relaxed. John leaves the courtroom, giving me a quick wink as he passes. Always the professional. I know he'll be right outside waiting for me.

The crowd disperses down the center aisle. This time, their eyes are soft and pitying as they look on us. We sit still, clutching each other's hands. Dennis stands and walks toward the door along with the throng of people leaving.

"You should be ashamed of yourselves," Dennis hisses, as he continues back to his mother. None of us acknowledge him. For once, I stay above the fray. This fight is over. Dennis walks over to Connie, whispers something to her and continues right out of the courtroom, leaving Connie sitting there.

We all stand.

Huston unfolds his body, stretching. His body finally relaxing, his smile easy, his hands reaching for the sky. Abigail stands, straightening her skirt, allowing her arm to rest around Huston's waist. He takes her hand and holds it tight. Abigail looks to Leo, tucking a stray hair behind his ear, soft and gentle. Leo bends into Abigail's caress.

I stand at the end of the row. My hand is sweaty now from Leo's tight grip never letting me go. I'm connected. We're like little paper dolls, strung hand to hand. Acting as one.

Huston starts to walk out of the courtroom; all of us file out like ducklings. Connie sits exactly where she was—utterly alone.

I, on the other hand, have a family.

epilogue

I take a deep breath and settle onto the table. The paper under me crinkles and folds. Under my body, against my body...into my body. I eye the door. Only the threat of public nudity makes me stay put.

"Why don't you go ahead and lie back," Dr. Singh asks, flipping out the dreaded stirrups. So vulnerable. Yet I'm oddly calmed by her commands. I stare at the ceiling, trying to get my breathing under control. I'm beginning to panic. I close my eyes—*Two times two is four. Four times four is sixteen. Sixteen times sixteen is...What the hell is sixteen times sixteen?* Okay, focus—carry the three and then the six...wait a minute...okay, count the dots in the ceiling, then.

John smoothes his hand down my arm and takes my hand. I hadn't noticed that my arm was raised in a knee-jerk defensive pose. I stop focusing on the dots on the ceiling, the times tables in my head. I breathe deeply and find John: my point on the horizon.

"You're about six weeks along," Dr. Singh says, motioning at the computer screen. Through the black-and-white static and bubbles of amorphous blobs, I can see a distinct little peanut. A little six-week-old peanut.

Our peanut.

"Six weeks," I repeat.

"Holy shit," John whispers, flushing as he apologizes to

Dr. Singh for his language. Dr. Singh presses a few buttons so we can watch our peanut come more and more into focus. Before I know it, a tear slides down the side of my face. I breathe deeply, trying to get control. Dr. Singh passes a tissue box over to me. Obviously, I've done a poor job with the control thing.

"Thank you," John says, taking the box and blowing his nose before he pulls out another tissue and wipes away the tears now streaming down his cheeks. Apparently he's not doing any better keeping his emotions in check. I find it adorable. I rest my hand on his arm, pulling him toward me, touching him, comforting him. He gives me a quick embarrassed smile and brushes my bangs out of my eyes, his hand lingering as we lock eyes. The tears fall. The emotions take over. Together we allow our little peanut to unravel us.

Life. A little life. Joy. Possibilities. Family. Trust. New beginnings.

The staticky image blurs as my eyes fill with tears. I bring my hand to my belly and look up at John. His face contorts. He's going to be a father. And I'm going to be a mom. Who would have thunk it: the juvenile delinquent and the lost girl are going to be parents. This'll be the luckiest little peanut in the world.

I think of Huston, Abigail, Evie, and Leo, who are in the waiting room. Sure, they're out there wrangling the twins. But they're here; they're trying not to get excited before our news is confirmed; they're thrilled for us. We're family, after all.

If it's a girl, I think we'll name her Evelyn.

And a boy?

Well, the world could certainly use another Ray.

about the author

I was born and bred in Pasadena, California. I've held every degrading job one could think of, until I finally realized my only talent lies in writing. Thank God, someone else thought so, too. *A Field Guide to Burying Your Parents* is my third novel.

Five Places I Would Rather Be than in the Midst of a Family Drama

1. Turkish prison

2. Receiving a colonoscopy

3. Devil's Island

4. Having a root canal with no anesthetic

5. Sitting on an anthill, covered in honey